DAFFODILS BEFORE SWALLOWS

This beautifully constructed tale of love and intrigue centres on the lives of Rosalind and Charles, born on the same day, but from very different backgrounds. Rosalind's family live modestly in Brighton, whereas Charles's father is a Lord, owner of the magnificent ancestral seat, Hathaway House and its legendary library, containing rare first editions and a copy of Shakespeare's first folio. Shakespeare plays an important part in their story, with a previously undiscovered manuscript being auctioned at Sotheby's, and there are echoes of Shakespearean themes, from issues of inheritance and betrayal to the redemptive power of love.

DAFFODILS BEFORE
SWALLOWS

Daffodils Before Swallows

by

Daniel Peltz

Magna Large Print Books
Long Preston, North Yorkshire,
BD23 4ND, England.

British Library Cataloguing in Publication Data.

Peltz, Daniel
    Daffodils before swallows.

A catalogue record of this book is
available from the British Library

ISBN   978-0-7505-3142-9

First published in Great Britain in 2007 by The Book Guild Ltd.

Copyright © Daniel Peltz 2007

Cover illustration © David Selman by arrangement with
britainonview

The right of Daniel Peltz to be identified as the author of this work has
been asserted by him in accordance with the Copyright, Designs and
Patents Act, 1988

Published in Large Print 2009 by arrangement with
Book Guild Publishing

Magna Large Print is an imprint of Library Magna Books Ltd.

Printed and bound in Great Britain by
T.J. (International) Ltd., Cornwall, PL28 8RW

For Max, Francesca, Isaac and George

CONTENTS

Part 1   Sotheby's –
The Present Day – 4 p.m.   15

Part 2   Rosalind   21

Part 3   Sotheby's –
The Present Day – 4.15 p.m.   61

Part 4   Charles   65

Part 5   Sotheby's –
The Present Day – 4.20 p.m.   113

Part 6   Awakenings   117

Part 7   Sotheby's –
The Present Day – 4.30 p.m.   189

Part 8   Rosalind Encounters Lear   195

Part 9   Sotheby's –
The Present Day – 4.35 p.m.   301

Part 10   Romeo and Juliet   307

Part 11   Sotheby's –
The Present Day – 4.50 p.m.   439

ACKNOWLEDGEMENTS

There have been many important influences in my life, not least my wife and my parents. However, when writing this book, I was inspired by Harold Bloom, celebrated critic and the author, amongst others, of *The Western Canon, Genius,* and *Shakespeare: The Invention of the Human.* These books have opened my eyes to the importance of Shakespeare to all of us today, not only in the way we speak, but also in the way we think and act.

Part 1

SOTHEBY'S, THE PRESENT DAY

4 p.m.

1

The main auction room at Sotheby's was filled to capacity. People from all over the globe had come to the famous old auction house to witness what many saw as the most important event in modern auction history. Investors, collectors, a few privileged friends, and a sprinkling of the general public who had queued for almost a week, all mingled together with the world's television and press, waiting for the drama to unfold. The anticipation leading up to the sale was at breaking point, with speculation over what price Lot 101 would reach. There was no precedent for such an item: this was something both unique and extraordinary. It was impossible to estimate the value; the market would have to decide. The reserve was one of the most carefully guarded secrets of that winter. Only four people knew: the auctioneer himself, Henry Smith Luytens; an antiquarian book dealer placed on the aisle in row three; and a young couple sitting in the back row, nervously waiting for their destiny to be decided.

2

As Lot 100 – a fine first edition of Emily Brontë's *Wuthering Heights* – was introduced to the sale room, the tension began to rise. This was no ordinary lot, and in a different auction on a different day would have generated a considerable amount of interest in its own right. It was signed by the author herself and preserved in fine condition in its original boards, and a comfortable six-figure amount was expected. Smith Luytens held up the item, boxed in a turquoise-blue leather casing with the gold letters 'HH' engraved on the spine. The bidding began at £50,000, quickly reaching £100,000 before it slowed down. Concentration on the lot was confined to two bidders, one of whom was the antiquarian book dealer seated near the front. The rest of the room remained quiet, desperate for the sale to finish, simply to hasten the introduction of the next lot.

The bidding on Lot 100 crawled its way up to £150,000, before finally stalling. 'I'm going to sell at this level ... do I hear any higher bids?' Smith Luytens looked around the room and saw that there was nobody else ready to take up the bidding. He slowly lifted the hammer, 'For the first, second and third time–' and as he brought the hammer down, 'Sold! ... to Mr Shapeman in Row three ... thank you.'

The book dealer sat back relieved. He turned around to the young couple seated at the back and smiled. They looked at each other, and then nodded to him. The afternoon had started as planned.

There was a faint ripple of applause, as people began to move around to get more comfortable. The time had finally arrived for the main event. For the next half an hour, the eyes of the world would be centred on London, fixed, more accurately, on this one room in St George's Street, Mayfair.

3

'Lot 101,' the auctioneer called out, smiling. 'The final lot of the day and I don't think I need to go through the details on this one!' The item had been brought out by one of the staff, who was dressed traditionally in the old auction-house overall. The audience laughed nervously. There was indeed no point in going through the description: there was not a person alive in the western world who did not know what it was.

'I am, however, going to lift it up, so that every-one can see it. Who knows, it might be the last time it is ever seen in public.' Smith Luytens knew exactly what he was saying. Representatives from the governments of Great Britain, continental Europe and the United States, as well as all the major museums, were all present. Luytens could also see a number of extraordinarily wealthy priv-ate investors appropriately well placed in the prime seating area, ready to bid for their own private collections.

As he lifted the framed exhibit up to the room, a burst of camera flashes lit up the room, accom-panied by gasps from the audience. For the first time, the auctioneer could sense the intense heat of the television lights at either side of the room. He noticed the cameras following the item as he held it aloft. It was so small, yet it somehow pos-sessed an aura of majesty. Holding it high above his head for thirty seconds – what seemed like minutes to the young couple at the back – he observed the expressions on the audience's faces. The energy in the room was almost tangible.

'Now then, where shall we begin? Will someone start me at, say, fifty – who will give me £50 million? Thank you, madam. I have £50 million from the lady in blue at the back. Is there anyone at £55 million? Yes, thank you, sir–' Hands went up as the price increased at a slow but orderly pace, before settling at £70 million, bid by a lady dressed in a smart navy-blue suit seated at the back. She remained calm; she was experienced and all too aware that the sale still had a long way to go.

So the bidding had begun. Arguably the most important treasure in Western cultural history was being auctioned. The young couple remained seated at the back, out of the public gaze where they would remain, but only temporarily. When the hammer did eventually come down, they knew that the world's attention would switch back from across the room, and on to them.

Part 2

ROSALIND

1

At midday on 5 May 1978, Rosalind Blackstone was born. It was a hot, muggy day that welcomed the long awaited arrival of the Blackstones' first, and what proved to be their only child.

'Seven pounds exactly!'

'Let me hold her– Come on, Catherine, give her to me,' Alan Blackstone pleaded impatiently as he took the baby into his arms. 'Well done Catherine, she's beautiful.'

The exhausted mother looked up at the doting father, her husband. 'OK Alan, that's enough, now. Give her back to me.' She wanted her baby in her arms.

There was no way that Alan Blackstone was going to give back the baby to her mother. He had been waiting for this moment for over 20 years. 'Wait, Catherine. All in good time.'

She smiled and decided to let him hold her. She had not seen him this happy for a very long time. The wait for a child had been unbearable for both of them: all those years of fruitlessness and frustration had taken a heavy toll on the marriage. But they had survived and now, as far as she was concerned, God had rewarded them with a beautiful baby girl.

Alan Blackstone was 23 years old when he arrived in England. Having recently lost both his parents to cancer within 12 months of each other, there was very little for him to stay in Ireland for. He was virtually penniless. His father was a labourer at the Dublin docks, and what little he had provided had been spent by his mother during her last days. Alan had no siblings, and very little close family to whom he spoke. He left school at 16 with no proper qualifications, took on a number of menial jobs, all of which offered very little prospect. It did not take long for him to make up his mind to leave. He scrambled enough money together to pay for the carriage to Liverpool, and without any second thoughts, promptly left.

After a year of travelling around, taking temporary jobs and staying in digs, he desperately wanted to settle down. For the first time in his life he came across real prosperity, when working as a bell boy at the Ritz in London. Wealth, however, did not impress him; he was not overly ambitious, and he knew his own limitations. A lifestyle without worrying about your next meal, or where to sleep at night, was what Alan Blackstone wanted. He didn't think that was too much to ask for.

Having moved down to the south coast during the summer of 1954, he continued with temporary work, this time at the Grand Hotel in Brighton as the lift operator. He immediately felt at home in the Regency surroundings of the famous seaside resort. Constantly looking at the vacancies board on the wall in the staff restaurant, he at last found a job that he thought would suit him.

'We are really looking for graduates, Mr Blackstone. The position of trainee concierge is highly sought after. Competition for this vacancy will be extremely tough. We have the luxury of being able to choose from a number of potential candidates who will be much better qualified than you.' He looked up and saw the face of utter dejection in front of him. 'Look, I don't want to put you off. You're a hard worker, and the management have been impressed by your timekeeping and presentation.' The personnel officer looked down at the file. 'Maybe this might be of interest to you?' He handed Alan a slip of paper.

'Listen, I know it's not at the concierge's desk, but being in Reception will be a start. It's a training position, but the entry level is not as demanding. In fact, Mr Blackstone, I could offer you that job as a permanent one. With Christmas coming up it's going to be very busy. It will be excellent experience for you– There is, of course, the chance of promotion if things go well.'

Alan looked up. He never really believed he would get the concierge vacancy. The assistant receptionist opportunity was a complete surprise. After all, it would be a start on the ladder and, most importantly, it was a permanent offer. At last, he could begin a settled existence, in a town where he felt comfortable.

3

Alan had been staying in lodgings, provided by

the hotel for its temporary staff. The new job offer meant that he had to move out, and look for somewhere a little more permanent, even if it did mean rental accommodation.

After four weeks of looking at flats, he finally found a first-floor two-bedroom flat in Kemp Town, near Eastern Road. The landlord was in fact a landlady in her mid fifties who owned the entire Georgian block. She herself lived on the ground floor, whilst letting the upper floors to respectable tenants who provided her with a generous income.

'Rent is payable on a monthly basis, in advance. I'll have to have a rental deposit of three months up front – I've had a little trouble recently with tenants.' This was a lie; she was extremely cautious in her selection of lodgers, and she never made a mistake. Everybody paid on time. 'You'll have to keep the place tidy, mind you,' she said, in a distinctive East-Sussex accent.

'That's OK. No problem. Can I move in next week?'

'You can move in as soon as your cheque's cleared,' she replied, smiling, but also with a hint of seriousness. This was not a woman who was going to be taken for a ride.

'Who do I make it payable to?'

'Mrs Davis – Mrs Emily Davis– Thank you.' She took the cheque before the ink had barely time to dry. 'So you'll move in next week, then?'

'Yes. I look forward to it.' Alan looked at the old woman who had already turned around and was walking, he assumed, towards the bank. He smiled to himself. Things were beginning to work out.

4

The following week Alan moved what few possessions he had into his new flat. Mrs Davis watched every move as he carried his belongings up the flight of stairs located outside her own flat. He could feel her beady stare fixed on the back of his neck. His first impression of the old woman was that of an eccentric, middle-aged small-minded busy body! He could not have been more wrong.

A war widow, Emily Davis had lived alone at the same address in Kemp Town for over 30 years. She had been a nurse all of her adult life at the Royal Sussex Hospital, a stone's throw away from her house, on Eastern Road. During the First World War she experienced horrors that most nurses would not see in an entire lifetime. Based in Bapaume, France, in a makeshift hospital, she worked for three years looking after the war-wounded. It was in France that she met her husband, a lieutenant in the British Army.

Following a whirlwind romance, they married, four weeks after meeting each other. Long courtships were not that common for a young officer on the Western Front, since the war had placed so much uncertainty on one's life expectancy. Their honeymoon lasted only a few days back in London, before he was sent to the Front on the Ypres salient. He left her at Victoria Station. It was the last time she would see him. He was killed at Paesschendaele during one of the bloodiest battles British troops were engaged in during the First World War. It was only after the war was over that she managed to travel to his gravesite. Unfortunately no body was found, or one that could be properly identified. His name was inscribed on the wall at the cemetery along with thousands of others. The annual visits to Tyne Cott continued uninterrupted until the present day.

He had left her the house in Kemp Town which they had shared during the brief weeks they had together. She had never moved, and although being too large for her, she converted the upper floors into flats and let them out. It provided her with enough money to lead a very comfortable life.

'Would you like a cup of tea?'

'Yes, that would be lovely,' Alan replied, brushing himself down and closing the front door. Having finished moving in, he welcomed the refreshment and followed the old lady into her sitting room.

'So, when did you arrive in England?' she asked, returning with the tea.

'Oh, just over a year ago. I've been everywhere, but I'm happy here in Brighton.'

'Why did you leave Ireland? I loved Dublin when I visited there.' Her questions were fired at him, rather than asked: more akin to an interview than a fireside chat.

'I had very little choice in the end.' Alan continued with his life story right up to the present moment. He began to relax, and as he provided her with more answers, she in turn warmed to him. Later that evening the young man was puzzled as to why he had opened up so easily to his landlady. He hardly knew her, but it all seemed so natural. She was certainly a very willing listener and coupled with an inquisitive, but not in any way intrusive, mind, she found out almost everything about him. There was method in her questioning; she now knew what she needed, before embarking on her plan.

'Would you like to come for tea on Sunday?' she asked, seeing him out. 'It's just that I would like you to meet someone.'

'Oh! Yes, that would be lovely!' Alan replied, slightly taken aback.

'Shall we say 4–4.30 then?'

'Fine.'

5

As soon as Alan left, Emily walked over to the phone.

'Hello. Catherine? It's Aunt Emily here. How are you?' And after a brief exchange of pleasantries, Emily continued, 'I was just ringing to see if you were free this Sunday. Perhaps in the afternoon. There is someone here I would like you to meet.'

'Oh no, aunt. Not again. Listen, I'm not interested in meeting anyone now. You know that the last man you introduced me to was a complete disaster.'

'Now, now, Catherine. How was I supposed to know he was a car thief on bail? After all, his cheque did clear!' She paused. 'Catherine, this one's very nice. A Catholic too – unfortunately not a very good church attendee – but very good manners!' She waited for a response.

'What does he look like?'

'Oh, very handsome. Strong, athletic–'

Catherine ignored her aunt's reference to his faith, since her own attendance at Mass had been very bad since her father died. It was not an exaggeration to say that her faith had been stretched to the limit, and as a result had effectively lapsed.

'Yes, yes ... all right! I think I've got the picture! Oh God, Aunt Emily, this has to be the last time, please!.'

Catherine agreed to come on the following Sunday. But she was absolutely right: it would be the last time her aunt would set her up with a date, but not for quite the reason she thought.

6

Arriving for tea, Catherine Davis sat herself down on the large armchair in the living room.

'Well? Where is he, then?' she asked, buoyed by the prospect that he might have cancelled.

'He'll be here soon, don't worry,' her aunt replied, carrying the tea tray. 'He's having to work late today. He's got a new job at the Grand, you know. I'm sure he's going places.' And then the door bell rang.

Catherine turned around as her aunt opened the door to let Alan in. As the young Irishman walked in, Catherine felt a rush of blood and her heartbeat race. Try as she did, she could not avert her gaze from the tall young man who had just entered. Her aunt had been right, after all. This one did look different.

'How do you do?' Alan said in a heavy Irish accent, stretching his hand out to Catherine. After stumbling her way through the initial pleasantries, Catherine managed to compose herself. It was too late, however, for her to try and conceal the cracks that had already been revealed to the potential suitor sitting opposite her.

Alan, although relatively inexperienced, realised quickly that Catherine liked him. To be fair, a blind man would have noticed. He looked at her: she was tall, slim and had auburn hair, which was tied back tightly behind her ears. Her face was pale in complexion, but this was more than made up for by her full red lips and clear blue eyes. He could see immediately how attractive she was, and was sure that she had no shortage of admirers. He was not wrong: she was inundated with telephone calls and letters from men asking her out on dates. She generally refused, determined only to go out with someone she genuinely liked. That person had not entered her life, that is, until the moment when Alan Blackstone entered her aunt's lounge.

'So you live in Hove?' Alan asked, desperately trying to appear relaxed.

'Yes that's right – in Brunswick Square. I have a flat.'

'You live alone?'

'Yes for the last 12 months – since my father died. I haven't seen my mother for 15 years. In truth I don't even remember what she looked like. She walked out on my dad without an explanation. Aunt Emily, my father's sister, has been my real mother. What about you?'

'Oh, my parents have both passed away. I arrived in England a year and a half ago. I've managed to get a job at the Grand, here in Brighton. I'm on reception – as a trainee.'

'How did your parents die?'

'Cancer. They both died within a year. I had very little family. Unusual really for a good Irish Catholic family.'

She looked at him. She liked his softly spoken Irish accent; his uneasiness as he tried to communicate with her. For an independent young man, he was shy and very unsure of himself.

'Well that makes two of us, then.'

'What? Being an only child, or being Catholic?'

'Both, really!' Catherine was beginning to take control of the meeting, as she usually did in this situation.

'Tea for anyone?' Emily was very pleased with how things were going. She had never seen Catherine look so at ease; certainly not since her father had died.

7

Emily Davis had indeed been a surrogate mother for her niece ever since her sister-in-law walked out on her brother 15 years earlier. Her brother had been a loving father to his daughter and although earning a modest income as a bus inspector, he managed to provide for her. He took her to school every morning; he managed to attend all her school plays; and there was never a parents' evening that he missed. However, the girl still needed a mother, particularly when she became a teenager and simple unconditional paternal devotion was just not enough.

Catherine was always grateful to her aunt for her support. Without her it would have been difficult for her to have got through school, achieved her A level results, and to have gone on to teacher-training college. It certainly would have been almost impossible for her to have carried on after her father's sudden heart attack and subsequent death. She was paralysed with grief, seemingly unable to carry on with life. It was Aunt Emily who picked her niece up off the ground, despite her own sadness at losing her brother, and made her look forward.

Although only 21, Catherine, like the young man having tea opposite her, was looking for a certain stability in life. She craved love and companionship, despite her public protestations to her aunt every time she tried to set Catherine up with a date. Her aunt, of course, knew this and took the protests with a pinch of salt.

8

As the tea moved on into supper, the two young adults slowly became more comfortable in each other's company. Everything was discussed, from the newly-crowned young Queen to the incumbent Tory government; from where to live locally, to the price of groceries; even former girlfriends and boyfriends were talked about. As the conversation became more fluid and relaxed, so the mutual attraction became more apparent. Catherine had already played her cards, but it was Alan who was now slowly revealing his. He was caught in her web, and was soon captivated by her.

'Can I see you again?' Alan managed to ask as Catherine was putting on her coat.

'Yes, that would be nice. You can contact me on this number.' Catherine replied, realising that she needed no more proof that Alan had now fallen for her. All the butterflies and insecurities she had first felt when seeing him had disappeared. It was he who was now nervous and lacking self confidence. She wrote down her name and address with the telephone number. Alan gratefully took the card from her, almost snatching it from her hand.

'Well, I thought that was most successful!' Emily said, tidying up the room. There was no reply as Alan was too deep in thought to respond. He had, of course, had a number of romances, none of which had lasted more than a few weeks. He thought he had experienced love, but it had always proved to be mere infatuation. But the feeling he had now was not the same: it was somehow more substantial and he was convinced that this was going to be different.

9

The first date followed a week later. Alan took

her for a drink at the well-established Royal Crescent Hotel. They both felt a little awkward and somewhat out of their depth. This feeling was made even worse by the attitude of the staff who took one look at them and treated them with disdain. Having decided that this was not the place for them, they hurriedly gulped their drinks down and left, walking briskly out on to the seafront.

The icy cold February wind lashed into their faces as they crossed the road and walked on to the promenade. The alcohol had certainly warmed both of them, but it had very little effect against the uncensored raw gale sweeping off the Channel. Alan put his arm around Catherine, a move made considerably easier by the weather. Instead of having to bide his time and carefully orchestrate the timing of the pass, he could use the arctic wind as an excuse for keeping her warm.

'Let's go on the beach,' she said, pulling him off the promenade and down the steep steps leading to the road across from the stony beach.

10

They ran down the stairs, both pairs of legs springing off each step. Landing with a thud, they tried to run towards the sea, but their feet sank into the pebbled beach, thus slowing their charge into mistimed chaos. It was only a matter of time before they fell together on to the stones.

She fell first, pulling him down on top of her. The pebbles gave way under their weight and

35

cushioned the impact of the fall. Catherine could feel the dampness of the rain-soaked beach seeping into her hair as she looked up into Alan's dark eyes. His head moved slowly towards hers. She closed her eyes as his lips kissed her. She responded, but this time with her mouth open. Tenderness was rapidly overtaken by a brutal passion as Alan began to move his hands underneath her jumper. He managed to pull down her bra, and clumsily began to grope her breast. Catherine tried to restrain him, but she was enjoying it too much. She could hardly breathe as Alan continued to kiss her. She moved her head and body slightly in order to catch her breath and regain some composure. But it was to no avail: Alan merely used the ever so slight adjustment in position to free his other hand which he used to unzip her trousers. She was powerless to stop him from inserting his fingers into her and wasn't sure that she wanted him to stop. Within minutes she was pleased she hadn't.

She shuddered with delight as he pushed his fingers deep inside her. As he continued to prod and stroke, she began to breathe more heavily. He could feel her fevered excitement grow inside her and finally, she arched her back and let out a groan of pleasure.

'Alan,' she whispered, emotionally drained from the experience. He stopped and watched her as she slumped back on to the beach. She lay there motionless. It was her first orgasm. She opened her eyes and saw that he himself was clearly in an extremely excited state.

'Here – take it,' he said, pushing his fully erect

penis into her hand. 'Go on – no. Like this. That's it–' She grasped his organ, and started to rhythmically pull her hand up and down the shaft, slowly increasing her speed. This was Catherine's first real sexual experience, and she was shocked by the power of Alan's ejaculation.

With the cold wind still blowing, they both suddenly became aware of the freezing temperature. Having readjusted their clothing, they slowly got up. Standing facing each other, Alan took Catherine's face in his hands and gently kissed her cheek. With a simple romantic gesture he had recovered something beautiful from the clumsy mess that had just taken place.

'I've never done that before.'

'What? You mean–'

'Yes. Alan, I'm still a virgin. You shouldn't be that surprised.'

'Do you want to remain one?' he asked, smiling with a glint in his eyes.

'Yes– Well I think I do–'

They both laughed as they ran across the beach and back up the steps and on to the promenade.

11

Alan moved in to Catherine's cosy two-bedroomed Brunswick Square flat a few weeks later. They were absolutely confident about their decision. Neither of them had ever felt like this before. Catherine, who by now had given herself to him, was determined to keep him; Alan, by no means an experienced lover but obviously more worldly than his partner, was hopelessly in love himself. He could not believe how quickly his life had changed.

The penalty of breaking tenancy agreement early was waived by his partner's aunt, who would have no problems re-letting the space. She was, however, more than a little concerned by the speed at which Alan had moved in – and of course, because of her faith, frowned on such behaviour.

'She's my niece and I am responsible for her, Alan. It's only been six weeks. She's so young and naïve.'

'Yes I know, Emily. But it feels so right – and we both know we're making the correct decision. I understand how you feel, but she is twenty-one, and I'm twenty-four. Not so young now, you know.'

'Well, as long as you're sure,' she paused. 'I'll have a lot of explaining to do,' she said cryptically.

'What do you mean?'

'Young Father Docherty has been going on and on about Catherine's wretched attendance for Mass. The excuses I've been giving are wearing thin. When he finds out about you and–'

'Why will he find out?' Alan interrupted, a little shocked. 'I mean Catherine hasn't been to church since I've known her.' This was a bolt out of the blue for a lapsed Catholic.

'I know, but she used to go every week before her father died. He will eventually find out – and when he does, he'll have plenty to say about it. He's a bit of a firebrand.'

'Emily, I suppose you can always say that I'm of the faith!'

'That's about all I can say!' She looked at him for what seemed an eternity. She then turned away and looked around the room. 'I suppose I'll be able to re-let the space pretty quickly!' Looking back at him, she smiled.

12

Six months later, Catherine and Alan were married at the Church of St Josephs, much to the relief of Father Docherty. The 35 year old priest had found out about the young couple just as Emily Davis had feared. Their wedding day, which took place on a mild summer's day in late June, was a small affair attended by what little family both sides had. The young couple had neither the time nor the money to go on honeymoon. Alan was working very long hours at his job on reception, whilst Catherine had graduated from teacher-training college and was now furiously looking for a position at local schools. Both of them, being only children, wanted a large family as quickly as possible.

'I want to enjoy them while we're still young. Can you imagine how wonderful it would have been to have lots of sisters and brothers. To have young parents who did everything with you.'

'No I can't. I never had that luxury. I hardly saw my dad. And like you, I had no siblings.'

'Well, I think we should start right away, and I know Aunt Emily will help.'

'Hold on there. I don't want your aunt to help.' He placed his hands gently on his wife's shoulders. 'Listen, I think I'm due a raise in the autumn because I'll be officially out of my traineeship. We'll certainly be able to afford one child immediately!'

The decision had been made, but it didn't quite turn out as expected. Months of trying turned into years of hoping. Nothing happened. Alan managed to persuade his doctor to check his sperm count, an unusual request at the time. The results were unremarkable, although it was true, he was on the low side. As far as Catherine was concerned, fertility checks were unheard of, especially for a modest couple with very little spare money. She was convinced that there was nothing wrong with her since she ovulated regularly, and would have refused to get checked out even if Alan had asked her.

13

As bad as things were on the family side, things could not have been better for both of them on the employment front. Catherine secured a teaching position in St John the Baptist primary school in Whitehawk Road, behind the general hospital in Kemp Town. It was literally no more than a hundred yards from her aunt Emily's house. Apart from being at the top of an exhaustingly steep hill, the job was perfect.

Alan, meanwhile, completed his traineeship and became a fully fledged member of staff working on reception. His pay, although not generous, was more than enough to cover the couple's expenditure. With Catherine's small salary, they managed to accelerate the payments on the residue of the mortgage that Catherine's father had left outstanding before he had died. Even after three years, they never lost hope, despite being childless, and looked to move to a house.

The ideal location would have been Hove. A house with a garden, for the future arrival of children, was of paramount importance. However, it was during this period that two events happened – or to be more accurate, two non-events – that would radically change their lives.

14

The expected arrival of Aunt Emily on Christmas Day was, as always, eagerly anticipated by Catherine. She loved her company, and Christmas lunch had become an annual event for the three of them since she and Alan had got married. Emily Davis was a very punctual woman. In fact she was never late for anything, particularly when it came to a family event.

'God! It's quarter past one. I can't believe it.'

'What do you mean?' Alan asked, struggling to pull the cork out of the wine bottle.

'Aunt Emily. She's late.'

'Only by 15 minutes. Give her a chance. The buses aren't great on the holidays. Though the traffic shouldn't be too bad down Western Road,' he replied, shrugging his shoulders without any show of real concern.

However, by 2 o'clock both Alan and Catherine had become anxious. After receiving no reply when telephoning, Alan decided to get in his car and drive down the sea front and up to Kemp Town. Ringing the bell constantly for five minutes, he finally went round to the back of the house and forced open the window of the ground-floor flat where Emily lived.

There was no sign of life in the kitchen, lounge or dining room. As he approached the bedroom, he began to smell a noxious odour that became increasingly stronger. It had become so powerful by the time he'd opened the door that he had to put a handkerchief over his mouth and nose to prevent himself from retching.

The sight that lay before him was one that Alan had never had to confront before. The old lady was lying across her unmade bed. Clad in a white cotton nightgown, her old pale body lay motionless. Alan stood transfixed to the spot, literally unable to move. The normal reaction would have been to call out her name, but there was no point. Although he had never seen a dead body before Alan knew that her stillness, the blue colour, and the foul odour emanating from the body were conclusive enough signs.

He did not approach the body, but slowly turned around and walked back out of the room. He picked up the telephone and rang the police, and then his wife.

'Darling, it's me. I have some terrible news – it's Emily.'

'Oh God! What's happened? Is she all right?'

'No– Catherine, there's no easy way of telling you this.'

'She's dead, isn't she, Alan?' Catherine interrupted, realising immediately what had happened. 'I'm coming over.'

'Are you sure. I mean I don't think you should. I mean–'

It was too late. Catherine had put down the receiver and was on her way.

Alan was surprised by his wife's reaction to her aunt's death. Her self-composure was extraordinary, especially since her aunt had been like a mother to her and was her last surviving close family relative. She didn't count her real mother as a member of her family as she hadn't seen her for years. She took control over everything, including liaising with the doctors and police regarding the post-mortem (which revealed that the old lady had died from a massive heart attack) and finally dealing with the funeral arrangements, making sure Father Docherty included her favourite hymns and readings at the service.

Perhaps it was because she was the only person who could take responsibility. Alan had known her for only four years, and was very busy at work. But it was more likely that the inner calm and self-repose was a result of a hormone change symptomatic of the early weeks of pregnancy. Catherine was late by a week before she started to feel different. She was two weeks' late when her aunt was found dead.

As the delay became longer, her excitement increased, and indeed managed to soften the massive blow of the loss of her surrogate mother.

43

The desire for a baby had become an obsession for both her and Alan. After two months she finally told Alan, who was equally ecstatic. The search for a house now became even more important to Alan. He wanted to provide for his family in a proper way. It had not entered his mind that his wife already had a place for all of them to live without him having to dig into his own savings.

'Absolutely not. I won't do it, Catherine.' His old fashioned Irish pride would not entertain the notion of him living in a house provided for by his wife. Although Brunswick Square was Catherine's, Alan had been paying the lion's share of the outstanding mortgage repayments.

'But it's a beautiful Georgian house with a garden in a quiet part of town. We could convert the flats back into one house. You can pay for that if it makes you feel better.'

'Yes it would – but it just doesn't feel right. I'm not comfortable with it.'

'You know it's what Aunt Emily would have wanted. She would never have left me the property if she knew I would just sell it. Her husband left it to her in his will, before he went to the Front. It meant so much to her. She would have really wanted us to live there. You know that.'

The Aunt Emily line of argument clinched it for Catherine: Alan agreed to move to Kemp Town. It was the obvious move, particularly with Catherine's job at the primary school being within a hundred yards. The monies raised from the sale of the flat at Brunswick Square, combined with Alan's savings, paid for the conversion of St

George Street.

15

It was two months later, just after they had moved in, when Catherine fell over the front-doorstep, carrying the food shopping. She lost consciousness for a few seconds, and then managed to have enough composure to remain still and not try and force herself up immediately. She looked around at the food strewn across the wooden floor of the hallway.

'My goodness, dear, are you all right?'

'Well, I'm not sure, actually,' Catherine responded, looking behind her at the elderly woman standing on the pavement and staring through the open door.

At this point Catherine put one hand on the banister and slowly pulled herself up. The old lady moved towards her, immediately seeing that the young woman was far from being all right. Noticing the small trickle of blood that was running down Catherine's tights, the old lady slowly walked her to the nearest room so that she could sit down.

'Now, dear, where is your telephone?'

'It's in the kitchen. Thank you for helping. You couldn't get me a glass of water?' Catherine hardly had the strength to finish off her sentence. She began to lose consciousness again.

The ambulance arrived in a matter of minutes. Unknown to Catherine, she had already miscarried.

16

The two crises, happening within months of each other, hit both Alan and Catherine hard. But of the two, it was the loss of the baby that almost proved unbearable. They couldn't afford private medical help, and the National Health did not provide for these situations, so coping with the losses was incredibly difficult for both of them. Alan spent more time at work, leaving home early and not returning until well into the evening. Catherine reacted differently, becoming morose, sitting at home, reading and watching television. The school was sympathetic and gave her as much leave as she needed.

As time went by, they both pulled themselves out of the depression that had threatened to drown them. Alan was first to gain some perspective.

'We'll try again. I know it won't be easy, but we're still young, sweetheart.'

'But what if I never get pregnant again? Remember how difficult it was.'

'I know, I know – but we must try. Everything seems terrible right now. Emily's death, and this–' He looked at his wife who had aged over the past few months since the tragedy. 'Listen, let's go away somewhere. Oh, I don't know – somewhere hot. What do you think?' She looked up at him, and smiled for the first time in weeks.

'OK, Alan. Maybe you're right. But don't expect too much from me – not yet anyway.'

The holiday, although not the panacea that Alan had hoped for, certainly helped both of them. Catherine started to emerge from her malaise, and began to look forward rather than back. The experience that she had suffered would not be forgotten, but she was now stronger, more resilient, and had a much clearer perspective on life. These were attributes, unknown at the time to her, that she would come to pass on to her child.

There would be other pregnancies, three, in fact, over the next 20 years of otherwise fruitless trying. None of the three ever went the full term, the longest being five months. The hurt and pain suffered after the miscarriages was terrible, and the last one meant that she had to go into labour and deliver. But she managed to get on with her life despite the latest tragedy. She was now a woman and was able to cope more easily. She carried on, immersing herself in her teaching, giving her all to the other people's children who attended her class.

Alan meanwhile began to climb the hotel corporate ladder. From the lowest rung, temporary junior lift operator, he had moved on to a permanent job at reception, and from there he regularly gained promotion. By the time he was thirty he had become the restaurant manager. He impressed his employers by not only his work rate, but also by his ideas. Over the following ten years he continued to progress, finally becoming the general manager of the hotel.

Earning an extremely good salary with a very good pension, coupled with the fact that there was no mortgage to pay off, the Blackstones slipped into a middle-class existence almost by accident. They only had themselves to worry about, and as such, made sure that they enjoyed life to the full. Adventurous holidays, an expensive car and antiques, were all part of their lifestyle as they approached their forties. And although nothing could compensate for the void left by not having any children, they both made the best of what they had.

18

Everything changed, however, during the autumn of 1977. It was Catherine's fourth pregnancy, but her first in ten years. This one felt different, and Catherine knew it. Her attendance at Mass dramatically increased during those first four months. Looking to God for the first time since abandoning Him after the death of her father over 24 years earlier, she began to confide in Him, praying to Him to allow her to go the full term.

'I don't understand why you bother. I mean, where was He before when you needed Him? How can you believe in Him, Catherine?'

'Alan, people have suffered far worse things than us and have still kept their faith.'

'Well more fool them. I think the whole thing is such a nonsense. If you–'

'Stop it, Alan. It's my choice. I want to go. It's

giving me strength. I can't quite explain it, but talking to Him and praying to Him has helped.'

'Oh! this is absurd. I just don't understand.' He looked down at his wife sitting on the couch with a cushion resting on her expanded waist-line. He genuinely could not understand his wife's recent surge in faith. He had left his belief behind in Dublin. Not since his parents had died at such a young age, leaving him an orphan, had he taken the Eucharist. His marriage in church had been a compromise for Aunt Emily, who kept her faith, despite her own personal tragedy at being left a widow at such a young age.

'You're right – you don't understand,' she said calmly. She felt an air of serenity, as if she was in total control, not just over the way she was feeling and in dealing with her self, but also over her husband. He would have to accept her, and her rediscovery of her creed. She continued to attend regularly, much to the delight of Father Docherty, until she gave birth on that early May afternoon.

19

Names for the baby had been discussed. Even this became a source of contention between the two of them. An agreement was finally reached if in the event a boy was born. The name 'Thomas' was one they both liked. However, if it was to be a girl, no compromise could be reached. Catherine, at this time in the clamp-like grip of the church, proposed three alternatives: Mary,

Virginia and Rose. Alan opposed all of them on principle, but could not come up with any choices of his own. He decided to leave it, and just hope that it would be a boy.

The pregnancy, which was now becoming more of an obsession for Alan than it was for the mother, seemed to be going according to plan. Catherine, now not working, spent her time walking along the promenade or on the piers, and going to the theatre or cinema. Alan frequently managed to get tickets for the Theatre Royal through the concierge and other hotel contacts. This proved particularly useful during the RSC season over New Year.

Catherine went to every performance during the period. Her appreciation of Shakespeare rapidly grew, helped in no small way by a great deal of reading about the playwright and his plays during the daytime. Her particular favourite was *As You Like It*, which she saw three times, twice on her own and once with Alan. She was captivated by the lead character, Rosalind, for her the most consummate of all Shakespeare's heroines. Beautiful and elegant, she possessed an irrepressible, if a little mischievous, nature, and an irresistible sense of humour. Her guile was undeniably greater than most other Shakespearian female characters, no small achievement given the fierce competition. In short, it was very difficult not to be captivated by her.

As the delivery date approached, the anxiety increased. Alan was desperate, trying to ensure that Catherine did not take any risks. By the 36th week, apart from taking her to church, he practically ordered her to stay in the house and not go outside for fear of her falling over. By the 37th week, he stopped her from going into the kitchen, just in case the heat from the cooking might make her feel unwell.

Thankfully, for Catherine's state of mind, her waters broke in the 38th week. Suddenly, with a real emergency on his hands, Alan had clarity of thought and purpose. Without panicking, he managed to get his wife into the car, and drove rapidly to the hospital (which was, admittedly, only 400 yards away).

20

Alan at last handed the baby back to Catherine, overcome by the emotion of the birth.

'Well – what about a name?'

'Of the three, I must say I like Rose the best,' she said, stroking the baby's matted hair.

'Hold on. I haven't agreed to any of those names. You know that.' He turned around and walked away from the bedside, sensing that if he were to stay, his resolve would disappear.

'Oh, Alan, don't be like that. You can see she's got Rose written all over her face.'

He turned around. How could he refuse her – she had just gone through nine hours of the most unbearable pain that no man could possibly understand. In fact she had endured nine months of hell, not to mention the 23 years of anguish. There was very little he could do, except say yes.

'Catherine, if you're really set on it, then OK.

But–' He paused. He couldn't resist it. The 'but' meant that Catherine was not going to get her own way without some measure of guilt.

'Oh, God, Alan! How could you! It means so much to me– You know it does.'

'Yes I do, but I just don't like the name. If anything, its just too short!'

'Well if that's the problem we can always lengthen it. What about Rosy?'

He looked at her in disbelief. 'I know you're a little emotional at this point, and you might be a touch mad having just given birth, but surely you don't expect me to take that suggestion seriously,' he said.

'No, I suppose not. What about Ros–alind!'

'Rosalind?'

'Yes. Rosalind.' She smiled, looking at him, and then at their baby daughter. She knew it was perfect as soon as she said it.

'Rosalind,' he chuckled. 'Just like the lead character in the play.'

'Yes. *As You Like It*,' Catherine replied.

'Rosalind.' He looked at the baby, and smiled. 'Yes, Rosalind will be just fine.' He laughed back at her. Not only was it an inspirational compromise, but the name would also prove to be prophetic.

21

After two days at the hospital, Alan brought both mother and child home. The Blackstone family – for that is what it was now – centred around the new addition. Rosalind, unsurprisingly, became the focal point in both Alan and Catherine's lives. Both their hopes and dreams had been fulfilled by the birth of their baby daughter and nothing would stand in the way of their love and affection for her.

The baptism took place six months later at St Joseph's, much to Alan's chagrin. What made it worse for him was that the christening took well over an hour. During those 60 minutes of religious ritual, all of his preconceived views on Christianity came to the fore. He feared Catherine's recently found, near obsession with the church, and wanted to make sure that his daughter would not fall into, what he perceived, as the same trap.

'I don't want her going to church every week, Catherine. It's not fair. I'm her father. I have a say too, you know.'

'I know you do, and I respect that. But I feel very strongly about this. I want her to be brought up a Catholic. It's important to me. I feel that my faith in God enabled us to have Rosalind– Anyway, you have no beliefs, and I do, so surely I should be allowed to follow that belief and encourage my child.'

Alan thought about the perverse logic in his wife's argument. He could understand that her view was a positive and proactive one, whereas his was essentially negative (although he felt more rational). Did he have a right to stop his wife from taking his child to church? And if he did, was it right to enforce his view on her? The longer he thought about it, the outcome was never going to be in doubt. After weeks of mulling it over, he finally came up with a proposal that bore a resemblance to a total concession.

'How about you have control over Rosalind's religious instruction up until her first communion. After that she can make her own mind up.'

'But she'll only be nine years old. That's ridiculous.' Catherine laughed it off, sensing victory was close. 'Of course, if you make it up until her confirmation when she can decide, that would be fine.'

'So at 13 she can do what she likes.' Alan stepped close to his wife. 'That means not even having to go to church.'

'Yes.'

'OK, then. I'll have to accept it. I can see you're not going to change your mind.'

That was the last that was said on the topic. It was never raised again, even when Rosalind started primary school at St John the Baptist, where Catherine still taught. A deal was a deal; and she was still only four.

22

It was one of the happiest days of Catherine's life when she took Rosalind to school for her first day. Only four-and-a-half, but brimming with self-confidence, the little girl was nothing short of precocious. She immediately fitted in and made new friends with ease. For the first two years she thrived in the school atmosphere, becoming the most popular girl in her class, as if it were the natural order of things to come. Everybody was delighted with her development. She was top (or close to the top) in almost all of the activities she took part in. However, in the third year, as she was approaching her eighth birthday, she appeared to accelerate at an even faster rate than before. Whereas in previous years she excelled but was still nevertheless part of the form, now she began to pull away and it was clear to all the teachers, including her mother, that Rosalind was something special.

'It's her reading, Catherine – and her maths. She's equivalent to a ten year old. Remember she's also had to deal with her catechisms for her First Communion.'

'Yes, I know,' she paused. 'You think she's that far ahead. You can't be sure– Look I know she's bright but–' Catherine looked through her daughter's workbooks with the Head. There was no getting away from it: Rosalind was more than just bright. If she continued her development at the same rate, she would be a scholar at any school in the country.

'What do you think we should do?'

'I suggest we give her extra work, expand her mind a little, and see how she gets on. But if she's as clever as I think she is, then you should start thinking about a top independent girl's school in two years' time.'

'Well, I better start putting my mind to it!' Catherine smiled.

She closed her daughter's class notebook and picked up her handbag. It was late, well past 5 o'clock. Rosalind was doing her homework in the classroom opposite. Catherine walked towards the door and peered through the glass window. Sitting at the desk, her daughter was feverishly doing her maths. Her concentration was never remotely threatened by her mother's presence. Her senses were totally absorbed in the arithmetic she was currently solving. Nothing would distract her. She was no ordinary girl.

When Catherine finally dragged Rosalind away, it was well gone half past five. The five-minute walk back down the steep hill towards home was usually taken up with the daughter asking questions and the mother answering. This time however, Catherine was too deep in thought to respond.

'Mummy, why did you and Daddy choose it?'

'What darling? Choose what?' Catherine finally answered, realising that her daughter had asked the same question three times and she was still unaware of what the question was.

'My name. Why "Rosalind"?'

'Your father and I named you after the most wonderful female character in a play called *As You Like It*. She was the most beautiful and clever girl; she was full of life, and she seemed to understand everyone and everything.'

'How beautiful was she?'

'Oh she was so beautiful, Rosalind.' She stopped walking momentarily. 'But you must understand, it wasn't just her beauty, it was her personality and her character that made it impossible for anyone not to fall in love with her.' She smiled and continued to walk back, holding her daughter's hand. 'You would be perfect for the part!' she said quietly.

'Why? Because my name is Rosalind?' The little girl knew the answer already, but wanted to hear it.

'No, sweetheart. Because you are just like her – you wouldn't need to act. The part will be so natural for you!' Catherine laughed. They had arrived at the house and Catherine was now looking for her front door keys.

'Who wrote it?' Rosalind's inquisitive mind slipped into second gear.

'What, dear? Ah here they are.' Catherine pulled the keys out of her bag and opened the door. The question then suddenly registered. She looked at Rosalind, who was still standing on the doorstep waiting for an answer. She crouched down and looked into her beautiful round blue eyes. 'The greatest playwright the world has ever known. His name was William Shakespeare.'

23

The two years that followed proved the headmaster right. Rosalind's academic ability was the best in the school. By the time her 11+ entrance exams approached, she had the pick of all the top private girls' schools.

'I don't want her to board. She's so young, Catherine.'

'Look, Alan, I'm not saying she should be sent away, but Roedean is the best girl's school in England and it's literally a mile-and-a-half down the road. I don't want her to miss the chance on some ridiculous excuse about her being so young, or so little. All the other girls who get in will be the same age, and approximately the same height! Listen, I'm also making a sacrifice.'

'How's that then?' he asked.

'Well, ideally I would like her to go to a Catholic school like St Mary's Ascot, but I know I've got no chance–'

'Absolutely none!' Alan interrupted.

'Exactly. Roedean has everything we would want. When she went for her interview, she loved the place – and I think they were very keen on her.'

'OK, OK, I get the message. Are you sure she's good enough? I mean obviously we have enough money to send her, but it's a very expensive place.'

'Alan, I don't think it will come to that – she'll probably win a scholarship.' She paused as he continued to look at her suspiciously. 'If you don't believe me, go upstairs, and come back and tell me what she's doing.'

Alan disappeared out of the room and came back downstairs five minutes later.

'Well?' Catherine asked, in a predictably triumphant manner.

'She's reading *A Tale of Two Cities*,' he said sheepishly. 'Is that normal for a ten year old?'

'Finally, the penny's dropped. There's no doubt she'll win a full scholarship. How many other ten-year-old kids read Dickens for fun? And she's now beginning to ask me questions on Shakespeare, since she's discovered the reason why she was named Rosalind. I can't answer them– I had to tell her to ask the teachers, but even they've told her to wait until senior school! Trust me, Alan, she's brilliant.'

'I suppose you're right. When is she sitting?'

'First week in January,' Catherine replied, knowing yet another battle had been won in her daughter's upbringing.

24

Rosalind did not disappoint. Although experiencing some nervousness before the big day, she performed as expected in the exams. She was awarded scholarships from a number of schools, but it was Roedean that the Blackstone family had set their sights on. When the formal letter of the award finally arrived, there was a certain feeling of anti-climax in the household. The problem was that there was never any doubt in the outcome. Both Alan and Catherine tried to be euphoric about the results, but it was clear that the anticipation and expectancy had taken something out of the event.

Rosalind, although sensing her parent's artificial exuberance and joy at the result, had a better understanding of the situation. Indeed, just like her alter ego in *As You Like It,* everything seemed so natural to her. She knew what she wanted to do and how to accomplish it. Like any other young girl, she had her hopes and dreams; but unlike most others, those dreams would now be attainable.

She was happy with her results, but was genuinely excited about going to her new school.

She was going to experience something that most people would never have the chance to go through. This was an opportunity that she would grasp. The school would provide her with a chance to express her talents in a way that she could not have done previously. Although not fully appreciating it yet, God had given her a brain that would open doors to certain rooms in life that were normally only reserved for the social elite.

Part 3

SOTHEBY'S, THE PRESENT DAY

4.15 P.M.

'I have £75 million with the lady in the blue suit.' Smith Luytens knew that the bidding would start slowly, but he could sense that the battle was still in its very early stages. The lady in blue was representing a museum in the midwest of the United States. She had already told him a week earlier that she would be bidding. He knew that she wasn't going to be anywhere near the price, but he was very grateful to her for starting the auction at the level he wanted. He expected the pace to quicken imminently.

'Do I have another bidder?' He looked around the room, momentarily glancing at his clients, the young couple seated in the back row to whom no one at that moment was paying the slightest bit of attention. He continued looking around, trying to entice the next bid. 'Do I have £80 million from anyone? All right, if you want to take it slowly I'll consider taking a smaller–'

'One hundred million!' a tall black American shouted from the back of the room. The bid was received with gasps from the audience.

'It's now against you, madam; I have £100 million from the gentleman at the back,' Smith Luytens responded without showing any emotion. He was the consummate professional and he knew that this was the bid that would electrify the sale. Most people in the room who were part of the art world knew that the identity of the bidder was the Los Angeles Getty Museum – the richest museum in the world.

£105 million was the next bid from the aisle near the front. The private Russian clients were now making their presence felt. Smith Luytens knew this one well; an oligarch who had made a billion pounds from Russia's state asset sale, and who was now desperate to make his mark in the more genteel surroundings of Western Europe's educated elite. But Smith Luytens had a feeling that despite his wealth he wouldn't stay the pace: there were too many big players out there ready to risk everything for the biggest prize available.

He momentarily glanced at his clients at the back, not long enough for the audience to notice but certainly long enough for the young couple to sense that things were going according to plan.

Part 4

CHARLES

1

As the hands of the clock came together at 12 midnight, signalling the start of another day – 5 May 1978 – the screams of agony could be heard across the plains of Wiltshire. Lady Longhurst's waters had broken at 8 o'clock in the morning, over 16 hours earlier. And now, after the most agonising and torturous labour, she had finally managed to push the head of her third baby out of her grotesquely distorted body. The final exertion was a desperate one. The family doctor and his nurse were becoming concerned for the health of the mother. She was now over 43 years old, and had insisted on having the birth without any medication, just like the others, at the family estate in Hathaway House.

The umbilical cord was cut a minute after the 9 lb baby boy had squirmed out of his mother's body. The new arrival was placed in the exhausted mother's arms.

'You better tell him to come in now,' the doctor said to the nurse.

'Right then. Are you sure you can manage?'

'Yes, yes, don't worry.' He was losing his patience, but at this point had no idea that he was about to lose one of his dearest patients.

The nurse left the doctor, who started sewing up the damage to the walls of the vagina, which had been torn by the stress of the baby's head.

'My lord, you can come in now.'

The aristocratic figure put down his copy of *Country Life* and placed it on the chair next to him. He uncrossed his legs and got up from his seat. Now over fifty, his once jet black hair had turned silver. Tall and broad, he still cut a very imposing figure indeed, though not the adonis he once was. He smiled down at the diminutive nurse who was opposite him and kept his eyes on her face as he walked towards the door. She felt uncomfortable as he came towards her.

'How long have you been working for the doctor? I haven't seen you before.'

'Uh – only three months, my lord.' Her response was interrupted as she felt his hand move slowly up her side and then cup her small but pert left breast. He left it there, waiting for her reaction.

'It's a little frantic around here at the moment. Perhaps we can talk later,' he said softly in her ear.

Before she could answer, he had withdrawn his hand and walked into the room where his wife had suffered so much pain over the last sixteen hours, but to which he was completely oblivious. The nurse momentarily shuddered as she followed him into the room. She resented his presence there. The disgusting audacity of his behaviour at that moment was incomprehensible to her.

'Ah, Lord Longhurst, you have another son,' the doctor called out.

2

Taking his newborn son away from the young

nurse, who was cleaning the infant carefully with cotton wool, he held him up above his giant frame and laughed.

'Well done, Davina. Just look at the size of him. This one's not going to disappoint me.'

The doctor turned around momentarily. He hated him. The only reason he remained the family doctor was because of his love for Davina. She was the antithesis of the monster standing beside him. Where he was tall and broadly built, she was slight and petite. His rugged pock-marked face, although attractive in a rough masculine way, stood in contrast to her smooth, silk-like skin and classical beauty. Where she portrayed an air of splendour and exquisiteness that was beyond a sexual dimension, almost surreal, his whole persona was about brutality and conquest. She was polite, warm and sensitive; he was rude, hard and a bully. They both represented the opposite ends of the human spectrum. She was forgiving and submissive. He was dominant, overbearing and remorseless.

The doctor had already told Lady Longhurst that after the baby was born, he would have to let them go as patients. He would always be available for her, but he wanted nothing to do with his Lordship. She understood completely. There were times when she had threatened to leave him, but as time went on, it was the easier option to stay. In the early years of marriage the threat of divorce kept him in check, but now it was an empty threat, and he knew it. Besides she lacked the necessary courage to abandon the family. There was no way that she would have been able to keep the twins, Gordon and Robert, when faced with the power of her husband. The establishment would have rallied around one of the oldest lordships in the realm. But it wasn't simply the social stigma attached to such a break, more the army of lawyers and a deep reservoir of professional advice that would make defeat so inevitable.

The decision to stay was not made lightly. She took comfort in the children, who were no angels. Indeed they were both naughty, to such an extent that even her patience was stretched. She blamed her husband for showing so little love towards them, and constantly belittling them. It was true that at school they were remarkable only in their ordinariness. Yet their places at Eton were assured since the family had been going there for over 400 years.

It was after a party at the end of the summer nine months earlier that James Longhurst, in a drunken state, forced his wife on to the bed and raped her. When she realised she was pregnant, she went to the doctor to consider an abortion. Once again – and despite the encouragement from her doctor – she lacked the courage to go through with it. And it was because of that fatal weakness that Davina Longhurst was lying on her bed at that very moment, beginning to fall into semi-consciousness from the loss of blood.

'Is everything all right?'

'No, I don't think it is. Please ring for an ambulance immediately. I hadn't realised how much blood she's lost.' He looked up at Longhurst, who for the first time showed some concern at his wife's condition. 'Lord Longhurst, did you hear me?' The doctor was now furiously working on his patient who was slipping deeper into a coma.

3

The Baron marched out of the room still holding the baby, and grabbed the nearest telephone. Inserting his index finger into the dial, he forced it round to the '9' three times.

'Yes, this is Lord Longhurst here, we have an emergency – yes, yes. We need an ambulance immediately. Yes, that's correct. Hathaway House – the gates will be open.' He hung up, paused for a moment and returned to the bedroom.

He opened the door slowly and looked across at the dreadful scene. There was blood everywhere, on the bed, the floor, all over the doctor's hands and arms, and now covering the nurse's tunic. Her left breast, which he had fondled barely ten minutes ago, was now covered by a harrowing claret-coloured stain.

'Well? How long for an ambulance?' the doctor shouted, while still desperately trying to stem the blood loss from his patient.

'Uh, they said ten minutes, but I think–'

'Ten minutes; Christ! I hope it's sooner than that. Jenny, I need more towels.'

The nurse grabbed the last two towels that were still clean. As she handed them to the doctor she glanced up at the baby, who was crying, but did not appear to be in too much distress. She refused the temptation of looking at the father, sensing that any form of recognition, even at such a catastrophic time as this, would have given him too much satisfaction.

'Are there any more?'

'No, doctor, that's it.'

'God! it's hopeless – Lady Longhurst – can you hear me? Davina, please nod your head or do something if you can hear me.'

4

The ambulance arrived seventeen minutes later. Ten minutes too late. Lady Davina Longhurst had lost consciousness when her husband had made the initial call. She was brain-dead within five minutes, and her heart stopped two minutes later. The doctor, the man who perhaps loved her more than anybody, finally pronounced her dead after a further seven minutes of desperate resuscitation attempts.

The doctor met the ambulance men outside the room and explained what had happened. What greeted them inside was something not even the most experienced of medics could ever get used to. Something akin to carnage was the best description of what lay before them. They carefully lifted the body off the bed and placed it on a stretcher. The doctor and the nurse began to clean up the room and complete the necessary bureaucratic procedures.

'Is there anything I should do?'

'Uh, no, your lordship. Just sign the necessary

forms. Should I take the baby now? Jenny can give him his first bath.'

'Oh, thank you.' He passed the baby over to the nurse. He felt an overriding sense of numbness. His inability to do anything useful compounded his confusion. Only half an hour earlier, this domineering, arrogant, giant of a man was holding aloft his third son in front of his wife in a triumphant, yet hubric moment. And now, at this moment, he was not at all in control of what he felt. His emptiness simply left him cold.

'I must go now, sir. The body's in the ambulance, and we'll have to do a post-mortem at the hospital. Obviously I can only wish you sincerest sympathies; she was such a fine–' He cleared his throat and paused, trying to regain his composure.

'That's all right old man. She was a fine woman. I'll miss her, too. You will come in to see on the baby, won't you?' James Longhurst was already beginning to feel better. For a man of his make up, 30 minutes was a long time to recover from such a loss.

'Yes, of course – but perhaps in the future, you could find a younger doctor.'

'No, no. Not at all. I won't hear of it. Now come on.' The ogre showed the reluctant grief-ridden doctor out of the hallway on to the driveway. He knew that the doctor loved his wife, and was now capitalising on the doctor's guilt to continue. The fact that the physician despised him gave him added pleasure. He watched as the doctor drove away, then turned away and went back into the house.

'Jenny!' he shouted as he walked up the stairs,

calling the nurse by her name for the first time.

'Yes, my lord. I'm in the bedroom with your baby.' She was sitting down now that the room had been cleared, with the baby sleeping on her lap. She was exhausted, and emotionally drained. The events of the past hour had removed the resentment she had felt for him, which was now replaced by sympathy.

'I am very sorry about what has happened.' He sat down next to her. 'It's not your fault. I am so sorry for you – that you have lost your wife, you must feel–'

'Oh, don't worry, I'm a strong person. Can I get you a drink?' His eyes were looking straight into her's. The stare made her feel uncomfortable. She wasn't entirely sure what he was feeling, but her confusion was telling her that she had to get out.

'No, I'm fine. I must be going. When is the maternity nurse arriving?' She was still hopelessly unsure of what the baron's motives were. It was impossible to determine whether he was going to make a pass, or if he was simply in dire need of some comfort. Her instincts now led her to believe that it was the former rather than the latter. The situation was so vile as to be beyond her comprehension. How someone could behave in such a manner whilst his wife's corpse was at that very moment undergoing an autopsy, almost made her convulse.

'Tomorrow morning. Davina expected to look after the baby until then, but now of course–' he tailed off, as he put his head in his hands.

'Well I'm sure you'll manage.' She got up, and

handed the baby back to the father.

Shocked at this total rejection, and not quite knowing what to do with the baby, he became slightly desperate.

'You can't leave me like this?'

'I can and I will. You'll find everything you need over there.' She pointed across to the table to the specially prepared baby milk, cotton wool and nappies.

'But how will you get home? At least let me call you a taxi.'

'No, thank you, I'm fine.' She walked quickly out of the room, leaving him with his baby sleeping on his shoulder.

5

The baron watched the nurse walk off down the drive. The lights of the house illuminated the night outside. It was now 3 o'clock, and it would be another five hours before the maternity nurse was due to arrive. He watched her body, dressed in her tight white tunic, until it slowly disappeared. Even at this nadir, he could not resist his sexual impulses. Her instincts to leave would normally have been correct. But in the event, she had been wrong. Unbeknown even to himself at that moment, the events of the evening had affected him deeply, and he was in desperate need of company. By the time the sun rose, he would be a different man.

He turned around and returned, with his baby, back to the room where the drama and tragedy had taken place. He placed the baby into its crib, and slumped into his armchair.

6

Lord James Longhurst, 37th baron of Hathaway House, came from one of the leading aristocratic families in England. Created a baronetcy in the sixteenth century by Queen Elizabeth 1, the Longhurst legacy had produced an unbroken line of male heirs for over 450 years. It was in the late-eighteenth century that the family reached its apogee in not only money and influence, but also the political sphere. Amassing huge wealth after speculating on the London Markets, the 15th baron then went on to make a second fortune exploiting Britain's fantastic gains after the conclusion of the Seven Years War. His great friend Robert Clive had effectively won India for the British at the Battle of Plassey, and as a result secured the foundation for the Empire itself. Clive was famous for looking after his friends and supporters, and Longhurst was no exception.

After the successes of the 15th baron in the financial arena, it was the turn of the 16th to concentrate on politics. He spent a small part of the family fortune buying up the 'rotten' boroughs, which enabled him to control six seats in the Commons, from the House of Lords. He ingratiated himself with the Tories under William Pitt the Younger, and managed for a period of three years to be in the government when the prime minister had to deal with the most tumultuous event of the century: the French Revolution.

The 16th baron's political career was cut short by smallpox; Jenner's vaccination experiment was still ten years away. His son did not have the intellectual capacity to carry on his father's political progress, and slowly and inexorably the family disappeared from the limelight. Over the following generations the Longhursts distinguished themselves in the battlefield more than anywhere else. A tradition was built up in the officer corps of the army, with the name 'Longhurst' being amongst the most notable for valour.

They hung on to the last vestiges of their great historical fortune. By the turn of the twentieth century, there had been a mini recovery in their financial status. Not that they were ever poor, but with a combination of excellent advice and some shrewd investment decisions, the family's position was secure. A network of trusts was set up before the war, which secured the family's wealth for the future.

Like most aristocratic families during the twentieth century, and after surviving two horrendous world wars where many fell, the Longhursts took comfortable city jobs in either stockbroking or investment banking, earning enough income not to compromise their inherited family wealth. Their lives followed remarkably similar paths, from Eton to Oxford, and then to the 'Square Mile'. They all had residencies in south-west London, as well as accommodation on the estate. The barons themselves lived in the mansion itself, whilst the others had houses on the estate. James continued this tradition to the letter, being a director at a major City bank, and having a house in Chelsea Square.

The family seat, Hathaway House, was one of the finest country houses in south-west England. The house had been continuously built-on from the time of the original ennoblement, and its characteristics displayed more than one style of architecture. Indeed, in some form or other, all five orders, from Doric through to Tuscan, had been incorporated. Inside the house, there were many memorable features, including rare and precious tapestries and sculptures. It was featured in all of the major country-house publications, for not only its architectural importance, but also the treasures inside. There was, however, one secret of which the public knew little. Located just off the main hall, away from the front of the house, was a room that contained the most valuable of Longhurst treasures: the library.

Embracing a collection of books that experts considered to be amongst the finest found anywhere in the world, it was rarely visited, even by the family, and was never discussed. Maintained by a team from the British Library, experts were allowed only to inspect the treasured tomes, but not to take them out of their habitat. This was part of the strict Longhurst code. The library was intrinsically part of the house. It could never be dismantled, nor the books be sold off separately. It had never been valued, but when an authority from the British Library came to visit, he considered the collection to be easily worth in excess of £100 million.

However, the house and its contents were not

the only jewels in the Longhurst crown; the land the house was built on was also unique. One thousand acres of the best Wiltshire countryside surrounded the mansion, offering the finest shooting, hunting, and fishing. The income arising from the estate had consistently increased over the years, and was very important to the family. The upkeep was enormous, and even with the trust income and their city earnings, there still would have been a shortfall had it not been for the well publicised shoots and fishing rights.

7

James was 30 years old when he met Davina Cavendish at a charity ball at the Grosvenor House Hotel, having just inherited the title after his father had met his death in a riding accident. James knew instantly that she would be the future Lady Longhurst. Tall, beautiful and elegant, demure and modest, to the point of self-deprecation, she epitomised everything that he wanted for, and from, a wife. After a whirlwind romance, where he quite literally swept her off her feet, the couple got married at St Paul's in August 1955, in what the society magazines called the social event of the year.

The Longhurst tradition was strongly patriarchal, and as such the young Davina would have to play a subservient role as James' wife. Being ten years younger than her husband, and more than a little in awe of the Longhurst family tradition, she was very happy to play this role. Producing an heir was paramount in James' mind. He did not want to be the first Longhurst not to have a son. However, he decided not to pressurise his young wife immediately. Wanting to let her settle down into married life, and to familiarise herself with her new and grand surroundings, he made no mention of children at this time.

Ensconced in the ancestral home, she happily played the dutiful wife, and made sure that the house was kept in the way that he wanted. She had never felt so happy. James was in London, at Chelsea Square, during the week, and returned home every Friday evening for the weekend.

During the first year of their marriage he treated her kindly, never shouting at her, buying her gifts, and making sure that she was looked after by all the staff. His attitude began to change during the second year when Davina suffered appendicitis. The operation was a success, but the 21-year-old's recuperation took a long time. She remained in her bed after returning from hospital for over six months, and James' patience was stretched to the limit. His frustration was further exasperated by Davina being too ill to have sex. He began to dread the weekends, having to be sympathetic to a bed-ridden wife. She felt his irritation and made desperate attempts to try and fulfil his demands. But it was to no avail; he had found alternative pleasures.

Weekends became less of a problem simply because he stopped returning to the estate. He stayed in London, going to parties and having affairs. There was no shortage of women. James had won a well-earned reputation for his sexual voraciousness during his youth. Rumours about how well endowed he was gave extra credence to his reputation, as he began to play the field. He felt neither guilt nor remorse at his behaviour. As far as he was concerned, she was failing as a wife.

The gossip did not take long to reach Hathaway House. Walking down the stone staircase to the kitchen, she overheard what was meant to be a private discussion between the family chauffeur and the housekeeper.

'His lordship is staying in town again, Wendy. He's got a party there this weekend. He doesn't need me to come up until Monday morning!'

'His carrying on like that – one day he'll get caught. Her ladyship would be devastated if she were to find out. It's most upsetting. She's much better now. If he bothered to come back and see her, he'd see how beautiful she looks.'

'That's quite enough, Wendy,' Davina said to the housekeeper. She then turned to the driver. 'Perhaps, Bill, you might take me to London.'

'Of course, ma'am. When would you like to go?' he asked, standing up immediately on her entrance, and brushing himself down in a manner similar to a schoolboy being caught with sweets in his mouth during lesson time.

'Now would be most convenient,' she replied.

8

The drive took just over two hours, but seemed like an entire morning. She instructed the chauffeur to park before they reached the house.

She wanted to give her husband as little warning as possible. She got out of the car and immediately felt the bitterly cold February wind bite across her face. She walked slowly towards the door, seemingly in slow motion. She overheard herself playing out the various scenarios in her mind before she reached the entrance.

She had no keys. There was no need for her to have them. During the past two years of marriage she had only stayed there once, and then it was only because of Hathaway House being redecorated. She pressed the bell in a determined fashion, and then waited.

'Hold on a minute; who is it?'

She made no reply, and waited for him to open the door.

'Hello – I'm coming, whoever you are.' He opened the door, not bothering to wait for a reply. As he opened it, she pushed it forcefully forward, knocking him back.

'Davina! No wait, don't go upstairs!'

She was already at the landing. She opened the bedroom door, and saw lying on his bed two naked women kissing and caressing each other. They didn't even bother to look up. Davina stood there paralysed to the spot, not quite knowing what to do. This particular scenario had not been rehearsed. She managed to maintain her poise. Slowly closing the door, she turned around and faced her husband.

'Get them out of here. You have 15 minutes to get dressed, and come back to Hathaway House with me. If you are not in the car when I leave, I will serve you with divorce papers on Monday morning.' She spoke in a calm, even manner.

There was a pause as he stared at her. He had never seen her like this before. It was the first time that she had confronted him on anything, let alone on something as devastating as this. He felt completely disarmed, almost frightened by her calmness, and her apparent capacity to absorb such a shock with such clarity and purpose.

'All right, I'll be there,' he said quietly in a pathetic manner.

She walked down the stairs slowly, with each step stressing how much in control of the situation she was.

9

She sat in the car waiting for him. After ten minutes the door opened and the two women scurried past the car. Davina looked at them, noticing that neither of them could have been much older than 16. She felt revulsion at what she had seen. She watched them go down the street and looked at her watch. Her husband had two minutes to go, otherwise she would be known in the future as 'Davina, Lady Longhurst'. It was the first and only time she had the conviction to carry out the threat. She knew that the threat of divorce would concentrate her husband's mind. The shame and scandal for the Longhurst family name would be too much for him to bear. That was the single most important thing in his life, and he would do everything in his power to protect it. And ironically it was Davina's most powerful weapon.

Almost running out of time, with seconds to spare, James locked his front door and walked briskly towards the car. He got in the front and put his seatbelt on.

'Bill, would you take us back to Hathaway House? You can then have the rest of the weekend off. Lord Longhurst will not be needing you.' It was she who was giving the orders.

'Darling–'

'Don't let's talk about it now.' She interrupted him, almost enjoying her moment of total victory. The guilt he was now feeling grew partly from the fact that, in his own warped way, he loved her. She was, for him, the perfect woman. He now saw it for the first time and he suddenly felt an admiration for her. He had no idea that she had that courage in her. He was at a loss about what to say or what to do. His previous carefree attitude had been cast aside by one confrontation which he would take a very long time to recover from. She had already made up her mind to forgive him, but she would never forget the episode. For the moment, she would keep the threat of her departure hanging over him like the sword of Damocles, in order to keep him faithful. It proved to be a successful strategy for a number of years.

10

Denying him an heir proved to be an extremely potent weapon, and concentrated his mind on behaving properly. It certainly worked for the lady of the household for a number of years. His demands were continual, but excuses were made. When no pretext sufficed, she calculated her cycle to perfection, never leaving anything to chance. However as she grew older, and with the time on her body-clock running out, she herself felt a desperate need for children.

Finally after seven years of waiting, Davina Longhurst became pregnant, and produced not one, but two male heirs. Gordon and Robert came out of her womb within 20 minutes of each other. There was very little argument over their names, since the parents only had five to choose from: all Longhurst men had a choice of James, Charles, Gordon, Robert or Hugo. And in this case, the choice was limited, to say the least, given that James obviously did not want to name either of them with his own name, one first cousin from the junior branch of the family was already called Hugo, and a very old uncle still alive was named Charles.

For a brief period, the twins brought Davina and James closer together. The pressure was off, and James could relax now that he had performed his most important duty for the family. He was extremely happy with his wife for providing him with two heirs. He showered her with jewellery and other expensive gifts. He gave her more attention, and showed more affection than at any time previously. For Davina, the events of seven years before had disappeared into the background. She felt that things could not be better.

Unfortunately the halcyon years were temporary. After twelve months, with the Longhurst male line now secure, James was back in London. The philandering began again on a much more discreet basis. He made sure that the staff, particularly his driver, never saw anything. He was very careful to cover his every move, ensuring that he left no clues. Davina noticed a gradual estrangement, but felt that this was normal in any marriage with two young screaming children. She never questioned him, nor did she suspect him. She believed that he had now changed his ways. She was also desperate for the marriage to work. Having children changed her position completely. She wanted the family to stay together, and any threat of divorce by her was a hollow one. Besides which she actually needed him. The twins were more than a handful, and there was no sign of improvement in their behaviour.

They inherited all of their father's bad points, and none of their mother's good ones. They were quite literally monsters. When they reached primary-school age there was a general uneasiness about them keeping their places. By this time James had given up disciplining them, mainly because it had no effect at all. It was up to Davina to try to contain them. It was to no avail, as they continued to steal, bully, and disrupt the other children during their time at primary school. It was no surprise when Davina received a call from the headmaster of Heathcliff Preparatory School asking to see her.

'Really, Lady Longhurst, if they were not your children, they would no longer be pupils.'

'I understand, Headmaster, but you only have them now for another year before they sit common entrance.'

'Yes, I do understand, but that leads me to the issue of their academic ability. I can safely say that their woeful behaviour record is superseded only by their complete lack of talent in the academic arena.'

'I've seen the reports, Headmaster. There is very little that I can say. I have tried, believe me, really I have.'

'Oh, I have no doubt about that. We have too!' He laughed sympathetically. He asked himself how two monsters such as Gordon and Robert Longhurst could have been produced by this beautiful, softly-spoken woman. 'But it's to no avail. It's a good job that they inherited the name otherwise Eton would never give them places. I only hope that they survive there.'

'Yes, that has crossed my mind. I can only hope that they mature over the next 12 to 15 months.'

'Who knows, they might. We'll just keep trying at this end. Thank you for coming, Lady Longhurst.' He got up and showed her to the door.

'Headmaster, thank you for all your efforts. Is there anything that we could do to help the school?'

'Well since you asked, we do need money in our scholarship fund. If you or Lord Longhurst are able to make a donation, it would be most welcome.'

11

The twins sat the exams in the following year, and as expected were given places at Eton. The Longhurst family connection to the school would continue, just as it had done for hundreds of years. It never crossed James' mind that the boys would not get in, although Davina had been more than a little worried. James' detachment from the family had slowly, but inexorably, increased. Davina had seen the familiar behavioural pattern for some time, but unlike twenty years previously when the courage of youth gave her the impetus to act, she decided to let it go. She had what she wanted. A beautiful home, a wide circle of friends who were supportive and who adored her, and the children who despite being at times intolerable, were still her sons, whom she loved more than herself. Her sexual needs had never been that demanding, even when she was just married, so she was more than able to live without her husband.

It was at this time, just after the boys had reached their 14th birthday, that she decided to move into a separate bedroom. He accepted her decision without complaint. He was bored with her in a physical sense, but recognised her virtues, both socially and as a mother, even if not as a wife. He was happy enough with the set up, enjoying his affairs in London (which had seemingly gone unnoticed) and having the family status and reputation unsullied by any family upheaval. Love as a concept had escaped his cognisant grasp; he no longer had the capacity to feel emotion, or indeed any kind of compassion.

But the finely balanced applecart was dramatically upset in the autumn of 1977, when, after a dinner party at Hathaway House, James became very drunk. With a glass of brandy in one hand, and a cigar in the other, he staggered up the giant staircase towards the first floor where Davina was sleeping. He knocked on her door, didn't wait for a reply and walked in. Davina woke up startled and grappled with the wire of the light switch.

'James! What's the matter? God, you look terrible.'

He didn't reply, but stumbled towards the bed. He managed to place his half-smoked cigar in a dish, and the brandy glass on the bedside table. Davina at once realised the danger in the situation, and moved across the bed. Her movement was not quick enough as James climbed on to the bed and grabbed her. There was nothing that she could do, as James overpowered her effortlessly. He ripped off the cotton nightdress that she was wearing, and then pushed himself, still fully clothed, on to her naked body. He hurriedly undid the buttons of his trousers and forced his way into her. The searing pain that Davina felt was like nothing that she had felt before. She stopped all attempts at resistance hoping that it would be over more quickly. Unfortunately the alcohol prevented a quick ejaculation, resulting in her suffering 15 minutes of agony until he slumped down on top of her. Such was the inauspicious environment in which Charles Longhurst was conceived.

12

Night was coming to an end, and James could see the sunrise in the distance. Holding his newborn baby in his arms, his mind ventured back to that evening nine months ago when he had raped his wife. She was dead, and he was now left with the harsh reality of bringing up three children on his own. He stood up, unlocked the door to the gardens, and walked out on to the giant grass lawn at the back of the house. A sense of bewilderment had overtaken him. He suddenly recognized what was facing him. Apart from one period of remorse after Davina had exposed him for what he was, he had lived a life lacking in any moral basis. To his wife he had been unfaithful, to his children, an absentee father, and to his friends, arrogant and uncaring.

For the first time he saw that he did not have anyone, either friend or family, to whom he could look for help and support. The sudden and tragic death of his wife had left him alone. He had to change. Many people had told him that, but he had ignored them. He could afford to do so then, but now it was different. The call for change came from within. It was not just out of necessity, but it was as if it came from his soul. He suddenly realised he still had a soul, even after the dissolute life he had led, and this realisation triggered an emotional upheaval within him. He felt tears well up. It was the first time in his adult life that he had cried. The sincerity of his feelings could not be disputed, and as he held the baby, it was nothing short of a spiritual conversion.

His thoughts were suddenly interrupted.

'Lord Longhurst! Sir – Lord Longhurst!' The shouts were coming from the house.

He turned around, and walked briskly towards Wendy who was beckoning back into the house.

'The maternity nurse has arrived, sir. She's waiting in the study.'

'What – already? What time is it?'

'It's 7.30, sir. Shall I take the baby from you?'

'No, Wendy, that's quite all right. I'll take young Charles to the nurse.'

'Oh? Is that the name, then?'

He paused and looked up at the old house-keeper. 'We didn't have much choice once my uncle died. It's the only one left on the Longhurst list. It's a shame Davina didn't know his name,' he said quietly.

'Sir, are you feeling unwell?' she asked, seeing a change in his manner.

'No, no, I'm fine, Wendy. Why do you ask?'

'Oh nothing, really, sir, it's just you seem different like.'

He chose not to respond. 'Now the nurse is in the study?'

'Yes. I've made her some tea. My lord, I and the rest of the staff want to say how sorry we all are about Lady Longhurst. She was such a fine lady. It's all so terrible and shocking.' Wendy broke down.

'Thank you, Wendy. But please – you have to try – all of us – we have to be strong, especially when the twins find out today and when they come home from Eton. Promise me that you'll be strong. I can't manage on my own, Wendy. I'll need your support.' He put his arm around her. It was the first time in thirty years that he had ever showed such warmth.

'Yes, I'll try, sir.' She looked up at him, puzzled by the transformation of her master.

13

James, still holding the baby, decided to go directly into the study by opening the giant sash window that faced out on to the gardens. He stepped into the room and looked up at the maternity nurse. She had seen him walking towards her, but she wasn't quite expecting him to make such an unusual entrance. She put the magazine down on the table, and got up from the sofa.

'Welcome to Hathaway House.' He half tripped over the step as he walked into the study. He was exhausted by the upheaval of the previous eight hours.

'Thank you, my lord. I am so sorry; I've only just heard about the tragedy. How is the baby?'

'Oh, he's just fine. I've been looking after him through the night. I've given him a feed, and he's sleeping beautifully. As you can imagine, it's been a terrible night. My other two children, the twins, don't know just yet. They're at boarding school, but they'll be coming home for the weekend this afternoon. I'm awfully sorry about the upheaval, but I suspect it's not going to be easy here for the next few days.'

'Yes, I quite understand. Please let me have the baby. What's his name?'

'Charles.'

'Well Charles, let's take you upstairs then, and give you a bath. Daddy might have given you a feed, but he hasn't changed your wet nappy, has he then!' She looked up and smiled at her employer. He didn't seem to be half the ogre that everybody had warned her about.

'Wendy will show you to your quarters. If you need anything, don't hesitate to ask. We have lunch at 1.30 sharp, and dinner at 8. Breakfast is not obligatory, but Wendy clears the table at 9.30.'

'That's fine. When would you like to see the baby?'

'Oh, I'll leave that to you.' He was about to turn to go away, but he suddenly stopped. 'By the way, I'm sorry, but what's your name?'

'Janet, my lord.'

'Well, Janet, I'll see you later.' He smiled. 'Oh, and by the way, please call me James.'

'Sorry?– What was that you said? Are you sure?' she asked, quite taken aback by his sympathetic manner. It was totally at odds with all the reports she had received about the monster from Hathaway.

'Never been more so,' he responded. The effects of his dramatic change were immediately being felt by the outside world. But this was only to be the start.

14

The journey down to Eton was the most difficult drive of his life. He had decided not to use Bill that afternoon, wanting to be alone when he broke the news to the twins. The full impact of the tragedy was now beginning to hit him. The hours of reflection that he had gone through had meant that he now understood the immensity of his loss. It was as if he had truly fallen in love with Davina, but only after she was gone. His love would remain unrequited. From never having cried before, he couldn't stop now. It was a tortuous two hours of self-inflicted loneliness. But it was necessary. He had to get the whole tragedy out of his system, if only temporarily, so that he could summon up the strength to tell the twins.

They were packing their cases, preparing for the exeat, when the housemaster knocked on the door and showed their father in. He sat down and opened his arms to the two thirteen year olds. They were confused, and knew something was not right. Their reaction to the news, as far as James was concerned, was unexpected. There were no tears, or any real sign of emotion from either of them. The only response was silence, as they sat facing their father. A silence so deafening, that James could hear things that normally would not register, such as the ticking of the bedside alarm clock, the dripping water in the basin, and even the electric current of the strip light on the ceiling. The three of them left to go back home. If the drive to Eton had been his most difficult, the drive back was the longest.

15

Gordon and Robert never did show any emotion over their mother's death. It was as if it had never happened. It worried James that neither of them spoke about it, or came to talk to him. He tried to be a good father, to speak to them. He even arranged for them to see a psychiatrist, but it was no use. They would not communicate. They had had a very poor relationship with their father before the loss of their mother, and although they did recognize that their father had changed and was making enormous attempts to repair the damage he had caused, they were in no mood to forgive, or indeed to help. They still feared him, and they were right to. Despite his conversion, James lost none of his authority – at various times his temper would explode, and there was not a person in the house who was not scared of him.

James tried everything that a father could do, but the bridge could not be built, and he soon realised that the twins would never let him get close. It was therefore obvious that he would not make the same mistake again with Charles. He devoted himself to the baby, and even looked forward to the weekends when Janet took time off. In short, he became a model father.

The relationship with his youngest son, from the very outset, was an extremely close one. Charles returned his father's devotion with tenderness, affection and trust. It was as if James' transformation was being nourished and kept alive by the goodness of his youngest son.

'I've never seen such a change in a person,'

Nelly said, whilst preparing breakfast.

'Well, it must have been. I mean, after Lady Longhurst gave me the job, people laughed at me, telling me that he was a complete bastard. But I have never seen a more loving father,' Janet replied.

'You should have seen him before. Mind you, he's still frightening when he wants to be. Did you hear him the other day telling off Gordon and Robert? He's still the boss!'

'Oh, I know that, Wendy, but with Charles, he's so gentle.'

'Long may it continue, that's all I can say.'

16

Janet remained at Hathaway House, becoming a full time nanny for Charles. She was the only member of staff who was directly under James' control, the others reported to Wendy. Over the next four years, Charles was brought up in a natural family environment, unlike his two older brothers, who had just finished school. Janet was close enough to him to act like a mother. She adored him, and her devotion was rewarded by Charles' love for her.

Both Gordon and Robert resented their younger brother, a feeling that would remain with them for ever. They always saw him as being the reason for their mother's death, and their attitude towards him, even at this tender age, was never in doubt. Charles picked up the signals almost immediately, before he had even begun to walk.

The resentment grew to hatred when they saw the developing relationship between their father and their brother. James saw the bullying, and constantly shouted at the twins. Janet also tried to put a stop to the incessant abuse, but she lacked the necessary authority. On leaving Eton the bullying stopped, as they moved to London to take jobs as stockbrokers in the city. From then on contact between the twins and their younger brother was minimal, and would remain so for a long time. At four years old, Charles started kindergarten locally, and then four years later, following the recent family tradition, set off to Heathcliff Preparatory School where he would remain before going on to Eton.

'Well, Headmaster, this is the last Longhurst of the next generation. I think you will find him easier than Gordon and Robert.'

'I do hope so, Lord Longhurst. I know it's been a good fourteen years now since they have gone, but I still remember them clearly – and let me tell you, it's not what I would call a happy memory.'

'Yes, I quite understand. They're a handful, to say the least.'

'How did they get on at Eton?'

'It was a difficult time for them, what with Davina dying, and the emotional upheaval that went on then. On balance, they coped pretty well. Neither of them were academic.'

'Yes, I understand. Did they go to university?'

'No. I got them jobs as stockbrokers in the city. They're doing OK. At least their behaviour has improved.'

'They must be well over twenty now, my lord,'

the headmaster laughed.

'Yes, that's true. Now this one here is totally different. Much more like his mother. He's bright, and has a very good temperament.'

'Well, he certainly looks like Lady Longhurst. If he's anything like his mother was, he will be a credit to Heathcliff.' He thrust his hand towards James, indicating that the meeting was over, and that Charles should remain in the office.

James gave his son a kiss and left his eight-year-old son to begin his boarding-school career. As he walked towards his car, he felt a deep sadness. He would miss him terribly, but he knew that the boarding experience would benefit him.

'OK then, Bill, take me back to London.'

'Yes, sir. How was young Master Charles?'

'Oh, he was fine. I was far more upset than he seemed to be. He'll be back in a couple of weeks,' James responded, picking up the *Financial Times*.

The chauffeur laughed as the black Rolls Royce drove off back down the M4.

17

The twins had very little problem establishing themselves in the city. With the Longhurst name, and the connections that went with it, they had a ready-made client base. They built themselves a reputation for quick deals, taking big risks, and gambling large amounts of money. They also traded shares on their own account, simultaneously borrowing against a margin, and thus dealing in very big sums of money. Being liked was not part of their remit. They wanted to make money, drive fast cars, and sleep with as many girls as possible.

James had heard about his elder sons' activities. He kept abreast as to what they were doing, particularly the personal trading, where they were taking huge risks on their own money. The trust fund capital on their own beneficiary accounts had now passed absolutely down to them. It was now their money and they had complete control over it. James was worried that they would lose the lot, but he could do little to stop them. They were independent now, not his responsibility, and in many ways that was a relief to him.

His own career had taken a perverse course since Davina's death. He was now spending less time in the office, and more time at Hathaway House. His more approachable attitude, and more relaxed nature, lent itself to a more public role at the bank. Whilst previously his hard-nose singular and ruthless approach was perfectly suited to Mergers and Acquisitions, his new modus operandi was far better adapted to client relationships.

It was at a board meeting just after Charles had started boarding school, that the chairman of the bank retired. Traditionally his replacement was chosen through a secret ballot by the board members. James was completely shocked not only by the fact that he was elected, but also that it was unanimous.

'I wasn't even aware that I was a candidate,' he said, smiling to the other board members.

'Oh, come on, old boy. You know it always happens like this. I can't remember when a person has been elected who was expecting it.'

'Yes, yes I know. But ... well, I don't quite know what to say!'

'How about accepting the job. You will be the fourth Longhurst to be chairman.'

There was silence around the boardroom as James surveyed the room. He felt enormous and justifiable pride. He hadn't really ever considered the chairman's job, but now that it was being offered to him by his peers, he realised how much he wanted it.

'When would I be taking over the helm?'

'At the next annual general meeting, James. Congratulations!'

James Longhurst was now in charge of one of the most important private banks in the country. He felt a sudden charge of guilt. It was at moments such as these, when his happiness reached a certain level, that his memory would lurch back to Davina. If only she were alive. But then again, he would immediately remember his old ways and behaviour, and realise that all of this would not have been possible had she still been alive. It was as if her death had cleared a path of righteousness for him to follow. The phoenix that had arisen from the ashes of that desperate May evening was Charles, an endless source of happiness and hope to him. For James, if Davina's death had pointed him in the direction of the path of propriety and goodness, then Charles had made sure that he stayed firmly on it.

18

Charles Longhurst thrived at Heathcliff Preparatory School. He was popular, excellent at sports, but more importantly was blessed with an academic mind. This more than anything differentiated him from the rest of his family. It came as a complete surprise to the headmaster, who had expected the worst, notwithstanding Lord Longhurst's introduction.

'Extraordinary. And you say that he did this under exam conditions.'

'Yes, Head, that's right. Nothing like his older brothers!'

'That's an understatement. I can't quite believe it. What was his mark again?'

'Ninety-seven percent. The top mark by a long way. Remember this was a common entrance maths paper. He is only just twelve.'

'Look how neat it is, as well. The time pressure doesn't seem to have affected him at all... How's his English and French?'

'Oh, first class, Head. Not quite as good as his maths, but he is comfortably in the scholarship scheme, not that his family will need the help!'

'That's not the point. Well, who could have believed it. A Longhurst scholar!'

'He's a very good sportsman too, you know. He's in the first fifteen for rugby and first eleven for cricket. In fact, all round he's a thoroughly decent young chap.'

The headmaster sat back in the chair and looked across the room. He had known for some time that Charles Longhurst was one of his best pupils, but his sudden and meteoric rise to being a potential scholar was something of a shock. His mind wandered back to the time when Davina Longhurst had been sitting opposite him. He realised that this boy was her son, and that it was her qualities that had formed his character. He did not know whether her ladyship was an academic, but even if she had had her son's talents, it was unlikely that, being a lady of that class, she would have been allowed to develop them.

'Thank you, Roger. Keep me informed about young Charles. I'll give the headmaster at Eton a ring.'

19

Charles' academic abilities did not come as a complete surprise to James. He had paid close attention to his youngest son's schoolwork during the weekends at Hathaway House. He had also been to a number of parent evenings where the teachers had given him glowing commendations. But the latest report he received, which would be the penultimate one from his prep school, made him rise from his chair.

'Janet, would you come down to the main study, please,' he called into the telephone intercom.

Two minutes later Janet appeared, her face made up and her hair flowing freely down, in a very smart suit. James looked up. Her appearance caught him unawares. He momentarily forgot why he had called her down: he had never seen her like this before, transformed from a nondescript, average-looking nanny, into an elegant and very attractive woman. She had been at the Longhurst's for over 12 years and was now approaching her 34th birthday. For the first time since he met her, he looked at her as a man would look at a woman.

'Janet – you, you–'

'What's the matter James? You're stuttering!' she laughed.

'Well it's just – it's just that you look so different. Are you going out?'

'Yes I am, actually. My sister is having a dinner party in London, and I promised I would go.'

'Oh, I see.' He felt relieved that she wasn't dressed up for a date. He couldn't believe that he felt like this. She was an employee, of whom he had the highest regard as a nanny, but not a woman he had ever looked at in a sexual way.

'Well? You wanted me?' she asked, responding more than coquettishly to his obvious interest.

'Ur, yes – it's Charles. Have you seen this?' He held up the pale blue-coloured report.

'Of course I have. I put it on your desk!'

'Oh, right then. Well, what do you think? He was always bright, but the school is putting him in the scholarship class. I must thank you Janet for all the work, not to mention the love, that you have given Charles. His success really is your success, too.' He couldn't help looking over the feline curve of her body, and down her nylon-covered legs towards her pointed slingback stilettos.

'Thank you, James. I'm really proud of him. Maybe we can discuss it later, but I have to be off. I'm getting the 5.30 from Chippenham.'

'Would you like a lift to the station?'

'What? No that's OK thanks; Bill will take me.'

It was on odd gesture. He had never taken her, let alone offered to take her, anywhere.

'No, no. Please. I would be happy to. Besides, we can speak about Charles in the car. It's a good 20 minutes without distractions.' He strode past her, and got the keys. She followed him out of the house to the car.

He opened the passenger door and watched as she sat herself down. He felt a sense of sexual excitement, something that had been relatively dormant over the past 12 years. From being a sexual predator for most of his life, he had led a celibate life since Davina had died. This was partly out of a lack of desire, but also due to the guilt of his infidelity during his marriage. In a perverse way he wanted forgiveness from his dead wife, and he genuinely felt that by being faithful to her memory, he would attain some form of redemption. As a result, he had lost his touch when making an approach to a woman, both actually and metaphorically.

As they drove to the train station, he kept glancing across at her. He desperately tried not to look at her legs and just managed to keep his eyes firmly fixed on the road, as they discussed Charles. Janet, for her part, would have to have been blind not to have noticed James' staring in the study, and giving her a lift was more than a confirmation of his sudden physical interest. She was enjoying it for now. His discomfort, from years of lack of practice, gave it an added edge. She herself had been involved with a number of men over the last number of years, but she had found nobody. She had thought of James, despite the very large age gap; he was a fine looking man. But such thoughts were only fleeting. It was a fantasy, knowing that any relationship with her employer would be out of the question.

'Well then, have a good trip.'

'Thank you. I'll see you tomorrow.' She undid her seat belt and got out of the car. He gave in to his lasciviousness, and managed to glance, albeit briefly, at Janet's legs as she swung them round to get out of the car. The skirt had risen, revealing her stocking tops. He quickly looked up at her, but she had turned around already and did not notice his voyeuristic glance. She didn't need to. She was aware of his sudden interest, and although flattered, she was a little confused about what she should do.

20

She returned 24 hours later, dressed in jeans and a loose-fitting shirt. She looked more like her usual self as she went up to her bedroom, and then on to see Charles. He was in his room, in the middle of making the most intricate model airplane with his father.

'Oh hello, Janet,' Charles looked up and smiled. 'Dad and I are nearly finished.'

'What are you making?'

'It's a Phantom F4!'

'You've been waiting for that to come out for ages.'

'Yes, I know. Dad picked it up yesterday.' He held it up to her as she walked in.

'My goodness! You have been busy. What colour are you going to paint it?'

'Metallic, I think. The paint's in the box. Dad, could you pass it to me?'

James reached over to the box and passed it to his son. He then looked up at Janet.

'Did you have a nice weekend?'

'Fantastic, thanks. It went so quickly... Oh Charles, you've missed a bit of the undercarriage... Look!' She averted her eyes and continued to concentrate on the model Revel airplane.

'Where? Gosh! You're right.' Charles took the plane back and searched for the missing piece.

'Well then, I'll see you at dinner.' She turned to go.

'Janet, can I have a quick word,' James said, following her out of the room.

'Yes, of course.'

'I mean in private,' he said quietly, gently taking her arm.

'Oh, right then,' she replied, slightly hesitant.

The two of them walked out on to the landing. His feelings for her remained puzzling to him. She was now dressed as normal, without any effort, but somehow she looked different to him. He couldn't put his finger on it, but he was certain that the sexual dynamic between them had changed. He sensed that she sensed it, too.

'I was wondering whether we might have dinner together.'

'Yes, James, well we are, aren't we? Tonight?' She was playing the game to perfection. Teasing him by pretending to be completely unaware of his interest.

'No, I meant alone. That I might take you out,' he said nervously.

'Oh, I see. Yes, well, why not? When?' Now feeling more comfortable with the situation, especially noticing his unease, she was eager to go out.

'Well, I was thinking about maybe tonight.' He smiled at her, warmly.

She looked into his eyes for the first time, sensing that this was an important moment. She had very little time to respond, and even less time to consider the proposal. She was undoubtedly flattered by his attentions, and she had not stopped thinking about him over the weekend. This was unusual in itself since prior to then, she had only thought of him as her employer. She admired him as a wonderful father, who dominated the house with the force of his personality and character. But she had never, up until this weekend, thought of him seriously in a different way.

'OK then. I'll get ready.' As soon as she answered, she felt an electrically charged sense of excitement.

21

He took her to a pub in the village. It was the perfect venue for a relaxed Sunday-night dinner. He felt no need to impress her, having known her for the 12 years she had been living at Hathaway House. The evening started well, that is until they began discussing Charles' future. She had strong views on which school he should go to, and Eton did not figure as one of them.

'I'm not saying that it's not a good school, but I would prefer him to go to Westminster or St Paul's. He might find a London school more enjoyable.'

'Well, I'm grateful for your views, Janet, but the subject is not for discussion. He's going to Eton, and that's final. Longhursts have been going there for hundreds of years. There is no way the tradition is going to be broken now. It's not as if I'm sending him to a second-rate school; it's still regarded the best in the land,' he replied, a little over defensively.

'Yes, you're right. I mean it did a wonderful job on Gordon and Robert!' she remarked sarcastically.

'Oh come on, no school could have changed them. Anyway, they have improved a lot. They're doing very well in the city. Making lots of money; they have now gone into property, which at the moment appears to be the only thing that motivates them.'

'What a surprise!' she replied. She had nothing but contempt for the twins, having seen how they had bullied Charles when he was younger.

'No, I think things are getting better. Listen, I've tried with them, and at least they still respect me, even though they're out of my control.' He knew that his elder sons were their own masters now that they had money, but he still demanded, and indeed received, their respect.

'When I see it, I'll believe it. I just don't want

Charles being anywhere near them. I certainly don't want him influenced by them.'

'Don't worry about that. You know that I have a special relationship with him. He's such a fine boy... I know I have you to thank for that.'

'Thank you, but you've been a great father, too. In fact you have been a very good parent, since I've known you, to the other two as well.'

'Only since Davina died.' He paused and looked up at her. 'I still miss her. Sometimes I think I only fell in love with her after she was taken away from me. I treated her so badly.' He sat back in his chair. He wanted to tell her about how he had raped his wife, and that Charles was conceived during that assault, but he lacked the courage. He was unsure what good it would do, apart from release some guilt from his system.

The evening became less contentious once they had stopped talking about schools and the twins. They walked back to the house. It was a warm night. James felt ill at ease, not knowing whether to put his arm around her or not. Finally, as they approached the gate, he held her hand and pulled her gently around. He kissed her. She didn't resist him and kissed him back. They stood in each other's arms outside the gate of the house for what seemed like a very long time. It was the first experience of intimacy he had had with a woman for over 12 years.

22

James slept in Janet's room that night, waking up

earlier than usual, and quietly making his way to his own bedroom before anybody had risen. He had a shower, and then wandered down to breakfast, only to see Wendy cooking him a full English breakfast.

'Good morning, my lord. The grilled tomatoes are on their way,' she said, with a noticeable smirk on her face, as she placed the plate of eggs, bacon and mushrooms on the table.

'Anything on your mind, Wendy?' he asked, picking up his newspaper.

'No sir, nothing at all,' she replied, immediately picking up the signal not to mention what she saw when her master and Janet came back last night arm in arm.

Janet woke up to an empty bed later that morning. She felt uneasy about what had happened, but also excited by that wonderful feeling of sexual fulfilment. He was the best lover she had ever had. She thought about his gentleness, his warmth, his touch, and most importantly his mouth, which ventured all over her body, kissing her so tenderly that with each contact she felt that she might climax. She soon began to lose herself to the memories of what had happened seven hours earlier, only to be interrupted by a knock at the door.

'Good morning.' He said it in a quiet, almost loving tone, as he walked over towards her and sat on the bed. She sat up, and attempted to kiss him, but he moved away. 'What is it?'

'I don't know ... it's just that these things can get complicated. I mean Wendy has already given suggestive looks. It's nothing to do with you, but

I feel uncomfortable. You are employed by me, and you are in charge of my son. I don't know whether it can work.'

'James, I don't want to put you under any pressure. If it's a problem, I don't mind.' She was being far more understanding than she felt, but she had little choice.

'Thank you. You know ... I haven't been with anyone since Davina. I haven't felt like this towards anyone for such a long time.'

'Yes, I understand.'

He got up and walked out. She had no idea where she stood. He had left the relationship in a state of purgatory. If there was any consolation, he was very confused over where it was going himself. He continued to leave matters unresolved. The relationship did not stagnate, but it certainly did not flow. Over the next 12 months James slept with her on a number of occasions. He had deep feelings for her, but unlike Janet, he was not sure whether he was in love. James could not commit, and he remained uncommitted. Janet could do little about it; she had fallen in love with him, and wanted to hold on to what she had. It was by no means ideal, but it was better than not having him at all.

23

14 September 1991 was a very important date in Charles' life. It was his first day at Eton. His final year at Heathcliff had been nothing short of glorious. He was captain of rugby and cricket,

and was selected by his teachers to be head boy. He had loved Heathcliff and was sorry that his days there were over. But now he faced a real challenge. The protection of a small preparatory school all but disappeared, as he looked forward to going to the most famous school in the country. He had, as predicted, won a full scholarship, but in agreement with both his father and the teachers, opted not to go to 'College' – the traditional base for the scholars – but to the main school, which was made up of 24 houses. This choice suited James, not only because he was happy to pay the fees for his son, but also since the school was a much more natural environment for him to develop (unlike 'College', which could be like a pressure cooker for the scholars).

As Charles entered his new school, it was exactly two years to the day since Rosalind Blackstone had made her way up the path towards Roedean College for Girls, to start her scholarship. She had now become fully integrated into her school, having made new friends and adapted fully to the rigours demanded there. Born on the same day, their lives over the next five years would follow parallel paths, meeting at times, and then diverging, but always going in the same direction.

Part 5

SOTHEBY'S, THE PRESENT DAY

4.20 P.M.

A bead of sweat formed and slowly rolled down the left side of his face. It had never happened to him before during an auction, but Henry Smith Luytens felt it now. The additional lighting for the television cameras and the sheer number of people gathered there combined to make the room at least five degrees hotter than usual. He was momentarily distracted from his free flowing style of taking bids in a rhythmical and professional way. With one movement of his index finger, he brushed the intruder away, hoping that he could keep his composure for the rest of the sale. Any thoughts he had were abruptly stopped by a bid that came from the front row of the room.

'*Cent-cinquant!*'

'Thank you, monsieur. You are a little ahead but I'll happily take your bid. I have £150 million from the gentleman in the front row. It's now against you, sir.' He looked towards the back where the black American, representing the Getty Museum, was standing. There was silence in the room as everybody waited for his response.

'It's against you, sir. I have £150 million from you, sir.' He looked down at the diminutive Frenchman who sat nervously in his seat. He had never seen him before, but he knew who he was bidding for. The Louvre had informed the auction house that it would be making an offer. He had made his representations known at the reception, and hence was given a front-row seat. Smith Luytens smiled at him. He got little response from the taciturn face, which reminded him more of Inspector Clousseau than a bureaucrat employed by the French government.

'One sixty!' There was another gasp from the seated audience.

'Sorry sir, was that £160 million?' He looked up at the new bidder. It was an American again, but a different one, and he was certainly not representing the Getty Museum.

'Yes, indeed it was.'

Smith Luytens took the bid immediately. He was amazed that the bidder had come himself. He attracted so much attention. For a man who loved his own privacy, it was positively perverse for him to be in this room and be bidding so openly. William Gaston, reputed to be the richest man in the world, had slipped into the room unnoticed. He was now the centre of attention as he made his move.

The young couple seated at the back smiled at each other. Like Gaston, they too had escaped attention, and watched the drama unfold until it reached a conclusion. However, that moment was some way off as Smith Luytens moved up a gear and looked down towards the Frenchman for a higher bid. If he did not have one in his armoury, he fully expected his old friend seated on the aisle in the seventh row to show his hand.

Part 6

AWAKENINGS

1

For the first three years at Roedean, Rosalind found the schoolwork unchallenging, to her surprise. She managed to come first in her form exams each year with very high scores. The teachers were very impressed not only by her spectacular academic ability, but also by her wide range of talents which included hockey and lacrosse (where she captained the school for her year).

It was not just her academic and sporting successes that drew their attention to her. Her energy and enthusiasm, together with her warmth and poise, set her clearly apart from the rest of the pupils. She dominated her year and was involved in all aspects of school life. Nobody appeared to resent her for her achievements; on the contrary, everybody seemed to love her and she attracted friendship and loyalty with ease, being by far the most adored girl in her age group. Her popularity was a result of her inclusiveness in everything she did. From playground games to midnight feasts in the dormitory, nobody was ever excluded. She was mischievous, but never to the extent where someone would get hurt. Her effervescent playfulness ensured that she was loved by everybody.

It was at the end of the third year, at 14 years old, that a genuine threat to her unchallenged supremacy suddenly appeared. It was not so much a group threat, but rather a singular one, in the form of Raveena Shah.

Born in Mumbai, a product of an extraordinarily aristocratic and wealthy family, Raveena was the quintessential Indian princess. Her face was made up of the most delicate features including a perfectly straight nose, high cheek bones, and wonderfully large dark-brown eyes. Her long, jet black hair was always worn tied tightly behind her face, accentuating her fine, angular features. Her English was perfect, spoken with a soft Indian accent, and people loved listening to her.

She had entered the school unusually late, at 14, and went straight into the middle school. Rosalind immediately saw that Raveena was no ordinary classmate, and was entranced by the girl's character and beauty. The threat to her supremacy was welcomed rather than feared, and the two girls instantly became best friends, sharing a room, and then creating a kind of duopoly over the school sports. Rosalind continued to captain both lacrosse and hockey, but Raveena took over tennis and cricket.

One area where the competition took on a different dimension was in the classroom. It started from day one, and would continue right up until O levels, two years later. And it was in the classroom, in the middle of the second term in their lower fifth year, that Rosalind, sitting next to Raveena, came into contact for the first time with what would be her greatest ever love.

2

'Good morning ladies.' The tall English teacher opened the classroom door.

'Good morning, Mrs Robinson,' the class responded in unison.

'And how is everyone today?' she asked, expecting as usual a mixed response.

'Fine, thank you, Mrs Robinson,' the class responded with a faint laughter. They had planned a uniformed response for a change.

'Oh!' She smiled at the girls, at the same time taking off her half-moon spectacles. She loved this class: not only were they an enthusiastic bunch, but also they were bright with a real thirst for knowledge. She also knew that it was a challenge to get the best out of them, particularly with Rosalind, who could reach levels of understanding she feared she did not possess herself.

Likewise, the class adored Mrs Robinson. She was very tall with grey hair which was tied in a bundle above her head. Her face was refined and delicate, but small in relation to her height. She always wore the same type of clothes, which when in ensemble, made up a long pleated flowing skirt, turtle-neck jumper, tweed jacket, and black pointed shoes. Her voice was unusually deep, and her diction was melodic and precise. When she spoke, people listened. She had a habit of walking around the class, whilst teaching her subject – English literature – leaving an impression that each pupil was having a private lesson. It was intimate, yet structured and formal. The effect was that the results in English at both O and A levels were among the best in the country. As a teacher she was, quite simply, a natural.

'Today is a special day in your lives.' She paused and smiled. 'Vanessa, will you hand out the books, please.' She passed the books over and looked up again at the class. 'Now, you have all heard of him, and some of you might have been to the theatre and seen some of his plays, but is there anybody in the room who has any real understanding of William Shakespeare?'

There was silence. The girls looked at each other.

'I was named after the lead character in *As You Like It!*' Rosalind blurted out.

'Have you read the play? Have you seen it?' She started to walk around the class, still awaiting an answer from Rosalind.

'No,' she replied, disappointedly. Rosalind considered herself very well read for her age, but it was true that she had never seen a Shakespeare play. Her curiosity, despite being named after one of the playwright's greatest heroines, had not been sufficiently pricked.

'Oh, don't worry, Rosalind. And for that matter, nobody should be concerned. Yes, you are all over 14, and you are among the brightest and the best teenagers in the country; and the fact that none of you have read the most important playwright, or preferably poet, in history is surprising. But not to worry, I'm going to teach you all about him, his plays and his poetry.' She walked back to her desk.

'I've picked this play, not only because of the

time of year with spring coming upon us, but also – well, it happens to be one of my favourites and I think you'll all enjoy it. It's a double lesson, so we'll read the play right through.' She looked at the cover of the book.

'*The Winter's Tale* by William Shakespeare.' She looked up again. 'Vanessa, you can be Leontes, and Helen you can be Hermione. Rosalind, you will be Perdita.' She stopped and smiled, and 'Raveena, you can be Paulina.'

3

Rosalind didn't realise it at first. She had never been interested in Shakespeare before; she had concentrated on reading the novels of Jane Austen and George Eliot. She had even avoided going with her parents during the holiday to see RSC productions, which her mother particularly enjoyed. She settled down in the chair and started to follow the text. Her mind drifted, and her attention was distracted by the strong wind that was blowing outside. She stared out on to the green lawns, and noticed the first daffodils of spring bending, but staying unbroken. What made her look at the flowers at that particular time would forever remain a mystery to her. But by coincidence, the combination of seeing the flowers and reading the role of Perdita, herself a poet of spring and rebirth, set alight her imagination, and catapulted her into what George Bernard Shaw called the world of 'bardolatory'.

She looked down at the text, and joined in the

reading, slowly absorbing the literature before her.

O Proserpina,
...Daffodils!
That come before the swallow dares, and take
The winds of March with beauty;...

She suddenly stopped in the middle of Perdita's speech. She looked out of the window and looked at those very same daffodils again. They were standing strong. They were in full bloom, and they were announcing that spring was coming. No freshness in the wind or coldness in temperature was going to break them.

'Rosalind! Why have you stopped? Please carry on.' Mrs Robinson prompted her, but she immediately realised what was happening. She herself had experienced a similar reaction when first reading Shakespeare, only with her it was Portia's brilliance in *The Merchant of Venice* that had hypnotised her. The beauty of the writing beguiled the young girl's imagination. She was a prisoner to the poet, and she would never be released.

'Oh, sorry – *Violets, dim But sweeter than the lids of Juno's eyes / Or Cytherea's breath, pale primroses / That die unmarried...*'

She continued reading, having now been infected by the genius of Shakespeare. At the end of the lesson they all handed their books back, except for Rosalind.

'Why are you keeping it?' Raveena asked.

'I want to read it again. Didn't it make your skin goose-bump? I mean the words, the text is so full of beauty.'

'No, not really. Listen, I'm better at maths and science. I'll always be good at them. Shakespeare leaves me cold,' Raveena replied. It was true; she was brilliant at maths and science, much better than Rosalind. But when it came to the arts Rosalind was the best, and now that she had found Shakespeare, she would devote herself to understanding him.

'Mrs Robinson?' She walked over the teacher. 'What's next?'

'Well, I'll start teaching you some background about him, and try to explain to everybody what an important figure he is, and the impact he has had on our lives. And then we'll look at the four big tragedies.' She got up to leave. 'Rosalind, why do you ask? What do you like about him?'

'I don't know ... it's just that the words ... they contain a magic.'

Mrs Robinson smiled. She had been waiting for a pupil like Rosalind for all her teaching life. A student who had a thirst to know more about the greatest poet in the English language, but also a student clever enough to understand him.

'I'll see you tomorrow.'

4

Two months later, the class had completed reading the four major tragedies, and she was keen to see how they felt about the playwright. 'It has been said that there are four great tragedians in history. Three of them are Greek; Aeschylus, Sophocles and Euripedes. The other is Shakespeare. So then, why do we all have to read Shakespeare? Why do we all have to study him?' Mrs Robinson looked into the faces of her fourteen-year-old pupils. Some of them were writing, some of them were looking blankly. Raveena Shah was gazing out of the window, but Rosalind Blackstone was staring right back at her. Her appetite for more knowledge was almost tangible.

'Well, I will try and explain it to you,' Mrs Robinson continued. 'The definition of "Genius" in the dictionary is as follows: "Extraordinary intellectual creative power – or a person endowed with transcendent mental superiority."' She paused and looked around her class. 'We have now read the four great tragedies over the last few months, and I hope you have seen that genius in the plays.'

She walked around the class. 'If one has to say what was so different, so special about Shakespeare from anybody else before him, we have to look at his characters. It's well documented that if one takes away the great names from the text of his plays, you can still tell who's speaking. Shakespeare's genius is the way in which he brings his characters to life. They overhear themselves just as we do ourselves, and by listening in on their soliloquies, we hear what they are thinking and can watch them change in front of our eyes, on stage. They grip us with their reality.

'Although the Renaissance in Italy had long before reached its climax, where artists such as Giotto, Brunelleschi and Masaccio had already rediscovered perspective and had put reality back into art, Shakespeare was finally about to do the same for literature.

'The fact remains that before Shakespeare there are no characters. Yes, there are representations, almost like cardboard, of a basic type. They don't change – they are single dimensional, unlike the multi-faceted characters in Shakespeare's plays. The Athenians invented drama, but not character in the individual sense. It was enough for the audiences in Ancient Greece to accept Oedipus and Agamemnon or in Medieval England the Wife of Bath; Dante's self depiction in the magnificent *Divine Comedy* entranced Florence,' she paused. The Italian poet deserved more than this. 'It is true that certain scenes in the *Divine Comedy*, particularly those between Dante and Virgil, exhibit the beginnings of characterisation. And indeed the very fact that the modern Italian language derives directly from Dante's pioneering use of the vernacular, gives him a special place in the history of western culture. T. S. Eliot once said that "Dante and Shakespeare divide the modern world between them; there is no third."'. She breathed in deeply. 'But it was nothing compared to the invention of real character in literature. Shakespeare's contemporaries, from Marlowe to Ben Jonson, did not have the intellectual or creative powers to portray lifelike people or express themselves in the same poetic manner. Yes, Chaucer, who some say was a precursor to him, did break new ground, and his characters are memorable, but he doesn't come close to Shakespeare's portrayal of character and personality.' She paused.

'The creation of people, and I mean actual

127

people who we can identify with, was Shakespeare's true inventiveness. They are creations that are so much bigger than the plays themselves. Hamlet's inwardness and intellectuality, Iago's evil, Macbeth's imagination, and Falstaff's humour, are so real that they explode out of their theatre roles.' She stood up and walked towards Rosalind. 'The language they speak, the thoughts they have, quite simply shape the way that we speak and think. Indeed some say he invented our language.'

'What do you mean, when you say "invented our language"? He must have used words that already existed?' Vanessa asked, from the back of the classroom.

'Well, I don't mean it quite literally. Shakespeare had no dictionary, and could not simply look up words, no. But he used an astonishing number of them, more than twenty thousand. More importantly, and this is what I really mean – can you imagine how much poorer our language would be without him today!'

Vanessa was scribbling down the answer when Mrs Robinson told everyone to put their pens down. 'Now you must listen and stop writing. It's important for you to understand that if any of you take English at A level, or go on to university to read literature, you will then fully understand the impact Shakespeare had on our great novelists. Jane Austen, Charles Dickens, Henry James and James Joyce to name but a few, are all heavily influenced by him. Poets including Wordsworth, Keats, and T. S. Eliot owe an enormous debt, and the list could go on and on...' She

128

walked over to Rosalind.

'Now your name, Miss Blackstone, is Rosalind. And you told me once that your mother called you that after seeing *As You Like It*, and after falling in love with the lead character, your namesake.'

'Yes, that's right.'

'I know we haven't done that play, but...'

'I've read it anyway,' Rosalind replied eagerly.

'Well, what did you think?'

'I understand why my mother loved the character. She's funny, beautiful, clever and intelligent, even mischievous, but full of life. She appears to have no jealousies or resentments. She keeps everything in perspective, allowing nothing to upset or disturb her. It would be difficult not to love her.'

Mrs Robinson looked down at the wide-eyed star pupil of the class. Rosalind had clinched it and she had understood it. She had seen the greatness and the genius of Shakespeare, and he in turn had captured her imagination. And Mrs Robinson knew that teaching her over the next four years would be a pleasure. She would learn to see the exhausting influence that he had on later novelists. It would not take long for her to understand the connection between a whole host of literary characters whom we talk about in everyday life, and how they owe their origins to the 'people' created by Shakespeare.

5

And so it started: Rosalind Blackstone's great

love affair with Shakespeare. It would never leave her. For Raveena, she remained relatively unmoved by Shakespeare. She did try to enjoy it, and on more than one occasion went to the Theatre Royal in Brighton to see an RSC production. But she failed to get excited by any of it. She never really enjoyed any of the 'arts', including history and French. What she did enjoy was maths and the sciences. These were subjects that came easily to her, and ones that she could enthuse about.

The competitiveness between the two of them continued, despite their interests being in different fields. It was always very satisfying for one of them to do better in a test, or a sport, where the other valued it much more dearly. Hence if Raveena scored more goals in hockey or got better marks in a history test, Rosalind would be distraught. Equally, however, if Rosalind took more wickets in cricket, or completed a physics test ahead of Raveena, the latter was more than a little piqued. It happened rarely, and after they had sat O Levels, it never happened again, since they both started to specialise in their chosen subjects. Games became less important to them as the girls approached their late teens. And as sport declined as a focus of physical activity, the adolescent interest in young men replaced it.

There was a problem in regard to this interest, in that Roedean was a girls' school. The only boys' school close by, or within a five-mile radius, was Brighton College, with whom relations were limited if not non-existent. The only real contact with the boys there was through informal coffees in town, or via family connections where one of the girls would have a brother or cousin at the school.

The main avenue for meeting boys, formal as it was, was through joint discothèques which the school arranged annually with various other schools. Traditionally this event was only for the sixth-formers, and the one arranged for 17 March 1994 with Eton was no exception. Rosalind and Raveena had been looking forward to the event with great anticipation. The date had been boldly written in both of their diaries, and as it got closer their excitement increased.

On the morning of the disco, the girls were called into the main hall for an *ad hoc* assembly called by the headmistress.

'For those of you who are attending their first discothèque, might I remind you of the rules. There will be no kissing or embracing on the dance floor. You will all behave in a ladylike manner, which means that no excessive behaviour will be tolerated. I will not stand for any bad behaviour. You will all be allowed one glass of wine each, and naturally there will be no smoking. Normal school rules apply!' She paused and looked around the hall at the hundred or so girls present.

'Well, have a wonderful evening; and remember that if everyone behaves in accordance with what I have said, there is no reason why these events cannot continue. If, however, I receive bad reports, this will be the last discothèque at the school. All right girls, you can go now and enjoy yourselves.'

'God, I must remember to invite her to one of my parties!' Raveena said quietly to Rosalind, laughing.

'I only hope she's not going to be there. I mean how do we dance a slow one with a guy we're not allowed to hold? It'll be like a monastery do, with monks and nuns as invitees!'

'You're right. You don't have to worry anyway. Robby's supervising, not her, so you'll be all right. The stories I hear from last year are encouraging.' Raveena had names for all the teachers; Mrs Robinson was no exception.

'Oh yeah? And what happened?'

'Kissing behind the back; smoking in the loos.' She stopped when Rosalind started to scoff in disbelief. 'No, I mean it Rosalind. I promise you we'll have a ball tonight. Look it's not as if either of us have had a lot of experience. I'd certainly settle for someone nice to snog!'

'You're right. Me too! Listen, I've got to get back to the library. I've got a history essay to give in this afternoon, and I haven't even started it yet. I'll see you at lunch.'

As she ran off, Raveena turned back to go to her room. It was true, and it was a sad situation, that neither of them had had much experience with the opposite sex. Being at a girls' school did not help, but even on holidays, neither of them had found anyone that interesting. It wasn't really surprising given their natural abilities, their expectations were extraordinarily high. However, despite having very little success, and being disappointed so often, hope breathed eternal for both of them. Raveena had a positive feeling about the coming evening. She was absolutely certain that she and Rosalind were going to strike lucky.

<h1 style="text-align:center">6</h1>

The small skinny dark-haired 13 year old was unpacking his trunk and putting his brand new school uniform away into the cupboard.

'Hello!' Charles Longhurst spoke crisply as he entered the room.

'Oh, hello there; it looks like we're next-door neighbours,' the swarthy young boy replied, turning around.

'My name is Charles, Charles Longhurst.' He put his hand out.

'I'm Sam Bernstein. Very pleased to meet you,' he replied, shaking Charles' hand. He recognised Charles from a previous occasion but did not let on, fearing it might embarrass his new acquaintance.

'Have you unpacked?' Sam asked.

'Yes, I got here this morning. I've unpacked already. My father brought me here early. He wanted me to get the "feel" of the place, in his words. I've done that but there's nothing really to do. I'm starving, and supper's not until seven-thirty. What do you think of the room?' Charles asked, looking around to see if it was any different to his, which it wasn't.

'Oh, it's fine. I'm not fussy anyway.' He smiled.

'Where are you from?' Charles asked, eager to find out more about his room-mate.

'I'm from London actually. I live in the West End,' Sam answered guardedly, not wanting to give too much information until he was more sure of Charles.

'Oh right ... and where did you go to school?'

'The Hall. And you?'

'Heathcliff, near Swindon. I know the Hall. We played you at rugby and cricket. I'm sure you look familiar.' Charles began to look at him more closely.

'Well you have met me before – on the cricket pitch.'

'God! How could I forget. Of course, you were the leg spinner. You took seven wickets that day. We'd never seen a leg breaker before. You tore us apart. You know it was our only defeat of the season.'

'I didn't get you, Charles. You read me pretty well.' Sam smiled back. There was an instant rapport between them. It looked incongruous to say the least – one was tall, blond and well built, a classical English public schoolboy; the other looked more like an Eastern European refugee, albeit with an English accent. But something had clicked, and although neither of them yet knew it, a friendship that would last for a lifetime had laid its roots on the shaven ground of a cricket square.

7

Sam Bernstein was the youngest of four sons of an extremely wealthy property developer. His father, Abraham, had left Europe before the outbreak of the Second World War, and barely spoke a word of English when he arrived on the island's shores. He was looked after by the Jewish agency in London who managed to find him a home in north London and he was educated at the local grammar school. He left school at 16, and started work in a commercial estate agents' office on Marylebone High Street.

He was quick to learn, and before long he began to make an impression on the retailers in the High Street. His aggressive deal-making abilities made the shopowners keen to instruct him on rent reviews and new lettings. His commission base grew rapidly, and as a result it was no surprise when the partners of the agency offered him a partnership.

He rejected it immediately, preferring to set up his own agency, taking with him his own clients. He saw that since he was earning the lion's share of the income anyway, he might as well have all of it rather than have to share it with three other partners who did very little. It was an inspired move: the agency expanded and became the leading retail specialist in the country. 'Abraham Bernstein & Co' red and white boards were everywhere on the main shopping streets in Britain, from Argyle Street in Glasgow to Northumberland Street in Newcastle, from Church Street in Liverpool to Oxford Street in London.

He married into one of the wealthiest Jewish families in Britain. With over 500 fashion shops nationwide, the Silverson family was a household name. By marrying into such an established family, Abraham felt that he had finally achieved a social status to accompany his rapidly growing wealth. But it didn't take long for him to realise that he would never fully be recognised, or indeed accepted by the establishment.

It had nothing to do with wealth or ability, but with his race. Being part of Jewish aristocracy was a world apart from being a member of the English establishment. He felt most offended when his applications for membership of clubs were always turned down. His wife, and indeed his children, did not share this unquenchable thirst to rub shoulders with the nobility. His wife in particular was comfortable in her social milieu, living in central London.

His drive for financial success never slowed down. His business ambition increased in parallel with his frustration at not, in his view, bettering himself socially. He orchestrated a remarkable takeover of one of Britain's sleeping giant property companies, at a huge discount to real asset value. Within ten years he was in charge of the 30th biggest company in the country. Money would never be a problem for him, his children, or even his children's children. It was no exaggeration to say that Abraham Bernstein had the Midas touch.

His four sons were, he hoped, to be the projection for his social ambitions. Unfortunately the first three did not live up to his expectations. They all excelled in ordinariness, none of them attaining a level in any subject, or indeed activity, which he would be proud of. However, with the birth of Samuel, Abraham knew that he had a son whom he would finally be proud of. A boy who might achieve excellence, and who might as a result mix with the social elite.

His belief was quickly confirmed by Sam's early success at the Hall; but his dreams were answered by his stunning entrance paper to Eton. A scholarship was offered, but turned down by his father, who passed it on to another boy of similar standard unable to afford the fees. Despite the different backgrounds and physical disparity between the two boys, it was therefore no coincidence that both the Honourable Charles Longhurst and Sam Bernstein were in the same House.

8

It was a real culture shock for both of the new boys. With 1,300 Etonians, the sheer size of the school and its accompanying playing fields was hard to take in at first. There was some comfort in that the boys' home was the 'House' which comprised of 50 boys, making the environment more akin to what they were used to. This was where most of their life took place, where they would make their friendships, where they would eat their meals, and where they would sleep. It didn't take long for Bernstein and Longhurst to make an impression. They were expected to do well in the classroom, and they did not disappoint. But it was on the playing fields that they really impressed.

Charles' talent for rugby football was immediately apparent after the first week. The teachers had known about his abilities from his previous school, and when they saw him, they knew that they had found their captain. Sam also liked to play football, but of the association kind. Slightly built but tenacious, and extremely fast, Sam impressed at the team trials.

'We need a winger. Now tell me, is he quick?' the games master asked his assistant as he walked over to watch the hopefuls play.

'Like the wind!' the assistant replied. 'Look at him now.' The assistant pointed to Sam as he ghosted past two defenders and sprinted into the penalty box. The games master watched in awe, and then blurted out: 'Select him. He's exactly what we want. You better let Tom know about him. He's sure to want him for the athletics squad. I don't think I've seen a faster sprinter.'

'There might be a problem there.'

'Why?'

'Well, by all accounts he's a brilliant cricketer. There's no way they'll get him for athletics.'

'Batsman or bowler? ... or both?'

'He's a leg spinner.'

'A what?'

'Yes, I know. Not many about these days, but if he's half as good as they say he is, he'll be playing for the Firsts.'

'Very good then. Well bring the boys together and tell them who's been picked. Bernstein needs to put a bit of weight on. Get him to eat a bit more, without losing any of that God-given speed.' The games master smiled.

9

Both Sam and Charles involved themselves in as many activities as possible. Although excelling in the major sports, neither of them reached the same level of excellence in the distinctly Etonian ones such as the 'Field Game', 'Fives', or the 'Wall Game'. When the Summer Half did arrive in that first year Sam elected for cricket, much to the chagrin of the athletics coach.

'Thank God!' Charles sighed with relief realising that the team would be immeasurably strengthened by Sam's presence.

'I'm not that good. You're probably the better player. I don't know why there's been such a fuss, Charles?'

'Sam, I am one of five very good batsmen in the year. I'll probably open. But there's only one leg spinner in the whole school. You'll get loads of wickets. You'll probably be playing for the firsts before the summer's out.'

Charles' opinion of Sam's exceptional cricketing talent proved correct. His figures were extraordinary, as he quite literally bowled schools out, never taking less than five wickets in a match. He was picked to go on a summer tour with the First Eleven in the holidays.

Charles himself had an exceptional sporting year, but it was only two years later that he managed to break through into the First Fifteen at rugby. This was no small achievement in that he was still only 16, and somewhat smaller than the sixth-form boys. However, his talent for kicking

139

the ball, coupled with his handling abilities, meant that the much coveted fly-half position was his for the taking.

10

Both boys continued to do well in the classroom, and in their O level year, they were in the top set for all the ten subjects that they took. It was no surprise when both of them achieved a string of A grades in their exams. As far as Abraham Bernstein was concerned, this was merely further confirmation of his son's talents. After taking his place at Eton, this was now the second stage of his quest for his son to be fully accepted into the establishment. Two more years of hard work and Oxford would beckon. After that, he would let Sam make his own choice over whether to join him at 'Bernstein Estates' or to make his own way in the business arena.

Sam himself hadn't really thought much beyond his A level options. Although being very good at all subjects, his ability for languages was outstanding. By sixteen he spoke fluent French, Spanish and Italian. He had a fairly good grasp of German as well, by virtue of it being his father's mother tongue. The old man broke into Yiddish, a form of High German spoken by his ancestors from central Europe, on frequent occasions, particularly in the family environment.

'Are you sure that's what you want to do?' his father asked.

'Yes, I'm quite sure. I'm not yet certain what I'll

140

do at university, but for the moment, French, Italian and Spanish are my best subjects.'

'OK then. Are your teachers happy with this?' Abraham smiled, not really waiting for the answer. He was an extremely proud man, not least of his own achievements. But that pride was nothing in comparison to what he was feeling for his youngest son. Out of all of his children, Sam was the only one who lived up to what he had dreamed about.

'My housemaster was the person who suggested it,' Sam replied, suddenly bringing his father back into the conversation at hand.

'Oh well, that's that then!' Abraham got up from his leather chair and walked across his gigantic office. Beautifully furnished, and lavished with the finest antique furniture, one would never have guessed that such refined and cultured taste could come from a property developer such as Abraham Bernstein. But it did; and that is what was so fascinating about the old Jew. Although leaving school at 16, he educated himself and read voraciously, realising that however much money he made, he would never be able to fully appreciate its power and what life had to really offer without some form of learning. His eyes were opened to culture. He became an expert on furniture and Impressionist Art. He loved History, having a particular interest in Ancient Greece. He studied Athenian Society, learning about the politicians, the philosophers, and of course, the tragedians. He stared out of the window, standing motionless, saying nothing, for what seemed like an eternity to Sam.

'Can I go now, Dad? I've arranged to meet Charles for lunch at the Brasserie in Kensington.'

'Sam, all this can be yours. I know your brothers are working here, and David is on the Board, but you know that I want you to take over. I have the controlling shares. It's my decision, you know,' he said, still gazing out of the window.

'I know, Dad, but at the moment I don't know what I want to do.' He had been through this conversation many times with his father. He understood his insecurities, and his desperate desire for his standing in society to match his huge wealth. His charitable gifts to many well-known causes, and his expertise in business advice to the Conservative Party, had, to date, all been in vain. There was no knighthood, let alone peerage, that had come his way. The establishment was not stupid. It would wait for more before it gave Abraham Bernstein what he wanted. Sam felt sorry for his father. He wished that he could just accept himself for who he was, and what he had achieved. But thoughts about him eventually taking over the business were very premature.

'I understand,' his father said, turning around and looking at him. 'So you're seeing Charles now. How is he?' The old man was always interested in Sam's friends; they fascinated him as they were from a background that he so much wanted to be part of.

'He's fine. I'm staying at Hathaway House tonight, but I'll be home in the morning.'

'Have a good time,' his father said, as Sam left the office.

11

Charles had spent the summer after his O levels in Tuscany, before returning back to Hathaway House prior to the start of the winter term. He had been looking forward to going back to school, and seeing all of his friends. He had no problems deciding which A levels to study, and he certainly did not need his housemaster to advise him. His mind was made up, and had been for some time.

'Latin, Greek and History!'

'Are they still subjects one studies today? I mean, what use are they?' Janet asked, completely bewildered by Charles's choice.

'Of course people still study them. Anyway I want to do classics at university, and these are the most appropriate A levels to take.'

'Well, I suppose you know what you're doing. You always do,' she replied in an almost resigned manner. Her control over him had obviously waned as he had got older, but she still felt like a mother to him. She certainly loved him as much.

'Janet, don't look so sad. I'll still need your advice on lots of things. It's just that on this, I really know what I am doing.'

'And what things do you need advice on? You're just saying that because you feel sorry for me.'

'That is just not true. There are plenty of things that I value your advice on. Oh come on, you know that I confide in you.' He went over to his nanny, who was now much more than just a friend, and hugged her. He did love her. He had had no mother, and Janet was the closest thing he had to that.

'Who else do you think I talk about girls to? Who else can I speak to about my father, or my dreadful brothers? Tell me!'

'OK OK, you're right. It's just that I want to be of help in everything you do, and I feel so inadequate when it comes to your work. I don't want to let you down,' she said, feeling more reassured.

'Janet, you'll never let me down. I wish you would be more open with me.'

'What are you talking about?' Janet asked, taken by surprise.

'You and Dad, of course.'

'What about me and your father?' she responded defensively.

'Do you really think I couldn't tell that there was something going on between the two of you?'

'That's total rubbish,' she replied, moving away, not quite believing what she was hearing. She and James remained very close, and she had now become more like a private secretary to him, looking after Hathaway House. During the previous year their physical relationship had virtually fizzled out, but they remained close friends.

'Is it?' Charles smiled.

'It is true that we are very good friends, but nothing more. I mean, my job as your nanny was over as soon as you went off to Eton. Your father has been very kind to me, and I won't have you say these things,' she said in a terse way.

Charles got the message and wisely decided not to pursue the current line of conversation. He was convinced, now wrongly, that Janet and his father were having an affair, but he really didn't care that much. Janet's happiness was more important, and he only hoped that his father was treating her as well as she said.

12

James Longhurst had been running the bank for almost ten years by the time his youngest son received his O level results. He had now had enough. Times had changed in the City. It was certainly less enjoyable than he remembered. Even during the late eighties boom, he began to find the work less interesting. Now with the Economy in a severe recession, and the bank losing money, his job had become even more unpalatable. He had already decided to retire before the crash, but now circumstances meant that he could announce it publicly, sooner rather than later. He would leave at Christmas and continue as a consultant.

'I'm quite pleased, actually. I've been wanting to give up London, and retire here for some time. After all, this was where I was born and brought up.' He was looking out of the floor to ceiling sash window, the very same window he walked through from the garden when she first met him.

'Well, I'm sure it's for the best, James. What will you do with your house at Chelsea Square?'

'I don't know yet. I've put a call into Francis Sutherland to discuss my estate, but he hasn't called back yet. It's time that I put things in order.' He paused. 'Yes I must do that.'

'Very good. When would you like supper?' Janet asked.

'Eight o'clock as usual. Who's here?'

'Well, Charles has his friend Sam, and I believe from Wendy that Gordon and Robert are coming down.'

'Oh yes – what a surprise!' he said sarcastically. 'I haven't heard from them for some time. They must want some help.' He looked up. 'I'm glad Sam's here. He's always good value!'

'Yes he is. I'll tell them not to be late.' She left the room. James sat down on the leather armchair, and put his feet up on the stool. He gazed out of the window. It was late summer, and everything outside was a melange of rich verdant colours. He felt very tired. Now in his seventieth year, James Longhurst suddenly felt every bit his age. He looked out on to the vast green expanse ahead of him. His thoughts were now focused on what he would do after Christmas. He would almost certainly stay here, and go to London only when necessary. His most important immediate task was to see Francis Sutherland, the family lawyer. Although the trusts were all set up, he had not yet decided who to leave the family's most valuable asset. Primogeniture was not an issue with the Longhurst Estate. Although the title itself went to the eldest heir, the land and the estate were in the hands of the incumbent lord. James could leave it to any of his sons, although it was true that tradition had dictated that it was passed on to the eldest child. He felt his eyelids get heavier, as he drifted off to sleep still thinking of the future of Hathaway House.

13

James woke up at 6 o'clock with a gentle nudge from Wendy.

'My Lord, it's Sir Francis on the phone.'

'Oh right, thanks Wendy. I'll take it in here.'

'I've made you some tea.'

'That's very kind, thank you. Oh, Wendy, can you shut the door behind you. I don't wish to be disturbed by anyone.' He picked up the phone.

'Francis, how are you? Thanks for coming back.'

'That's a pleasure, James. I trust all went well this morning at the bank. I see that the *Standard* has given you a very nice write up.'

'Oh did they? I haven't seen it. I left for Hathaway House before the last edition. I've had all the broadsheets on to me. Fortunately I dealt with all of them in the car... I'm very happy to go. It's difficult out there. Besides I've done my bit. The climate's very bad at the moment, but the bank's pretty solid. My successor has a real chance after we get through this wretched recession.'

'I have no doubts about that. What are you going to do now? You're only 69.'

'I'm going to relax, Francis. Go away a bit, perhaps, but mainly run the estate from here. Actually that's what I want to talk to you about.'

'Oh yes?'

'I know the Trusts are all safely set up, but I really ought to start thinking about my will, and who to leave what?'

'Yes, well you know I've wanted to get you to write your will since Davina died. Have you had any thoughts about Hathaway House itself?'

'Yes, of course. You know that traditionally the Longhurst family leave the house and the grounds to the eldest son, but it's not sacrosanct. There have been instances where it has been left to the middle, and even the youngest son.'

'Well, that was some time ago, James. If you aren't going to leave it to Gordon or Robert it will be a significant break with precedent. But I wouldn't blame you. I suggest you think it over carefully, and maybe talk to them.'

'The thought of talking anything over with the twins is not one that fills me with warm antici- pation. Every time I speak to them, I end up lending them money. I don't quite understand it.'

'Why not? As you are the settler of the Trusts, it would not be inappropriate for me to tell you that both boys have almost drained their re- sources. There's hardly any money left at all.'

'I don't believe it. How much?'

'Maybe a million left in each account. Hardly enough to last more than a year with their lifestyles.'

'A million each? They had over 15 each 10 years ago. I thought that they were doing well with all the financial press. It just shows you, there's no fool like an old fool... Are you sure, only a million each?'

'That's what I said. Whatever you have lent them in the last two years, you might not get back. Even I hear rumours, James. You must have had some inkling. They're playing a big numbers game. You're in that business, you know about these things.'

'Well obviously I didn't. I assumed they wouldn't have been so stupid to have used up all their money. I thought their borrowings would have been ring-fenced around their company.' James was beginning to get angry.

'I wouldn't bet on it.'

'No, you're probably right. I really ought to think very hard before making any decisions over Hathaway House, and the rest of my will – including the library, of course.'

'But that's always been indivisible from the house.' Francis was shocked at James' implication. 'Surely the library would remain in the house – I mean the books, they're priceless, part of the heritage.'

'Yes I know, but– Well, let me think about it.'

Sir Francis had once again given sound advice, and had led James to think very carefully before making any decisions on the great estate. He had been relieved that James had already considered the dangers of leaving the house and its lands to Gordon and Robert. It could make the Longhurst grip on its home very tenuous indeed. However, as family lawyer, his first duty was to get his client to draw up his will, and then give advice on its contents. James' view on the library had indeed taken him by surprise, but he would use it later to his advantage.

Charles met Sam at Chippenham and they took a taxi to the house. Sam had spent a week the previous summer at Hathaway House, after Charles had gone with his family to the Bernstein villa in Villefranche. However beautiful the south of France village, and however magnificent the view that overlooked the bay that separated Nice from Cap Ferrat, it was always a poor second to the grand lustre of Hathaway House. As they came down the long gravelled drive and Sam caught his first glimpse of the stately home, his heartbeat would accelerate. For Charles, the excitement his friends would experience was a welcome reminder for himself not to take the house for granted.

'We'll go riding, shall we? Cleo is waiting for you in the stables!' Charles said mischievously, knowing Sam's discomfiture with horses.

'Oh, let's not. I haven't ridden a horse since I was last here. Please don't make me, Charles!'

'Come on. I need to take Harry out. You were great last year, and Cleo will remember you. I learnt on her, too. She's very gentle.'

'All right then, but don't gallop off and leave me behind not knowing where to go.' Sam was referring to the previous year when Charles did exactly that.

'Don't worry!'

After two hours of riding gently around the estate, and with Sam just about staying on Cleo, a dark brown filly, the boys returned to the stable. It was a glorious late afternoon, the sun still high in the sky, its light still strong enough to pierce even the most foliated areas of the gardens. Having tied up the horses, the two of them went into the house.

'Charles, dinner will be served at 8. Make sure you and Sam are ready. By the way, your father's back, but he's resting.'

'OK, we'll be ready.'

'I'm going for a bath. I'll see you in the study at 7.30?'

'Fine,' replied Sam, as they both went upstairs.

Sam was ready by 7, and wandered down the great staircase to the main marble hall. The floor resembled a giant chessboard with black and white squares symmetrically arranged corner to corner. He walked on the squares, trying to avoid the lines, in an aimless fashion, stopping only when reaching the walls of the hall. He looked around at the vast open space, and then towards the various doors that led into the main rooms. He was familiar with all but one of these entrances. He stopped suddenly, when his wanderings had led him to that particular door.

He looked around, and then slowly stretched his hand out towards the gold handle. Any hope of him entering the room without anybody noticing were immediately dashed by the un- usually loud creaking sound the door made when opening. Sam pressed ahead regardless, thinking that he had now gone too far to pull back.

As he stepped into the dark room, he immediately sensed that there was something different. Whether it was the distinct musky smell that pervaded the chamber, or the surprising darkness of the room itself, Sam felt anxious enough to jump when the door suddenly closed shut behind him. He desperately felt his way around searching for a light switch. Salvation was at hand, quite literally, when his fingers located the metal square panel, which had six switches. He immediately pushed all six of them down, thereby lighting the room immediately.

He stood fixed to the spot. The room had been dark because there were no windows. The reason behind there being no windows was that every inch of wall space, from ceiling to floor, had been taken up by shelves of books. There must have been thousands of leatherbound volumes beautifully arranged around the room. At first glance, it looked as if all of the books were of the identical size, bound or boxed in the same turquoise-coloured leather, but on closer inspection, each one was different.

He stood still in the middle of the great room. He looked down at the floor, and noticed that the marble hall squares had now been replaced by triangles, in the same black and white colours. Looking up he saw that the shelves, fixed above each other in perfectly measured intervals, were painted in the same turquoise colour as the books themselves. The only embellishment was the gold leaf trapping that decorated the corners of the shelves.

It appeared that the books had been placed in categories, comprising Geography, Literature, Nature and Science, Medicine, Philosophy and – most importantly and by far the largest section – History. The separate classifications were defined by gold-leaf busts of famous writers, philosophers, historians, poets and playwrights. Plato was placed proudly at the head of the philosophy section, whilst Herodotus watched over history; Newton governed science, and Shakespeare, the literature category. Darwin looked down on the nature shelves, and Vesalius guarded the literature on medicine. He slowly walked around, occasionally brushing the tips of his fingers across the bindings. He then noticed the golden letters 'HH' etched on every book, thus giving each tome a common identity.

Simply being there was like an education, where titles that he had only heard about, suddenly tangibly existed. Diderot's *Encyclopaedia* was just one of those titles, with one shelf bearing the full weight of its twenty monumental volumes. He tried to pull one of the books out, but the *Encyclopaedia* was so tightly packed, that he had to use all of his strength to dislodge it.

'Magnificent, isn't it, Sam?'

Sam turned around. He had been so captivated by the books and the library, that he hadn't heard the door creak open.

'Do you mean, sir, the Diderot or the library?' Sam replied, trying to keep some measure of composure.

'The library, of course! Hardly anybody comes in here these days, but when I was a boy, this used to be the most important room in the house,' James replied, walking over towards him.

'I don't think I've seen anything like it. There must be thousands of them.'

'Oh at least twenty.'

'What, twenty thousand books?'

'Yes, at least.' He walked over and took out a large volume, one of a set of six. 'This is a particular favourite of mine. Gibbon's *Decline and Fall of the Roman Empire*. It's signed by the author, and the original boards have been kept. Come here and look.' He beckoned him over.

'It's a box. I see, you've kept it in its original condition, and preserved it in the leather box.'

'That's right. A lot of the books have been rebound, but some are in boxes. Look... You see that Sam..."HH", ... Hathaway House has been engraved in every volume, on its binding.' James breathed in deeply.

'Can you smell it?'

'You mean the leather? Of course I can.'

'I love it. This room is the hidden jewel in my estate. The outside world, apart from a number of experts and collectors, have no idea of its existence. I want to keep it that way.' He walked around gazing at the shelves. 'It's been a long time since I've been in here. The boys aren't really that interested, but that's my fault. I've never fully explained it to them. I really ought to. It's part of their birthright. I mean it's probably worth as much as the house – and more!'

'Forgive me for being so intrusive. I was just curious about the door. It's the one door I hadn't opened before!'

'It's not a problem, Sam. I'm delighted that you've seen it.'

'The books must be worth a fortune.'

'Indeed. Come on, it's 7.30, let's have a drink,' James replied, as he led the 16 year old out of the room.

16

'Where have you been?'

'We've just been to the library,' Sam said in a somewhat triumphal tone.

'You're joking. I haven't been in there for years. I thought the door was always locked anyway.'

'It usually is locked, but obviously Wendy must have left it open after dusting. We'll all go back later,' James said, smiling. 'Your friend here was very interested, and I think very impressed.'

'Yes I was. There's some unbelievable treasures in there.'

'Such as?'

Sam was just about to launch into what he had just seen, when the study door opened and Gordon and Robert entered the room. The only way one could spot the difference between the brothers was quite literally by a dark brown mole on Gordon's cheek. Otherwise, at six foot, broad and fair, the brothers were identical, and their presence in the room, imposing. Sam felt that the room had become darker, and a cold air suddenly brushed across his face. His senses were not completely playing games with him; the sun had disappeared behind the clouds just as the twins had entered.

'Hello, Gordon.' Charles went over to the elder brother and shook his hand. He turned around to the other twin. 'Robert, how are you?'

'Yes, good thanks, Charlie.' Robert turned round to Gordon and smiled in a patronising fashion.

'Who's this then, Father?' Gordon asked, pointing to Sam.

'Oh, sorry, this is Charles' friend Sam, Sam Bernstein.' James replied.

'How do you do?' Sam got up and shook both the twins' hands.

'What was your name again?'

'Bernstein – Sam Bernstein,' he replied.

Gordon shot a glance across to his twin, and smiled. Sam merely thought it was a reference to him being a Jew, and chose to ignore it, not realising that there was something more sinister than that.

'Are you at Eton with our "holier than thou" brother?' Robert asked sneeringly, continuing the conversation.

'If by that you mean Charles, yes I am.'

'Is your father in property? Any relation to the Bernstein of "Bernstein Estates"?' Gordon asked.

'Yes, that's him. Why, do you know him?'

'No, just heard of him, that's all. I must say Charles, he speaks rather well for a person of his race.' Gordon laughed.

'That's enough now. Sam is a guest in my house, boys. Try and behave.'

Sam felt distinctly uncomfortable. He had never really experienced anti-semitism in his life before,

156

in stark contrast to his father. He was at a loss over what to say or do. Fortunately Charles ushered him away before he could think of a stinging response.

'Ignore them, Sam. They're so insensitive. I wouldn't worry.'

'I'm not worried, just a little surprised. I didn't think people still thought like that.'

'Well they do. I don't think my brothers have a monopoly on racism. The establishment is riddled with it. You only have to go to the golf club nearby, or even the tennis and country club to see it. There isn't one black member, and come to think of it, I can't think of a Jewish one either.'

'I think I am only now beginning to understand my father for the first time! He's been obsessed by not being accepted by, what you call, the establishment. I've always laughed at him, but maybe he's not so paranoid after all.'

'I don't know why he's so anxious to be part of it. Your dad is an incredibly successful guy who built up a fortune from nothing. He's got nothing to prove. If people can't accept him for what he is, that's their problem.'

'You tell him.' Sam smiled. The two of them followed on behind the others, as dinner had just been called.

17

Dinner was served in the dining room. The five men sat at one end of the table, with James at the top in front of the magnificent eighteenth-century marble fireplace. The discussion at the start of the meal was relatively congenial, with James discussing his imminent retirement, and the twins talking about their latest business plans, which were becoming even more expansive and aggressive.

'You do realise, boys, that we are in the grip of a very severe economic recession. I can't see it getting any better for some time,' James said cautiously.

'We know that, father, but there are still opportunities out there.'

'Oh yes, and what are they?'

'The property market is going through a credit squeeze. There's a lot of buildings being sold, particularly in the fringe city area. We reckon there's a lot of money to be made,' Gordon continued.

'Really. I thought every business was contracting at the moment. Who's going to take the space?' James asked, not quite understanding his sons' optimism.

'At the moment you're right, but things are bound to change. Both Robert and I are convinced about growth in these areas.'

'But Gordon, the city fringe has had an explosion of growth already ... I was under the impression that it's been hit the hardest.'

'That's my point. We reckon the recovery is going to be spectacular. The only thing is that we need some money to take advantage of it!'

'Ah! Now I understand why you've come down here! I thought for a mad moment that you both came to see me and talk about my retirement.

How wrong I was. I must say it was a little foolish of me to think otherwise.'

'That's not fair, Father. We did want to see you anyway, but the opportunities we're seeing are too good to be true, and we want you to be part of it,' Robert replied.

'Have you spent all your money?' James asked directly.

'Father, Gordon and I would prefer to talk about this alone with you. Certainly not in front of young Charles and his friend.'

'I understand. Well since we've all finished, perhaps Charles and Sam can leave. Charles, take him to the library and look at the books whilst I talk to your older brothers.'

'Good idea... Oh and Charlie, make sure Shylock doesn't actually take anything with him!' Gordon laughed.

The boys left the room, Sam ignoring the offensive remark from Gordon. Even at his tender age, he had the maturity not to respond. Besides he was relieved to leave, as was Charles, who had always been embarrassed by his elder brothers.

'How can you stand them?' Sam asked, as they went through the hallway.

'With difficulty! Look, they're ignorant. That's all. They haven't been disciplined, and they mix in a real moneyed set in London. I feel sorry for them. They lost their mother when they were in their early teens.' He looked down at the floor. 'Sam, I'm not condoning their behaviour, but if my father was a little stronger with them, and didn't turn such a blind eye to their selfishness and rudeness, they would have made better human beings. They'll never change. I wouldn't be surprised if father backs them again now.'

'You must be joking. It's obvious to me that they don't know what they're doing. I know it's a long shot, but my father could give them some advice. He would love that!' He had no idea of the irony in his remark.

'It's best to stay out of this, Sam. Come on.' The boys unlocked the library door.

18

James remained seated as Gordon and Robert started to discuss their ideas and plans. It was not long before his two sons explained their financial predicament.

'All of our money is in the business. At the moment the cashflow will support the debt interest, but there is nothing left for us to buy new developments, like the one we're looking at in Farringdon. It's an office building complex providing five hundred thousand feet of space.'

'I'm surprised you haven't raised money on your houses!' James laughed sarcastically.

'Actually Father, both of our houses have been mortgaged for some time.'

'What? You must be mad. I bought you those houses. You had no right–'

'We had to, Father. The banks in the past have given us no choice. Father – we need to make this investment. It will throw up lots of cash, and will loosen the bank's hold on our other assets.'

James looked at his two sons. He could tell that

they were desperate for help. He also knew their shortcomings, and that any money he would lend them would probably never be repaid. Yet, they were his eldest sons, and despite their deficiencies, he felt a devotion to them. He could see that it would be wrong to lend them the money, but he felt it was his duty to support them.

'How much do you need for this deal?'

'Ten million. We've managed to persuade the banks to put up a lot of debt,' Gordon replied tersely and without emotion.

'You won't give any personal guarantees, will you?'

'Of course not! We're not completely mad,' Robert replied, privately knowing that his and Gordon's personal guarantee had already been given.

'OK then. I'll lend it to you, but I want it repaid in five years. That's long enough for any investment to prove itself, in my experience. I'll get Francis to draw up an informal document.' James was following a pattern he had always done, namely letting his patriarchal feelings overcome his common sense. They would eventually destroy the entire family heritage.

'Thank you, Father.' The twins almost said it in unison, such was their relief. Gordon looked at Robert and smiled. He couldn't believe his father, as a chairman of a bank, had accepted what they had said at face value. The loan documentation for the bank was extremely restricted, and riddled with personal pledges that were signed over despite the boys' perilous financial position.

In order to feed their grotesque egos and their

161

desire to attain wealth by whatever it took, the twins had no choice but to accept the conditions laid out before them. But there was no need to let their father know; with luck he would never have to know. Five years was a long time, and by then their financial position might be completely different.

19

'Promise me one thing, Charles. If, as you say, tradition dictates that your brothers will inherit Hathaway House, you must make a claim on this.' Sam opened his arms as if to embrace the room.

'I agree. It's magnificent, but I don't think they'll let me. You see, Sam, historically the library has always gone with the estate. It won't be split, not even by my father, who I'm sure would give it to me if I pressed him. He would be the first Longhurst in years to break the tradition.'

'What do you mean, Charles? The twins will have absolutely no interest in any of this. I doubt that they've even heard of Diderot. You have to promise me that you'll seize the chance. Don't let this pantheon of knowledge fall into the hands of those barbarians,' Sam insisted.

Charles let Sam's words ring in his ears. He walked around the room he had barely been in himself. It had an air of greatness about it. He looked at the treasures on the shelves, clothed in their turquoise-coloured leather boxes and bindings. He suddenly realised that it wasn't the room itself that reeked of greatness, but the books that gave the space its wonder. It was at that moment he took his oath.

'Sam, I'll make this promise to you. Whatever happens to Hathaway House, whatever happens to this room, these books will be forever mine... I don't know how or when, but I promise.' His fingers brushed the bindings. His eyes glanced at the inscriptions: Austen, *Pride and Prejudice,* Brontë, *Jane Eyre,* Dickens, *Tale of Two Cities;* he walked on, and looked up: Adam Smith, *The Wealth of Nations,* Grotius, *Mare Liberum,* moving down to Keynes and the *Economic Consequences of the Peace.* He walked across the marble floor and stared at the great European writers: Cervantes, Montesquieu, Racine and Voltaire. He looked up at the top shelf which was protected by glass and housed the most valuable books and manuscripts in the collection, including a Gutenberg Bible, Chaucer's *Canterbury Tales,* Vesalius' *De Humani Corporis Fabrica,* The Rothschild Prayer Book, and, unknown to him, the first folio edition of *Shakespeare's Comedies, Tragedies, and Histories.*

Sam walked over to Charles and put his arm around him. Their friendship had been well established after boarding together for three years, but in that half hour Sam Bernstein and the honourable Charles Longhurst became brothers-in-arms.

20

Charles and Sam went back to Eton to start their A level courses. Sam's gift for languages was clearly apparent from the outset, whilst Charles' ability for the classics was never in question. They were both in auto-pilot during their lower sixth year. The boys appeared to take everything at their own pace; a pace that was severely disrupted by an event that suddenly loomed in the calendar.

'It's a week to go,' Charles said to Sam who was lying on his bed reading the newspaper.

'Yep, I know. March 17th. I only hope those Roedean girls are ready for me.'

Charles looked at him with disdain. He knew that Sam talked about having lots of girlfriends at home, but he had never seen him with one. He had suspected for some time that his friend had never had a relationship, and was either deluding himself or too embarrassed to admit the truth.

'Oh, I'm sure they are, Sam. They're just waiting for someone like you!' Charles responded with the air of someone who had had experience of the fairer sex. His friend looked up from his newspaper, not sure if he had seen through his bravado and had guessed that he was still waiting for his first relationship. He decided to continue on the course of 'bluff' and hope that he could carry it off up until the event, where he would finally get off the mark.

The days leading up to the 17th accelerated to such an extent that everything appeared to be geared to the disco. It seemed to the invitees – those hundred or so young men and women – that the whole world was waiting for the music to start. Nature itself was waking up; daffodils lit up the playing fields at Eton and the grass lawns of Roedean. The days were getting longer and tangibly warmer. People all around were leaving their coats at home and wearing brighter spring-like clothes. It was as if the momentum of the Ball was going to bring in spring itself. And indeed for four young students, spring was about to start in more than one sense.

21

The alarm clock rang at 8.30. A long slender arm emerged from under the covers, reached out, and with the palm of her hand, banged down the button to shut off the noise. Raveena Shah turned back over, not quite believing that it was time to get up. She closed her eyes and began to drift back to sleep. However, any chance of her actually falling asleep was dashed by a loud knocking at the door.

'Go away!'

'Oh come on Rav! I'm coming in.'

Rosalind didn't wait for a reply. She burst into the room, went straight over to the window and drew back the curtains.

'I can't believe you're not up. I've been awake since 6.'

'Oh, go away, Rosalind. I can't cope with you when you're like this.' She put the pillow over her head to black out the light and drown out the noise.

Rosalind sat on her best friend's bed and looked at the pathetic bundle underneath the covers. She started to nudge her gently, but after a few seconds, she lost patience and threw back the blankets.

'Don't you realise that this is the big day. Now get up, and let's go to breakfast. We've got lots to do. I've booked the hairdresser in the Lanes for 11, and then I've arranged manicures for both of us.'

'Oh God! What did I do to deserve this! Why don't you just go on your own?'

'Because you promised me!' Rosalind replied. In truth there was no way she could afford the luxury of a hairdresser and a manicurist, but Raveena had promised her that it was her treat. It was not unusual in their relationship that Raveena would pay for such things, given their respective backgrounds and wealth. What made the friendship so special was that such inequalities didn't seem to matter. It was Raveena's pleasure to spend money on her closest friend, and it was Rosalind's obligation to accept her generosity. The absence of resentment on both sides was a key component in their relationship.

Slowly, Raveena stirred herself and finally managed to get herself out of bed. Rosalind breathed a sigh of relief: the day had finally got off the ground and her plans could now be set in motion.

'Hurry up! I'll see you down at breakfast,' she shouted from outside the bathroom, where Raveena had her mouth full of toothpaste and was unable to answer her over-excited friend.

22

The girls spent the morning exactly in accordance

with Rosalind's plans. Before going into town, they stopped off at the Blackstone house in Kemp Town. This was a regular weekly appointment that both the girls had kept since they had started at sixth form (and had been given more freedom to be allowed out at weekends). Catherine and Alan were pleased to see their daughter so often, especially as Alan, in particular, feared that they would never see her during term time. Their love for their only child remained boundless, and was the main ingredient that had made Rosalind the complete person she had become.

'Hi! Now we can only stay for half an hour, because we're off to the hairdressers at 11.'

'Oh, of course, it's your disco tonight. You must be very excited, both of you,' Catherine said, as she opened the door and welcomed them into the house.

'Well your daughter certainly is. Do you happen to have any coffee on, Mrs Blackstone? I'm in desperate need of caffeine,' Raveena said, marching past her friend's mother into the kitchen.

'How many times have I told you, Raveena, call me "Catherine". I've known you for three years now.'

'OK then, *Catherine*.' She stressed the name as if she was announcing it. 'Thank God, it's made,' she said, on seeing the full percolated pot of coffee on the kitchen table. Raveena poured herself a cup, and collapsed on to one of the kitchen chairs.

It was strange but she felt so comfortable here. Her own home could not have been more different. The palace outside Mumbai, with its own private lake, was magnificent by anyone's standards. The wealth of the Shah family was world renowned, but it was in India where its true impact was felt. When Raveena returned home for the school holidays, it would appear as a separate event in the gossip columns of the Indian press. Met by a retinue of staff, she was driven home in a cavalcade that would make any president content. Arriving home, she would look around and know that as far as she could see out on to the vast horizon, her family owned everything. Her eyes would turn to the stables and see the hundred horses cantering around the paddock, and then on to the lake where a flotilla of boats were at her family's disposal.

Mumbai was thousands of miles away from Kemp Town, but Raveena Shah felt just as at home here as she did in India. The Blackstones had made sure of that.

'Good morning, girls.' Alan Blackstone had been on night duty at the hotel. He looked exhausted, but his mood was brightened by the arrival of his daughter.

'Hi, Daddy; we can't stay for long. We have–'

'I know, I know; I've heard everything from upstairs while I was changing. Now, this disco, you're not going to do anything–'

'What do you mean, Mr Blackstone?' Raveena asked mischievously.

'You know what I mean, Raveena.'

'No I really don't, Mr Blackstone!' There was an air of formality about her relationship with Rosalind's father that she respected. But this didn't mean she couldn't gently pull his leg.

'What's for breakfast, Catherine?' Alan knew

this was a battle he was not going to win, and he smiled to himself. Life could not be better.

23

The girls arrived at the hairdressers late, but not late enough to lose their appointments. For Raveena it was almost an irrelevance anyway, since her beauty could not be improved by any hair stylist or beautician. Her hair was pulled back tightly, revealing a face that was so perfectly structured, that to try and tamper with it would be pointless. And it wasn't just the structure of her face that appeared so perfect; her hands and fingers, when placed on the beautician's cushion, were so beautifully proportioned, that the manicurist simply looked at them and smiled.

For Rosalind, however, the visit was almost like an event. She was looking forward to the fuss, and there was no way that her friend was going to stop her from enjoying it. Rosalind Blackstone, from an unpromising start, had grown into a striking young woman. Whilst Raveena's stunning aura was there for all to see, Rosalind's attraction was a little harder to detect. Her hair – auburn, long, and left free to flow down over her shoulders – needed constant care, hence her excitement at the visit. Her face was soft and blessed with an immaculate complexion. Pale blue eyes were accompanied by a straight nose and full mouth. Her head was held aloft by a long neck, and a wonderfully straight back. Her breasts were non-existent, a source of great concern, particularly as Raveena boasted a very full bosom. But any inferiority complex was easily countered by a small bottom, and legs that appeared to go on forever. She measured five foot nine, a full inch taller than Raveena.

The two girls, not quite yet women, turned heads wherever they went. Their height alone would have commanded attention, but it was their beauty that held it. There was absolutely no reason why the reaction would not be the same that evening in the assembly hall. Raveena was taking the event in her stride, whilst her friend as usual oozed irrepressible confidence. It was a mystery to Raveena where this confidence came from. It wasn't a confidence that was born out of arrogance. No, it was a confidence that gave one reassurance; something that was needed to help one get through certain situations. Raveena at first thought that the church was responsible since Rosalind had remained a devout Catholic (much to her mother's delight but her father's chagrin). However, as a non-believer herself, Raveena dismissed this reason and was resigned to never finding out the answer.

Nobody, not even Raveena, understood how Rosalind managed to possess all her gifts. They were not necessarily things you were born with. But for Rosalind herself, she knew exactly where the source could be found: it was in the English classroom where Mrs Robinson had introduced her to the world of Shakespeare two years previously. The lodestar of her nature, through some magical transference, rested with her dynamic namesake from *As You Like It*. Fleet-footed, strong-willed, intelligent and good natured, irrepressible and full of life, Rosalind was the perfect romantic heroine to adopt, and the English scholar knew it.

24

The coach arrived at 7.30. Some of the girls were looking out of the windows. The boys, knowing this, desperately tried to ignore them and thus retain some sense of cool as they disembarked. Last off, Charles and Sam were an incongruous pair at first sight. Charles – fair haired, six foot two inches, slight and gangly, but nevertheless a physically imposing figure; Sam, no taller than five foot seven, well-built, dark and swarthy, but with an attraction about him that was hard to define.

The two boys had had a quiet day. School lessons on a Saturday had a relaxed feel to them, particularly in the lower sixth form where the pressures of A levels still seemed a long way off. They had walked into Windsor for lunch and relaxed all afternoon in their rooms. There were no games that afternoon, much to the relief of Sam who was keen to listen to radio coverage of the football, with his beloved Arsenal playing in the commentary match.

'I don't know why you get so nervous. You can't do anything about it ... you might as well just relax and enjoy it.' Charles walked in to Sam's bedroom, laughing at his friend's tortured appearance, which seemed to oscillate between pain and death with each rise in the commentator's voice.

'Please. A period of silence would be most welcome from you at this point. Even better – piss off!' Sam had no time for Charles' philosophy, but he did wonder if there were better ways of enjoying oneself.

'Absolutely not. I want to talk about tonight.'

'You can – to yourself! I will be available for all the advice you need at twenty-to-five.'

Realising that his presence was causing Sam more than just an irritation, Charles decided to leave. 'I'll be back later, then.' Sam put his arm up to signal relief at his departure.

At exactly a quarter to five (allowing Sam an extra five minutes for injury time) Charles re-entered his friend's bedroom. A smug look of triumph on Sam's face as he sat at the bottom of his bed meant only one thing.

'They won. What a shame!'

'Do you want to hear about it?' Sam asked, not waiting for a response. 'Excellent result, it sets us up for a good end to the season. I'm telling you, if this evening goes anything like this afternoon, I'm going to really enjoy it.'

'Look – about tonight, I don't want to cramp your style. I realise you're regarded as a God by the opposite sex, and I just want you to know that I'm going to watch and learn,' Charles said with a straight face, trying very hard not to laugh. Sam always boasted about his success with girls, although strangely this only happened in school holidays and never in front of anybody he knew.

'I'll try and teach you. Just don't get too close and give me some room,' Sam replied nervously.

He realised his time might well be up that evening. He hadn't really been looking forward to the disco and unlike Charles who had had experience with a number of girlfriends, Sam had been singularly unlucky in love. Shyness was the main culprit in his quest to meet the opposite sex. Getting past 'hello' was an ordeal in itself. Although Charles suspected as much, Sam never told his friend just how bad he was at chatting girls up. But tonight, he realised with an air of complete resignation that he would be found out.

'Well, I'm looking forward to watching the master at work,' Charles said, not letting his friend off just yet.

25

As the boys got off the coach and mingled outside, ready to be chaperoned to the main assembly where the disco had been set up, a number of the girls were looking out of the windows.

'Anyone you like the look of?' Rosalind asked, as she walked into Raveena's bedroom and caught her friend peering at the spectacle.

'Come over here,' Raveena replied.

Rosalind walked over to the window and leaned against her friend so as to get a view out of the same opening.

'Who am I looking at?'

'The two at the back. Can you see? It's as if all the others are waiting for them.'

'You mean the ones that look like Abbot and Costello?' Rosalind said giggling, only able to see

173

the backs of the boys.

'Yes, that's them. But wait until they turn around. Look – look at the way the others are following everything they do, and yet they're at the back... Rosalind, they're different. Can't you see?'

At that moment the Honourable Charles Longhurst turned briefly around and looked directly up towards the very same window Raveena and Rosalind were looking out of.

'Yes, I can now,' Rosalind replied, looking directly into the cold crisp blue eyes of the tall young man from Hathaway House. Their glance at each other was as straight as a ray of light and as piercing as an arrow, which Cupid seemed now to be directing.

'God, he's so attractive,' Raveena muttered, in a barely audible tone.

'You're so right. Look how tall he is! And the blond hair–'

'No! I'm not talking about him ... the other one. He looks so uncomfortable, but he's really got something.'

'You are joking, aren't you? How can you compare the two of them. One's absolutely gorgeous, the other one is ... well I don't quite know what the other one is.'

'Rosalind, beauty is in the eye of the beholder. You can have your stereotyped English schoolboy, I'll stick to something a little more interesting.'

'That's fine by me,' Rosalind replied, her eyes still fixed on Charles. She had never seen anyone so handsome. She was convinced that he was her Orlando.

26

For an event that everybody was looking forward to, it began as a disappointment. The girls joined the boys in the assembly hall, but neither sex really mingled. There were isolated pockets of coexistence, where a girl knew the sister of one of the boys. Otherwise both sides lined up against opposing walls looking across the room at each other. Rosalind and Raveena had held back from joining at the outset, and had decided to remain in their room for a cool half hour before entering. Charles and Sam spent the first 30 minutes at the bar drinking the first of their permitted two glasses of wine. Every so often Charles looked around the room to see if he could catch sight of the beautiful, if fleeting, image he saw at the window earlier. But to no avail.

The music was loud in the main area but at the bar, located just outside the main area, it was possible to talk.

'No one you like, Sam?' Charles asked.

'No ... hey, it's difficult. You know, I've been thinking, I don't want to be disloyal to Jane at home.'

'Who on earth is Jane?' It was the first time Sam had mentioned 'Jane', and it was clear that she was a figment of Sam's imagination. An excuse for him not to enter the fray.

'Oh, nobody you know. A girl I've been seeing. You know how it is, living in London, always dating ... you know.'

'No, I don't really,' Charles replied, not quite believing the audacity of telling such a gigantic bluff. He was about to try and make life even more uncomfortable for Sam, but was forced to stop. His attention was diverted by the presence of two women who had come to the bar.

'Well, it's not a difficult situation to explain, Charles. She's a girl called Jane, and–' Sam realised that his friend had ceased paying him any attention and was staring at something behind his shoulder. He turned around, and immediately realised why he had moved on.

'Two glasses of white wine, please.' Raveena placed two vouchers for the drinks on the bar.

'No, let me,' Charles said, brushing past Sam, and placing the last of his vouchers into the hands of the girl serving at the bar. Raveena looked across, smiled, retrieved her vouchers, and then took the drinks, handing one of them to Rosalind who was standing beside her.

'My name is Charles, and this is Sam.' Charles pulled Sam's arm, and managed to bring him into the conversation.

'Hi, I'm Raveena, and–'

'Yes, and I'm Rosalind. Thank you for the drink.'

'My pleasure,' Charles said, staring at the face that he had caught a glimpse of at the window. She was more beautiful close up. Her hair seemed so free, as if it had a life of its own. Her pale blue eyes were wide open, looking straight at him. Although not noticeable to anyone else, he felt himself shaking with excitement and he couldn't take his eyes off her.

'So, when do you break up?' Raveena asked.

'On Thursday. What about you?'

'Tuesday,' Rosalind replied. 'Are you going away anywhere for the holidays?'

'No, I'll be staying at home in the country at Hathaway House.'

'Where's that?' Rosalind was captivated by him. She couldn't believe her luck. This was the boy she was convinced she had fallen in love with from that first fleeting sight of him in the courtyard.

'Oh it's in Wiltshire. Hey, would you like to dance?'

'I'd be delighted.' She took his outstretched hand and walked into the disco with him.

As they left the bar area, Raveena looked at the relatively short, swarthy dark-haired boy facing her. She had liked him as soon as she first caught sight of him earlier. He appeared so anxious, yet it was that very anxiety that she was attracted to.

It seemed like an inordinate amount of time that they stood together without speaking. She could see – even feel – his unease, but did nothing except sip her drink and look at the dancers on the disco floor. As ever she felt very much at ease, full of confidence, and now perversely enjoying his discomfiture. Sam, however, could feel the sweat gather above his lips, form beads on his forehead and down his temples, and concentrate on the palms of his hands. He didn't know what to say or do. He certainly didn't want to dance; at least not until his hands were drier.

'Can you speak?' Raveena broke the excruciating silence, with a hint of gentle sarcasm mixed with a little sympathy, to alleviate Sam's obvious anxiety.

'I can,' Sam replied, and then stopped.

'Very good! Would you like to talk?' Raveena continued, trying to open him up.

Sam looked up at her. She must have been at least three inches taller than him in her high heels.

'Where are you from?' he asked.

'Mumbai ... actually just outside the city. And you?'

'London. Central London.'

'How central?'

'Berkeley Square. It's a little unusual.'

'Why? It sounds fantastic to live in such a great spot.'

'Oh no, it is. But what I meant was that we're the only family who actually lives in a house on the square. We are surrounded by offices and consulates. Opposite us are car showrooms and banks. It obviously has its advantages, but it also has its drawbacks. I don't have many friends who live nearby. Do you have many friends where you live?'

Raveena thought before answering. She had always been cautious about giving too much away about her family background. Wealth had given her a wonderful life, full of privileges and luxury, but she also knew that it had its pitfalls and was painfully aware that a lot of people would be attracted to the money rather than to her as a person. Nevertheless, she felt ready to open up.

'I've lost touch with most of my friends since coming to Roedean. Anyway, it hasn't been easy for me to have friends. My family are very protective of me and we lead a relatively privileged life in Mumbai.'

'Join the club. My dad was an immigrant from Europe. He's incredibly successful, but hugely demanding. He has ambitions for me, and as a result, you could say he's had quite an interfering influence on my life and friends,' Sam replied. He was feeling more relaxed and his palms were no longer clammy, so was now in a position to ask the Indian princess for a dance.

'Believe me, however successful or ambitious your dad is, and however wonderful your house is, you have no idea how much easier you have it than me.' She drank the last of the wine in her glass and placed her hand on his. 'Come and dance with me.' He followed her on to the dance floor.

27

The disco was in its final stage with slow, romantic, tear-jerking songs bringing hopeful couples closer together. Some had already ventured outside to break through the friendship barrier and embark on a more exciting physical adventure. It was a clear but very cold night. The wind meant that the temperature dropped even further, bringing tears to some of the girls' eyes.

It was strangely quiet among the ten or so couples who had made it outside. The most audible sound was that of the sea crashing on to the pebbled beach. Although the stars were out – and there were a great many of them on that crystal clear night – it was still surprisingly very dark given the lack of any artificial light.

Charles started to talk about his background and tell Rosalind about that tragic night when his mother died giving birth to him.

'What date was that, did you say?'

'May 5th 1978—' he replied, wanting to continue, but was interrupted again.

'That's amazing.'

'Why?'

'That's my birthday ... that's when I was born ... but I came out later that afternoon.' She shuddered from a combination of the excitement, and from the cold wind.

'Do you want my jacket?'

'Thank you,' Rosalind replied, gratefully taking it and putting it around her shoulders.

'That really is a coincidence—'

'Yes!' She laughed and looked at him. It was further confirmation for her that destiny was playing its part here.

Charles turned away from her stare, worried that he was losing himself to her magic. 'God, you can smell the sea here. It must be beautiful in the summer.'

'Actually, it's easy to take it for granted.' Rosalind breathed in deeply and looked out towards the dark sea.

...thou deep and dark blue ocean.

She smiled, and turned to Charles.

...sweep over thee in vain;
Man marks the earth with ruin – his control
Stops with the shore.

Charles looked straight back at her.

'You know your Byron?' she asked him, thrilled that she had found a kindred spirit.

'I know all the Romantics, but Keats is my favourite by a long way. How about you?'

'English literature is my favourite subject. I love all of it! But there is one poet above all who casts his shadow over all of them.'

'Shakespeare?' He was now facing her with his arms around her waist. She was leaning back so as not to be too close to his face.

'Yes.'

'Do you love all of his work, or just certain plays?'

'Everything he's written. For me, he's peerless. The ultimate genius.'

'No question. But there's an awful lot of him!'

'I've read it all,' she said, in a slightly triumphant manner.

'I'm sure you have. I'm in fact feeling a little inadequate. I mean, poor old Keats compared to the mighty Bard. Perhaps I should have–'

'Oh, don't be silly, Charles. You don't have to worry, Keats was–' Charles put his finger to Rosalind's lips, stopping her in mid sentence. It was the last thing he wanted to talk about. All he wanted her to do was to come forward and kiss him, but she wasn't going to do that.

'I'm not worried, Rosalind.' He smiled as he took his finger away from her lips and gently kissed her. It lasted less than a second. She was slightly taken by surprise, but significantly had not moved away as he leaned in towards her. She stayed locked in position, her face so close to his that both could feel their warm breath caress each other's mouths and cheeks. He looked into her dark eyes, and for the first time felt the power of total attraction. He once again moved his mouth towards hers, but this time slightly adjusting the angle of approach, and with his lips apart. She opened her mouth, and accepted his tongue, responding with her own.

28

Raveena had taken the lead from the very outset, and it was time for Sam to make some sort of move. He had never felt so comfortable with a woman before, and for that he was grateful. He privately thanked God that he was feeling so calm, not realising for one moment that he should have been thanking Him for Raveena. It was nothing to do with the Divine, or any outside factors, that Sam was feeling so at ease. Raveena Shah was the only reason for Sam's promising debut in the world of romance.

After the second dance, Sam managed to catch Raveena's glance long enough to seize his chance and clumsily plant his lips on hers. The relief he felt after his sudden exertion was exhilarating – it was no mean physical feat for him to reach her mouth with his, given the three-inch difference in height. She, on the other hand, was so surprised by the offensive that she almost stopped dancing.

'Have you never kissed a girl before?' she asked, laughing.

'Of course I have! There've been many victims, but I'm far too modest–'

'Sam Bernstein!' She looked at him. He was adorable. 'Don't lie. If you kissed other women like that, the dental profession would have a field day with teeth capping.' She took her hands off his shoulders, and placed them around his face. 'I don't care Sam ... I really don't. It's not important to me.'

'Can we go outside for some air. We can talk more easily.' Sam knew it was time to come clean. They walked outside, passing Charles and Rosalind, but were completely oblivious to their presence. They sat down on a bench, which in daylight afforded wonderful views of the sea.

'OK then, I'm not that experienced ... in fact I've only had one girlfriend and that was two years ago. I can't even remember her now. I've certainly forgotten how to kiss. I know it's a bit pathetic.' He looked across at her. Sitting down, she was no longer taller than him. He then reached over and kissed her. Only at that moment did he realise some things in life don't necessarily need to be taught. Raveena was already aware of that. After half an hour of perfecting his technique, Sam took her hand and walked her back to the disco.

'God! Look at those daffodils. Amazing how they survive the weather,' Sam said, as he looked at the bank of flowers illuminated by lights from the building.

Raveena stared back at him. 'Christ! It's like being with Rosalind. Have you been talking to her?'

'No, why?'

'Oh, don't ask. For the last three years I've had to listen to her rattle on about Shakespeare, and Perdita's speech in the Winter's Tale on daffodils was her "thing". Every spring I've had to hear her drone on about them.'

'I won't mention them again!' he replied privately, noting to himself not to mention Shakespeare. She needn't have worried – he couldn't stand English literature, much less the theatre.

29

The coach back to Eton that evening left at 11.30. The drive seemed to last much longer than the two hours it actually took.

'Well, Sammy, it looks like even you managed to score,' Charles said, quietly mocking his friend. 'Sam ... well, what was she like?'

'She was something else. She was... I don't know how to explain it, but I've never felt so comfortable, so at ease, with a woman before. What's more, she's beautiful. Didn't you think?' Sam looked back at Charles. This was no time for frivolity or mockery. He was being deadly serious, as only someone who had fallen in love could be.

'Yes, she was beautiful,' Charles replied, sensing the tone.

'What about Rosalind, did you like her?'

'Yes I did.' He then paused. 'Very much.' He reached into his pocket and took the scrap of paper on which her phone number '01273 45555' was written. He carefully folded it and pushed it back in his pocket. He smiled, looking out of the window. Sam saw the reflection of his friend's face. He quickly rolled up his shirt sleeve and saw Raveena's handwritten number written across his forearm. He thought back to the moment when they were all leaving and was desperately looking for something to write on. He remembered looking at Raveena holding a biro, waiting for him. Completely demoralised, he returned empty-handed, but she immediately pulled his hand towards her, pushed his sleeve up, and wrote the number down. He now sat back holding on to that last impression of her saying goodbye. He rolled the sleeve back down, relieved that the previously unchecked writing was legible.

The two young men sat at the back of the coach were completely oblivious to the fact that the women they had just met would play such a significant role in both of their lives.

30

Raveena sat at the bottom of Rosalind's bed. 'He better call me,' she said, looking down at the plastic cup of wine.

'Well, he might not, Raveena. Calls to Mumbai can be rather expensive,' Rosalind replied, now pouring herself a drink. The bottle was hidden under the bed, in case a teacher walked in.

'Don't be ridiculous. He's not poor. And if he doesn't ... well I'll–'

'What? Go to Eton and scream at him? I don't think so! I'm sure he'll ring, but I don't know why you didn't just give him your address. It would have been the normal thing to do.'

'There was no time. You didn't give Charles your address, did you?'

'Kemp Town's a touch closer than Mumbai, Raveena.'

'Oh God! You're right. I knew it. The first guy I really fall for – and I mean really fall for – and I–'

'Hey Rav, don't cry, I was only joking. He'll ring.' Rosalinmd got up from her pillow, and put her arm around her friend. 'I didn't realise how much you liked him. He's not really your type.'

'I know. I don't really understand it. He's everything I would normally laugh at. He's short, swarthy, nervy, and shy and yet when he speaks, and let me tell you, Rosalind, trying to get him to talk was no small achievement, he completely changes. Physically and mentally, he becomes a giant. I've never met anyone like him.' She rested her head on Rosalind's shoulder. 'And what about Charles?' she asked, after a pause.

'Oh, I fell in love with him when I first saw him from the window.'

'What... Just like that? Didn't anything change when you met him?'

'No, Rav. I fell in love with him at that moment, and nothing he said or did changed my feeling for him.' She looked at her friend. 'I'm in love with Charles Longhurst, and I will marry him.'

'I hope you didn't tell him all of this.'

'No, of course not, but it won't be long before he knows,' she surmised, completely discarding the uncertain thoughts and nervousness that lie in a young man's psyche.

'Rosalind Blackstone, if it were anyone telling me this and saying such things, I would call her mad and conceited, but coming from you, I suppose I'll have to believe it.' Raveena laughed and charged her plastic cup against Rosalind's. 'To Sam and Charles,' she said. 'To you and me,' Rosalind replied.

Part 7

SOTHEBY'S, THE PRESENT DAY

4.30 P.M.

The room had an air of unreality about it. It was as if everything was suspended in time as the audience waited for the next move. Every pair of eyes was now firmly fixed on the diminutive Frenchman. He was clearly uncomfortable with the attention that was now focused on him. But his instructions were lucid, and he knew what he had to do. He looked up at Smith Luytens, who in turn was staring at him.

'It's against you, monsieur. I have £160 million from the back of the room.'

The Frenchman turned around and saw Bill Gaston, the most televised human on the planet, who was standing behind the last row. He was instantly recognisable, standing at six foot four, and it was extraordinary that he'd managed to enter the room unnoticed. He turned back, loosened his tie, and then looked up to the auction-eer.

'Cent soixante-cinq.'

'I'm sorry, sir, I didn't quite manage to hear you.'

'Cent soixante-cinq millions!' he shouted back.

'Thank you, monsieur.' The price was approaching its reserve, but there was plenty of bidding left in the room. Smith Luytens sensed it; he could feel, almost smell, the money in the room. He looked up and saw Gaston look at the Frenchman in the front row indifferently. There was no contempt, merely a disregard for the civil servant's anxiety at the level of bidding.

'Hey, come on now, let's get this thing really moving. Two hundred million,' Gaston shouted out. His words fired out like bullets into the room and had an immediate effect. The Frenchman would not be able to respond. He now waited for his next rival.

'Thank you, sir. I have £200 million,' Smith Luytens replied quietly. He didn't even glance at the Frenchman now – he was out. He knew where the next bid was coming, but he was concerned that the person in question had not yet made his move. He somehow had to entice his friend into the field of battle.

'I will sell at this level, ladies and gentlemen.' The bait was set.

'Two hundred and ten,' a crisp aristocratic voice declared. The old Etonian stood up from the seventh row next to the aisle, and finally entered the fray.

'I now have £210 million from the aisle, and it's now against you, sir.' Smith Luytens pointed his hammer at Gaston aggressively. The auctioneer's relief was palpable. He was momentarily worried that the British Government was going to leave it too late. Like all Englishmen, he was desperate for the treasure to remain in this country. He didn't want the nation to suffer the embarrassment, the humiliation, of losing a fundamental part of its heritage to some American tycoon, even if it was William Gaston. Now, finally, his schoolboy friend, Hugo Samuels, had come on to the stage to save the day. But did he have enough in his arsenal to gun down the American intruder, or was there someone else biding his time and about to come in? Smith Luytens waited anxiously for Gaston's response.

Part 8

ROSALIND ENCOUNTERS LEAR

1

Placing the receiver on the phone, Sir Francis Sutherland walked across his drawing room towards the window and looked out over the gardens. It was almost six years since James Longhurst had last raised the subject of his will and Hathaway House, but since then his client had prevaricated and procrastinated. But time would no longer wait for the 37th Baron of Hathaway House. The 75 year old Lord was racked by cancer, with primaries in the spine, and secondaries in the lungs and kidneys. He had a matter of weeks to live, and he was, as far as his lawyer knew, still intestate. Sir Francis genuinely had his client's interest at heart over the previous years, whilst he tried to persuade him to write a will and settle the future of the great baronial estate of Hathaway House. But it was to no avail, as James would always have a reason for delaying his decision.

Tradition in the Longhurst family dictated that primogeniture should govern his choice. However, there had been isolated instances in the Longhurst history where a younger son had inherited the estate, even if it was rare. Yet Sir Francis Sutherland – loyal friend and family lawyer – now felt, despite his earlier reticence, that this was one of those instances. He, more than anybody else, knew that Gordon and Robert were totally unfit for the inheritance. Their company was a hair's breadth away from going into receivership. Their trusts, after 16 years of unadulterated hedonism, had nothing left in them. But, most importantly, he had never met anyone as hateful as them, and they appeared to have no morals. His main task over the previous two years was to try and convince James to leave the estate to Charles. At first it was James himself who felt that the twins should be left out, but now with the weight of tradition on his back, he was very unsure, and Francis' words had fallen on deaf ears.

He continued to stare out of the window. The gardens below were filled with young children celebrating a birthday party. He turned around and waited for the phone to ring. It wouldn't be his advice but the cancerous tumour that would finally bring James to the table to write his will.

2

'Francis?'

'James, thank you for calling me back. We have to do this thing, you know. You can't keep putting it off. It would be a disaster to leave it all up in the air.'

'Yes, yes, I know. The medication is fantastic. I'm not in any pain. In fact the doctors think I've got a few months yet but I don't believe them.' His voice tailed off.

'James, let me come down this afternoon, it won't take long. We can sort it out once and for all, very quickly.'

'Very well then, Francis, but I'm not going to be browbeaten by your criticisms of the twins. I know their shortcomings, but they're not as bad as you think. Listen, I was the one who told you that I was considering leaving them out of the will in the first place.'

'I know James but–'

'I agree with you that Charles is a super kid, but he's been blessed with his mother's temperament. Life's been easy for him – he's doing extremely well at Oxford, they're predicting a first, you know. He's got a new girlfriend he's very keen on. But the twins need to be protected, you do understand that?'

'Let me come over there and we'll chat.' Sir Francis hurriedly hung up, picked up his case and left the flat, realising that his client might be ready to make up his mind.

The drive from Knightsbridge to Hathaway House usually took just over two hours, but that August afternoon Sir Francis covered the 110 miles in 90 minutes. He had been waiting six years to bring this affair to a head; he wasn't going to let it slip from his grasp now. Even if the old man decided to leave everything to the twins, at least it could be finalised and documented. This was a far better scenario than the chaotic mess of his dying intestate.

As he approached the estate and drove past the giant wrought-iron gates, a nervous anticipation suddenly struck him. In the distance, barely discernable, he saw the dishevelled figure of James Longhurst standing at the door. He slowed down as he approached, and thought back to when he first met him, over 40 years ago.

Francis despised his client during the first 20 years of their relationship. Arrogant, ruthless and insensitive, he treated people with disdain, particularly his professional advisors. A lot of that character had been passed on to Gordon and Robert, but the twins lacked the charisma and the standing of their father. He could just about get away with his behaviour, but only just. The twins could not.

After Davina's death and James's subsequent dramatic change of persona, Francis' relationship with his client also shifted. Respect replaced condescension, warmth thawed the coldness, and a mutual regard formed a friendship, which rapidly developed into a very close personal relationship. James rarely made a move, both personal or in business, without discussing it first with Francis. In return, he received the best advice that was available: counsel that was mixed with astute professionalism, but given out of the warmth of friendship. And it was that counsel which Sir Francis Sutherland hoped his client would listen to now.

3

'Francis, how was the drive?' James came out from the doorway slowly to welcome his friend, resting on his walking stick.

'Very good, actually. Hardly a car on the motorway.' Francis looked at his old friend, and felt sadness. The illness had clearly taken its toll. It seemed like he had literally shrunk. Bent over, thin to the point of frailty, haggard and grey, James Longhurst was a shadow of his former self.

'How long did it take you?'

'Oh, about an hour and a half.' Sir Francis glanced at his watch. 'Thank you for finally listening.'

'Well I can't put it off any longer. Hathaway House has to be sorted out. Come on, Francis, don't look so grim, it's not really as bad as all that.'

'No?' Francis was dismayed by James' mood. He seemed so cavalier, so nonchalant about the future of the very thing that he had agonised about over the last few years. And now, when facing his own demise, he seemed to have shrugged off Atlas' world that had been lying on his shoulders. He appeared to be ready to make the necessary decision.

'No. I've decided on what to do. It's all very clear to me now. The last hour or so has been conclusive. Come. Come into the study and let's discuss it.'

The two men walked into the study and sat down at the eighteenth-century bureau. They started to go through the old man's personal possessions, as opposed to the estate itself. To Francis' surprise, despite the physical deterioration of his client, his mental capacity for the moment appeared to be unimpaired. He had already drawn up a list of everything that he owned, and had divided it up for his heirs in equal fashion. He had also provided for the staff, particularly for Wendy who had looked after Hathaway House for 50 years. Special provisions were made for Janet, who had started working for the Longhurst family as a nanny for Charles, later becoming a mistress and companion to the master of the house, and had now become his nurse, helping him through his final weeks.

'It's absolutely vital that all those mentioned must be protected, especially Wendy … and, of course, Janet.'

'I understand James, completely.' Francis was writing everything down.

'Now, Hathaway House. Before I finally decide on this, have you had any change of mind?'

'Have you?'

'It's difficult to change a decision when one hasn't made one.'

'So you are still undecided.'

'The loan I made to the twins for the Farringdon property deal five years ago has remained unpaid. Interest has rolled up, making the figure outstanding at well over £13 million.'

'I am well aware of that, James, and I don't believe you will ever get it back.'

'Yes, yes, I'm sure you're right. The development is highly speculative. There haven't been any pre-lets and I doubt if the banks will see their money back.'

'But doesn't that deal alone underscore my point? The twins are unfit to inherit the estate. It would be utter madness for them to have something as great as this. They have proved themselves incapable of keeping anything of value. Everything they touch seems to turn to stone. It's as if they have the Midas touch in reverse.'

'Maybe, but they have been very caring

recently, particularly after my diagnosis.'

'Oh come on, James. You must know them better than that. Of course they're going to be caring. They have their eyes on the prize. They've always feared that Hathaway House would go to Charles. Now that you're dying, this is their one last throw of the dice to win you over.'

'Maybe, but that doesn't alter the fact that they've been staying over much more than Charles.'

'Charles has got finals in a couple of weeks. He's been a model son to you all of his life. You can't penalise him for working for his exams, something that might determine his future.'

'I'm his father!' James retorted angrily.

'I know that; he knows that. I don't think anybody in the world knows it better than him.' Francis was suddenly conscious for the first time that James' mental health was unstable. The cavalier attitude, the nonchalance displayed on his arrival earlier that afternoon, and the decisiveness in his preferences were all part of his madness. The cancer was finally affecting his judgement and his arguments now seemed irrational.

'Well, I genuinely believe that both Gordon and Robert, notwithstanding their record, love me unconditionally, and have proven that over the last few weeks. I cannot deny them their birthright. Technically Gordon should inherit everything since he's the oldest by 15 minutes, but I haven't got it in my heart to deny Robert. Anyway, as I said, it's a technicality, so they'll both inherit it. Gordon will naturally take the title ... I mean, you can't split that, can you!' James laughed, but

Francis found nothing funny about the situation.

'Is this your final word on the matter? And the library? I mean, I've always maintained that the library should always go with the estate, but maybe now in this instance—' Francis asked softly, now resigned to the fact that his client was obviously not fully compos mentis.

'No. The library remains, the books stay here. The twins will respect that.' He paused. 'Yes that's my final word... Don't worry, Francis. I appreciate your concerns, and I know that Charles is a very good son, but—'

'What?' Francis interrupted, seizing the opportunity for a last attempt at making his client listen to some sense. 'What is it that has made you so certain about leaving this place to them? What has Charles done? Has it ever occurred to you that your illness could be affecting your judgement?'

'Ah! Is that what you think, Francis? That I've gone mad. Well I haven't. I'm perfectly sane, and I want you to promise me that you won't contest the will in any way after I am dead. You must promise me that, Francis.'

Francis stood motionless, staring at James. If he agreed to this, he knew that he could never help Charles inherit the estate. He wasn't even sure that Charles wanted it, but he was certain in his own mind that he was morally the rightful heir. By promising James, he would be denying Charles his only chance. But he didn't really have a choice. If he refused, James would have instructed another lawyer who would confirm his soundness of mind and general sanity. He realised that

204

he owed his friend some comfort in his last days.

'Oh very well, James, I promise. But if you have any second thoughts, please call me. We can draw up a codicil very quickly.'

'I won't, Francis. I'm doing the right thing. Hathaway House is in the twins' blood. Charles rarely stays here any more and, as I said before, he's very busy at Oxford – what with his girlfriend and his exams, he has no time.'

Francis sensed an air of bitterness in James' voice over his youngest son. It was strange that he should feel this way. Charles had been a perfect child, always dutiful and respectful, but also caring and loving. During the last few weeks with his finals days away, it had been impossible for him to get away. With his brain being invaded by the cancer that had by now almost destroyed his other organs, Lord Longhurst, the 37th Baron of Hathaway House, was going insane. Francis was right: James was not able to think straight and his reason had become distorted. The twins were first to see this vulnerability in their father and had taken advantage of it, by seeing him and coming down frequently to stay with him. Their plan to ingratiate themselves with him would work, and their dreams would be fulfilled when Lord James Longhurst's will was read out.

4

Francis Sutherland drove home after dinner the same evening. He started to reflect on his own life. Single, never having been married, he had enjoyed living alone. His experiences and past relationships with the opposite sex were few and fleeting. He simply wasn't interested. His real love in life was opera. It consumed him, taking up almost all of his leisure time. He would travel the world, from Milan to New York, to see productions. Such was his expertise, that he was frequently asked to write reviews for *The Telegraph*. There was no time for anyone, or anything else. He smiled to himself as the automatic CD changer selected one of his favourites, the overture from Beethoven's only opera, *Fidelio*.

He slowed down at junction three, and turned off the motorway at the Heston Service Station. He parked the car and went into the dining area where he ordered a coffee. He rarely stopped when driving, but he was exhausted. The meeting with James, although decisive, had not produced the outcome that he had hoped for. He sat down at the table, opened his case, and took out the 'active' Longhurst family file. He went through his notes. There was nothing that had been omitted. He would draw up the official document tomorrow, and send it to his client for witnessing and signing within a week.

He slumped back in his chair. A sudden wave of depression accompanied his fatigue, creating a cocktail of overwhelming sadness. He put his hands over his face, and began to think of Charles. Over the last three years, his relationship with the youngest member of the Longhurst family had developed into a close one. The trigger for the friendship was Charles' acceptance at Worcester College, Oxford. Being an alumni and a trustee of that establishment meant that they at once had something in common. Francis frequently made trips to the College for trustee meetings, and often visited Charles.

'Do you want a refill, sir?'

'Sorry?'

'Your coffee.'

'Oh ... yes that would be very kind.'

The waitress poured the black fluid into the white mug, and then added the milk. He moved the cup back towards him. He looked at his watch. It was one thirty in the morning. He raised his eyebrows; no wonder he was tired. Looking across at the papers once again, he realised why he had been thinking of Charles. The title was never in anyone's gift, but the only person who deserved to inherit the estate, the only son who really did care about his father, and the only human being who had any compassion and love in the family, was hardly mentioned in the notes, apart from a few derisory chattels left to him. True, he had his own trust, and would never be poor, but that was not the issue. Charles Longhurst was the finest young man Francis had ever met. He was the natural successor, and yet he was being ignored by a sick father who could not be challenged, now or later. And that was where the real tragedy lay. The will would be incontestable given the promise that Francis had made. Drinking the last drop of coffee, he slammed the cup down on the table, attracting the attention of the two staff still working. It was unethical, but he felt obliged to inform Charles about what his father was planning to do. He would drive up to Oxford in the morning.

5

'Francis! How are you? What a surprise. I didn't expect you today,' Charles said, opening the door to his room.

'No, it's more like a flying visit.' He walked over to the window, which overlooked the beautiful sunken grass quad. 'How are you?'

'Yes, very good thanks. Now what's up? You know I haven't got too much time. Finals are days away.'

'Yes I know, Charles. I understand. Can I sit down?' he asked, turning away from the window.

'Good lord, Francis, what's wrong?' Charles looked at the man, who had effectively been like a mentor throughout his time at university, and saw the ashen complexion of his face. 'You look terrible.'

'It's your father. I think he's—'

'What, Francis?'

'I think he's lost his mind.'

'Why? What has he done?'

'I'm sorry, Charles. I shouldn't be telling you this, but I felt that I had to. He's left Hathaway House to Gordon and Robert. The whole thing, lock stock and barrel. And, dare I say it, that means the library is theirs too. They don't even know its true value, but if they did, it would almost certainly be dismantled and sold.' Charles looked at Francis, but said nothing. He slowly walked over to his desk and without thinking, picked up a pen. 'I'm sorry, Charles, but there was nothing I could do. Really. You know I've been trying to persuade him to break with tradition, but yesterday was my last chance, and I failed. He's mentally not well. I'm convinced of that.'

'First of all, Francis, please stop apologising. But more importantly, what makes you think that his mind has gone. I only spoke to him three days ago and he sounded perfectly normal. I know the cancer is terminal, and admittedly I haven't had the chance to see him for a couple of weeks now, but–'

'But that's just it. He's upset – no, more piqued than upset, about you not seeing him enough during his illness. I tried to explain to him that you're busy with exams and all that, but he didn't listen. Meanwhile Gordon and Robert have almost taken up residence there, and have managed to convince him that they are, and have always been, loving and caring sons. No matter their failings and their shortcomings, your father has wiped the slate clean and embraced their love as if they were newborn babies. You didn't stand a chance.'

'No, I probably didn't,' he replied quietly. 'What do you want me to do about it?' Charles asked quietly.

'There isn't much you can do. When I questioned his judgement, he made me promise that I would not contest the will after he had died. It's a tragedy that such a man, such a father, should make such an error of judgement over his children.'

'Would you like a drink, old man? It looks like

you do.' Breaking the tension, Charles got up, walked over to the cabinet and took a bottle of brandy out. It was only ten o'clock in the morning, but he could see that Francis needed something to alleviate his stress.

'Thank you.' He gratefully took the glass. He never drank in the morning, but at that moment, he wanted nothing more than to consume the golden brown liquid in front of him. As he took his first gulp, he felt the cognac ooze its way down his oesophagus and rest easily in his stomach. Its soothing effect was immediate. 'Is there anything in Hathaway House that you want? Perhaps I can manage to persuade your father to give you something from it. The art, for example, or the furniture? At the moment, apart from a few chattels, everything is going with the estate.'

Charles sat back and tried to weigh up the extraordinary situation he had suddenly been confronted with. He, of course, had always known that the eldest had always traditionally inherited the estate. But given the way Gordon and Robert had behaved, and the very nature of their characters, he genuinely believed that he would be left Hathaway House. Indeed his father had frequently led him to believe that this would be the case. As a son, his relationship with his father was exceptional. The news he had just received from Sir Francis simply didn't add up.

'Are you saying that there's nothing that can be done, not even if I were to go up there and see him?'

'Yes, a visit would be pointless. He would soon

realise that I had spoken to you, and any trust that I have with him would be irrevocably broken. Besides, I'm sure that he would have told the twins by now.'

'But Francis, you don't understand. They might–'

'What?'

'I know it's unthinkable, but they could quite easily sell it or even lose it. I mean, what if one of their mad property developments goes wrong, and they're personally exposed to the debt? It might be taken from them. Hathaway House might end up in the hands of some bank.'

'I'm afraid Charles, it's not possible – it's more likely probable.'

There was silence in the room as both men looked at each other and imagined the unimaginable. For the first time, Charles suddenly woke up to the fact that he desperately now wanted to inherit the house. The very realisation of his loss, and the near certainty that the twins would sell it, triggered a fresh desire within him. Charles got up and began to pace around the room. He still could not quite believe the news that Francis had brought him, and he began to question himself. Where had he gone wrong? Why was he being punished? Why had his father waited so long before deciding on the future of the estate? Why hadn't Sir Francis seen this coming? He turned around, his frustration and anger was now rising up inside him, and about to explode into a verbal assault on the only person upon whom it could be vented, his old and trusted friend.

'Why couldn't you have–' Before Charles could

finish his opening salvo, there was a knock at the door. 'Who is it?'

'It's me.'

'Oh!' Charles walked over and opened the door. 'Rosalind, come in. Let me introduce you to Sir Francis Sutherland.'

'I'm very pleased to meet you.' She walked into the room, smiling, her hand outstretched towards Sir Francis.

6

Rosalind's entrance saved the old man from suffering the full force of Charles' resentment and anger. He looked up at the girl about whom Charles had spoken in such glowing terms and at such great length. She did not fall short of expectation: tall and slim, appearing wonderfully poised, elegant and refined, she majestically breezed into the room in the same manner as summer breathes its warmth into the air. There was a sense of wellbeing that pervaded the room as soon as she came in. He stared at the vision before him, realising that Charles had found someone quite exceptional.

'I'm very pleased to meet you. Charles has not stopped talking about you, and I can see why.' Sir Francis stood up and shook the outstretched hand with both his hands, expressing a warmth that normally he wouldn't know how to show.

'Thank you. He's very flattering about you, Sir Francis.'

'Well, I don't think he'll be thinking the same

way now!' he said, immediately regretting being so indiscreet.

'Don't be ridiculous, Francis. It's just such a bloody shock, that's all.' Charles felt a certain remorse for his earlier outburst. Rosalind's presence was also having an effect on him.

'What's happened?' she asked.

'It's what I feared but never really expected,' Charles replied.

'What?' Even Rosalind's patience was being tested.

'Hathaway House... My father's left the estate to Gordon and Robert.'

'But I thought he had always said he would leave it to you. Why has he done this?'

'Well, apparently, according to Francis here, he's gone slightly mad. It seems that he's extremely angry that I haven't been to see him enough in the last few weeks, ignoring the fact that I've been a devoted son my entire life. I've shown him love and affection at all times, I really don't think I need to prove it.'

'That's it, in a nutshell, I'm afraid. I should have pushed him more forcefully to write the will earlier, but he always refused,' Sir Francis added.

'Gordon and Robert have hardly spent any time there – apart from the last few weeks, that is! They now have the prize. It's a tragedy. They have no love for the place, no sense of attachment. They'll probably either lose it on some mad property venture, or sell it. You don't know how awful they are ... selfish, arrogant ... they're evil.' Charles looked at Rosalind. He held out his hand to her. She took it, and smiled at him, giving him reassurance.

'Lear,' she whispered under her breath.

'What?' Sir Francis asked, puzzled.

'Oh, don't worry, Francis. Rosalind lives her life in the world of Shakespeare. She's convinced that everything in this world is a re-enactment of a Shakespearian play in some form or another,' Charles explained. He suddenly felt conscious of his hand, which was still being held by Rosalind's. He felt a strength being transferred from her, injecting a certain perspective to the current situation. 'Francis, you asked if there was anything in the house that I want. Well, I must have the library. I want those books. In a way, although I care very deeply for Hathaway, it's the books that are really important to me.' Charles now remembered his vow to Sam six years previously.

'But he won't let it go. Originally, I must admit, I advised him that the books must stay with the house, but as time went on and having seen the finances of your brothers, I realised it was not sensible. After he had made his decision, I did ask him to separate them, but he was adamant. I really tried.'

'You have to try again, Francis. You don't understand – have you ever been in it?'

'Once, many years ago, but I am aware of its contents. Rosalind, you'll like this. There's a First Folio, a Shakespeare First Folio that is, in there!'

'You're joking! Charles, you never told me. There are only three hundred in existence.'

'And only six in private hands,' Sir Francis interjected.

'I didn't know myself. The entire library is magical, Rosalind. There is something ethereal and intangible, even sublime about the place; I don't know what it is, but I made a promise to Sam six years ago, and I want to keep it.'

'What promise?' Francis asked.

'I swore an oath to Sam – Sam Bernstein. You've met him, Francis, haven't you?' Francis nodded. 'that I would never let the books go. I must keep that oath.'

'Well I'll go back, but I don't hold much hope. The value of the collection is over £100 million. The inheritance tax on the twins is going to upset them.' He smiled at the only upside in the whole affair. 'Maybe I could get him to pass some of the books over to you,' Sir Francis said, opening his file.

'Just do what you can. Maybe the twins, not knowing what they're worth, will give me some books.'

'I doubt it. And they'll know soon enough.'

'Look, why don't you see what you can do, Francis. Speak to me after you've seen Father.' He looked across to Rosalind. 'I'm sorry, sweetheart, you might never get to see Hathaway House. I really wanted you to see it, but I doubt my brothers will let me set foot in it. How many Shakespearian characters suffer the fate of being completely passed over?'

'Apart from Cordelia?'

'Yes. Or rather, tell me about someone who does slightly better!'

'There're a number, but Orlando does rather well,' she said, as she put her arms around him.

215

'Which play is he in?'

'*As You Like It.*'

'And–?'

'He does a lot better, but it's a complicated tale. He marries the right girl in the end though!'

'And who was that?'

She smiled and kissed him. 'Rosalind.' They both looked around for Sir Francis, but he had already left. He had to salvage something from the debacle, and he had to move quickly.

7

It was over five years after they had first met in that March of 1994, before Charles made his move and actually asked Rosalind out on a proper date. Unlike his friend Sam, who made contact with Raveena during the Easter holidays a week after the disco, Charles suffered a sudden loss of courage and decided not to contact her. He had never felt like this about anyone before. The sense of longing, the anguish of desire, and the gut-wrenching pain of simply not being with her, almost destroyed him during the ensuing months. But time slowly weaved its magic, and the angst was reduced to an ever-present dull, aching pain that remained with him until he saw her again.

He sought refuge in his work, the only thing that really challenged him. His exam grades went from very good to excellent, and he decided to read Classics at university, committing himself to Oxford in the Longhurst tradition. After achieving two 'A's and a 'B' at A level, there was never any doubt that he would pass the Seventh Term Oxbridge exam, but he still had not yet decided on which college he would go to. He visited most of them with his father, who wanted him to follow in his footsteps and select Balliol. However, Charles wanted to break with this particular precedent and looked at other colleges. It was left to a chance meeting in Queen Street with Sir Francis Sutherland, returning from a trustees' meeting, who suggested that they look at Worcester College.

One of the smaller colleges in the University, it remains one of the most elegant. As soon as Charles visited the buildings, a blissful blend of old and modern with its capacious grounds and stunning lake, he instantly fell in love with the college. An interview followed, and a place was guaranteed subject to his passing the entrance exam. This proved to be a formality; in the event he won an exhibition, an achievement which so impressed his father that the old man recovered from his initial irritation of his youngest son passing up on his old college.

'You're the first Longhurst to go to Oxford, and not go to Balliol. I can't say that I was happy about it, but as usual, Charles, you have made me so proud of you.' He opened up his arms and hugged his son with all his strength. 'At least you're going to Oxford, unlike the other two. Still, one can't expect too much from life. Have you told anyone yet?'

'No, apart from Janet, who opened the envelope before I got it!'

'Yes, that's pretty typical. She can't help it!' he laughed. Janet had been like a mother to Charles, and could not resist the overwhelming impulse of finding out the result before anybody else.

'I must tell Sam.' He paused. 'Father, would you mind if I went to London tonight?'

'No, not at all. Send Sam my best, won't you?'

'Of course I will.'

8

Sam Bernstein, two months after the disco, found himself in a full blown romance with Raveena Shah, which would continue throughout his final year and a half at school. It was an unfamiliar situation for him to be in, but perversely, it felt completely natural to him. The first phone call was always going to be the most difficult. And whilst Charles had lost his nerve, Sam held his, but nevertheless agonised terribly about making contact.

'They've broken up now,' Sam suddenly said to Charles during tea on the penultimate day of term.

'Who?'

'Roedean. Their end of term was Tuesday.'

'Interesting,' Charles said sarcastically. He really didn't want to discuss it. Slightly ashamed at his failure to call Rosalind, but more worried that he knew he would not be contacting her in the future, he just wanted to move on.

'I've got to ring her. I just don't know what to say. She'll be in Mumbai by now.'

'Don't look at me. I can't give you any advice. Also Sam, I don't really want to talk about it, sorry.'

'I don't understand. You're so much more experienced and more confident than me. Why can't you discuss it? What did she do to you, Charles?'

'That's just it, Sammy, I just don't know. I'm in a place that I haven't been to before. I'm at a loss over what to do. I can't even eat!' He looked at him. 'She was so perfect, in every way. Physically I've never been so attracted to anyone like that. Compared to previous girls, she was so different, almost perfect... I can't deal with that kind of sublimity.'

'So there's no chance of going out in a four then!'

Charles laughed and nodded. 'No Sam, no chance at all. But you go and ring.'

Sam held back from making that call until he went home for the holidays. He felt tortured, his heart pumping the anxiety all around his body, but somehow managed to find the strength to pick up the receiver. He pushed the buttons on the phone with deliberate care, subconsciously hoping beyond hope that the number would prove to be unobtainable or engaged. But it wasn't.

'Hello, is Raveena Shah there, please?'

'Who is calling?'

'Sam. Sam Bernstein. Just tell her it's the boy she met last–'

'Hold the line, Mr Bernman.'

'Bernstein!' Sam shouted to no avail as the

phone was put on hold. The tension he felt during those 30 seconds was almost unbearable. He held the phone closely to his ear; the long-distance line was not completely clear.

'Hello... Sam?' Suddenly, as if by magic, the fuzziness and the crackling disappeared, and the familiar voice ran through the communication cables in crystal clear fashion, into the ear pressed near the receiver. The effect of her sweet-sounding tone was to simultaneously cut the wings away from the butterflies that were ravaging Sam's stomach, and to release a surge of assurance, smothering the angst that had governed Sam's behaviour up until then.

'Raveena. It's Sam; you know the guy–'

'I know.'

'Ah, right. I'm sorry I hadn't rung before, but it's a lot easier to make long-distance calls from home than from school. Mind you, when my dad finds out, maybe it's not such a clear-cut decision!'

She laughed. 'Are you well, Sam?'

'Yes, very good thanks, and you?'

'I'm happy to be home. But I would be happier if you were here, too.' It was unusual for her to be so open about how she felt, but for once it felt right for her to say it.

'Me too,' he replied, collapsing on to the chair next to him.

9

It started as a weekly call, but by the end of the fourth week they were speaking every day. At first

220

the conversation would last ten minutes, but by the end the calls lasted over an hour. The reckoning was never going to be far away, and when it came, Sam felt the full impact unleashed upon him.

'Twelve hundred pounds! Twelve hundred pounds!' The ranting started on the ground floor, slowly and inexorably working its way up the winding staircase to the first floor; and just got closer and closer until it forced its way into Sam's room located on the top floor.

'Dad! Hi, what is it?' Contrived innocence was not a strong card to be playing at that moment, and it was easily trumped by a much more powerful combination of anger and outrage.

'What is it?' He repeated his son's words in a parodic manner. 'You might well ask "what is it", but I think you know exactly what it is. It's one thing to tell me you are really keen on some Indian princess, and how wonderful she is. It is entirely a different matter spending twelve hours on the telephone to Bombay at a cost of–'

'Twelve hundred pounds,' Sam interrupted.

'Yes, quite. Now I don't know what you think you're doing, Sam, and you've never disappointed me before, but you better pull yourself together. This relationship can't go far.' He looked his son in the face. He adored him so much, and because of that, the hurt he felt when angry with him was even harder for him to bear. 'There's over five thousand years of unbroken heritage and tradition in our family. From Mount Sinai to the concentration camps, no one has broken away from the faith. If you think I'm going to stand by and let my

221

son break away ... well, you have to be joking.'

Sam sat motionless as his father turned around and closed the door behind him. He never realised how strongly his father felt about him going out with a gentile. He wasn't entirely sure whether he was more upset with the fact that she was Indian, or the fact that she wasn't Jewish. He was even more uncertain what his reaction would have been if she had been a member of the English aristocracy. What made it all the more baffling was that the family had never practised the religion. When Abraham Bernstein fled Eastern Europe he also turned his back on Judaism.

His grandfather on his paternal side had been a rabbi, and as such his family were relatively religious. However, when he arrived in England, he was determined to hide his religion, almost blaming orthodox Judaism on his family's misfortune in Europe. His distress at losing almost his entire family in the gas chambers at Belzec, one of the six death camps constructed by the Nazis in Poland, seemed to justify this antipathy towards the religion. He continued with the distorted belief that if his co-religionists had assimilated more readily into society, they would not have been subjected to the heinous crime that occurred during the war years.

As a result of this tragic loss, Abraham Bernstein never went to synagogue, never fasted on the Day of Atonement, and never said Kaddish, the memorial prayer for the souls of one's parents. He forbade his wife from lighting the candles on Friday nights, or having the annual Seder night, a ritual at Passover when all Jews celebrate the exodus of the Jewish people from Egypt. And yet, perplexing to the extent of being paradoxical, he had always been adamant that none of his children would be allowed to marry out. He knew deep down that although not Jewish, he was still a Jew. Nothing would change that. Whether it was because of this profound sense of identity, or whether it was due to a more easily understand-able matter of respect for his dead parents' mem-ory, even Abraham Bernstein himself was unsure. His first three sons, who were such a disappoint-ment to him generally, all towed the family line, marrying Jewish girls from socially acceptable families (even if they hadn't presented him with a bride from society's elite). Sam, his one great prospect, whom he expected to fulfil his own dreams and mix with the elite on his own terms, would prove a far more difficult proposition.

10

The relationship between Raveena and Sam began much the same way as a match when struck. It had started with a spark, turning quickly into a bright burning flame, and then finally blazed with energy. However, unlike a match, it hardly flickered or waned, and it certainly failed to burn out. When Raveena returned for the sum-mer term, Sam managed to see her in Brighton on several occasions. Exeats rarely coincided, and the time spent together never lasted longer than two or three hours during the afternoon. School was completely out of bounds, and so all their meetings took place in public places, the most common being Browns restaurant in the Lanes. The affair was therefore cramped physically from the outset. Apart from the kiss at the station on arrival and at departure, the most intimate bodily contact was the holding of hands.

Yet it was precisely this physical frustration that fuelled the flame of desire, and increased the anticipation and excitement. Locked in love, but unable to express or fulfil their emotions, the two became metaphorically inseparable. The pattern was set, and continued for almost a year. Sam managed to play down the relationship to his father, whilst the latter also adopted a more mature attitude to the affair, realising that they were both young and that inevitably time would take care of matters. However, all of this changed on a cold February evening at the end of half-term.

Sam had decided to stay in London instead of going to St Moritz with the family on the annual skiing week. He had a lot of work to cover, particularly as the constant weekend travelling to Brighton, the prodigious letter-writing, and the endless phone calls were taking their toll on his grades. Unknown to his father, Sam had lowered his sights from going to Oxford, to staying in London and reading languages at Kings College. His choice was in no small way influenced by Raveena's choice of reading medicine at the same college.

'Why don't you come up – both of you?'

'When's your dad coming back?' Raveena responded, knowing the way he felt about her.

'The family doesn't get back until Monday. I'm here on my own. You know that.'

'But what about Rosalind? I can't just leave her here. She's put me up all week.'

'She can come too. Honestly, I don't mind. It's not as if she'll feel uncomfortable.' Sam was very fond of Rosalind. Who couldn't be? He was delighted for her to join them, especially if it meant that Raveena would come up.

'OK, I'll ask her, and see if the Blackstones mind.' Raveena felt her stomach tighten. She sensed the immensity of that moment. She knew that the Blackstones wouldn't mind, and that Rosalind would jump at the chance of going to London. She also knew that if she were to go, the purity and innocence of her love for Sam would break, and that something romantic would be lost for ever.

'Great! Ring me back.' Sam was certain that they would come. He had worked incredibly hard during that week. The daily phone calls to both of his parents allayed any suspicions they originally had that their youngest son was going to exploit the week alone and use their house as a base for parties. On the contrary, he had had nobody, not even Charles, across the front doorstep. He now waited for Raveena to phone back, and announce his reward. He did not have to wait long.

'Hi.'

'Can you pick us up from Victoria?' The temptation had been too great for her to resist.

'Of course. What time?' he asked excitedly.

11

The two girls were last off the train. Sam waited at the gate whilst a full Saturday train from the coast disembarked for the weekend in the capital. Craning his neck, trying to catch a glimpse of the two girls, proved to be in vain as there was no sign of them. Finally he saw them walking idly up the platform, at least 50 yards behind the rest of the passengers. Both of them were deep in conversation, seemingly without a care in the world. Sam smiled and watched them slowly amble up to the gate. Even if they had been in the middle of the crowd pressing through the barrier a minute before, he would have had no trouble spotting the two of them. Tall, hair flowing freely and strikingly beautiful, their radiance would have shone through any crowd.

'Raveena,' Sam said almost in a whisper, as they walked past.

'Sam!' Raveena dropped her bag, and enveloped him in a tight embrace.

'What about me?' Rosalind asked, feeling somewhat left out after two minutes.

'Oh sorry, Rosalind,' Sam said, walking over and kissing her. He picked up their bags and the three walked back towards his car.

'I haven't been in the car with you since you passed your test. Is this it?' Raveena stopped short of the racing-green Mini. 'Couldn't you have done a little better, Sam? I mean your dad... I thought you were the favourite! What did he get the others?'

'Funny. You don't really get it, do you? This,

Raveena,' he pointed to the car, 'is cool. It's a cultural thing. I can't explain it but I can't think of a motor car I would rather have.'

'I can!'

'Raveena, be quiet. You sound awful,' Rosalind wisely interrupted, and then whispered quietly in her friend's ear, as Sam was unlocking her door, 'he probably chose it himself.'

'Relax, I was only joking. God, you guys, where's your sense of humour?' Raveena got in the car, now trying to recover from digging a larger hole for herself. Sam shut the door, and ushered Rosalind to the other door so she could get in the back behind the driver's seat. As he opened it, he caught her eye, and smiled. They both knew she wasn't joking, but neither of them were going to let her know that. After all, the weekend hadn't even started.

Arriving at the house, Sam parked the car in the only available resident's parking bay in Hill Street. Letting the girls out, he took both their bags, and led them around the corner into the famous square. His excitement, laced with anticipation, was almost palpable. As he approached the black front door, he fumbled with the keys and dropped them, before recovering his composure and unlocking the door to the house. Rosalind gasped in wonder as she caught her first glimpse of the marble hall.

'My God! It's magnificent, Sam. Does your family own the whole building?' she asked, suddenly realising the extent of the Bernstein wealth.

'Yes. Is it up to your standards, your highness?' Sam asked, bowing to Raveena with no small

227

hint of sarcasm.

'I would like to see the bedroom,' Raveena replied, ignoring his unsubtle humour and revelling in her superiority. She turned towards the giant staircase and started to make her way upstairs. Sam looked at Rosalind, hands open in a gesture of disbelief, and laughed. 'Come on, Rosalind, I'll show you to your staff quarters where you will be at her majesty's command.'

'Oh, thank you, master. And where will you be sleeping?'

'Hopefully with her, but–' Rosalind placed her finger on Sam's lips, stopping him from going any further. She knew that Raveena had decided to sleep with Sam that night, but she had promised her best friend that she would say nothing to Sam. He put his arm around her. Although he had talked to Rosalind on many occasions over the previous twelve months, it was only at this moment that he really began to appreciate her friendship. She was with him and Raveena a lot, but never so that it became intrusive. There was no malice in her, and no jealousy about Sam's relationship with her best friend. She only once asked about Charles, and that was at the very beginning; she'd never mentioned him since then. He took care not to talk about him, as Raveena had told him how she felt.

He now suddenly understood what sort of friend she was, not only to Raveena, but also to him. Without realising it before, Rosalind had always pushed aside her own pain and hurt, and promoted both Raveena's, and his, happiness. She was, and would always be there to help and support them. Walking up the stairs together, he thought of Charles, and felt sorry for him. If he only knew what he was missing out on, he surely would not have let her go. But that was the heart of the matter. Charles did know, and it was precisely for that reason – he feared he would fall short in keeping her. And to lose her, after having her, would have been too much for him to bear.

12

They left San Lorenzo late that evening and took a taxi to a local pub near the house in Mount Street. The pub was full, and noisy. They decided to have a quick drink and then go back home. It had been a long day, particularly for the girls, and they were all relatively tired. As they stepped out of the pub, it had begun to snow. It wasn't settling, but, having drunk a fair amount, the three teenagers had to be careful walking back, so as not to slip.

'For God's sake, Sam, I'm freezing; open the door!'

'The lock seems to be stuck, hold on ... that's it.'

'About time. You were quicker opening it this afternoon.' Raveena had always felt the cold. She had never really got used to it, even though she'd spent four winters on the exposed Channel coast where the wind mixed with the icy cold sea frequently pushed the temperature down to extreme levels.

Sam disarmed the alarm and ushered the girls

into the house. 'I'm going straight to bed,' Rosalind said, as she kissed both of them goodnight and went up to her room. She was sleeping in Sam's bedroom, whilst he and Raveena would take his parents' room. Both of them watched Rosalind go up, and then looked at each other, knowing that the time had come. He reset the alarm, took her by the hand and led her up the staircase to the bedroom.

Raveena went into the bathroom, while Sam hastily got undressed and got into bed. He dimmed the lights and put on some soft music. Desperate to create the right environment, and yet very conscious of not making the whole scene too contrived, he waited anxiously for Raveena to come into the bedroom. It seemed like an age while he waited. Unwelcome thoughts suddenly presented themselves: the sheets would have to be changed, and the whole room cleaned so as not to leave any evidence that his parents might find when they returned. The condom packet that was lying so obtrusively on the side table, his cigarettes placed next to the contraceptives, and his towelling robe, which now lay across his father's armchair, would all have to be removed first thing tomorrow morning.

Still he waited. The thoughts became worse. He suddenly realised that Raveena was a virgin. 'Oh Christ,' he thought. Forget the sheets, what about the mattress! He hurriedly put on his pants, and ran down to the utility room. There he found three dark towels. 'Perfect!' He grabbed them and raced back up the stairs and into the bedroom. Turning up the lights, he suddenly found himself in a state of panic. He pulled the blankets down, and lay the towels over the bottom sheet. He was just finishing when, for some inexplicable reason, the music level suddenly shot up. He scrambled around for the controls on his hands and knees, in an effort to stop the deafening noise. He finally found them, lying beneath the blankets, which he had thrown off in his haste to lay the towels down, the weight of material adjusting the highly sensitive volume control. He grabbed the remote and placed his finger on the button.

'Sam? Sam! What's going on?' Raveena entered the bedroom to be greeted by 'Bridge Over Troubled Water' at a cacophonous level, and to find her Romeo in his pants on all fours in a heap of blankets at the bottom of a bed now laid with ruby-coloured towels.

'Raveena! Oh er, nothing really.' He had managed by now to get the music back to its original level.

'What are these? Why are these here? Your parents like this colour?' she asked, picking up the towels.

'No, no, we haven't used them for years. I just thought that ... you know.' He was struggling to find the appropriate words. He wasn't sure whether to feel simply embarrassed, or deeply humiliated. Much would depend on her reaction.

'Oh, Sam, you don't have to worry. It's going to be fine,' she laughed. 'I've been riding horses for the last ten years. It'll be all right.' She threw the towels on the floor, leaving the mattress covered by a single pristine white sheet. She got on the bed and lay in front of him. Sam stood and looked at her. She was wearing nothing but a simple white oversized man's shirt. Even in such a shapeless and inchoate garment, she still looked sensual and seductive. In fact, if anything, she looked even more sexy at that moment than at any time before. His eyes stared at the marvel that lay in front of him. Her hair was now loose, but not a strand lay across her face. Her body, hidden by the nebulous mass of cotton, was left to his imagination. He looked down and then saw her legs visible from her thighs down to her ankles and feet. He had never seen her feet before. It was almost involuntary, but his hand reached out and gently took one in his hand. He placed his lips on her ankle, and then moved down around her heel, kissing her sole and instep, before finally arriving at her immaculately pedicured toes. She lifted her upper body up so as to take the garment off, and having done so threw it on the floor, and lay back down again.

He looked up at her face, and then pulled himself up so that his mouth was on hers. He kissed her tenderly on the lips, and then on her cheeks, trying very hard not to move too quickly. He flicked her ear lobes with his tongue, and then gently kissed her neck, moving down to her breasts. His hands, meanwhile, seemed to be everywhere, stroking her body, smoothly massaging her stomach and sides, and then moving down around her thighs. She was shivering with excitement as his mouth made first contact with her bosom. He started softly, kissing each nipple, gently enclosing them with his lips. Using his tongue, he licked them softly, and then he engaged his whole mouth, providing Raveena with a level of pleasure that she had never experienced before.

Sam felt imperiously in control. This was his first time, but it felt so natural. Oozing with confidence, and having brought Raveena to such a level of excitement, he now went down to her naval, not letting an inch of her body escape his attention. Writhing with ecstasy, Raveena could hardly control herself as he probed her naval, but it was the anticipation of what he was going to do next that fuelled her excitement. As his mouth reached the black triangle of her pubic hair, he looked up again, and saw the expression of fevered excitement on her face. She was completely at his mercy, begging for him to continue. For the first time, such was his concentration and need to give her pleasure, he felt his own aching desire in his loins. He suddenly wanted to stop the oral adventure, and drive himself into her. But he continued with his mouth. The lust governing his libido was more interested in her taste at that moment, as he plunged his tongue into her velvet warmth, licking and stroking her clitoris.

Raveena was now screaming with excitement, unable to contain her emotions or any semblance of self control as Sam savoured the sweet tang of her juices as she climaxed for the first time.

'Please Sam, I want you inside me ... now,' she managed to whimper.

He got up and reached over to the side table to pick up the condom. He undid the packet and quickly put it on. In his first awkward moment, betraying his innocence, he thrust inside her vagina. At first he struggled to keep it inside as it seemed to have a mind of its own, whether to stay in or out. Unlike his oral performance, no book or film could teach him the necessary experience in this technique. But slowly nature took over, and he gained a rhythm which became more regular as his pleasure began to rise to a higher level. The strokes became faster and faster until he ejaculated in an explosive rapture. The culmination of his climax was so physically draining, that he could hardly move from off her.

'Sam, are you OK?' she asked, after a minute had passed and Sam had remained motionless. He looked up at her.

'Yes ... I think so. You?' he whispered into her ear, nibbling on her lobe.

'Me? Oh I feel pretty good!' She laughed. 'Come on, you have to get off me, I want to shower.' She pushed him off, and stumbled into the bathroom. He looked at her walking away, and felt an unfamiliar serenity take him over. He rested his head on the pillow and let his mind wander.

13

It was 10.30 the following morning when Sam was woken up by the sound of voices and the alarm being switched off. At first he thought he was dreaming, but as the voices became clearer, the Eastern European accent became louder and more familiar. He did not want to believe it, but reality was forcing its way into his subconscious.

'Sam, your mother and I are back!' the voice bellowed up from the hallway.

Sam lay still, not sure whether he was dreaming, or whether the nightmare of his father's roar was a reality.

'Sam? Oh I'm sorry, I thought my son was here.' He quickly closed the door, not quite understanding why a young woman was getting dressed in his son's bedroom. He walked across the landing and, not bothering to knock, opened the door of his own bedroom.

'Oh!' his father exclaimed, standing rooted to the spot. For once lost for words, he simply stared at his son, who had now woken and was sitting up, calmly looking back at him. Raveena, who had just returned from the shower in Abraham Bernstein's towelling robe, turned around to see the expression of horror on the seventy-year-old father of her boyfriend. 'And who, might I ask, is this?'

'Ah, this is Raveena,' Sam replied serenely. He had never felt so calm and collected. It seemed very strange that on the brink of Armageddon, Sam felt totally at peace.

'Well, maybe Raveena can get dressed and leave, with her friend, as quickly as possible so that we may speak,' he replied, straining every nerve and sinew that he possessed in order that he might control his temper.

'Yes, absolutely... I'll make sure that–' His father had already gone. He looked at Raveena, who was still trying to work out what was happening.

'Shit! You better get dressed. I'll get Rosalind,

and see you in the kitchen.' He washed, and quickly got dressed. His main concern at that moment was not for Raveena. She was confident, and more worldly than her friend. She could handle the situation. Rosalind, on the other hand, was different. Delicate, exquisite, and composed, and yet so finely balanced that he feared that something as cataclysmic as this might upset her graceful but fragile equanimity. He left and went straight to his bedroom.

'Rosalind? Are you OK? I'm so sorry. I had no idea that they were coming back early.'

'Don't worry, Sam. I guessed that's what had happened. Poor man, he didn't quite know what to do ... or say. He's nothing like I imagined.'

'No?'

'No, not at all. The man you've always described seems like such a tyrant, a type of German army officer. He seemed to be quite sensitive ... and calm. Where was the famous temper you keep going on about?'

'You don't know him. Look, you're ready. Meet me in the kitchen. It's best that you leave as soon as possible.'

'OK,' she replied. She followed him out of his bedroom and went downstairs. She left her bag by the door and walked into the kitchen where both Abraham and his wife Leah were sitting having coffee. 'Hello, my name is Rosalind.'

As soon as she entered the room, the old man felt a sudden sense of tranquillity. His whole mood of pent-up anger and frustration lifted, as if by magic. He looked at her, and immediately saw her elegance. But it was more than her appearance that had enchanted him.

'Who are you?' he asked, in a manner that was more akin to a little child asking a stranger.

'I'm a friend of Raveena and Sam. We're all very sorry, Mr Bernstein, but we had no idea–'

'No, no, of course you didn't. It really isn't your fault.' He was so spellbound that Rosalind could have said anything and he would not cast any blame at her. The bewitching effect that she had on him would never disappear, and would have a considerable impact on all of their lives. She stood quietly by the kitchen table, looking around, before her eyes settled on the book lying next to Sam's father. She picked it up.

'*The complete Greek Tragedies, Aeschylus Volume 1.* Do you read a lot of Greek drama, Mr Bernstein?' she asked, flicking through the well-known Penguin classics edition.

'Yes, yes I do ... I love it–' He hesitated and found himself staring at her. 'My favourites are Aeschylus, Sophocles and–' He stopped when Sam walked in followed by Raveena. There was a period of silence as everybody looked at each other, waiting for the first person to speak.

'Sam, have you anything to say for yourself?' his father asked him.

'No, not really.' Sam couldn't think of anything to say that would help his cause. To apologise would have sounded glib, even insincere. To try and fight his corner would inevitably lead to a tirade and then punishment.

'Well, I suggest you take the girls to the station, and we'll have a chat when you get back.'

Sam picked the keys up from the side table, and

led the girls out to the car. He started the engine, and slowly drove off.

'What's going to happen?' Raveena asked, clearly worried for Sam.

'I don't know ... but it'll be fine.' He smiled reassuringly at her, but inside he felt his stomach tighten and his heartbeat quicken as he feared the worst.

14

Having dropped the girls off, he returned to the house. The sense of trepidation overshadowed everything as he opened the front door. The welcome sight of his mother – by far the favoured preference in this situation – was short lived.

'Your father's expecting you in the study.' She stepped towards him, and gently kissed his forehead in a manner that told him to expect the worst. He walked on into the wood-panelled room to confront his father, who was sitting behind his giant-sized bureau. The old man didn't need to look up as he entered; he was waiting for him.

'You know how I feel about this relationship. I mean it's almost been a year now, and you show no signs of moving on. What happened here last night was disgusting and disrespectful to me and your mother. You will be grounded for the Easter holidays as a punishment. There's no discussion about this.'

'Can I go then?'

'What? No of course you can't go. What are you going to do about this girl?'

'I don't understand? I thought you didn't want to discuss it.'

'No you fool ... the punishment is not up for discussion. No what about ... what's her name?'

'Raveena.' Sam paused. 'I love her.' He stared directly at his father, waiting for a reaction. For the first time he wanted to see his father squirm in his seat. He wanted to expose, and then exploit, his hypocrisy. He had no idea until then how deeply flawed his father's standards on religion were, and how much he resented them.

'You don't know what love is. It's not just about what you are feeling now. That's just lust and infatuation. Love is about friendship, companion-ship, loyalty, devotion. It's all these things. You can fall out of lust very quickly. You'll see. This girl is from a different background. Remember how I feel about our tradition. It's inappropriate for you to think of her in this way for such a long time. I won't allow you to get too serious.'

'But I am. Dad, you don't understand. Every-thing you have just said merely endorses what I feel. It's a confirmation that I do love her. There is no one else I would rather be with. I'm afraid ... she's the one.'

'This is ridiculous.' The agony on the old man's face was perceptible. 'You better get out.'

'There is just one thing I would like to ask you, and if you give me an honest answer then I'll give her up.' The confidence in the young man's voice betrayed the fact that this was no gamble.

'What?' His father had began to go through the mail, which had built up over the previous week.

'You keep playing the Jewish card with me, and

239

yet we as a family have kept none of the traditions. Yes, we're Jews but are we Jewish? Do you fast on the Day of Atonement? Do we celebrate Jewish New Year, or any of the festivals? At Passover do we give up bread? No! We don't even have a mezuzah on the door post of our house. Is it really about Raveena not being one of us?' He got up from his chair, and stepped towards the desk. He placed his hands on the edge of the bureau, and leant over towards his seated father. He was looking down on him, as if to symbolise the moral high ground. 'If it were really that important to you, you would not have turned your back on the religion.' He paused, 'You see, I think it has nothing to do with her not being Jewish. I'll even give you the benefit of the doubt that it's nothing really to do with her being Indian. You've seen the cruellest type of racism, face to face. It's hardly possible that you could be a racist. No, I think this is all about you. If Raveena's name was Natasha; and instead of Shah, it was Astor or Cadogan, would you be taking the same position?' He waited for his answer.

'Of course I would. All of your elder brothers have married within the faith ... I have always been consistent on this point. Listen. I know you ridicule me for trying to be part of the establishment, but this has nothing to do with it.' Sam pushed himself up. His self confidence had been justified. It was never a gamble; always a safe bet. 'Well? Will you give her up now?' The old man asked weakly, betraying his doubt at the response.

'Why would I do that?'

'Because you said if I answered your question you would finish it.'

'That's absolutely true, and you didn't.'

'Yes I did, I've just told you–'

'No you didn't,' he interrupted his father. 'You replied, but not truthfully. Dad, you were not being honest. I feel I'm free to continue and if it means you doing what you say you have to do, then so be it.' He walked out of the room. The relationship had been shattered. From being his greatest hope, Sam Bernstein had now become his greatest disappointment. His love for Sam was never in question, but his pride had pushed him to the brink of losing him. It was something that Abraham Bernstein would take a long time to come to terms with. On the one hand, he had a grudging respect for his youngest son that would never leave him; his independence and strength of character revealed a courage so absent in his elder brothers which impressed him. On the other, his disobedience, bordering on recalcitrance, damaged his pride to such an extent that a barrier now came down between them.

15

Sam went back to school, uncertain of where he stood with his father. Only time would reveal his position. He discussed it with Charles who had no such worries. Faced with none of the distractions of his close friend, he concentrated on school life, not only academically, but also in the sporting and social arenas. He captained the

First Fifteen, was elected to 'Pop' (the self-elected prefect club distinguished by each member wearing a waistcoat of his own choice) and was chosen as Head of Oppidans, effectively meaning that he was joint headboy along with the head of the college scholars. It was no surprise when he achieved three top grades and went on to do the seventh term and go on to Oxford.

Sam's last year did not follow the same path as his friend's. It was true that he was also elected to 'Pop', and played in the First Eleven in both soccer and cricket, but his heart wasn't interested in the playing fields of Eton. His innate talent carried him through, and his real sporting potential was never fully realised, particularly in cricket, where his performances bordered on the ordinary. Nowhere was this lack of commitment made clearer than when, for the first time in four years, he failed to win the school steeplechase. It was unthinkable that a boy blessed with his speed could lose the race, but he fell short of a top three place by some distance.

His academic work also began to suffer. His ability in languages was not in question, and he knew he would pass his A levels without too much trouble. If he had put his mind to it, even in his last term, he could have recovered and recaptured the necessary grades and then gone on to do the Oxbridge term. But there was nothing to entice him there apart from the companionship of his best friend, Charles, and that was not enough.

The real prize as far as he was concerned lay in London, and not in Oxford or Cambridge. He

242

had subsequently looked up the best colleges in London, and found that the languages degree at Kings was an extremely good one. He completed his UCCA form accordingly, and was offered two 'B's and a 'C' for a place. This hardly represented a challenge to a young man who, if put under any sort of pressure, could achieve anything he wanted. With his heart directing every move, he made sure that he got the grades he needed. Nothing more, nothing less.

16

Rosalind Blackstone started her final year at Roedean with a heavy, but unbroken, heart. She knew that she had met the boy of her dreams, and although her passion was left unrequited, she had the presence and equanimity of mind to move on and detach herself from her emotional turmoil. She now set her sights on Oxbridge, and like Charles, she wasn't going to let any distractions divert her from her goal. She knew what she wanted to read. There was very little competition, and although she was a straight 'A' pupil, English literature was her real calling. History and French were subjects she paid lip service to, never spending more than the absolute minimum time revising the relevant topics. She counted herself lucky in that at least in French there was a literature paper, an examination on Racine's *Phedre* which she voraciously devoured.

But it was English, and most importantly Shakespeare, that captivated her. The lessons with Mrs Robinson were the highlights of her week. Each lesson opened up a new avenue of delicious ideas and thoughts, and led to adventures down untrodden paths. It was a poignant moment when Rosalind finished her last lesson before her exams. She was last to leave the classroom, and was just about to say goodbye when she was stopped by her teacher.

'Are you ready? Is there anything you want to ask me, Rosalind?' The old lady closed her class notes and looked down at her star pupil who was about to leave. She knew she was ready, but strangely wanted to hear it from her.

'One last thing on Shakespeare. What is it that makes him so unique... I mean, why do you think we all need him?'

'Because he was so far ahead of his time. He is part of all of us. His influence on us is enormous – the way we speak and the way we think has been shaped by him. Don't you remember our first class on Shakespeare when I talked to you about the intrusion of reality in literature? This is the real key to understanding his greatness. His creation of multi-dimensional characters that we can sympathise and empathise with ... people, who we can listen to, even monitor ... eavesdrop on their inner thoughts through their soliloquies ... and, as a result, finally identify with. He was the first to do this, just as the artists of the Renaissance had brought reality and expression back into painting and sculpture many years before.'

She shut her book and smiled at her. 'I would say good luck, but you, above everyone else, really don't need it. I have never gained so much pleasure from teaching anyone as I have from you.'

'Thank you, Mrs Robinson. I know it's your job to teach me, but by opening my eyes ... and not just to Shakespeare, but also to all the other poets and writers ... you've changed my whole life. I now can't imagine a world without Keats and Wordsworth, Dickens and Jane Austen.'

'And just remember who influenced them!' She smiled as she interrupted her, knowing that Rosalind knew the answer.

17

When the brown envelope arrived at the Blackstone house on a sunny August morning, the family was having breakfast.

'Was that the post?' Alan Blackstone asked, getting up from the table and going towards the hallway. It was a rhetorical question: he had clearly heard the mail being pushed through the door. Catherine sat opposite her daughter. She smiled at her, knowing that this was the day the A level results were due to arrive. She could see the anticipation in her daughter's face. 'Rosalind, this is addressed to you,' he said, handing her the brown nondescript envelope. He knew exactly what it was, but was desperately trying to be indifferent to the situation.

Rosalind snatched the pale-brown envelope from her father and tore it open in a rather dramatic manner. She then pulled the white card out and read the contents out loud.

'History A 1, French A, English A 1.'

Alan Blackstone took the card from her, and looked at the results himself. She had got straight A's at O levels, but this was different. A levels were so much harder, and far more difficult to predict. It was never a certainty that a top student would get what he or she was predicted. Even the love of her life, Charles, with all of his academic ability, and hard work, had missed out on a clean sweep, falling short in one of his exams and ending up with a B.

'What are the '1s' for? What do they mean?' he asked.

'They're special papers. Those who are predicted the best grades can take them voluntarily. You don't have to revise for them. You can get a 1, which is a distinction, or a 2, which represents a merit. They're the icing on the cake,' Rosalind replied as she sipped her coffee, trying to maintain her composure. She knew that she would achieve the top grade in English, and also expected one in History. But French, despite the literature content, was a different story. Her vocabulary and grammar were marginal, and an A was no certainty. To achieve what she had was not a surprise, but at the same time, it had still been a chimera. There was only one other girl at Roedean to achieve such a result.

'What can I say, darling? You never cease to amaze me.' He opened up his arms and embraced her. He looked across at his wife, and at that moment Alan Blackstone realised what a lucky man he was. From the Docks in Dublin and Liverpool, to the breakfast houses on the

South Coast, he had finally found a permanent job in Brighton and had worked his way up the greasy pole to be manager of the finest hotel in the city. But his greatest achievement was in meeting Catherine, his wife for over 35 years. She still radiated a beauty that he would never grow tired of. Intelligent, selfless and kind, she had devoted herself to him and her daughter. The prize that was Rosalind was down to destiny, rather than chance.

'Where are you going to go?' Catherine asked, getting up and joining her husband in the embracing of their child.

'Oxford ... I'm going up there next month to look around and see which colleges I like. Will you come with me?'

'I'd love to... God, how exciting!' Catherine said, as a tear welled up in her left eye and rolled down her cheek.

18

Rosalind started her Oxbridge term, her seventh in the sixth form, with ten other girls who had attained high enough grades for the universities. Unfortunately for her, Raveena was not among them. This was in no way due to her best friend not achieving the grades she needed. On the contrary, Raveena Shah was that 'other girl' who achieved straight As and had secured a place to read Medicine at Kings College. This was exactly where she had wanted to be, with the added bonus of Sam now being there as well.

They had spent the summer together at the Shah palace ten miles outside the swollen oppressive metropolis that is Mumbai. The contrast between the palace grounds and the city could not have been more manifest. The difference between old Abraham Bernstein and Rajeev Shah was crystal clear, never more so than when Sam arrived at the Shah compound for the first time that summer's evening. A party had been arranged for his daughter's return, and her father welcomed Sam in as part of the family. He was immediately shown to his quarters in the main building, located near Raveena's rooms, and was then led downstairs and introduced to the rest of Raveena's family. Sam had never felt more at home than he did that evening, 10,000 miles away from Berkeley Square. He must have met at least a hundred of Raveena's relatives, and not remembered one name.

As the evening drew to a close, Sam reflected on his new-found happiness. 'It's as if I've lost a friend ... a companion.'

'What do you mean? I would have thought you've gained at least 50 tonight!' she said, kissing his cheek.

'Not people ... I wasn't talking about people. I was thinking about me, the way I feel. It's as if I'm a different person.'

'You're more relaxed, that's all. You're more normal. Sam, you're growing up.'

'But that's just it. I've lost all my anxiety; I feel ... like everybody else.' There was a moment of sad introspection as Sam came to terms with the fact that he was no longer a child, and that adulthood was upon him. Whether this sudden maturity was a result of his severing the umbilical cord with his father, or due to his boundless love for Raveena, he was uncertain. But the combination of the two had meant that Sam had now discovered an independence that he had no idea existed. 'It should be a great few weeks.'

'Oh! it will be! I'm going to take you everywhere, meet all my friends, and have a real blast!'

He laughed, and then kissed her, softly stroking her cheek.

19

That summer holiday in Mumbai was a memory that neither Raveena nor Sam ever forgot. It was one that they always referred back to, and one that would always be etched in both of their hearts. They returned to London, ready to embark on what the future had in store for them. Raveena rented a mews house off Wimpole Street, which she moved into immediately. Sam remained at home, still under the shadow of a somewhat strained relationship with his father. He remained there for the first of his three years at Kings, managing to maintain some semblance of communication. What he didn't realise was that it was hurting his father far more than himself.

Abraham Bernstein loved Sam, more than anyone else. His youngest son provided an outlet for his otherwise repressed emotions. He would be his successor, his encapsulation of his aspirations, hopes and dreams. Sam's sudden, newly-found intrepidity had knocked him back, and he was unsure how to respond. The conversation he had had with Sam that morning, had left him in no doubt about the way his son felt. More importantly, his son's words were so axiomatic, that he knew that the truth was being spoken. All through his life he had fought battles to gain wealth and acceptance, and he had won them all. He doubted if he could recognise defeat, even if it stared him in the face. But now he was up against someone whom he practically canonised. What was more, he knew that it was only his pride that prevented him from retreating. He realised that this was a conflict he couldn't win. Here there were no winners, only losers. He knew that Sam loved Raveena, and there was nothing he could do about it.

He slowly tried to repair the damage. From a position where they hardly spoke to each other during Sam's final year at Eton, his father visited him during the weekends, particularly in the summer when he watched him play cricket. In truth, Abraham loved going to Eton where he could mix freely with society's elite, but what his son was not fully aware of was his father's prodigious admiration for him. Watching him bowl his devastating array of deliveries, varying from leg breaks, googlies and sometimes a flipper thrown in for good measure, was a delight even for the non-aficionado.

'I've seen him bowl entire teams out, you know,' the headmaster commented to Abraham, sitting in the pavilion. 'But it's a little strange ... he hasn't been quite on his game this term.'

'Yes, I know, but I still hope he gets a blue when he goes to Oxford.'

'Oh! You don't know then.'

'What?'

'He's applied to Kings in London, to read languages. I think it's a good choice. He hasn't been working hard enough for Oxbridge. Kings will suit him well.'

'Yes, yes ... of course. Well, whatever he wants to do,' Abraham said quietly, trying hard not to show his disappointment. He never let Sam know his feelings about his choice of university. He could not afford to lose him completely; matters were strained enough. Besides, there was an upside to the situation in that he would remain in London, where he might be able to repair some of the damage already caused.

Sam never actually told his father that he had chosen London as his choice of university. He couldn't bear the thought of another argument about not going to either Oxford or Cambridge. He was surprised, after receiving his results, that his father supported his selection and that he already knew. The fact that he chose not to adopt an adversarial position certainly helped the relationship, which over the following twelve months improved enough for Sam to touch on the thorny issue of him moving out of home.

'Yes, of course, I understand you want some freedom, but maybe after you graduate?'

'Dad, I really would like to move out now.'

'Where then?'

Sam dreaded the question, but like being tied to a railway track with a train rapidly approaching, he knew that it was coming.

'Raveena has a flat off Wimpole Street, in a mews. It's rented, and obviously I would contribute–'

'OK, then. You have your own trust, and there's plenty of money for you to settle any payments.' He interrupted him, alleviating him from further torture.

'You're not upset?'

'You're in love. She seems very decent.' He got up from his chair. 'Educated, from you say a very good family, beautiful, and extremely polite ... how can I stop you?' he replied softly.

'Thanks, Dad.' Sam went over to his father and embraced him. He smiled at him. They both understood. For the old man, it meant reconciliation, whatever the price; for Sam, it was tacit that his father was beginning to acknowledge his own bigotry, and was now effectively conceding that sometimes on certain issues, there is no right or wrong. The relationship was slowly being repaired, and although it would never quite be what it was, it was certainly healthier than it had been for some time.

20

It did not take long for Rosalind to choose her college. Arriving in town with her mother, the first steeple she saw was that of the historic chapel attached to Christchurch College. She stepped out of the car and walked towards the college with its bell tower overseeing the surrounding edifices.

As she walked through the entrance, she immediately came out on to the famous quadrangle – the largest in Oxford – with the picturesque pond, its water covered with lilies. The concoction of its colossal structure and vast open space, mixed with its tradition and history, made a heady cocktail for her to drink. The names of Locke, Auden and Carroll danced around her mind, as she wandered through the grounds of the college.

'This is the place where I want to study,' she said to her mother as she walked around the building, with its sixteenth-century staircase, medieval cloisters and its dining hall where the famous alumni's portraits hung on the walls.

'But you haven't seen any of the other colleges yet.'

'I know, but it feels right here.' She stood still, looking around, inhaling the academically-charged atmosphere.

'Aren't you going to look, then?' her mother asked, amazed that she could be so certain after seeing only one college.

'I suppose so ... come on.' She took her mother's hand, certain that she had no need to visit any of the other colleges, and convinced that her choice was the right one.

They spent the whole day in the city. With only one college left to see, none so far had struck the same chord with Rosalind as did Christchurch. She was pleased with herself and absolutely sure that her choice was the correct one. It was at that moment that Catherine led her into Worcester College. They walked through the gates and looked down on to the main quad. They then turned left and soon approached the extensive gardens that had so captivated Charles recently. For the first time that day, Rosalind felt a sudden trepidation. She sensed her confidence begin to ebb away as she strolled around the grounds looking up at the unusual blend of medieval cottages coalesced with the neoclassical structures surrounding her. There was something she liked about the place, and it was more than just the buildings and grounds.

She sensed a presence here that she was unfamiliar with. She grappled with the feeling that there was something special, almost preternatural, here. It was as if it had nothing to do with the college itself, but more to do with someone being here. Unknown to her, Charles Longhurst had chosen this place as his home for the next three years, and although he was not there at that moment, his selection was being picked up by Rosalind's extraordinary antenna.

'Well darling ... you like it here, don't you?'

'Yes, mother, I do. It's special. I don't know why, but it is.' Feeling more comfortable now, sensing what she was feeling, and regaining her poise, she walked out of the college, turned around to her mother, and said, 'but it's Christchurch I'll be going to.'

21

They never spoke to each other during the first two years at Oxford. To say that it was not deliberate was extremely hard to argue. They frequently saw each other, but their eyes never met. Whether it was in a coffee shop, at a party, or going in and out of lectures, destiny seemed to guide them away from each other. There were moments, many of them, when Charles wanted to call out her name on seeing her tall, willowy frame walk by. His desperate desire to try and make contact, to confide in her, to put his arm around her and walk with her, consumed him at times. But he was crippled by a devastating lack of self-belief, so alien to his character, but so palpable when she entered his mind.

Rosalind threw herself into university life, joining a number of societies, including a Shakespeare one, which gave her the first chance to act in a play written by her idol. At Roedean, the school had never put on Shakespeare productions, and as a result she never experienced performing in the plays she really loved. Now she was given the opportunity to express herself on the stage in roles that she'd only dreamed of acting. Unsurprisingly she showed a talent for acting that enabled her to win the lead female roles.

Learning the lines for Cleopatra, Lady Macbeth, and, of course, Rosalind, was hardly taxing; she knew them all already.

Like Charles, she often saw her loved one, but was more composed, and controlled. This innate composure was not purely down to genes and character, but also due to the fact that she knew she would conquer him in the end. However much he felt the pain and anguish of cupid's arrow piercing his already damaged heart, Rosalind just grew stronger and more confident.

'Do you ever want to speak to him?' Raveena asked her in the October of Rosalind's third year at Oxford.

'Of course I do ... and I will do ... but only when he's ready. He's not yet.'

'God, I admire your assurance. How can you be so confident? What makes you so sure? You're in your final year now, and he hasn't made a move yet.'

'He will,' she replied. 'Raveena, trust me, he will.'

Raveena, in this situation, always knew that it was pointless to go any further, and simply dropped the topic. For a woman whose ethos was based on science and practicalities, and whose understanding of the world was empirical rather than deductive, she quickly realised that Rosalind was on a different planet. Nevertheless she could not help but be fascinated by the relationship, or rather the non-relationship, between her friend and Charles. She often discussed it with Sam, who had similar difficulties in understanding it when he raised it with Charles.

'For a person who professes to be so successful with women, isn't it about time you made your move on Rosalind? I don't quite get it? You're like a broken record when it comes to discussing her.'

'Forget it, Sam. I remember when you weren't so sure of yourself ... it wasn't so long ago.'

'All right, all right, but Charles, I know her. I see her often in London, and she's warm, irrepressible, loving ... she's almost perfect.'

'Don't you know that I realise that. I just

haven't got enough for her … I'm not up to her standards.'

'All this you know from three hours of meeting her at a school dance?'

'Yes,' he paused. 'Yes, I do. You don't understand–'

'Oh, I think I do. For god's sake! You've got six months before you finish here. If you don't make your move you might lose her for ever. Read some Shakespeare sonnets … or go to one of his plays … or, I don't know, just go and see her. I wouldn't mind, but,' he paused. 'You know somebody told me that in his plays, the common rule is that the great heroines always marry men who are inferior to them.' He laughed. 'If that were the case then you would actually fit the bill quite well!'

22

He was in the pub. He had ordered a pint of bitter, and sat himself down by a small round table next to the window. He always came here alone at the start of every term, to gather his thoughts, think about what lay in front of him. His studies had gone well, and now in his final year, he was entering the final stretch. A first was probably beyond him, but he knew that he was up to date on his reading and in his essays, and that most of the topics for his finals had already been covered. An upper second, the absolute minimum requirement for his own academic satisfaction, was assured. He languidly sipped the beer, enjoying the local drink, much as he did whenever he came here. He looked outside, through the window, and saw the soft September sun slowly setting.

Finishing the last drop, he placed the glass on the table, and got up to leave. He pushed open the door, and was about to walk out, when his attention was diverted towards the events board that hung by the doorway. He let the door swing back and close. He walked over to the announcements and looked at the yellow poster advertising an amateur drama production in the gardens behind Wadham College.

The Bard Society presents an Autumn production of The Merchant of Venice, *by William Shakespeare. One night only, October 4th, 7pm.*
Principal players include...

His eyes glanced down, and there, in yellow and black, playing the role of Portia, was the name 'Rosalind Blackstone'. Having seen the poster, it was no surprise; he had expected it. But the fevered anticipation fuelled a far more compelling sense of excitement than any sudden surprise. He put his finger on the paper, and brushed it against her name. He felt a surge of electricity emanating from the writing, through his finger into his hand and arm, and then through his body. He stared at the letters, and then read them as a name, and he only then finally understood. It was now time.

Charles walked through the main quad at Wadham, under the archway and into the gardens towards the small crowd of people congregated around the makeshift stage, where the play was just about to begin. He had fought all afternoon against his instinct of getting there too early, but to arrive just as the production was about to start. He wanted to be part of a crowd, so as not to be identified, and remain anonymous to the players. His fear of being seen by Rosalind and facing the humiliating prospect of a potential rejection would have been too much to bear. It had been so long since they last met, but it was precisely this length of time that made any future reconciliation all the more fragile.

There were no more than thirty students sitting on the grass as the play began. Charles sat near the back. He always enjoyed Shakespeare, and having studied the *Merchant* for O level, he remembered the play well. He waited for Portia's entrance. Clever, very witty and very beautiful, she possessed the virtues of many of Shakespeare's leading female characters. Charles was desperate for the first scene to end, knowing that scene two opened with Portia complaining about her father's rules and stipulations over her future choice of husband. He longed to see her; it seemed like an eternity before the opening scene ended. And when it finally did, the interval between scenes seemed to be protracted. The temporary curtain was drawn back.

'By my troth Nerissa / My little body is a weary of

this great world.'

He stared at Rosalind as she played the role of Portia as only she could. Her husky deep voice melodically uttered the lines. At times he found it hard to separate actress from character. Although she always liked to be identified with her namesake from *As You Like It* there was so much of Rosalind in Portia, not least her quick wit, her elegance and her beauty. As Bassanio picked the correct chest, filled with lead, thereby winning Portia's hand, he could not help but feel a tinge of jealousy at the young suitor's good fortune.

As the play continued, his eyes followed Portia, admiring her ability to stick to the rules and requirements, and yet still retain her free spirit. How could Bassanio have won her love? And if he could win Portia's heart, surely he himself would have some sort of chance of winning Rosalind's? Confidence grew inside him. The anxiety of rejection disappeared, as he based his hopes on what Sam had told him, and the Shakespearian formula where the great female heroines almost always fall in love and marry inferior male characters.

The play ended at 9 o'clock. The audience mingled with the actors during the final act, drinking wine from plastic cups. Charles wandered across to the drinks table and picked up a cup of red wine.

'There was a time when a young man would offer a girl a drink before getting one for himself.'

Charles looked across. 'I don't have any spare vouchers.' He remembered the allocation allowed at the Roedean disco.

She laughed. 'I prefer white.'

He handed over a cup, and then took her arm and led her away from the table.

'How have you been?'

'Did you come for me?'

'Yes.'

'Charles, it's been over six years.'

'Look.' He took from his pocket a scrap of paper. It was creased with the folds that had been opened and closed on countless occasions, in hope and in despair. She took the fragment from his hand, opened it up carefully, and looked at its contents.

'I remember writing this out–'

'01273 45555.'

'Yes.' She handed the note back to him.

'I'm sorry, Rosalind.'

'I know.'

'I've missed you ... there hasn't been a day when I haven't thought about you.'

'Why didn't you call me?' She knew the answer.

'I lost confidence. I fell in love with you... I was frightened, I suppose.'

'About what?'

'Falling in love.' He sat down on a bench, and took her hand, pulling her to sit beside him. 'At 16, you're not really prepared to meet the perfect woman. I mean, your biological make-up is that you meet girls, have crushes – make out, and have a good time. The girl of your dreams is meant to come along a little later. Unfortunately for me, or maybe fortunately, it depends really, I met that girl when I was 16. I know this now because every girl I've met since is a pale imitation of what I experienced during that cold night by the sea in Brighton. That ... that was the real thing. Rosalind, it's probably too late, and that's probably why I have the confidence to say it now, but I am in love with you. I always have been.'

She turned away from him, scarcely able to control her excitement. Victory had never tasted so sweet. She had held firm despite the temptation – and the advice from her friend – not to contact him. Finally, after six years of heartache and emotional torture, she had won. The exquisiteness of the triumph was sublime. She looked back at him. Like a golden chalice of wine, ready to be drunk, she cupped his face in her gentle hands and kissed him. 'I'm in love too, Charles.'

24

Unlike Charles, Rosalind was a certainty for a first, and even an intense relationship with the man that she loved, would not divert her from the pursuit of academic excellence in English literature. Apart from Shakespeare, she concentrated on what came naturally to her. She studied the Ancient Greeks, and spent a great deal of energy on the classics, realising through Aristotle the debt the theatre owed to the fathers of dramatic tragedy. The Roman theatre was also researched, where she read Seneca and Ovid with particular zeal, given their influence on her favourite poet.

In poetry, she retained her love for the Romantics, relishing their mythology and emotion, and identifying easily with their imagination, and their concept of nature. She also spent time on nineteenth- and twentieth-century literature, studying Austen and Dickens, and in particular James Joyce with whom she empathised (in regard to his obsession with Shakespeare).

The two lovers embarked on a relationship that was the total antithesis to that of their friends Raveena and Sam. Whilst the latter was physical, practical, mature, and brutally real, Charles and Rosalind experienced an affair that was ethereal, romantic and quixotic. That was not to say that it was not physical, but in a more sensual than sexual way.

'So you haven't slept with her yet?'

'No, Sam, I haven't. Listen, I thought we were here to talk about your job.'

'Forget that... I've decided what I want to do anyway. Even my father's pleased.'

'What, the interpreter's role at Brussels?'

'Yes. It suits me down to the ground. I'll be away during the week, and back for weekends. Rav's started her clinical training now, so she'll be working all hours. I'd be getting in her way if I hung around.'

'Is it good money?'

'About £30,000. Much better than doing accountancy or law. Now, come on, what about you and Rosalind?'

'What about it? I saw her in *The Merchant of Venice*, and we talked, and–'

'Did you kiss her straight away?'

Charles looked at Sam. He had never seen his friend so enthused. It was almost as if he was getting some form of vicarious pleasure from the story. 'Actually, she kissed me.'

'Really! So how long have you been seeing her?'

'A couple of months, I suppose.'

'And you haven't slept with her yet?'

'No.'

25

Raveena spent Christmas that year with the Blackstones in Brighton. It was the first time in months that she had a chance to properly catch up with her friend, and find out how things were going with Charles.

'I'm glad you're happy, Rosalind ... it's so exciting!'

'I know, I'm really happy. But you sound surprised, or perhaps relieved ... why?'

'Well, I just didn't think you were ever going to get it together. You can't blame me. I mean, you met each other in 1994, and in a week's time it's going to be the year 2000.'

'Funny!'

'What is? Who is?'

'You are! Rav, I never had any doubt that I would marry Charles.'

'Marry him?'

'Yes ... it's quite clear to me. I'm even sure that he knows it.'

'But you haven't even slept with him.'

'I won't until we're married. I can't – you know I'm a Catholic.'

'Yeah, right.' Raveena dismissed her answer, and questioned her religious conviction.

'What do you mean? You know I take communion. You know I believe.'

'Of course I do, but you won't be able to resist it. Lust is so consuming ... you won't have a chance, believe me.'

'Oh, I'll resist. It's the only way that I'll be able to preserve our love... I have to keep it pure. Rav, for me, the whole thing has an important religious significance. It's holy and I must remain *in tacto* to preserve its dignity. It's not the same if I surrender. He understands.'

'I'm sorry, Rosalind, but I don't.' She smiled. She was a woman of science. She had no time for religion. She had nothing but contempt for the bigotry and narrowmindedness, which she believed religion was responsible for. She could not understand that someone as brilliant as Rosalind could fall for superstition and magic. She had always thought that religion should be the preserve of the ignorant and superstitious. But as usual Rosalind broke the mould, and was forcing her to rethink.

'One day Rav ... one day, you're going to need something to believe in. One day something will happen, that science, or medicine, won't be able to answer. You'll have to search for the answer, but you won't find it ... unless you have some faith ... something to grasp on to, which can't be explained.'

26

It was six months later when Sir Francis Sutherland left Worcester College after having met Rosalind for the first time, and having discussed with Charles his omission from his father's will. He felt uplifted from meeting Rosalind, and was now optimistic in the hope of trying to persuade James to leave the library to his youngest son, and not with the rest of the estate to Gordon and Robert. An artificial air of optimism filled the car as he drove down to Hathaway House. As he approached the wrought-iron gates of the grand estate, he was positive about his chances of persuading the old man to leave the treasured library to his treasured son.

'Absolutely not. Francis, we discussed this yesterday. It was crystal clear. It's absolutely ludicrous to think that I would separate the library from the house. Sometimes, Francis, I just don't understand you. At the start you actually advised me that the library should remain with the estate and now you're saying the complete opposite. If anybody here is going mad, it must be you.'

'James, I agree that I haven't been consistent in this matter, but the books are extremely valuable. Some of the items individually are worth many millions ... look at the valuation. The Gutenberg Bible, Chaucer's *Canterbury Tales,* and the First Folio, of course.' Francis handed the document to James.

'What for? I know all this.'

'Has it not entered your mind that Gordon and Robert will sell them, as soon as they get possession of the house, in order to feed their huge, failing property scheme. It would be so easy for them to raise a lot of money, without the outside world ever really knowing. James, you must understand that as soon as the twins inherit, the library will be dismantled and sold off. It's true that my advice was not to separate the library from the estate, but the reason behind that advice was always to keep the library controlled by a Longhurst. The only way that will happen is if Charles inherits the library. In a way I have been consistent in my goal, but perhaps not in the way of how to achieve that goal.' He looked at his client, and knew that his advice was going unheeded.

'The library is integral to the estate. I fully appreciate the value of the books. I seem to remember that I bought Newton's *Principia*. But Francis, I do think you are worrying unnecessarily. The twins haven't asked for any money from me for a long time now. I think that they might be turning the corner.'

'Probably because they know they are about to inherit an estate worth over £125 million, and a book collection almost as valuable. Look James, I've known you for a very long time now. This will be my final piece of advice on the matter. You obviously have made your mind up, but I am only interested in the Longhurst name, and its integrity. I believe by leaving the library to Charles, at least one component of the legacy will remain intact, and in family hands.'

'I've heard you, Francis, but *alia iacta est*. Now, have you seen Charles, and if yes … how is he?'

'Yes I have and he's fine, working terrifically hard. And I met Rosalind.'

'Ah! The new girlfriend. What's she like?'

'Extraordinary.'

'Really ... in what way?'

'In every way. She's beautiful, intelligent, clever, and possesses ... I don't know how to say it, but–'

'For God's sake, man, you're a lawyer! I thought you could talk your way out of everything!'

'I know, but this is different. James, she has a presence that one cannot easily describe. She's so full of life, but at the same time, irresistibly composed. I thought I would never say this, but Charles is a lucky man to find her.'

'Well maybe, when he has time he can introduce her to me, before it's too late.'

'Oh, I'm sure he will.' Francis looked across at his client. Despite looking aged and decrepit, hunched over holding a walking stick for support, this dying man had beaten him. Blinded by a filial love, and a distorted perspective, he was about to let one of the greatest birthrights in existence pass over to two equally undeserving beneficiaries. The consequences would be immense.

27

Charles was not surprised by the news, relayed to him by Sir Francis on the telephone. His resentment increased as he realised that Hathaway House would soon become a memory. Even if the twins, whom he had not spoken to in years, held on to the estate, they would never invite him. His communication with his father became less frequent as the bitterness inside him grew. Perversely, James Longhurst, unaware that Francis had told his son of the contents of the will, felt that this abnegation by Charles justified his decision.

In contrast to his youngest son, the twins moved into Hathaway House in midsummer. Unbeknown to their father, the Farringdon development, which had first germinated seven years earlier, was finally completing. Beset by planning difficulties, critical delays, funding problems and legal complexities, it had taken six years to rise up from the ground. However, the damage had been done as the debt burden rapidly increased by the lack of income received. The money that Gordon and Robert put in, including the ten million pounds from their father, was now under threat as the interest on the debt remorselessly devoured into the equity. The office complex was effectively owned by the banks. The success of the development depended on the London office letting market, in a location that was as yet unproven.

'I understand the maths, but unfortunately not your confidence,' the young merchant banker muttered in an audible aside.

'Look, you are just one of six banks funding this project. The other five are relaxed. Our equity has now been reduced to five percent after the refinancing. We have very little to offer you except to say that we are still fully committed to the project – and believe in it.' Gordon sat back in his chair. His mettle was being tested. During the day he had indeed met the other five banks, who were anything but relaxed. He was under severe pressure, he was now juggling the balls, hoping that he could catch at least one of them.

'And what do you think?' The banker turned to Robert, adopting a divide and rule posture.

'Oh, I fully agree with my brother. I am convinced that in three months time when the *Millennium Tower* is complete, the topping out will be a major event.'

'Really? Don't you think you should rename the bloody thing. I mean the Millennium was last year. These delays have killed any hope of the development being financially viable.' He could see through Robert, who unlike Gordon's steel-like demeanour, revealed a fragile brittleness that was cracking under the pressure. 'Listen, you know the score. You must get a pre-let, otherwise we'll be forced to call in.'

'Oh, come on, you can't be serious! We've hocked everything on this. There's nothing left to give. You've already got our shares in our company, and first call on the houses. What more is there?'

The young banker looked at the two brothers with contempt. He had heard about their shady deals, their womanising and gambling and their rich lifestyle; they were like dinosaurs in an increasingly sophisticated jungle. There was no place for people like them in the modern market-place, and he was now witnessing a Darwinian selection where they were the least fit.

'Hathaway House. I can speak on behalf of the consortium ... we want that as extra security.'

'But it isn't in our gift. The old man is still alive,' Robert replied.

'Well then, I suggest you keep daddy happy, and make sure you inherit the great estate, otherwise, I'm afraid it's all over.'

Gordon looked into the cold eyes of the young banker. He tapped Robert's arm, signalling him to get up. The meeting was over. The inheritance had to be secured for their very survival. 'You'll get what you want.' The brothers left the office, defeated and deflated.

As the twins departed, he asked his secretary to set up a conference call with the other banks. They all knew they were at crisis point where a bloodbath was about to take place, and they wanted to make sure that there were no personal assets overlooked.

28

The crisis for the twins was easily concealed from their father in that until the massive complex had been completed, all of the interest payable on the mountain of debt was rolled up. The banks had agreed to this at the outset. But as soon as the building was available for occupation, the interest would be payable on demand. With the senior bank debt amounting to over £200 million, the annual interest bill was fixed at £15 million. As soon as the development was completed, interest would be called in on a quarterly basis. Any remaining equity that the Longhursts had in the deal would be swallowed up in months. Unless they could find a tenant for the space, catastrophe was fast approaching, and only Sir Francis Sutherland was aware of the dangers the twins would face. His law firm was acting for one of the banks involved in the lending, and was painfully aware of the personal guarantees that Gordon and Robert had given. However, confined by the restrictions of client confidentiality, he was unable to tell James of the imminent dangers of the situation. Warnings had been ignored, and that was the best he could offer.

That autumn, the complex was finally reaching fruition, with the building becoming available for letting in January 2001. As the final tower rose into the sky, its glass windows reflecting the harsh winter sun, the development had become an extremely impressive landmark. The press had been kind, but rumours were beginning to circulate in the property journals that all was not well with the letting. Fortunately for the twins, their father was now too ill to realise what was happening. Blind to newspaper reports and deaf to Sir Francis' warnings, James was living out his final months in glorious ignorance.

29

Charles remained at Oxford after completing his finals, where he achieved a very good second, as expected. He had had a number of interesting job offers, including one from the bank where his father had chaired.

'You should take it, Charles. I'll make sure that you're looked after.'

'I don't know what I want to do, though. I'd like time to think.'

'Well, you'll have to make up your mind soon.

What else have you got?' His father sensed that there was an unfamiliar distance between them, although he could not understand why.

'I thought I might stay here. My tutor is publishing an extremely interesting thesis on the Cicero's Catiline Orations. He needs help, and he asked me if I were free for twelve months. What do you think?' Charles was trying very hard to be more intimate, but he found it almost impossible to freeze out the feeling of neglect that his father had displayed with the will. The tragedy was that his father never realised Sir Francis had told him of his omission.

'Well that could be interesting. But I must say I know very little about it.'

'Don't worry, it's fairly specialised. I wouldn't expect you to know about it.'

'You sound distant, Charles. Is anything the matter?'

'Oh nothing... I just hear things ... rumours mainly about my brothers and the development in Farringdon.'

'Exactly, rumours, that's all. You sound like Francis. Listen, I managed to get down to the site in Farringdon. It will be completing at Christmas. I must say it looks very impressive. It's completely transformed the whole area. I'm very proud of your brothers. You should be, too.'

Charles remained silent. This reaction from his father typified his tragic demise. Weakened by the cancer, he was now completely manipulated by both Gordon and Robert. They controlled the family situation, with Charles himself now just a part player stuck on the periphery. There was nothing he could do. The only light that could be seen at the end of the dark tunnel was that held by his girlfriend. In truth, she was the principle reason for his decision to stay at Oxford.

30

Rosalind achieved a brilliant starred first, and had decided to stay on at Christchurch and do a PhD. This would entail a further four years at the university city. When Charles told her of his decision to stay as well, she was overjoyed. In October, they rented a picturesque cottage in the small village of Woodstock, a few miles outside the city. The village was an easy choice for its historical setting as well as for its aesthetic appeal – it was famous for its proximity to Blenheim, the seat of the Dukes of Marlborough since the early eighteenth century, when Queen Anne rewarded her most brilliant general, John Churchill, after he defeated Louis XIV's army.

'I can't believe that we'll actually be together. I thought we'd fall into a commuter trap, seeing each other at weekends, and during the odd evening in the week ... but Charles, isn't this great?' She wandered around the house, with a wide-eyed expression that beamed so much pleasure, it almost took his breath away.

'Listen, Rosalind, it's only for a year. I mean, I don't think David is going to take any longer than that on his publication. After it's finished, I'll probably get a job in London. I am so lucky to have you.' He grabbed hold of her, and kissed her.

'I know, but let's just enjoy it.'

'And then there's also father to worry about.'

'I know, but you could help yourself. Why don't you go and see him? I know you're upset, but he obviously hasn't a long time left.'

'I should do, but the thought of seeing Gordon and Robert there, sitting smugly, waiting to take everything as soon as my father breathes his last breath ... it's too much.'

'Listen to me. You have to go. You'll never forgive yourself if you don't see him. Have you spoken to Francis?'

'Yes I have. He told me that he would be lucky to make it into the new year. He also said that father had told the twins everything – the will, its contents, the beneficiaries – everything.'

'You still have to go. He's still your father ... and until the last few months, he's been a very good father. His illness has not only distorted his mind, but it's also distorted your own view of him. You must make allowances.'

'How can I, Rosalind? How can I? Unwittingly he has deprived not only myself, but every future Longhurst of their birthright.'

'How can you be sure of that, I mean, I know it's unlikely that the twins will keep the estate, from what you've told me ... but what makes you so sure?'

Charles handed Rosalind a copy of the *Estates Gazette* that had been sent to him by Sir Francis. She took it from him, and slowly read the relevant article. After digesting its contents she handed it back. She remained silent. She had no idea of how close to crisis Robert and Gordon were. The building was effectively weeks away from completion, and there were no tenants interested in the space. Rumours abounded about the banks baying for blood, and the vultures were out for the landlords.

The situation demanded all of Rosalind's skills in diplomacy and tact. Her judgement and intuition were needed, but, how could she help? At first she was bewildered, not knowing what to say or do. It was so unusual for her to be confused that she found it difficult to deal with that emotion in itself. But slowly, she regained her composure, and began to appreciate what was needed.

'I'll come with you.'

'What?'

'If that's what you want, of course.'

'Would you really?' Charles had never thought of her coming with him, but it now made perfect sense. Her being there would be an immeasurable support for him, notwithstanding a bulwark against the double threat from the twins. Above all she would bring her sublime attributes to the great estate.

'There's nothing I would like more.'

31

It was another month before Charles managed to secure an appointment to see his father. The relationship over the last few weeks had further deteriorated to such an extent that his father preferred to let Janet speak for him when Charles called.

'We'll be there late afternoon.'

'OK darling. I'm looking forward to meeting Rosalind.'

'You'll like her!'

'I'm sure I will. She's obviously got good taste.'

Charles laughed at Janet's compliment. She was the only sane person remaining at home, and without her being there he was not sure whether he would have had the strength to face the latent hostility that pervaded the atmosphere. She had been instrumental in bringing him up, as caring as any parent could have been. Loyal, supportive and loving, Charles knew that he owed Janet a great debt. He would now need her support more than ever before.

They left Woodstock at 2 o'clock, and arrived at the black wrought-iron gates of Hathaway House at four. The weather had gradually worsened during the afternoon, and by the time of their arrival, a storm was beginning to brew. The thick dark-grey clouds were accompanied by a powerful gusting wind, which produced a dramatically foreboding effect around the estate. Rosalind, for the first time in her life, felt frightened. It was as if she was about to go on stage, to perform in some tragedy, but unlike the theatre, this was real life.

'Hello. Charles Longhurst here.'

The gates opened, and Charles proceeded down the sweeping drive, parking his car outside the main doors of the house. The first person they saw was Janet, who had stepped outside to greet them. Her friendly face and warm smile contrasted starkly to the dark tweed suit, opaque brown tights, and heavy walking shoes that she was clothed in.

'Christ! What are you wearing?' Charles asked. He had never seen her look so old fashioned and formal. 'It looks like you're off to walk with the hounds!'

'Thank you, Charles!' she replied sarcastically. 'In truth, I think that the adage that one dresses in the manner of how one feels, holds true.'

'What – old fashioned?'

'No, just old.'

'God, I'm sorry, Janet.' He embraced her, feeling a mixture of guilt and stupidity at his initial reaction.

'That's OK. It's so good to see you after so long.' She smiled again, waiting for Charles to introduce her to the girl standing beside him.

'Oh! Sorry ... I almost forgot. Janet, this is Rosalind.'

'I've heard so much about you ... he's never talked about anyone as much as he has about you.'

'Thank you. Well for what it's worth, he's very fond of you, too. Without you I don't think he would have come here.'

Janet put her arm around the young woman and walked both of them into the house. Charles immediately felt uncomfortable once inside the hallway. He felt like an intruder, an unwelcome visitor in his own family house. The sight of Gordon and Robert coming out of the study confirmed this feeling.

'Ah, I knew it wouldn't take long for you to turn up! Who told you? Sir Francis, I suppose.'

The twins were now aware that the rewards for their endeavours were tangibly close. The old man had informed them that they were inheriting the estate and its contents, including the library.

'What do you mean?' Charles retorted. 'I just thought I'd come and see father. Don't worry, I'm not here to steal your prize ... although God knows what will happen to it once the receivers take over your affairs in the New Year.'

'You've been reading too much in the papers, boy. We've got everything sorted out. Tenants are lining up for the development,' Robert replied rather too quickly to sound convincing. 'Who's this?' he asked, pointing at Rosalind.

Charles looked on, but said nothing. He didn't want to introduce her to the twins. He had no desire to contaminate her by letting them communicate with her.

'Janet, could you do me a favour and show Rosalind to her room, and then get Bill to take the luggage from the car. I'm going to see father.'

'It will be my pleasure,' Janet responded, taking Rosalind up the stairs. The relief of having Charles back in the house, albeit temporarily, was palpable. Having suffered the company of the twins over the past several weeks, she felt exhilarated at the way he had handled his brothers with such contempt.

32

'How long have you been seeing each other?'

'Fourteen months.'

'You're not counting then!' Janet laughed as she opened the cupboards showing Rosalind where to hang her clothes.

'And twelve days!' Rosalind replied.

'I suppose you're aware of what's going on here. It's quite terrible, you do understand.'

'Yes, I know everything.' She walked across to the window, and looked out into the darkness. She could see nothing except a branch of a tree, which was lashing against the window due to the force of the gale blowing outside.

Janet watched the young woman, observing her demeanour and poise. There was a sense of command about her, but one that did not offend. Her composure was consummate, but in no way arrogant. She exuded warmth, but her reactions were guarded enough not to mislead one into thinking that she was a soft touch. She seemed so confident in her responses that it led one to believe that she really did know everything but had no way of knowing how. But above all, she emanated light, that was all the brighter in the gloom that surrounded them.

'There's a storm brewing,' she said, turning around from the window, and smiling at Janet.

'How has he taken everything?'

'I think he now fully realises what he has lost, but–'

'But what?'

'I don't think he'll ever understand why.'

'I think he'll have a clearer view now.'

'Why do you say that?'

'Over the last few days his father has deteriorated rapidly. The cancer has entered his brain. He has moments of clarity, but–' Janet broke off, her voice cracking under the intense strain.

'He's gone mad.' Rosalind finished the sentence that Janet hadn't the courage to complete.

'I'm afraid so.'

'Rosalind!' The shout came from Charles downstairs. 'Come down. My father would like to meet you.'

33

Rosalind gestured to Janet, who indicated that she should go. She left the room, and walked slowly down the staircase. The fear she felt when she arrived had now disappeared. Arriving in the hallway, she glanced across at the twins, who looked back sneeringly at this intruder. She walked past them, and then knocked on the study door, opening it without waiting for a response.

'Rosalind, this is my father, Lord Longhurst.'

She looked at the dishevelled creature sitting on his throne. Dressed in a white tunic, covered by a thick cashmere rug, he beckoned her closer. He tried to stand up, but was unable to do so. She approached him, until he lifted his arm, signifying that she was close enough.

'Hello, I've looked forward to this moment. Charles speaks about you often.'

'Does he? I hope he's kind.' His voice was far softer than she had imagined. It was barely audible above the noise of the lashing rain outside.

'You already know the answer to that,' she said

smiling. Although his eyesight was failing, he could see the attraction in the woman who faced him. She gave off a light and purity that Hathaway House had not seen since his wife, Davina, had died.

'Yes I do. Here, come and sit down.' Although sanity only visited him rarely, everything appeared so lucid to him now. It was as if her presence generated a passage of clarity that cleared away the confusion in his brain. 'If only he could have shown me his love when I needed it.'

'But surely he didn't have to prove it to you.'

'Yes he did... I needed him to. I wanted confirmation. But he had you ... and his exams, and...'

'Unhappy that I am, I cannot heave / My heart into my mouth. I love your majesty / According to my bond; no more nor less,' Rosalind interrupted him.

'For God's sake Rosalind, now's not the time to start–' Charles whispered in her ear.

'No!' his father shouted, summoning up an energy and strength that had been absent for months. 'Tell me, is that what you think? Does he?' The old baron knew his literature; the quotation was not lost on him, having himself studied English at Balliol.

'Yes, he does love you.'

James Longhurst sat motionless, his great frame hunched over, not knowing what to say. He was, for the first time in a long while conscious of everything around him. Cordelia's words from *King Lear* suddenly struck home with such a force that he was determined not to make the same mistakes as Shakespeare's tragic colossus had made.

'Charles, forgive me. I have tried to do the right thing ... to be a good father to you all, but I have made a terrible mistake. Get Francis down here immediately. I must change everything.'

34

Rosalind and Charles left the study thirty minutes later, to find Gordon and Robert hovering outside.

'Haven't you moved in the last two hours?' Charles asked the twins.

'We're going in. What have you said to him?'

'Well actually, if you must know, we've been discussing a different premise for *King Lear.*'

'What?'

'You know... the play ... Shakespeare...'

'Yes, yes, I know,' Gordon said dismissively, not quite knowing where this was all going.

'Well then, you'll understand.'

Gordon looked at Robert, and then again at his younger brother and Rosalind. 'What are you talking about, Charles? Have you gone mad too?' He tried to work out what his brother meant, and then without any warning his rudimentary knowledge of the play he once acted in school, suddenly kicked in. 'Christ! He's asked for Francis – he's changing the will.'

'Exactly, Gordon. Maybe you're not so stupid as I thought.'

'Why don't you just piss off!'

Charles smiled and took Rosalind by the arm, and led her to the safety of the kitchen, where

Wendy was preparing dinner.

'Hi Wendy, how are you?'

'Master Charles, it's wonderful to see you. I'm sorry about your father. Are you here to stay?'

'Well, hopefully for a few days. Let me introduce you to Rosalind.'

'Very nice to meet you, dear.' She robustly shook Rosalind's hand. 'Oh yes ... a great improvement on the last ones!'

'Um, thank you, Wendy, that's quite enough!' Charles said, not a little embarrassed. Rosalind, however, found it altogether quite amusing. 'Wendy, it's going to be quite stormy tonight.'

'Yes, I can see, Charles, but to be honest a blind man could have told me that!'

'Wendy, I meant the mood in the house rather than the weather outside.'

'Oh! Well, we're all used to that with Gordon and Robert around.' The phone ring interrupted her. 'Hathaway House? It's Sir Francis for you, Charles.'

'Hello – yes – that's right – as soon as Rosalind spoke to him, he appeared crystal clear – that's fine – tomorrow morning, then.' Charles replaced the receiver. 'He'll be here at nine.'

35

The family met later that evening for drinks. First Gordon and Robert, and then Charles and Rosalind came downstairs into the drawing room. The atmosphere was on a knife-edge. The only sounds that could be heard were from outside, with the cracking of thunder, the howling wind and the lashing rain against the windows. The four remained split into two pairs at either end of the room, neither wanting to speak to the other.

'Look, I have a gift for you.' James Longhurst entered the room, carrying under his arm a turquoise-leather box, and presented it to Rosalind.

'Oh, thank you. But what is it?' she asked innocently.

'Be careful, my dear, it's extremely valuable.'

'Father, I thought you didn't want–'

'Quiet Charles. The library will survive. After all, it's only one book.' He glanced across to Charles. He was still clearly wrapped in the comforting blanket of sanity, and whilst in this condition, wanted to start putting things right between himself and his youngest son.

Rosalind looked at the box, and noticed the gold letters 'HH' engraved on the binding. She stroked her fingers over the leather cover and then placed the box on the table, realising that she had to handle it with the utmost care. She pulled open the top half of the container, and put it to one side. The object inside, clearly a book, was wrapped in tissue. She lifted the book out of its home, and delicately pulled the tissue away.

It measured approximately eighteen inches by twelve. It was a contemporary binding of brown calf leather. There was no title on the front cover. She opened the book, shaking with excitement. The title page stared at her glazed eyes.

Mr William Shakespeare's Comedies Histories &
Tragedies,

She looked up at the old man. 'But you can't be serious? You can't give this to me.' She held the priceless tome in both hands.

'Oh, but I can. You will appreciate it more than anybody else. I want you to have it.'

'Father, you have to be joking – that's the First Folio, it's worth millions.'

'Three and a half, I believe, Gordon. That's what one fetched at auction recently,' James replied, hitherto unaware that Gordon knew anything about books, and their value.

'But she's not even a member of the family,' Gordon shouted.

'Oh I think she will be,' the old man said with such confidence that it was almost deliberately prophetic.

Charles moved closer to him, and whispered in his ear, 'Thank you'.

'The rest will be yours, I promise,' his father said under his breath, in a voice that could be heard only by Charles.

Rosalind placed the book back in its box, embarrassed by the magnificence of the gesture, but also overwhelmed by the greatness of the gift. She desperately wanted to devour the contents of the treasure, but knew it would incite the twins, who were on the brink of a violent response. She certainly was in no mind to accept it. 'I don't want to seem ungracious, but you can't expect me to actually take this?'

'And deny a dying man one of his last wishes?' He paused, and seeing that Rosalind was not going to change her mind, 'Fine, I'll merely include it in the codicil when Francis arrives.'

'Take it sweetheart ... you never know.' Charles pressed Rosalind. Something – he didn't know what – was telling him that she should accept it, before it was too late. There were twelve hours until Sir Francis's arrival when matters would be formalised. That was an awfully long time, when there was so much evil around them.

36

The twins sat through dinner without eating. Their father, who hadn't had an appetite for months, finally found it again and consumed a meal fit for a king. He felt that he had recovered his authority, his power to make decisions. The mist and confusion that had surrounded him over the last year had suddenly dissipated with the arrival of Charles and Rosalind. The love which he felt emanating from the young couple, that had been so absent in the house previously, had opened up the pores, letting in light and clarity and enabling him to regain a sense of complete control. He sensed that God had given him a second chance, and all he needed to do was to stay alive until Francis arrived in the morning, to document his final testament.

After finishing dinner, he bade good night to his children and Rosalind, and retired to bed. Charles nodded to Rosalind, who immediately understood and got up to leave. Before departing from the room, Charles swiftly passed the turquoise box to her.

'Take it ... he wants you to have it ... please.' He was almost imploring her.

She looked at him, sensing a foreboding that he was already feeling. She accepted the gift, and kissed him on the cheek.

'Well I suppose you're very pleased with yourself.' Gordon sneered across the table.

'No not really. But you're both in deep trouble ... you'll lose the whole estate to some faceless bank,' Charles retorted.

'What are you talking about? If this is about Farringdon Millennium, you're wrong, because we've got plenty of tenants lined up.'

'For God's sake, Gordon, do you take me for a complete fool? There's nobody in the market even close to taking the space. The interest on the debt will amount to tens of millions when practical completion triggers the end of the roll-up period next month. How on earth are you two going to pay for it?'

'Oh, so you're now an expert on real estate! Who have you been talking to?'

'I've read the papers.'

'Well once Hathaway House is in our hands – and don't think your paws will be anywhere near it, because he's not of a sound mind to change his will. We'll contest any change, and we'll win.'

'Maybe, maybe not. I'll take my chances. But answer me this – how are you going to pay off the debt?'

'We thought initially about taking a mortgage on the estate, and its contents. We could easily raise £150 million against the property and the books. The valuation will be way ahead of that.'

'Oh, that's sensible, borrow from Peter to pay Paul. You'll have to sell in the end. You do realise that?'

'Yes, you're probably right young Charles–'

'But don't you care?'

'No, not really. I never liked the place anyway. I don't think I'll miss it.'

'But what about–'

'What, Charles? Family? Heritage? Tradition? Quite frankly I don't give a shit about any of it, and neither for that matter does Robert.'

The twins rose and left the room, leaving Charles sitting alone at the table. He sat back, suddenly realising that the home he was brought up in, the house his family had owned for hundreds of years, and the baronial seat that was theirs since Queen Elizabeth 1 bestowed the estate, was about to be lost forever.

37

The storm was unrelenting, raining its venom over the house and causing its inhabitants to experience a restless night. Charles, the last to retire, didn't go to bed immediately. He chose to go into the library, and breathe in the smell of the leather, knowing that he might not be able to experience it in the future. Charles walked around the great room, looking at the vast array of books. He sensed that this would be the final time he would see them.

Rosalind had placed the box on the side table, not opening it, almost frightened of contaminating its contents by merely exposing it to the light. The gift assumed almost a holy significance to her. It was akin to a priest being given a contemporary edition of St Paul's Epistle. She went to bed, frightened, distraught, worried, but also curiously excited. She was excited for Charles and for the future of Hathaway House. She was however scared by the pent-up violence of the twins, in her mind the very embodiment of Goneril and Regan. She was consumed with anxiety over the health of James Longhurst, who seemed to be experiencing the kind of peace that happens before tragedy strikes.

And then finally there was the elation over the possession of the First Folio, something that she never hoped to have owned in her lifetime: a treasure that she, above anybody else, could appreciate.

For a woman who was only familiar with a warm and loving environment, this was a worrying time. But however disturbed both Charles and Rosalind were, their disturbance paled in comparison to the catastrophe that faced Gordon and Robert. Only they knew the impending disaster that faced them. The personal guarantees that had been given to the consortium of banks now included the promise of Hathaway House as security. Indeed, it had only been the promise of the great estate that had kept them alive.

'We have no choice,' Gordon whispered.

'But how?' Robert asked, his voice shaking with panic.

'All I need you to do is to keep a look out.'

'What are you going to do?'

'Let me worry about that. I just need you to make sure that nobody sees me.'

Gordon left his twin's room and tiptoed his way towards his father's bedroom. He had to strike, and there was no time to lose. The stakes were so high that this was his only chance. He alone had the strength, and the conviction to do the necessary evil deed. As he slowly turned the doorknob, he glanced down the hallway and saw his twin standing, looking on.

'Father?'

'Who is it?'

'It's me. Gordon.'

'What is it? What time is it?'

'You were crying out for me.'

'Was I? No, no–'

As the old man reached out to turn on his bedside light, Gordon's hand wrenched it back, and placed his own hand gently around his father's neck.

'For God's sake, what are you doing, Gordon? Have you gone mad?' he tried to shout, but his son placed a hand over the old man's mouth.

'Quiet! Father, you are the one who's mad. You promised us our birthright. Hathaway House should pass to Robert and me. Charles has no right. I can't let you give it to him.'

'Wait! You're right... I'll speak to Francis tomorrow. We'll sort something out.' James was now in a state of panic. He really believed that his son was capable of patricide.

'I wish I could believe you... You don't understand. We're ruined, bankrupt. Without the estate, we're finished.' Gordon put his hand back around his father's neck, ready for the final act.

'But you said–'

'I know, I know, but we were lying. The development's a catastrophe. There are no tenants, and the banks are all over us.'

'But why? It's in a company... You shouldn't have to worry.'

'We gave personal guarantees. Did you honestly think, you old fool, that they would lend us so much without us pledging our inheritance?'

The words, which slowly came out of Gordon's mouth, were like bullets aimed at the old man's heart. Searing pains shot through his chest, causing him to convulse. His back arched upward as the pressure increased, producing an unbearable tightness around his chest. Gordon released his hand, not knowing what was happening.

'My God!... My heart – my–'

James tried to speak, but was unable to do so. Oxygen was being prevented from circulating around his body, and thus feeding his vital organs. Unable to breathe, and suffering from a pain that he had never experienced before, he began to lose consciousness. His body collapsed, and slumped back from its arched convulsions, on to the bed. Lord James Longhurst, 37th Baron of Hathaway House was dead.

Gordon stepped back from the corpse. He tried to gather his thoughts, not quite believing his luck. He quickly looked at the old man's neck, and saw that there was no trace of a mark where his hand had been. If he could leave the room, and join his brother without being seen, it would be the perfect result. He quickly left the room, and walked back to Robert who was still waiting for him in the hall.

'It's over – he's dead. Hathaway House is ours.'

'What? You killed him?'

'Shut up! No I didn't. He had a heart attack.'

'What do you mean? How?'

'I threatened him, and told him the truth about Farringdon. It's the perfect result for us, don't you see? Our hands are clean. I didn't physically kill him.'

'My God, you've done it! He's dead! We're home and dry!'

'Yes, we are. We have nothing to fear!'

38

As James exhaled his last mortal breath, the storm outside suddenly abated. The deafening silence was first noticed by Charles in his bedroom. He got up and pulled back the curtain. He opened the sash window and looked outside, not having seen anything like it before. The black, dark storm clouds, were now replaced by crystal clear night, lit up by thousands of stars, illuminating the whole estate.

James remained there looking at the astral phenomenon, marvelling at the spectacle for five minutes, until he was distracted by what he thought were footsteps on the landing. He stepped back into the room and opened his door. Looking up and down the landing he saw nobody, and thought little of it. He walked over to his bed, and lay fully dressed on top of the blankets. He suddenly felt overcome with tiredness, and within minutes fell into a very deep sleep.

He was woken by screams, five hours later, when Wendy discovered the old baron's cold and stiff lifeless body. He got up and ran to his father's room, where already his twin brothers, and Bill, the chauffeur, were standing by the bed.

'What? What's happened?' Charles shouted.

'It's father, Charles. He's dead.' Gordon looked at him sombrely.

'But he was fine last night. What happened?'

'Looks like he had a heart attack,' Robert responded.

'How do you know?'

'We don't–'

'But it's a reasonable assumption.' Gordon interrupted his brother, realising immediately the possible exposure of knowing too much too early.

'Wendy, call the doctor ... and tell Sir Francis. He'll be on the mobile in the car,' Charles said.

Wendy walked out, passing Rosalind who made her way into the room.

'What's happened?'

'It's my father ... he died.'

'What? But he seemed so strong last night. I don't understand, Charles. I don't know what to say – I am so sorry.' She put her arms around him, realising that nothing she said would help, and embraced him, holding him tightly so he could feel her support.

'Thank you.' He walked over to the bed and looked at the cadaver. The body of James Long-hurst was now so alien to him: it was no longer his father, but a cold carcass, pale and emaciated, already affected by rigor mortis. Charles hardly recognised his father lying before him. For the first time he understood what people meant by the soul. James Longhurst's body was laid out starkly on the bed, but his father had long departed from this world.

39

The doctor arrived, followed shortly by Sir Francis Sutherland. Both of them dealt separately with the death, and the subsequent burial arrangements.

'There'll have to be an autopsy.'

'Why?' Gordon asked.

'It's normal practice, especially if the death was unexpected.'

'He had terminal cancer!'

'I know, but it's a little unusual that he should have suffered a heart attack at this cycle of his illness. His cardiographs showed no abnormality in his heart. The scans had shown no damage to his heart muscles, and the angiogram showed his arteries to be clear. As a protective measure, I even put him on beta blockers.'

'How long will the autopsy take?' Gordon asked impatiently, belying a sense of nervousness that Charles did not understand.

'Forty-eight hours, I suppose. I'll have to talk to the hospital.'

'Very good. The quicker the better. We ought to have the funeral, say, in a week. That will give family and friends plenty of time.'

'What's all the rush, Gordon? After all, you've got what you wanted,' Francis said, realising that any hope of contesting the will on behalf of Charles would be futile, with no written evidence of James' volte-face.

'Nothing ... nothing, of course. I just thought for the sake of good order. Father would have wanted it all done and dusted as speedily as possible.'

'Done and dusted? Well no one could accuse you of being the sentimental type, Gordon.' Charles, walked out with Francis, leaving Gordon alone with the doctor.

'He gave Rosalind the First Folio last night.'

'God! Why?'

'He didn't think it was that significant since he was about to leave me the entire estate, including the library.'

'No, I suppose not. What are you going to do?'

'Nothing, of course.'

'But, he obviously wanted you–'

'No, Francis. He wanted her to have it. You see, he saw something that I thought only I knew.'

'What? I mean anybody who meets her can see that she is a wonderful–'

'He could see that I was in love with her, and that I was going to marry her. This was a gift to his future daughter-in-law.'

'Well, she'll certainly appreciate it!'

'Yes, but can the twins claim it's theirs? I mean, is the gift legitimate, given that there's a written will expressing the desire to keep the library intact with the estate?'

'No– It's a gift in his lifetime. The will only

takes effect over what he owned at the time of his death. It's quite clear he had already given the Folio to Rosalind. It's really not a problem.'

'Yes, but–'

'Don't worry. I know your claim on the estate is now futile, but they'll still be a little uneasy. I mean, look at Gordon this morning. I'll certainly make sure as a quid pro bono that, in return for not contesting the will, they make a written undertaking not to have any rights over the Folio.'

'Very good, I'll leave it to you then.' Francis nodded, and carried out his instruction. The twins in the event were happy to confirm the gift in writing, having successfully inherited the entire estate.

40

The autopsy showed that James Longhurst had died from a massive cardiac arrest, one which a fit young man would have found difficult to survive, let alone a man in his seventies racked with cancer. The family doctor remained slightly perplexed as to the cause, but there was no uncertainty about the effect of the arrest.

'Was there anything he did? Can you remember if something happened that evening to bring on the attack?'

'Well, my youngest brother, who hadn't seen him for a long time, arrived at the house. But he seemed to be fairly calm when he went to bed. Isn't that right, Charles?'

'I'm as shocked as you are, doctor. Sometimes,

perhaps, there are no answers.'

'No, quite ... quite. Well, I assume you'll want to go ahead with the funeral.'

'Yes. Thank you, doctor.'

The arrangements were made for the burial of the thirty-seventh baron. Taking place in the family mausoleum in the grounds at Hathaway House, family and friends paid tribute to the life of James Longhurst. Gordon, the 38th baron, was one of them, reading passages from the Psalms, expressing his grief in front of the hundred people present.

Charles, the only member of the family who was suffering real grief, stood silently, accepting the condolences that were being offered. He looked across the land, on to the Hathaway House estate, and realised that this would probably be the last time he would see his home. Feeling a gentle tug on his arm, he glanced at the graceful figure next to him, and slowly began his walk to the car.

'You know, it's strange, but when dad died, the storm ended, almost simultaneously, and in the silence that followed I almost thought I heard footsteps outside.'

'You did!' Rosalind replied.

'What? You heard them too?'

'Yes, I was awake. I heard whispering.'

'For God's sake! Why didn't you say something, Rosalind?'

'Well, I didn't think it was relevant ... and to be frank, I had no idea it was at that moment your father passed away.'

'Well... What do you think now?'

'What do you mean? Do you really think your brothers were in your father's room? Do you think they could have had something to do with his death?'

'I don't know, Rosalind ... but what's the point? Nothing can be proved now. But to put it in words that you would appreciate, *Something is rotten here...*' He stopped walking, and turned to her. 'Are you ready to leave?'

Part 9

SOTHEBY'S, THE PRESENT DAY

4.35 P.M.

The relief Smith Luytens felt as Hugo Samuels made his bid was palpable. He waited for William Gaston to respond. He watched the six-foot-four dark-haired American, and tried to read his next bid. A billionaire a hundred times over, he could afford to buy nation states, let alone the most authentic piece of Western culture. He waited, looking directly into the great man's cold blue eyes.

'Two fifteen.'

The words came out evenly, almost melodically, from Bill Gaston's mouth. He remained cool, unmoved, almost as if in a trance. He seemed imperiously in control. There was no way he could be beaten. Smith Luytens looked away from the American, although it was difficult, since Gaston exuded such an enormous presence that he seemed to be everywhere in the room. He saw Hugo, who was standing fifteen yards behind Gaston, very much in the American's shadow. His old friend from school stood fixed to the spot, mulling over what strategy would be the most effective.

Smith Luytens had known Hugo Samuels from the age of thirteen when both started at Eton together. They remained close throughout school, even though they were in different houses. They followed different paths, but both well-worn ones, with Smith Luytens going to the Courtauld to study history of art, and then to Sotheby's, where he was now their leading auctioneer. Samuels, a superior academic, went to Kings College Cambridge where he read law, and then joined the civil service. He had been selected to oversee the move of the British Library to Kings Cross, and was now in charge, amongst other things, of acquisitions.

'£250 million.' Samuels, unknown to his friend the auctioneer, had been given a very large arsenal, from which to fire.

Gaston for the first time reacted to the counter offer, the level of which surprised him. He turned around to the refined-looking gentleman, dressed in a dark grey suit, white shirt, and navy blue tie. He looked like, and indeed, was the quintessential Englishman. Samuels nodded to the American, inviting him to better his bid.

'Two sixty!'

'Thank you, sir.' He looked over Gaston's shoulder at his friend, 'And it's against you, sir.'

Samuels smiled. Should he take it more slowly, or maybe consider another leap. It was difficult to call, knowing that the American had unlimited funds to play with. As a result, if he really wanted it, there was nothing he could do to stop him. He waited, and used the little time he had to make up his mind.

'It's against you,' Smith Luytens said, in a quieter, more friendly manner. He felt a surge of sympathy not only for his friend, but for the nation, which was about to lose a most extraordinary part of its heritage. He glanced up at the back of the room where the young couple remained seated. They were winners whatever happened now. The reserve had been reached and passed long ago.

'Three hundred million!' The words rang out around the room.

Part 10

ROMEO AND JULIET

1

'Oh, I'm not at all worried by that.'

'But it's been over two years, and you've only let 10,000 feet. Even with that letting, the rent-free period is reportedly over twelve months. The whole thing must be costing you a fortune,' she said, placing her whisky on the hotel bar.

'Listen, my dear, when you are as rich as Robert and myself, one can afford to carry the burden.'

'Gordon, don't speak to me like I'm a village girl with no idea of the real world. I'm a leading bloody property lawyer, for Christ's sake!'

'All right... All right... I'm sorry. Since when have you been so touchy?' He looked at the smartly dressed women sitting opposite him. She had long dark hair, large brown eyes, a full mouth and an aquiline nose. She had a pale complexion, made to look even paler by the overdone black eye-liner. Gordon had always found her very sexy, but today the more so, because of her tightly-fitted suit, black stockings and very high stiletto-heeled shoes.

'Well, I'm not usually.' She changed position on her chair, crossing her legs, revealing slightly more of her nylon-covered thigh. 'But I can't stand you treating me like an idiot. I should never have slept with you. We should have just maintained a professional relationship.'

'Why should I be different to any of your other

male clients?' He smiled at her, in a superior manner, and placed his large hand on her leg, moving it up under her skirt, feeling the suspender clip attached to the stocking. He gently moved his hand around the top of her stockings, and felt her cold, bare thigh.

'You can be such a bastard!' She got up to leave.

'Sally! Don't go, I'm sorry. I didn't mean it, really.'

'Forget it, Gordon. You're a bore.'

'Sally–' He grabbed her hand. 'Don't go! I need you. I beg you, please!'

She looked down at him, and saw an image she had never thought that she would see. Gordon Longhurst, 38th baron of Hathaway House, the most arrogant man in London, was asking her to stay. She slowly sat down again, leaving her hand in his.

2

He opened his hand and looked at Sally Fulton's long, red-painted fingernails. His voice became hushed. 'Farringdon is a disaster. It's really the reason why I wanted to see you tonight. Things are very bad, very bad indeed.'

'Gordon... You're scaring me. How awful can it be? I mean personally you still have the estate, and all of its contents. The equity must still be worth a fortune.' Sally Fulton had never seen her client like this before. She could feel his hand shake with fear. She looked up at his face and saw the beads of sweat that had formed around his temples.

'The interest coupled with the capital repayments, has meant that I have very little cash left. The money raised from the mortgage on Hathaway House is almost exhausted. I'll have to either take a second mortgage, which the banks are not happy about. Or–'

'What?'

'Listen, never mind. More importantly, three weeks ago you told me you met an antiquarian book dealer. Do you remember? You kept telling me how attractive he was, but he wasn't interested.'

'Yes ... and he's still not. Shame really, but I suppose if you're married with three kids, and you have a large mortgage, you are a little bit more cautious about having an affair. Why do you ask?'

'There's a library at Hathaway – a very valuable library.'

'You've kept that very quiet. I've never heard of it.'

'You wouldn't have. Even the banks are unaware of its true value, otherwise they'd be all over it.'

'Well, how valuable?'

'It's been valued in excess of £100 million.'

'What? You're joking.'

'No I'm not. I have to raise money now, and quickly. Robert and I plan to leave the country in the next twelve months. The debt mountain at the bank will just grow, and by the end of next year Hathaway House will be owned by the banks themselves. Before that, the upkeep of the estate is exhausting huge amounts of money. And then there's the–'

'There's more?'

'I'm talking to you as my lawyer now. I wasn't going to tell you this, but the Revenue are chasing us for the final payment of the inheritance tax, which we were liable for late last year. I thought I could strike a deal, but they're not moving.'

'So, you have to sell the books and you need a buyer?'

'That's where you might be able to help.'

'Well, of course. I'll speak to him tomorrow.'

3

They took the lift to the sixth floor. She felt an unusual wave of sympathy come over her. By nature she was no sentimentalist. On the contrary, affection never came easily to her. She revelled in her lack of feelings, especially being a woman in the professional arena. She believed it gave her the cutting edge in the ruthless world that she lived in. She had no attachments, or relationships of note. These would have been a handicap in her current environment. Her success was based on a triumvirate of selfishness, toughness and total disdain for others. The only pleasure she gained, involving other people, was from the transient cheap one-night-stands, that she was a master at.

Men enjoyed her company, primarily because, although there was no doubting her feminine, feline appearance, she was essentially one of the boys. She could drink like them, enjoy sport, tell filthy jokes, and talk about sex without being embarrassed. They also knew that she was available, but only on a selective basis, and it was her selection, not theirs. She was very clever, and without having to use her sexual skills, she had made it to the top of the greasy pole, and was senior partner at a mid-sized West End law firm specializing in conveyancing. Her relationship with Gordon was well known in city circles, since he was the only man to have managed to sleep with her on more than one occasion.

Malicious talk said it was his title and his wealth that had given him this special position in Sally Fulton's heart of stone, but this was wide of the mark. There was something brutal and unpleasant about Gordon Longhurst that attracted her to him. Maybe she saw something of her in him which she empathised with. She wasn't sure, but as she stood in the lift, she couldn't help but feel a certain amount of admiration for him. He had so far refused to buckle under the immense pressure of failure, but now he appeared broken and facing denouement. Yet in spite of the troubles he currently faced, he still wanted her, and wanted her now. She understood him and he spoke her language. She was desperate to reciprocate his wanton desire, and was happy to be part of his unacceptable world.

He slipped the plastic key into the door and led her to the bed. He held her tightly in his arms, and pressed his lips apart, on hers, forcing his tongue inside her mouth. He hated kissing, or any form of foreplay. He pushed her on to the

313

bed, stood up and undid his trousers, letting them drop to the floor. He then moved over to her, and placed his hands on the outside of her thighs, then pushing them up to her waist, simultaneously dragging her skirt up with them. He wrenched her G-string down, and pulled it off over her stilettos. He stood up, lifting her legs up and placing her ankles on his shoulders.

He looked at her, momentarily, and then thrust his fully erect penis into her vagina. She gasped at the simultaneous excruciating pain and ecstatic pleasure of his organ inside her. He pushed rhythmically into her, each time relieving an element of the strain he had been suffering from. She treated the pleasure and the punishment in the same way, releasing groans at every thrust. This was how she liked her sex; savage, untamed and without sensitivity. He pushed harder and more quickly. She could almost feel him in her throat, so deep was he pressing inside. After 90 seconds, he let go of her legs, and fell on top of her, releasing his orgasm with such a force that even she struggled to cope with.

He remained still, on top of her. She welcomed the respite, as she began to lose the feeling of his penis as it shrunk back to a flaccid state.

'Gordon ... come on, get off me.'

He groaned as he got up. 'So, will I hear from you soon?' he asked, pulling his trousers back up.

'About the book dealer? Yes, of course. I'll call you tomorrow.'

'Thanks.' He turned towards the door.

'Where will you both go? Assuming it all works out.'

'South America probably. Extradition isn't so easy from there!'

She nodded, and started to readjust her stockings and suspender belt. She rolled over on the bed and reached out to her bag, from which she took a Kleenex. She then wiped away the residue of his lust, which had began to seep out and roll down the inside of her thigh. Getting up, she picked up her G-string, still lying on the floor, and then pulled down her skirt, and followed him out.

4

Bernard Shapeman received the call very late on a Friday evening. He was the last person left on the premises, as he went through his papers one last time before the weekend.

'Hello? Yes, speaking.'

'It's Sally Fulton. You might not remember me, but I was introduced to you three weeks ago at a book launch in Holland Park.'

'Yes, yes, of course I remember you. How are you?' He vaguely recalled the tall, dark, slightly vampiric woman from the launch.

'I'm fine. I was wondering whether I might meet you. I think I have something that you would like.'

'Oh, I'm sure you have, but I've already told you that I'm unavailable!' he laughed.

'Are you free now?' She wasn't laughing.

'What, now ... this very moment?'

'Yes.'

'Well, I suppose so. Let's say 15 minutes, then?'

'No, I think five would suit me better.' She cut him short, and put the mobile phone back in her bag. She looked across the street, and saw Bernard Shapeman place the receiver back on the phone. He turned his office light off, and then went downstairs to the shop floor. She waited until he was settled in the shop, and then got out of her car and walked over to meet him.

He glanced at his watch, not quite understanding the almost surreal situation. He certainly wasn't used to intrigue and subterfuge, but the phone call from this woman reeked of artifice. Now in his early forties, married with three young children, Bernard Shapeman had finally established himself as one of London's leading antiquarian book dealers. Beginning at school, his passion for books started with travel, as he traded independently in Baedeker guides. After leaving school, he opened a shop in Holland Park, where he attracted a rich, but more importantly, loyal clientele.

He expanded the business to include manuscripts, then maps and drawings. The business grew exponentially, and as a result he moved to St George Street opposite Sotheby's, into a large Georgian building which could house his burgeoning stock. The financial pressure of having so many books and other works of art, which by their very nature failed to provide any income, meant that he had to trade all the time to create a sufficient cashflow to feed the overdraft. He worked tirelessly, travelling all around the world, meeting the rich and famous, selling his treasured books. Intensely ambitious, and having tasted the

316

luxury that his clients enjoyed, he was desperate to have a similar lifestyle for himself and his family.

'Come in.' He welcomed Sally Fulton into the shop. 'Would you like a drink?' He looked at her, as she took off her coat and hung it on the back of the chair.

'No thanks.'

'Well? How can I help you?' he asked, pulling a chair from the wall, and sitting down opposite her.

She reached down into her bag, pulled out a list and handed it to him. She watched his reaction as he looked down the index of books typed out. His face, soft and attractive – the very antithesis of Gordon Longhurst's – began to reveal astonishment as he took it in. 'Miss Fulton, this is a list of arguably the most valuable books in the world. I suppose it's someone's wish list. Well believe me, I can't help you. It can take years to find some of this stuff. I advise you to go to the auction houses and take your chances.' He looked at her. She stared straight back at him, smiling. 'What's so funny?' he asked.

'You! Have you finished?' She liked him. He would be a rare commodity in her world of property. He appeared honest and gentle. There was nothing guileful or shady about him. Perhaps that's what she found attractive about him in the first place. She wasn't sure, but she was taking great pleasure in playing with him.

'Well ... yes.'

'I have those books.'

'That's impossible.'

'In perfect condition, all in their original cloth or boards. The manuscripts are all–'

'But it's impossible. I mean, I've never seen some of this stuff. The only thing missing is Shakespeare First Folio.'

'That's another story.'

'How can you be so sure of all this?'

'The list represents the hundred most valuable in the collection. It's estimated that there are twenty thousand books in the library. Most of the value is in that list.'

'I'm not surprised, and forgive me if I seem a little suspicious, but have you seen them yourself?'

'Of course. They're in the safe room at my law firm. When would you like to see them? Tomorrow would be good – Saturday is quiet at the office. We can go through them together.' There was more than an element of flirtatiousness in her voice.

'Yes ... yes, of course.' He wasn't at all interested in her. All he could see at that moment was the piece of paper with 100 titles of the most famous books in the world.

'There is one thing. You cannot talk about this to anybody – not even your wife.'

'Yes, yes, of course, I understand.' He was too intrigued by the list to be suspicious.

5

The following morning, Bernard Shapeman arrived at the offices in Berkeley Square. He had hardly slept the previous night, unable to contain his excitement at the promised treasure, although still retaining a measure of suspicion at the veracity of her claim.

'Sally Fulton, please. She's expecting me.'

The receptionist picked up the phone and dialled the four-digit extension. 'Yes, of course, Miss Fulton, I'll send him down.' She replaced the receiver. 'Can you go through the glass doors, and take the lift down to the basement. Miss Fulton will meet you there.'

'Thank you.' He walked briskly through the doors and into the lift. He pressed the button marked 'Basement' twice, his impatience now getting the better of him. Finally the doors closed, and the lift made its way down to the lower level. Again, there was a delay before the doors opened.

'Good morning, Bernard.'

'Good morning, Miss Fulton.'

'You can call me Sally.'

'Oh, fine.' He suddenly felt awkward, being alone with her. She was dressed in a cream-coloured blouse, very tight denim jeans, which hung over her dark-brown cowboy boots. He noticed her sexuality for the first time, and he felt slightly exposed. If she were to make a move on him, he wasn't sure how strong he would be in trying to resist her. They reached the reinforced steel door.

'Before I open the door, you must sign this.'

'What is it?'

'It's a confidentiality letter.'

'I don't understand.'

319

'You will ... sign it. You can – you have to trust me.'

He took the document and scanned its contents. It appeared fairly standard. He had very little choice. He was desperate to see the books, still not quite believing that such a collection existed. He took the pen which she was holding out to him, and signed it. He gave it back to her. 'Right, can we go in now?'

'Of course.' She unlocked the door and pushed it open.

He stepped into the room and gazed at the piles of turquoise-leather boxes that lay in front of him on the floor. He immediately noticed the gold letters 'HH' on all of the bindings. 'God! You were telling the truth. It's extraordinary!' he muttered as he walked over to the books. 'Is there any order to all of this?'

'No, not really, but the most valuable are over there.' She pointed to a separate section where the boxes were individually laid out on the table.

He moved towards the table and slowly opened the first leather container. He stood staring at its contents. His fingers brushed the cover of the most famous bible in the world. *The Gutenberg* he whispered. He left the lid open and walked over to the next box. Opening it again, in a slow, almost melodramatic way, he gasped as he gazed at Vesalius's *De Humani Corporis fabrica libri septem*. He looked at the lawyer standing behind him. 'Go on, it only gets better. Look, I believe this one's very impressive.' She opened the next box and took out a cloth-bound book and gave it to him. He opened the cover and saw the frontis-

320

piece. After a few seconds he recognised the unbelievably rare suppressed edition of Charles Lutwidge Dodgson's, better known as Lewis Carrol's, *Alice in Wonderland.* 'Yes, I've never seen this before – I've never seen any of these before!' He opened the boxes far more quickly now, satisfying a surge of what amounted to nothing less than inquisitive lust. His amazement grew at the treasures that were revealed in the first twenty boxes including a 1476 edition of Chaucer's *Canterbury Tales,* Audubon's *Birds of America,* Newton's *Philosophiae naturalis principia mathematica, Don Quixote* by Cervantes, and Copernicus' *De Revolutionibus orbium coelestium.*

'The manuscripts are over here.' She pointed to two very large receptacles at the end of the table. 'If you think the books are something else, wait until you see these.' She lifted the first manuscript out. Protected by a transparent plastic cover, she handed it to him. '*The Rothschild Prayer Book* – this is priceless.'

'Wait ... look.' She passed him the next one.

'What is it?' he asked.

'It's the Gettysburg address written by Lincoln.'

He stood fixed to the spot. 'Is there anything else of this magnitude?'

'Yes, somewhere there's the final proofs of Nabokov's *Lolita,* with the author's corrections.' She looked around trying to remember its location.

'Don't worry, I'll find it.' He wandered around the room. He had never seen anything like this in his entire life. There was, however, something missing. And then he remembered. 'What about that *First Folio?* You said something about it.'

'Yes. Obviously it was part of the collection ... a very fine copy, but it was given away.'

'Shame, but it's incredible anyway. Where's it all from? I mean a collection like this ... every book dealer would know about it. And tell me, what does "HH" stand for?'

'You're right, but it's always been kept a very closely guarded secret.' She looked at him. He had signed the confidentiality letter, but could she trust him? She thought for a few seconds, and decided to gamble. 'Have you heard of Hathaway House?'

He stared at her. 'So it really does exist ... it's real, then.'

'What?'

'The Hathaway collection. Nobody knows in the book world whether the fabled Hathaway Library is genuine. It's acquired mythical status.' He stopped and looked around him. 'Seeing this here is ... well, it's almost like a classical scholar being led to the ancient city of Atlantis.'

'Well, it's all yours, Bernard. The latest valuation is here. You have to get close to it. My client is in a hurry, so you'll need to put your skates on.'

'Do you want me to sell it as a collection, or individually?'

'My client wants absolutely no publicity, so I presume it would be best to sell the books individually to your private clients.'

'What's the deal for me?'

'A straight ten percent on all sales. You can, of course, buy yourself, but only at valuation.'

'And the money?'

'Here.' She handed a slip of paper with the Swiss bank account details on it.

'There's nothing illegal in all this, is there? I mean, it's not a laundering exercise, is it?' Bernard was always alarmed when Swiss bank accounts were mentioned.

'No – no, of course not, Bernard. Everything is perfectly proper and correct. You have nothing to worry about. I am a lawyer, Bernard.' She looked at him, seeing that he had taken the bait. 'Just remember everything has to be carried out quietly.' She put her hand on his shoulder, adding to her comforting tone.

'Very good.' He paused, not completely reassured, but certainly less worried. 'One final question.'

'Yes?'

'What about the rest?'

'When you've sold this lot, you will get the remainder. As I said the real value is in this room, but obviously there is a lot left at the house which is worth millions. Oh, and by the way, you have exactly one year to complete.'

'Fine, I'll get on with it.' He rubbed his hands, and like a bee to a honey pot, went back to the books.

6

Shapeman knew what he had to do, and the time limit meant that he had to deal with it quickly. He started to make a list of his richest clients and prepared various menus for each one, matching up their individual collections with the books that were now on offer. He had no doubt in his own ability to sell all of the books substantially above valuation. Keeping it quiet would be a problem, but fortunately the clients he had in mind were relatively low key and would be more than happy not to have any publicity.

And so the sale of the Hathaway Library had begun. One of the finest book collections ever to be assembled in one room was about to be dismantled, to feed the greed of its inheritors. If anything positive could come out from the sale, it would be that it was orchestrated by the shrewdest antiquarian book dealer in Europe. Intelligent, scrupulously careful, Shapeman would ensure that each sale was handled with the utmost care and attention. Prices gained were the best in the current market conditions, especially with the prerequisite limits set on privacy and time.

Raising over £50 million in the first five months, he was well on his way to disposing of half of the collection. Never being allowed to see the books in their historic environment and always collecting them from Sally Fulton's office, the operation assumed a covert nature. This was exactly how both Gordon and Robert planned it. Nothing could go wrong: impersonal and untraceable, controlled by a ruthless advisor who ensured that the monies were arriving at the right place and at the right time.

Over the following three months the operation was running so smoothly that it was becoming dangerously easy. And it was at this moment, when everything appeared in perfect order and the end was in sight, that a glitch appeared. It was almost unnoticeable at first, but like a dot on the horizon, as it came closer, it grew into a large black mark. The first sign of it came in August 2002, when most of London was away. Bernard Shapeman had just returned from a family holiday. He was always relieved to be back in the shop with his feet up on his desk, finally able to relax away from the noise of his demanding children.

Thumbing through the coming autumn auction catalogues, he suddenly stopped at lot number 39.

Pride and Prejudice *by Jane Austen.*
First Edition in the original boards.
Very fine copy

It was extremely rare to find a book of this nature in the original boards, but it wasn't the scarcity or indeed the value that caught his attention. There was a further detail that set the alarm bells ringing. He picked up the phone and rang Sally Fulton.

'Sally? It's Bernard.'

'Hi Bernard. Congratulations, things seem to be going very well. I assume you're ringing about the final third of–'

'No, Sally, I'm not.'

'Well, what is it then?' There was the tiniest sense of concern discernable in the lawyer's voice.

'There's a *Pride and Prejudice* First, in its original boards, in the Christies' auction for September.'

'Well, I realise that must be an extremely

valuable book, but I'm not interested. I prefer cars myself.'

'No, you don't understand – I sold this copy two months ago.'

'But there must be more than one. How can you be sure it's yours?'

He picked up the catalogue and read out the final description of the lot. *'Boxed in turquoise leather with the letters HH engraved in gold leaf on the binding.'*

There was no reply from the other end of the phone.

'Sally, are you still there?'

'Yes, yes, I'm still here. Let me think.' She tried to collect her thoughts and remain calm but couldn't resist her anger getting the better of her. 'You should have done a more thorough job, Bernard. Didn't you tell your clients that reselling was problematic?' She was now shouting, realising that even the best laid plans can go wrong.

'Of course I did, but these are very rich people. How do you think they got rich in the first place? They're ruthless, they don't care about breaking a promise. You should know that better than anyone.'

'Why do you say that?'

'Well, I don't know... It's just that–'

'What?'

'Oh, nothing.' Bernard instinctively knew when he had overstepped the mark, and immediately retreated.

'Look, it's no good worrying about it. I'm going to speak to my client, and I'll get back to you. In the meantime I suggest you monitor the auction, and speed up the rest of the sales as quickly as possible. My clients will be even more anxious to complete now. Don't worry about getting valuation, just push on and sell what you can at the best prices possible.'

'Fine.'

7

Bernard Shapeman continued with the quietest sale of the century, picking the relevant buyers from his massive database of clients. The disposal became progressively easier, as the lesser valued items, ranging between ten and twenty thousand pounds attracted a greater number of buyers. Speed was now of the essence. All Gordon and Robert wanted was to get as much money as quickly as possible into the Swiss bank account, and then leave the country. At the end of the year, what remained of the fabled Hathaway Library were a few very old books with limited value and appeal. Bernard himself had made an offer for the remainder, at valuation, which was readily accepted.

Gordon and Robert Longhurst had prepared meticulously for their departure. The book sale had been carried out according to plan, even though the final third went rather more quickly than they had originally envisaged. Nevertheless, the panic that accompanied the appearance of Jane Austen's *Pride and Prejudice* proved to be unnecessary, as the resale passed by without any real attention. A profit was made for the vendor, but nothing material. It all proved to be a storm in a teacup, from which Bernard Shapeman heaved a huge sigh of relief. The result of the mini storm, however was that the disposal of the collection was completed well before the 12-month deadline.

By the end of January the following year, the brothers were ready to leave. They had nothing to stay for. Unofficially bankrupt, with interest bills and bank debt mounting daily, their interest in Hathaway House was negligible. But even worse than that, Hathaway House itself was rapidly becoming a liability. Not being able to pay for its upkeep meant that the house started to decline, both inside and outside. Stonework was either crumbling, or actually falling off. The roof was covered in moss, and showed early signs of decay. The gardens, at one time the most spectacular in the country, began to look more like a wild, untamed forest. The lawns and driveways were overtaken by weeds. Even the giant wrought-iron gates were beginning to rust.

'We're leaving tomorrow morning.'

'OK, then. You have everything?'

'Yes. Sally, are you sure you don't want to come? Buenos Aires has a wonderful climate. You'd have a great time. We've managed to buy a fantastic country house as well.'

'No thanks, Gordon. I'm fine here.'

'Well, if you ever change your mind, you have my address there.'

'Yes I do. Have you told anyone?'

'Not a soul. And you?'

'Of course not.'

'Listen, nobody will find us. You've set it up perfectly. Even Wendy the housekeeper here hasn't got a clue. She thinks we're just going on a skiing holiday to Switzerland. Well, of course, we are, but only for 24 hours! By the time the banks realise, we'll be cattle-ranching on some pampas! And if they do find us, which I doubt with the identity changes, extradition will take years.'

'I know the score, Gordon.' She sounded tired. Over the past few months she had had enough of Gordon Longhurst. Whether it was because of the selfishness or the general unpleasantness of his character, she was not quite sure. It was true that they had planned their departure, but she had done the work, using contacts, pulling favours, enabling them to have different passports, driving licences, even new birth certificates. In truth she had been paid an enormous amount of money for her work, but it was not enough to wash the spots of treachery from her hands. She would be happy once they had gone.

'Yes ... yes, I'm sure you do,' he said, picking up on her mood. 'And I am sure you will keep your confidence.' There was an air of malice that Sally Fulton could not miss.

'Oh, don't worry, Gordon. Your secret is safe with me. You could ruin me far too easily.'

'Yes I know that.' His response had a threatening tone to it that was not lost on Sally Fulton. She put the phone down and walked over to the window of her office. She took a cigarette out of her pocket and then struck a match. For the first

329

time in her life she noticed her hand shake as the flame attempted to light the tobacco.

8

The flight of the two brothers had very little immediate impact. Friends assumed, like the staff at Hathaway, that they had gone on holiday. It was only when the quarterly interest payment demands were met with a deafening silence at the end of March that the banks woke up from their complacent slumber. From a period of tranquillity, there suddenly erupted a flurry of activity. The speed at which the banks acted to seize what remained of the brothers' assets was akin to a vulture swooping down on its dead prey. From the law courts to the television studios, from the radio stations to the newspapers, from the street cafes to the Michelin-starred restaurants, everybody had become obsessed with the whereabouts of the Longhurst twins.

Hathaway House was the first casualty in the fall out. It was inevitable as it was the only asset that the twins had left, which although encumbered with a sizeable debt, was not completely mortgaged. The historic country estate was seized with alarming alacrity by the finance houses, who saw that this one prize would certainly all but clear the twins' debts. Photographed in its former glory, in all the property press, as well as receiving full exposure from the leading estate-agent publications, Hathaway House became front-page news.

Charles heard of Gordon and Robert's disappearance from the police, two days before the news broke. He had no idea when or where they had gone. His first thought was of Wendy, and the rest of the employees at the estate.

'So you and Bill are the only ones left. All the others were laid off.'

'Yes, that's right, Charles. Before Christmas the twins said that they couldn't afford a full retinue, and they were going to lay off everybody except the two of us. We could manage anyway, there was nothing left here to do.'

'What do you mean?'

'Well, come down and you'll see.'

9

Charles and Rosalind arrived at the house the following morning. He stopped the car outside the gates. They were left open, rusty and crooked, clearly not in use. He got out of the car and looked at the house, that was once one of the grandest, and most impressive country estates in the entire land. It was a shattering sight for him to see his old home in such a state of disrepair.

'God! Look at it.'

Rosalind held his arm firmly, ensuring that he knew she was there, to support and comfort him. She looked around the front drive, and the garden, which had been overtaken by weeds and over-grown grass. One flower did, however, stand out, emitting warmth and colour on that cold and grim March morning. The daffodils that had been planted all those years ago, which had made their annual appearance at the start of every spring, but were normally overshadowed by the cascade of colours from other spring blooms, were now the only beacons of light on that grey morning. The exotic and more fragile plants had failed to stand the test of time, without the care of a team of gardeners nurturing their flowering. And although the grass, with its weeds, had overgrown their borders and had eaten through most of the bedding around the garden, the daffodils seemed to have flourished and multiplied.

'Yes, but look at the daffodils,' she replied, pointing to the flowers standing tall, exuding light and beauty, braving the cold March winds.

He stood silent, his despair at seeing the house momentarily diverted by Rosalind's favourite flower. He couldn't count the number of times since his father had died that she had lifted him out of the depression that had accompanied his loss. The irrepressible nature of her character was hard to resist, and at moments such as these, her ability to see through the darkness and bring forward hope to the situation had the effect of liberating him.

'Funny, I've not noticed them before.'

'Look how many there are.' They walked down what was left of the drive, leaving the car at the gates. 'Charles, if you ever own this house and restore it to its former glory, you must keep them. Promise me.'

'Keep what?'

'The daffodils.'

He took his arm away from hers, and put it around her shoulder. 'Of course I will. That makes two promises I'll have to keep if I ever get control of this place again. This one though will be a lot easier to keep.'

'What was the other?'

'To Sam, that I would keep the library intact. That shouldn't be too much of a problem ... they'll all be–' He stopped. A sudden fear enveloped him. A thought that had never previously entered his mind crept into his brain, causing him to shudder. He quickened his step.

'What is it, Charles?'

10

'Hello, Wendy.'

'Charles, how are you? Where are you going? There's nothing there, the books are gone.' He left the empty hall, not noticing that the furniture had disappeared, and opened the library door. The words that Wendy had thrown out echoed around the marble floors, and bounced off the bare walls, but evaded his ears.

He walked into the dark room, and turned on the lights. Shelf after shelf was laid bare. The leather musky smell had gone, to be replaced by a stale odour emanating from the unclean marble floor. He walked around, discovering for the first time just how large the room was. He looked up and saw the golden busts of the great philosophers, writers and scientists, which had now been left to watch over bare empty spaces. He paced the length and breadth of the library, realising now that the first of his promises could not be kept. There was no way he could ever replace what had been there.

'Charles?'

He looked up and saw Rosalind. Even she couldn't help now.

'Everything has been sold, even the china. The house is completely empty. What are you going to do?'

He walked towards her. 'There's not much that I can do, sweetheart. It's strange, but I couldn't really care less about the antiques, or the furniture; even the condition of the house itself, and the grounds I can live with. They can all be replaced or restored.' He stopped and turned round. 'But this ... this is catastrophic.' He looked up at the naked shelves. 'The books were irreplaceable. How will I ever get them back?'

'I don't know.' She placed her arm around his. *'The greatest of all woes / Is to remember times of happiness / In wretchedness,'* she whispered to him.

'Shakespeare?' He looked at her.

'No – Dante.'

Both he and Rosalind walked around the house with Wendy. There was nothing cathartic about the tour. It was more poignant than uplifting as Charles went from room to room, remembering childhood experiences with his father and Janet. When he had completed his visit, he could not leave fast enough. His thoughts turned to Janet, who was now living alone in Scotland. He had managed to keep in contact with the woman who had been a mother to him during his childhood. They would speak at least every month, and sometimes more often. However, he had not seen her since his father's funeral, and he missed her, never more so than at that moment at Hathaway.

'Wendy, here's something to tide you over. And give this to Bill.' He wrote two cheques, each for ten-thousand pounds. 'Please stay in contact, and if you are ever short of money, you will tell me. Ask Bill to do the same. I rather suspect that the new owners will want you to stay.' He smiled. 'Come on, Rosalind. I want to go. This isn't my home anymore.' He kissed Wendy goodbye, and took Rosalind's hand.

'Oh, you don't have to worry about these,' Wendy replied, handing back the cheques. 'Your father provided for us in his will. It was kept separate from your brothers. We have been well looked after. Thank you, anyway. If you want, Charles, I'll tell you who comes round to view the house if you wish.'

'Don't bother. I'm no longer interested in the house,' he called out, walking back to the car.

11

It took a long time for Charles to recover from the visit to his ancestral house on that bleak March day. Having finished helping his tutor at Oxford, he had now moved down to London and bought a four-bedroom house off Mount Street in Mayfair. His trust had been unaffected by his brothers' folly, and as such, he was financially secure. Sir Francis Sutherland was retained as a trustee, and had given him sound advice on his investments. Sir Francis had no idea where the twins were, and given the debacle which they had previously created, he had no real interest in pursuing their whereabouts. The house was almost certainly lost, and the books also. He had, however, managed to keep Charles out of the press using all his contacts, not to mention favours, so that his client preserved a measure of privacy that he felt he was entitled to.

Charles had decided that he wanted to pursue a career in television journalism, and applied for a place on the highly competitive Trainee Assistant Producer programme at the BBC. When he received the news that he had won a place for the following September, it meant that he had four months of free time to play with. Unsatisfied with her weekend trips to London – the only time when he saw Rosalind – his frustration at not being able to see her more often began to gnaw at him. Just when all the other parts of his life were beginning to attain some sort of order, the most important aspect of his happiness, Rosalind, wasn't playing a leading role.

'I miss her during the week. I just don't know if I can wait another two and a half years.'

'Well, don't then.' The old man refilled his client's glass with the 1982 Château-Margaux he had opened for dinner.

'Francis, please don't speak in riddles. What do you mean?'

'You know what I mean. She's a devout Catholic. Charles, you know she won't fully commit to living with you ... and I mean living with you in the conjugal sense, until you–'

'Yes, yes, I know. But I'm only twenty-six.'

336

'So is she.'

'Yes, but marriage, Francis. It's such a big step. I mean, look at Sam and Raveena. They've been living together for five years, and haven't tied the knot.'

'What's the matter, Charles? Aren't you sure?' The question did not warrant a response. There was nobody in the entire world who was more certain of being in love than Charles Longhurst. 'It seems to me, dear boy, that you need to ask that wonderful young lady a very important question.' He lifted his glass of claret and raised it to his young client. 'Cheers! Come on, drink up, man, we've got a whole bottle to finish. I'm not wasting a drop!'

Charles left at ten, straight after dinner. He hailed a taxi, and went straight to Paddington. Catching the next available train to Oxford, he sat in the empty second-class compartment as it shuffled interminably along the line, eventually arriving at its destination after an hour and a half of mental torture. In his eagerness to disembark he leapt off the train before it had properly stopped at the platform, and then dashed across the concourse to the taxi rank. Hands in pockets, pulling down his dark-blue Crombie coat, he paced up and down the taxi rank, waiting for the next car to arrive. It had begun to rain, which added to his anxiety about the obvious lack of available taxis. The angst was short-lived as a maroon-coloured licensed Vauxhall slowed down to pick him up.

'Where to?'

'Woodstock ... the village ... Blenheim?' He

337

wasn't sure if the driver was being stupid, or whether he was a complete novice and simply didn't know the area.

'I know, I know. Well, get in then.'

Charles opened the back door and got in. The contrast to the train journey could not have been more marked. The car raced through town and on to the ring road. 'We should be there in five minutes now,' the bald-headed overweight driver commented, as if he were talking to himself.

'Very good,' Charles replied, sitting a little uneasily at the speed at which the taxi was swallowing up the miles. As happy as he was at the rapidity of this final leg of the journey, he began to wonder whether he would reach the village of Woodstock alive, let alone in one piece. 'Tell me, how fast does this car go?'

'Oh, about 90,' the driver replied, suddenly pushing the gear up from fourth to fifth.

'And how fast are you going now?'

'Oh, about 93!' He turned around, and smiled, revealing a row of uneven teeth, with varying colours ranging from yellow to black.

'And how far is it?' Having seen the red colour of his face and preferring not to think about the colour of his teeth, Charles just wanted the journey to end.

'Oh, it's only a couple of miles, won't be long now. Anyway, I have to get back to the pub.'

Charles closed his eyes and prayed for the first time since his father had died. 'If there is a God up there, please just get me there,' he thought to himself.

The car arrived at the picturesque village,

slowing down as rapidly as it had taken off outside Oxford. 'Thank you very much.' Charles got out of the car and gave the driver 10 pounds, which included a 20 percent gratuity. He wasn't sure why he had been so generous to the person who had put him through such a purgatorial experience. Perhaps it was because of the relief he felt that he was still alive. What was certain was that the driver with the red face, and with the multicoloured teeth, would be drinking away any gratuity he received in a very short time, if he survived the return trip.

12

He waited until the taxi had disappeared, and then turned around and looked at the cottage. It seemed so small, now that he had moved on to the capital and lived in a relatively substantial house in one of the most desirable areas of London. It was pouring with rain, making him feel even more grateful that he had survived the car journey from Oxford. All the lights were off. It was well past 11.30. He suddenly felt uncertain. He hesitated. Indecision overtook him. He stayed frozen to the spot, staring at the dark-brown timber door. Slowly he lifted his hand and pressed the doorbell. He waited, for what seemed like an eternity. He sensed the conflicting emotions of not wanting her to come down so that he could go back home and think about the entire situation more carefully; but also the desperate desire for her to open that door and see her face, see her exquisite beauty, feel her radiant warmth, and let her presence overtake him, as it always did.

She opened the door, her face, in his mind, suddenly lighting the immediate area. 'Will you marry me, Rosalind?'

She stared back at him. She had waited for those words for the last ten years, ever since she first saw him from her bedroom window at Roedean. The words, sweet-sounding, almost lyrical to her ears, made her laugh.

'What?'

'Didn't you hear me?'

'Yes, of course I did. But I want to hear it again!'

'Do you want me to go down on one knee?'

'No, I just want you to ask me again!'

'Will you marry me?'

She stepped towards him and put her arms around his neck. She felt the rain falling on her hair, and then all over her face, and on to her dressing gown. He was soaking, the water relentlessly falling on him, forming a drip at the end of his nose. She withdrew her hands and caressed his cheeks. She pulled his face gently towards hers, brushing her parted lips against his. She kissed him, not once, but over and over again. He responded, kissing her back, his tongue returning the pleasure, losing himself in the luxury of the moment. He suddenly pulled his head back.

'Well?' he asked.

'Of course I will.'

He held her waist, and began to shiver. 'Charles, are you all right?'

'Yes, I think so. It's just the excitement.'

She pulled him inside into the dry and warmth. 'Come on, you have to get these clothes off, they're soaking.' She took his coat off, and then his jacket.

'Wait. Rosalind, you know what I've been through, and the mess the whole family's in. You understand that there will be more press, and more exposure in some form or another. Are you sure you want to commit to me with all the baggage?'

'I've never been more sure. I've wanted to marry you since I first met you. This is the happiest moment of my life, Charles.'

He was holding her hand, staring deep into her large dark-brown eyes, searching, desperately wanting to know, how and why someone could be so perfect. He touched her cheek with the tips of his fingers, and then stroked them down around her mouth. Delicate and refined, her beauty was consummate. 'I love you,' he whispered.

'I know.'

He kissed her again, but this time, with more passion, his mouth meeting hers fully open, their lips together in unison, their tongues searching inside, exploring each other more forcefully. He pulled off her dressing gown. She was wearing a cotton nightgown. 'I want you now, Rosalind.'

'I can't, Charles. You know that.'

'It's been almost three years now since we started going out. You don't know how hard it is not to–'

'It's no easier for me. You must understand that.'

'Well frankly I don't. This is your decision, and I've accepted it throughout the relationship. But now that we're going to get married, surely that's enough for you.'

'Charles, I won't break my vows. You know that, you know how important it is to me ... and to my mother. I gave her my word. I promised her.' She was resolute, and would not compromise. Born a devout Catholic, she had never lost her belief in Christ, and the sanctity of marriage. There was no way that she would break her vows now. She was so close, she wasn't going to throw it all away in a mad moment of salacious wantonness. She was better than that.

He realised that she would not give in. He slowly took the straps of her negligee, and lifted them from off her shoulder, and let it drop to the ground. She was standing naked in front of him, and yet she remained out of his reach. He kissed her neck gently, accepting her decision. The passion of the moment had seemingly disappeared, as his lips moved down to her breasts. She quivered, as she experienced the pleasure that his tongue on her nipples gave her. He moved down further, kissing her, his lips like a butterfly hovering above her skin, making contact intermittently. Reaching her naval, his tongue probed the orifice, and she responded in a similar manner. 'You have to stop,' she gasped, as she collapsed on to the floor. She was losing her control, as he continued his attention around her stomach, moving slowly downwards.

She desperately tried to move before he reached her inside, and finally succeeded in pull-

342

ing his face up to hers. 'Charles, my darling,' she said as she kissed him, 'you have to stop.'

He smiled and nodded. He had waited for so long, a few more weeks wouldn't matter. She embraced him, more closely and more tightly than ever before. It was an envelopment of love; a seal on their commitment; an acceptance by her of his devotion. Marriage was the natural outcome for this relationship, which had now run its course as a mere courtship.

13

Raveena Shah was studying at home for an exam, in her final year at medical school, when she heard the news of her best friend's engagement.

'I can't believe it!' she screamed down the public telephone in the hospital waiting area.

'Why?'

'You're going to beat me to the altar!'

'Oh I never doubted it! After all, it's been over ten years!'

'Rosalind! How could you have been so sure? You weren't even seeing him for seven of those years.'

'I know. But I just knew!'

'When is it going to be?'

'In the summer some time. We haven't got a date yet, but probably July. It will be in Brighton at St Joseph's. It was where my parents got married, and my mother has already promised Father Docherty that he can marry us. He must be at least eighty by now, but I'm pleased. He married Mummy and Daddy, and he confirmed me, and has literally known me all of my life.'

'A white wedding, a truly white wedding, in an English summer. It doesn't get more romantic.'

'I can't wait.'

'I bet you can't. You must be the last virgin to get married in their mid-twenties. Definitely the last, as good-looking as you.' Raveena still could not understand how Rosalind had kept her chastity. She could not comprehend the willpower, and strength of resolve that her best friend had in her beliefs.

'You would be surprised.'

'I would be – if there was another one around!' She paused. 'Do you think he would have married you, if you had slept with him?'

'I don't know. I never really thought about it,' she replied, slightly puzzled by the question. 'Do you think Sam would have asked you, if you hadn't.'

'Christ! that's a good question ... why do you keep doing that?'

'What?'

'Turn the tables back on me. I'm going to have to ask him now!' She paused. 'Listen, why don't you come down this Friday? It's Sam's father's birthday, and he's having a big dinner party at home. He'd love to have you over. He's always going on about you, and asking how you're getting on, since meeting you that time when he caught me and Sam in bed. He was captivated by you. That makes a change,' she said facetiously.

'I'd love to come. I'll speak to Charles, but maybe you should check first?'

'Don't worry. Listen, I have to go. And Rosalind, it's so great, I can't tell you how happy I am for you.' Raveena's pager was bleeping. She hung up hurriedly. She rushed to the ward, where her patient needed her. She felt elated. Her best friend, her soulmate and confidante; the most complete person, certainly the most virtuous, was attaining what she had always wanted. 'A prince, for the most Christian of princesses,' she whispered to herself as she ran.

14

Sam met Charles at a local Italian restaurant in Mount Street. They had maintained a closeness, despite Charles having been at Oxford and Sam being away in Brussels. They always managed to meet up somewhere, making time to keep in contact. Their friendship, forged in those five years at school, was as strong as it always had been. It was different to Raveena and Rosalind's relationship, which was as perfect an example of female bonding as one could achieve. Nevertheless, there was little that either boy would not talk about to the other.

'So, you finally asked her.'

'Yes, Sam, I did. And just to stop you from asking; no, I haven't slept with her ... in the conjugal sense.'

'Well, that explains it, then.'

'What?'

'Sex, of course ... or the lack of it. Don't beat yourself up over it. You're a normal man, who has needs. I don't blame you. But there are other things to consider in a relationship–' Sam was talking as if he were the doyen of partnerships.

'Sam,' Charles stopped him from carrying on. He sounded preposterous. 'I accept that there is an element of truth in what you say, but it really isn't just the pent-up desire and frustration that has driven me to this decision. We do have sex, just not full intercourse.'

'Oh, right then.' Sam was taken a bit by surprise. He had an image of Rosalind not letting Charles near her. She was so perfect, almost inviolably so, that the thought of his friend committing some sexual act, upset him. It was appalling to think that Rosalind would let him touch her.

'It's much more than that.' He paused. 'I don't want anyone else. I can't even conceive of a moment when I would even think that that I would want anybody else. She is everything to me. Do you understand?' He looked at Sam.

'I can't think of a better reason.' He drank his water, thinking about what Charles had just said. He suddenly felt envious of his friend, in that he could feel such passion and love, even after being with her for almost three years. Maybe they were right to have waited. Marriage to them would truly be a sacrament.

'Will you be my best man?' He waited for his friend to respond.

'Will you be mine?'

'What? When?'

'When I ask her, and she accepts!' Sam had suddenly realised that living with Raveena, and sharing her bed, had chilled the passion and had blunted the intensity of their love, jeopardising the one thing in the world that he wanted. His wish to share the rest of his life with Raveena Shah was being compromised by the carefree, easygoing relationship that they were now experiencing. He needed her commitment, and Charles' decision focused his mind on attaining it. Both he and Raveena in the past had ridiculed their friends' relationship, and in particular Rosalind's religious beliefs on purity and the sanctity of marriage. But now Sam had woken up to the fact that the joke could be on them. He was not going to allow it to happen. He resolved to follow their example. He only hoped that Raveena would accept, and after which, his father give his blessing.

'Good luck,' Charles responded.

'I'll need it. Listen. My father's having a birthday dinner. Rav mentioned it to Rosalind, I forgot to tell you, but he said I could invite you both.'

'I'm surprised he wants us there. I haven't seen him for such a long time!'

'Well he does. I think its more for me and Rav. Anyway, Friday, eight o'clock.'

'We'll look forward to it.'

15

It was while they were walking down Davies Street on the way to his father's party, approaching the north end of Berkeley Square, that Sam asked Raveena to marry him.

The response was nothing if not predictable.

'I suppose Charles had something to do with this?' She stopped him from going any further.

'Yes, he did ... but not in the way you think.' He continued to walk towards the square.

'What do you mean?' she asked, following in his footsteps.

'I mean, you are the most important person to me. I can't think of a life without you. By living the way we do, there's a danger that we're taking everything for granted. The commitment, the responsibility, the obligation, even our love for each other, is at risk while there is no vow to keep us together. Don't you see, Rav? It's all just a bit too easy.'

'But there are no guarantees, anyway. What difference does a piece of paper make? You know my feelings on religion. I don't believe in any of it. If you want a young virgin to promise undying love, be my guest and go and look for one.'

'So you don't believe in undying love then.'

'I didn't say that.'

'Yes you did. You're so obsessed with the absurdity of religious sanctity, that you've missed the point. I'm asking you to marry me – nothing more, nothing less. We can do it in a temple, a synagogue, a mosque or a registry office – I really don't care, darling.' He paused. 'But I would very much like you to come out of the road because your very existence is in significant danger!' He was so calm, so assured in his manner, he knew that he had won the day. It was only a question of how long it would take her to realise it.

She looked at him, fixed to the spot. She

suddenly became conscious of the fact that he had just asked her to spend the rest of her life with him, and she had responded in the most brutal and undeserving fashion. He was making a commitment, and it was that very pledge that she found difficult to make herself. She would have to make that covenant if she wanted to keep him. Pulling herself together, she walked slowly across the road, opened her arms, and jumped into his.

'I'm sorry, darling.' She kissed him forcefully on the cheek and then on his lips.

'Is that a "yes", then?' he asked, laughing.

'It's a yes!'

16

Sam and Raveena entered the party, holding each other's hand tightly. Forty of the fifty guests had already arrived, and were enjoying the vintage Krug champagne that was being poured liberally into their glasses. The Bernstein parties were sumptuous white-tie affairs. The food was prepared by the best chefs in the city, and the wines were carefully selected by the old man himself, brought up from his cellar. The perfectly chilled Montrachet was normally the preferred white, whilst a Petrus was the favoured red. Abraham Bernstein had come a long way from the shtetls of Eastern Europe, and he knew it.

Although still not being fully welcomed by the establishment, he was happy to invite its members into his home. But these guests were his friends, who had recognised his achievements in industry, as well as his generosity in charity. Constantly rebuffed from being honoured, despite enormous donations to hospitals, museums and schools, the length and breadth of the country, he had now resigned himself that it was the one war he would and could not win.

Sam saw his mother first and asked her to join him and Raveena in the study. He quickly searched around for his father, and having found him, prised him away from the chief executive of Britain's largest clearing bank and led him into the study.

'Mother, father. I wanted tell you that Raveena and I are going to marry.'

'That's wonderful!' His mother got up and hugged her youngest son, and then her future daughter-in-law.

Sam looked at his father, waiting for the reaction. He had accepted the relationship for what it was. He had come a long way to full acceptance. His other three sons, who never came near to his ambitions, had dutifully married within the faith. Perhaps it was because of their mediocrity that they chose what their father wanted, lacking the courage to do anything else. Although his own religious beliefs were nonexistent, it still hurt that his greatest hope, the one son who had fulfilled his own dreams, was seeing someone who could not trace their ancestry back to Moses. This was the ultimate test for him. The choice was to jettison the hypocrisy of his own position regarding the faith and keep a son whom he loved more than life itself, or stand by the false standard he had set himself and lose everything. He sat motionless, weighing everything up.

He got up, and walked towards Raveena. 'Welcome to our family.' He embraced her, closing his eyes, and felt a tear roll down his cheek. It was the first time he had cried since leaving his mother 65 years earlier. He let go. 'Come on, then, let's really enjoy tonight! Leah, will you accompany me, my dear?'

'It will be my pleasure.' They walked out, followed by his heir and his fiancée.

17

Charles and Rosalind arrived late, to the slight consternation of their host, whose penchant for punctuality was well known.

'Where have you been?' Sam asked them, clearly ill at ease with their tardiness.

'It was Rosalind – she took hours.'

Rosalind looked at Charles disdainfully. Rising above his accusation she chose not to respond, and walked forward to reacquaint herself with Sam's father. She managed to find him sitting in the corner of the room, chatting to a number of guests.

'Mr Bernstein, thank you so much for inviting us. And happy birthday. No, don't get up.' She bent down and kissed the old man's cheek.

'Thank you, and I am very pleased that you and Charles could come. I assume you've heard about Raveena and Sam?' He looked up at her, and felt the same way as he did all those years ago. She radiated a quality that was ethereal, and the effect on him was electrifying.

'Well, I knew they'd get married, after I'd decided to tie the knot!' she replied in her usual irrepressible manner. Both Charles and she knew that Sam was about to pop the question some time that evening.

He laughed. 'Well I'm glad you finally have arrived because we can now go and eat!'

'Yes, I'm sorry we were late ... but men, they're so slow.' She took his arm as they followed the rest of the guests into the main room where the tables were laid.

The sight of the silver cutlery, placed alongside the Copenhagen Flora Dannica china, and Baccarat crystal, was dazzling. 'What do you think?' he whispered into her ear.

'Impressive – spectacular,' she replied.

'Mr Bernstein, thank you for inviting us. I am very sorry we were late but–'

'Don't worry, Charles. I've known you long enough. You don't have to stand on ceremony. It's not a problem.' Charles looked at him, knowing that the complete opposite was true. He had been at the Bernsteins' house many times, and was well aware that formality was the acknowledged norm. 'Anyway, Rosalind has told me that you were the one responsible. You should never keep a lady waiting, especially not your fiancée, and particularly not one as beautiful as her!'

'What?' Charles looked at Rosalind. He knew the truth, but whatever he said would not make any difference. As usual she had captured both the host and the high ground and would not be moved. He could never win against such formidable opposition. Perhaps that was one of the reasons why he loved her so much.

18

The evening was one that very few people would ever forget. The main reason was not due to the announcement that his son was getting married, but because Abraham Bernstein, at the age of seventy-three, had decided to retire. He would leave his company, and sell half of his vast shareholding, to concentrate more fully on his philanthropic duties. The Bernstein Foundation would keep its share-holding in the company, now worth over £250 million, and give out more than £15 million annually to charitable causes.

'It's been a wonderful voyage. I started in rough waters...' He paused and reflected for a moment, '...stormy waters. But I found a smooth passage, here in this great country of yours. It has been very kind to me, and my entire family.' He smiled and looked towards his children. 'I've had a very good navigator, without whom I would never have achieved what I have done.' He then looked down to his beloved wife, seated next to him. 'Still, it's now time to move on. My two eldest sons will go on to the board, to look after the family's interests. Thank you, everybody, for everything. God bless you all, because each and every one of you has helped and been part of it.' He sat down to tumultuous applause.

The men later retired into the library, and some

of the elders started to reminisce about the ups and downs of the past property cycles.

'Well you can be relieved that you never got Farringdon.' Sir Evelyn Carter sat down with his brandy, and continued, 'It's an absolute disaster. There'll be no lifeboat, I can assure you. Those Longhursts have left a real bloody mess.'

Abraham Bernstein looked up, and saw Charles looking at the books with Sam. He saw the tall, fair, statuesque young man glance across at the mention of the Longhurst name. Charles had indeed overheard the comment.

'Steady, Evelyn. You might upset one of my guests.'

'Why is that then?'

'Charles.' He beckoned him over. 'Let me introduce you to Sir Evelyn Carter, chairman of the Bank of England. Evelyn, this is my son's closest friend. Indeed he has become a friend of the family. His name is Charles, Charles Longhurst.'

'Oh, I'm frightfully sorry. You must be the youngest son. I know that you're not involved. But your brothers have–'

'I know.' He cut him short. 'It's nothing to do with me though. All I have lost is my family house, and all its contents ... apart from a solitary book, which father gave me before he died.' He paused. 'Actually even that's not true.'

'Why is that then?'

'Well, he gave it to Rosalind. It's a First Folio edition of Shakespeare, and she just loves Shakespeare.' He smiled.

'It's a very valuable book, Charles.'

'Yes, I know.' He stood uncomfortably in front of the two older men. He then remembered the original comment. 'Mr Bernstein, can I ask you a question?'

'Of course, but you can now call me Abraham.'

'What did Farringdon have to do with you?'

'I never told you this before, Charles. I respected the fact that it had nothing to do with you, and I also knew how fond Sam was of you.' He lifted his glass of cognac and drank a large gulp. 'The Farringdon site was one of the greatest opportunities I have ever come across. It was an unbelievably large, unencumbered site. I made the highest bid. I had the best architect, and we had produced the best model – a mixed scheme composing of retail units, residential apartments, as well as offices. We also had leisure in there with a sports centre. I was so confident. The vendor, a consortium of old private trusts and local authorities, had even told me that I was the preferred bidder. But then something went wrong. My telephone calls went unanswered, and everything went quiet. I subsequently found out that your brothers had won the bid.'

'Had they done anything wrong?'

'Well, at first, I thought not. But then I found out that they had bid significantly less than I had done. It also later transpired that various people had taken bribes – up to £10 million. It was rumoured that your father might have been involved. I later had investigators look into the money transit. It transpired that your father did invest in some equity, but it was his money, unbeknownst to him, that they used to grease the palms of those selling.'

'But as Sir Evelyn says, you must be relieved. It's a catastrophe.'

'That's because they developed the wrong scheme. Putting up an office tower, with so much space, was bound to be a disaster. The plan was driven by greed. With hindsight it was a monumental error. Still, the banks are now licking their wounds. And after the way they behaved, particularly with me, I can't say I'm sorry.'

'Nor can I,' Charles replied, looking at Sam's father and at once feeling a certain amount of empathy with him. 'It's strange, don't you think, that you and I share the same bitterness with regard to that episode. I lost everything because of their avarice and folly.'

'In some ways, yes, and in others no. Materially you have lost much more than I did. But emotionally, I was hurt, and scarred. For me it was a wonderful opportunity to change the landscape of an area of London that really needs investment. But actually, Charles, it was more than just that. Certain issues were confirmed to me there and then. The establishment closed ranks, and I didn't stand a chance. Yes the behaviour of your brothers was disgusting, but I could sense that the banks, the institutions, everyone, was against me. I've now learnt that however successful I was, however much charity I give, and as hardworking and industrious I am, I will never be accepted ... and for that, I am resentful, bitterly resentful.'

'I understand,' Charles muttered, for the first time beginning to understand the complexities of the old man.

'Do you?' He looked at the young aristocrat. He was part of everything that he now despised with a hatred that would not be sated until he had his revenge. And yet, looking at Charles Longhurst, he also understood that he was innocent. Although physically he could not hide his background, he realised that Charles was a world away from his genetic roots. Here was an honest, decent young man, who had also almost been destroyed by his own people.

'Yes, I think I do.'

'Christ, Abraham, I hope you don't think we're all against you!' Sir Evelyn said rather loudly.

Abraham looked around. 'Of course not. Everyone here is an exception in his own right. Supportive and loyal, they are my real friends. That's why you have been invited. But – I mean it Evelyn – I will get my revenge, and innocent people might get hurt.'

Evelyn raised his eyebrows and glanced at Charles. The young man nodded at his host, and wandered back to Sam who was talking to one of his brothers by the books.

19

'My father been giving you a hard time?' Sam asked Charles, who looked slightly shaken.

'No, not really. It's me really. I think I understand him a bit more now. It's about time ... I've only known him for over ten years!'

'You'll never fully understand him, Charles.'

357

'Probably not. Sam, did you know about his involvement in Farringdon?'

'Not at the time, of course not. The first I knew of it was when your brothers left the country. I didn't want to raise it because of what you'd been through.'

'No, I understand.' Charles looked at the books. He was reminded of the Hathaway Library, as he looked up and down at the rows of books, shelved in immaculate order. He walked slowly away towards the far end of the room. Alone, deep in thought, his attention was suddenly diverted by the sweet voice of Rosalind. 'Charles, are you all right?'

He turned around, and saw her. He felt relief and then gratitude, when he heard her voice.

'Yes. I am now.' He put his hand through her free-flowing auburn hair.

'Look at these books. Oh my God! I don't believe it!'

'What?' Charles asked, turning towards the shelves.

'Look!' She pointed to a turquoise-coloured leatherbound boxed book on the shelf.

Charles said nothing, but pulled the tome down from the shelf. It was, in fact, a box. The inscription on the front described its contents. *'The History Of England From The Accession Of James the Second. Volume One. Thomas Babington Macaulay.'* But it was the engraving on the binding of the box that struck like a thunderbolt. He placed his finger, and stroked it against the gold letters *'HH'* that were emblazoned across the front cover of the box. He opened the lid, and saw a perfect copy of one of the great histories written by western man.

'It's beautiful. At least it's found a good home.' He turned around and called out to Abraham Bernstein, who was now in deep conversation with Sir Evelyn Carter. 'Excuse me, Abraham,' (he still had difficulty in calling his host by his first name). 'When did you buy this?' He held the book aloft.

'Is that the Macaulay?' He recognised the box.

'Yes.'

'My dealer procured it for me. I had been looking for one in perfect condition for years. If you look on the frontispiece you'll see it's been signed by the great man himself. He did very well. Mind you, he demanded payment within 24 hours. A bit unlike him.'

'Why?'

'I've been dealing with him for years. He's never actually asked for payment. He's always assumed, knowing who I am, that he would get paid. He's a very good man though. If you ever want to collect first editions, or manuscripts, I would recommend him – Bernard Shapeman. He's in St George Street.'

20

Charles and Rosalind left the party late that evening. Walking slowly through the streets of Mayfair, their conversation was mostly taken up with the news of Sam and Raveena's announcement.

'Aren't you a little put out?'

'No. Should I be?'

'Well, it's just that it might take something away from you.'

Rosalind laughed. She hadn't even thought about that. 'No, not at all. I'm really happy for them, particularly for Rav. It's just wonderful that we are all moving along the same path. I'm really excited.'

'I think I was responsible for it.'

'Why? What did you say to Sam?'

'I just pointed out the error of his ways, I suppose.' He opened the door, and waited for her to walk in. 'I was being slightly judgemental, but he seems to have taken the point!'

She laughed as they went upstairs. She was exhausted, and knew that when her head hit the pillow, she would immediately surrender herself to sleep. He went into the study, and poured himself a brandy, and walked over to his own bookshelves. He went straight to the turquoise-leather box, lying against a book rest, separated from the others. He pulled it down and opened it. He rarely looked at it. The memory of the library was still very raw. But tonight, having seen one of the books in somebody else's study, a sort of closure appeared to have been brought down to bear on him. For the first time, on opening the box, he didn't feel the terrible wrench of agony and bitterness, nor the misery and resentment of his misfortune.

He took the book, the first collected edition of Shakespeare's works, and opened it. He was no expert, but he felt the weight of greatness in the book, and saw the beauty in the words. He had never discussed it with Rosalind, who had left the book with Charles for safekeeping at his house. He went straight to the *Tragedy of King Lear,* the play he had studied at A level, and read through some of the more famous passages in the first act, grimacing at Kent's brief but candid remark of what happens when *'majesty falls to folly.'* He continued, but was feeling tired. He laughed ironically at Gloucester's poignant, and prophetic speech in scene two. Finally he placed the book down, open, and retired to bed.

Love cools, friendship falls off, brothers divide; in cities mutinies; in countries, discord; in palaces, treason; and the bond cracked 'twixt son and father. The villain of mine comes under the prediction: there's son against father. The king falls from bias of nature; there's father against child.

21

The First Folio, published in 1623, seven years after the poet's death, was unprecedented at the time since there had never been a folio devoted entirely to plays. It was the first collected edition of Shakespeare's drama and contained 36 of his plays. It was probably the brainchild of Shakespeare's fellow actors and friends in the King's men, his acting company, in particular John Hemminges and Henry Condell. The 900-page volume took over two years to complete, and was so successful at the time that a second, third and fourth folio followed in the following 60 years. But the most valuable edition is the first. With 600 printed, only 300 survive, most of which are in institutions. Over 80 are housed in the Folger Shakespeare Library, the world's leading institution on the playwright, located in Washington. The number in private hands is estimated to be five, and not all of them are in a complete state. None of them could compare with the immaculate condition of the copy lying on the table, opened, in Charles Longhurst's study. The value of it ranged from £3½ to £5 million depending on its condition: an enormous amount of money, but a realistic sum in light of the fact that this was the most important work in the English language.

All of this was not lost on Rosalind Blackstone. Soon to complete a spectacular thesis on 'Shakespearean tragedies and the birth of modern psychoanalysis' for her doctorate, she was well aware of the significance of the book. The monetary value was of no interest to her, but its relevance to contemporary life – its impact on the way we think and speak, and its influence on the way we react and relate to others – was very important to her. It was quite simply the canon upon which her entire life was based.

She woke early the morning after the party. Seeing that Charles was still sleeping, she carefully pulled on his towelling robe over her pyjama bottoms and sleeveless white cotton vest. She hadn't fully moved in as yet; that would happen after the wedding in the summer. She then tiptoed out of the room and down the stairs. Going straight into the kitchen, she put the coffee on. She went to the front door to fetch the paper. She turned round with *The Times* under her arm, and walked back to the kitchen. She sat waiting for the coffee to percolate through to the jug. She scanned through the headlines of the morning paper. When the coffee finally finished brewing, she slowly wandered into the study, with the cup in one hand, and the paper in the other.

As she entered the study, she noticed the First Folio, out of its box, and opened at Gloucester's speech in *King Lear.* She had rarely opened the box since that dreadful night when Charles' father had died. She was too in awe of its contents to enjoy it. If she had let herself go, and gorged herself on the feast that was on offer in the turquoise-leather box, she would never have had time to read or do anything else. It was a treasure in its own right, but to her, a student of the poet and an avid devotee of his writing, it was a prize, a nonpareil.

She placed the newspaper and the coffee on the table and then went towards the Folio. She lifted the front cover from its resting place, and brought it forward to close the book. As she did so, something caught her attention. With the movement of the binding, a page, unlike the others, moved out. Not straight, jutting out at an angle, it looked like the edge of a manuscript rather than a page from the folio itself. She placed her fingers towards the loose sheet, and pulled back the pages. She breathed in deeply as she saw the offending leaf, now resting loose from the rest of the book. She felt her heartbeat quicken as she tried to absorb the writing on the paper. It was written in black ink, the body of which was clearly legible, from a different age. She lifted the manuscript away from the book, and walked towards the window, to let the spring-morning sunlight illuminate the scrawl.

She already knew what was written. Moving to the window was a manoeuvre to give her more time to take in the enormity of the words that were inscribed on the paper. To an unread person, the writing might have appeared familiar, but to an expert in Shakespeare, it was an integral part of one's reading. The top of the page was worn out, but the first words were instantly recognisable:

With love's light wings did I o'er perch these walls;
For stony limits cannot hold love out.

Her eyes moved down the script, skipping over the deletions and various stage directions, faster than she wanted, eating up the most beautiful poetry written by man. She managed to stop briefly at certain lines:

O, swear not by the moon, the inconstant moon,
That monthly changes in her circled orb,
Lest that thy love prove likewise variable.

And then:

This bud of love, by summer's ripening breath,
May prove a beauteous flower when next we meet.

She finally reached the bottom of the page, and a tear formed as she read the most celebrated poetry of this most famous scene:

My bounty is as boundless as the sea,
My love as deep; the more I give to thee,
The more I have, for both are infinite.

She held on to the manuscript, staring at the words. At the bottom right hand corner were the initials *'WS'* scribbled in the same handwriting as the rest of the script. She knew immediately what it was, and how important its consequences would be. The excitement made her shake. She called out for Charles, but her larynx was paralysed by the sheer enormity of the document she was holding. She took in another deep breath, and screamed his name.

Charles sat upright in a sudden jolt, woken by his name being screamed across the house. He ran down the stairs, wearing only his boxer shorts, dashing into the kitchen.

'Where are you? What's the matter?'

'I'm here, in the study!'

He ran into the study to find her sitting in a chair holding a brownish manuscript in her hand. He could see that she was shaking and that she had been crying. 'What is it, Rosalind? What's in your hand?' Charles was disturbed not just by her present state, but also because the reaction was so out of character for the woman he loved.

'Don't worry, Charles. I'm not upset ... just dumbstruck. Look!' She carefully lifted the manuscript and showed it to her fiancé.

He took it from her and looked at it. 'Romeo and Juliet. Where did you find it?'

'In the Folio. It was inside the text. Someone had obviously put it there, and had forgotten about it.'

'Great. But why the reaction? It's as if you had seen a ghost or something.'

'Look at the initials. This will finally put an end to all the prejudice and snobbery. It was a working-class boy, a son of a glovemaker from Stratford who wrote the plays after all. God, I hope this is real. Charles, look at the writing – think about its context and location,' she said, trying to make him see what she already in her heart knew.

He looked at the bottom right-hand corner of the paper, and saw the initials. He looked up at her. 'No! You surely don't think that this is–'

'Yes– Yes, I do, Charles,' she interrupted him. 'Proving it will, I admit, be a problem. Currently there is a whole conflict on "who" and "what" Shakespeare was. The controversies surrounding the textual theory, and involving reviser and catholic arguments, dominate intellectual and academic debate. If I'm right, a lot of people, some of whom have very large reputations, with even larger egos, are going to be very disappointed. But I'm convinced. I can feel it.'

He looked at the script. 'Why are you so sure?'

'The folio was put together by the Company of the King's Men, an acting group of which Shakespeare was part. They were his friends, and they wanted to keep his memory alive. To get the thing published, they had to collate, from the manuscripts, complete and incomplete, all the plays. In reality, only they would have had the originals, since they learnt their lines from them. When the Folio was finally published, they probably felt that it was unnecessary to keep the manuscripts. It is perfectly possible that one of them missed out this sheet, and kept it in his copy of the published Folio, and simply forgot about it.' She paused. 'Look – I might be adding two and two and making five, but it's a possibility!'

'But are there any other manuscripts he wrote that survive?'

'No... Well at the British Museum there's a manuscript of the play *Thomas More* which some believe was written in Shakespeare's hand. There are a number of legal documents around, like his will, which was signed by him. In fact that is the one piece of handwriting that we are certain was Shakespeare's – his signature.'

'It's amazing that no manuscripts were saved. I mean, you would think someone would have realised how important he was.'

'That's just it, Charles. Nothing like this has survived ... if, of course, it's real.'

'What shall we do?'

'We must get some advice. What was the name of the book dealer in St George Street who sold Abraham Bernstein the Macaulay?'

'Bernard Shapeman.'

'Why don't we talk to him? He's supposed to be an expert in old books and manuscripts. I mean I've never heard of him, but if the old man uses him, he must be good.'

'Yes, OK then, get dressed and we'll go.' He was anxious to meet the antiquarian book dealer anyway. He wanted to learn what had happened to the library, and he was sure that Shapeman could provide him with answers.

'Right. What – now?'

'Why not? I mean, if you're right and it's real, the manuscript could be one of the most important finds ever.'

22

Having washed and dressed, Charles carefully put the manuscript into a plastic cover and placed it in his briefcase. Rosalind was already waiting for him at the door. The short walk across Mayfair to St George Street took just over fifteen minutes. There was not a cloud in the sky on that early May morning, as the young couple arrived at the bookshop. Rosalind felt that it was a special time. Spring was now being overtaken by summer. The days were now somewhat brighter than in April, and the temperate breeze that brushed through the branches of the trees, had a newfound warmth to it.

Charles pushed open the glass door. 'Hello. Is Mr Shapeman available?'

'Yes, sir. Who, might I ask, wants to meet him?'

'My name is Charles Longhurst.'

'Very good, sir. Please wait here and I'll try and locate him.' He disappeared upstairs. Charles wandered over to the sash window, and looked out across the road. Sotheby's, opposite, was advertising a major Post-Impressionist Sale the following week, and their back entrance had a giant sized Seurat hanging on its wall. He stared at the giant painting, and then watched various people go into the showrooms.

Rosalind had walked in the opposite direction and was looking at the shelves of books. And it was not just the shelves that were packed with them. The wooden floor, particularly at the back end, was covered with piles of books. There was very little space to walk around and appreciate the vast array of what was on offer. Most of the books related to travel. The Literature section was at the back of the shop. She managed to walk around, climbing over the various stacks, and finally immerse herself in the Austen section.

'Good morning. Oh, I'm sorry about the mess back there. It looks chaotic but, I promise you, there is some method in the madness!' Bernard Shapeman, dressed in a light grey suit and a white open-necked shirt, had come down from his office.

'Oh, don't worry. You have a lot of books,' Rosalind responded to the genial book dealer.

'This is just the rebound stuff.' He stopped for a moment, having set eyes on Rosalind. He was taken aback by the young woman. She had a presence about her that he was unfamiliar with; it wasn't just that she had a rare beauty and elegance. It was more than that, but he didn't know what. He recovered his composure. 'Most of it is made up of collections, and libraries that I've bought. The really good stuff is upstairs.'

'Really?' She looked across to Charles, who had now turned round, and was looking on.

'Mr Shapeman–'

'Bernard, please!' he interrupted. He hated

formality, without compromising correctness.

'Bernard, this is my fiancée, Rosalind Blackstone, and my name is Charles Longhurst.' He continued, 'We need your advice, but I would prefer it if we could go upstairs.'

'Certainly – but what is it you want?' The antiquarian book dealer, at first, made no connection with the name and Hathaway House.

'Well, it's more about what we already have, but I really would like to show you in private.'

'Yes, yes, of course. Follow me.'

23

The three of them walked upstairs to the first floor. They walked through another showroom, which housed artefacts as diverse as old globes, maps and manuscripts. The shelves were filled with giant encyclopaedic tomes, beautifully bound in various leather bindings. After walking through, the shop owner took his key out from his pocket and opened the locked door.

'Please, come in.' He ushered in his visitors. He didn't know what all this was about, but he felt something special was about to happen. He sat down behind his bureau, and waited for Charles to tell him what he had.

Charles lifted the briefcase up, and placed it on the desk. He undid the buckle, and pulled out the plastic file. 'What do you make of this?' He handed it over to him.

Bernard Shapeman had seen many things in his twenty-year career. Books and artefacts of extravagant beauty had crossed the door. After being involved in the sale of the Hathaway Collection, very few things could knock him off of his stride. But as he took the plastic-covered manuscript from Charles, he did so with a sense of trepidation. He at first tried to look at it with a sense of detachment. He wanted to preserve a certain aura of professionalism. However, as the contents were absorbed into his brain, any pretence began to vanish. He looked up at Rosalind, and then across to Charles, but said nothing. He looked back down at the script. His index finger going through the deletions, the stage directions, the alterations, and punctuation errors, all of which necessarily added to its authenticity. But it was the words that captivated him.

'Act Two, Scene Two,' he whispered.

'The very heart of the play,' Rosalind responded.

Shapeman nodded in agreement. He appeared extremely composed, but beneath his cool exterior, his body was in turmoil. He could feel his hair bristle against his cotton shirt, one of his legs begin to shake underneath the table and his stomach starting to turn. 'It's even signed with his initials,' he said quietly.

'Well, what do you think?' Charles asked.

'What do I think? If this is genuine, it would be the greatest discovery in western cultural history. There's nothing like this in the entire world. Unless I'm mistaken, none of his manuscripts survived, apart from the 'Hand D' Thomas More extracts, but even with that, scholars are divided.'

'I find it incredible that nothing of his survives. I mean he was a colossus in literature–'

371

'You don't understand,' Shapeman interrupted Charles. 'In his own time, he was quite well known and some of his plays were printed in his lifetime. The heyday of Shakespearian idolatry came much later. But the scripts were actually used by the actors at the time. When the plays had finished their various runs, there were much better uses for the paper in those days than simply keeping the manuscripts for posterity. Paper itself was made by hand and mostly imported from France, and was relatively valuable. The new paper was only used for writing or printing. Once it had been used, it was a marketable commodity that could be sold for a number of uses, such as wrapping or packaging. Anyway, once the Folio had been published, there was no need to keep the originals. Can I ask you where you found it?

'It was hidden in our First Folio,' she said innocently.

'You have a First Folio?'

'Yes. And it's in immaculate condition. Anyway, I found it lodged behind one of the plays.'

'Where did you get the Folio from? They are extremely rare, you know.'

'Oh, I do know. You should understand that I love Shakespeare, and I'm continually studying him—'

'She's doing a doctorate at Oxford, for God's sake! She's an expert, Bernard. There's nothing she doesn't know about him! She was even named after one of his characters.'

'Ah! Rosalind, from *As You Like It*. Yes, I see now. It's appropriate,' Bernard said, nodding and smiling.

372

'I'll take that as a compliment,' she responded.

'It was meant to be.'

'When you two have finished, perhaps we might get back to the manuscript,' Charles intervened, not at all amused by the book dealer's flirting.

'Yes, of course. Now where did you say that you obtained the First Folio?'

'It was given to us by Charles' father, Lord Longhurst.'

'The Hathaway Collection,' Bernard said, in a barely audible voice. The penny suddenly dropped. 'You must be the youngest brother,' he whispered.

'That's right. I believe you are already aware of its existence,' Charles said, carefully noting the book dealer's reaction.

'Yes, yes, I am,' he replied, looking back down at the manuscript. 'So you had the Folio. I was told it had been given away.'

'Who told you?'

'My client. Her name is Sally Fulton. She's the lawyer who orchestrated the sale of the books. I handled all the disposals.'

'Did you know the actual vendors – my brothers?'

'No, I didn't. The first I knew about your brothers was when it hit the press a few months ago. Then everything fell into place – the secrecy, the speed, the Swiss bank accounts, and, of course, the anonymity.'

'Do you have a record of where all the books went?'

'Everything and everywhere. And nobody is allowed to sell ... although one book did reappear recently in an auction.'

'Good!' Charles replied. Something told him inside that he would need that information, if not now, some time in the future.

'Listen. I am very sorry that the collection has been sold, but if it is any comfort to you, each book has found a good home. I even have a lot of the library stored in my warehouse. I bought it. It's all being kept in impeccable condition, I promise you. I'd be happy to sell it back to you, at my cost price.'

'Well, maybe in the future, but not now. Listen, don't feel guilty, it's not your fault. I understand, you did nothing illegal,' Charles replied, with remarkable perspective.

Bernard looked at Charles, and decided to return to the matter at hand. 'OK, but ... well, the Folio is worth, if in good condition, well over four million pounds. But that's small beer compared to this.' He pointed to the manuscript.

'Do you think it's real?' Rosalind asked.

'To be honest I just don't know. But it was found in a First Folio, which conceivably came to the Hathaway Collection directly from one of the actors. He might well have forgotten about it, and have left it in the book. The manuscript itself looks like the real thing, but I can't confirm it.'

'What should we do?'

'You have to get it authenticated. That will not be easy. Scholars these days hardly agree on anything.' He thought carefully, before continuing. He wanted to help, particularly after his role in the destruction of the Hathaway Collection, to alleviate the guilt he felt. 'I would go to the

Bodleian Library and get the age of the manu-script determined. If it's verified scientifically as being of the early sixteenth century, we can then go and see some experts on the subject.'

'Thank you. I'll ring the Bodleian. I know a lot of people there,' Rosalind interjected.

'I'll also try some of my contacts, and between the two of us, we should get a response,' Bernard replied, standing up. 'Oh, and by the way, you'll have to bring the Folio as well. They'll want to test that too – particularly the place where the parchment was found.'

The book dealer turned to Charles, and offered him his hand. Charles accepted the gesture, and shook it. He could not help but like him. He had been honest, and showed genuine remorse about what had happened. If he had not taken on the sale, someone else would have, and almost certainly would have been less circumspect about to whom he or she sold. 'Just one thing. If it is real, how much would it be worth?' Charles asked.

'I don't know. Nothing has ever been seen like this. It would be a national treasure. The government might declare it as such. But in value terms, hundreds of millions of pounds.'

24

An appointment was made at the Bodleian in Oxford for the following Wednesday morning at 10 o'clock. It was Bernard's contact in the manu-script department, located in the Duke Humfrey's section of the great library, and not one of Rosalind's many colleagues she had met as a current Reader, who proved to be the only one worth pursuing. Charles had already opened a safety deposit box at the bank for its safe keeping; it was clearly too valuable to keep at home. They waited anxiously for three days, not telling a soul about what they had found.

Arriving at Oxford on the Wednesday morning they went straight to the Old Library, entering the institution from Broad Street. Walking past the Sheldonian Theatre, they made their way into the quadrangle. Bernard Shapeman was waiting for them by the famous Pembroke statue in front of the main building.

'Bernard – I didn't know you were coming,' Rosalind said, surprised, but genuinely pleased that the antiquarian book dealer was there.

'Well, I thought you might need some guidance. I know you come here a lot, but since it's my contact in the manuscript department, I thought I should make an appearance. Believe me, to get an appointment in three days is a record.'

'Thank you for coming, Bernard,' Charles said, patting him on the back. The pressure of the whole situation was beginning to tell on him. Seeing Bernard there was a welcome relief. 'Who are we seeing?'

'His name is Gerald Crispin. He's a very nice man. You'll like him. Come on, he's waiting for us.'

They walked into the reception. Bernard nodded to the receptionist, who rang through to the department. 'Please take the door on the right, and go upstairs. Mr Crispin will meet you,' she said, replacing the receiver.

The three of them made their way out of reception, and walked towards the department. As they walked up the narrow staircase, a very large, rotund man was waiting for them at the top. Balding, bespectacled, his cheeks flushed, Gerald Crispin had the look of an affable and convivial giant.

'Bernard, it's good to see you again.' Gerald Crispin greeted the book dealer.

'Hello, Gerald. Let me introduce you to Rosalind Blackstone and Charles Longhurst.'

'Hello. How do you do?' He shook both their hands vigorously. 'Please come ... come in to my office. I'm sorry about the mess here. And you sit there. That's it.' He directed everyone to various seats cluttered around his desk. 'Now, how can I be of help?'

'We need a certain manuscript authenticated.'

'Yes, yes, so I understand. Do you have it?' he said quickly.

Charles opened his case and handed it over. 'I've left it in a plastic cover, but if you want to take it out, be my guest.'

Gerald Crispin took the parchment out of the plastic, without really listening to his guest. Charles noticed his hands. They were remarkable in that they were so refined, almost feminine, for such a big and clumsy man. His fingers were delicate and his nails appeared perfectly manicured. The expert began to concentrate, and remained silent staring at the document. Both Charles and Rosalind watched with baited breath as the expert examined the manuscript.

'Well?' Bernard broke the silence. He had known Gerald Crispin for years, and had worked with him on numerous manuscripts. Ironically he had been most useful in regard to the Lincoln Gettysburg Address, when the Hathaway House collection was being disposed in a hurry, and he needed some form of authentication without delay. Gerald's name had been enough to convince the buyer.

He looked up at Bernard. 'If ... if it's genuine... Well, it's the most beautiful thing that I have ever seen. We'll need to do some scientific tests, to accurately gauge how old it is, and we'll take it from there. Bernard has told me where you found it, so I'll have to take the Folio as well, just to make sure everything marries up. There's bound to be some residue from the manuscript on the Folio which will confirm its location as being genuine.'

'Yes, of course. But your initial thoughts?'

'If it is four-hundred years old, then who knows? To get it properly verified you'll have to go to the best Shakespeare scholars. I can only tell you if it is authentic in relation to the linguistic style, to its age, and the materials used.' He looked up. 'You know – the ink, for example.' He looked back down. 'There are records of his signature – on his will and other legal documents, so we could look at the handwriting, but the problems arise there because there is so little written by him that survives. We're not convinced about the "Thomas More" at the British library.' He felt the paper carefully. 'I must say, it feels and looks genuine.'

'How long do you need?' Charles asked.

'A week, just to make sure. After which, I can recommend some scholars.'

'That won't be necessary. I think I know just about everyone who could qualify,' Rosalind said, laughing. 'I'm attached to Christchurch, doing a doctorate.'

'Oh, fine. Just one thing though – where did you get it? The Folio, I mean.' Gerald Crispin had waited to the very end to ask perhaps his most pertinent question. He wasn't going to waste his time on it if the response did not intrigue him. As he listened to the answer, he looked again at the manuscript, realising for the first time why his friend Bernard Shapeman had been so insistent on seeing him, and also, more importantly, understanding that he was about to become a part player in perhaps the most extraordinary discovery in the history of western Culture.

25

They left the Bodleian and went to get a coffee in town. It was important to start putting a plan together. They had to prepare for a situation in the event that the manuscript was genuine. Although each of them had no doubt of its legitimacy, it was too farfetched, up to then, for them to seriously consider a strategy for an announcement, and with it the implications for the general public.

'Have you both considered what you might be getting into?' Bernard asked them.

'What do you mean? Shouldn't we just wait until we hear from Gerald, the results of the testing?' Charles replied, anxious to try and delay any decisions, and not daring to think that it was genuine, hoping to avoid the inevitable disappointment if it turned out not to be.

'Listen to me. I've been in the business for a very long time, but I've never seen anything like this before. This is all new to me. But one thing I do know is that you have to be prepared. If the manuscript is real – and let's face it, given its origins and where you found it – we all think it is, then you will lose all privacy. You'll be public property. Every newspaper and television station will want a piece of you. Every government in the western hemisphere will want to be part of the show, offering you money to purchase it for their respective countries. You must understand the enormity of the find.'

Rosalind smiled. 'Do you really think people will be that excited? I mean, I entirely appreciate the greatness of what we have, but I breathe, eat and drink Shakespeare. I always have done. The problem is, as a result, I have no perspective when it comes to discussing him.'

'There's no question, in my mind, that the public interest will be unprecedented.'

'What do you suggest?' Charles asked.

'I don't have any answers, but I'm happy to front everything until you're happy to go public. It's up to you. But with, I presume, a wedding coming up, perhaps you want to keep some privacy.'

Charles nodded at Rosalind. Whatever unwitting part he had played in the destruction of the Hathaway Library, he was more than making up for it now. 'Thank you, Bernard, but shall we wait and cross that bridge when we come to it?'

'Yes, absolutely. I just want you to be aware of what we are facing and what might happen.'

26

A further week passed without any news from the Bodleian. Rosalind had gone down to Brighton to stay with her parents, and to make initial pre-parations for the wedding. Raveena joined her for five days. She had just completed her final exam, and was herself waiting for the result, before qualifying. The excitement in the house was at fever pitch. Every time the telephone rang, or the letterbox rattled with incoming mail, a mixture of tension laced with anticipation gripped the family.

'I can't stand it any longer, Rosalind. I'm more nervous about your news than I am about my results.'

'That's because you know you've passed.'

'Maybe ... but you never really know, do you?'

Rosalind laughed. 'Yes you do.' She knew Raveena had passed, and so did her friend. But it was impossible not to be caught up in the excite-ment of the situation. It wasn't enough that Catherine, her mother, who was remarkably calm, was taking full responsibility for the wed-ding. Everyone's thoughts were dominated by the manuscript, which the outside world, apart from the privileged few, was blissfully unaware of.

The two girls managed to get out a lot during the week, shopping in town, or going for walks along the South Downs. Time was slow to pass, as the wait slowly took its toll. The torture was finally broken on the fifth day when Rosalind's mobile rang.

'Hi, Charles. You'll never guess where we are?'

'Where?'

'We're just walking up past the gates of Roedean about twenty yards from where you stood when I first saw you.'

He smiled. 'Listen, Bernard's just rung.' He waited, taking pleasure in her increased anticipation.

'Yes?'

'The Bodleian has contacted him.'

'Yes? For God's sake, Charles! I can't stand this!'

'The manuscript is genuine! It was written at any time between the end of the sixteenth, and the start of the seventeenth century. The paper, the ink, the materials ... they all add up. Its authenticity, regarding its age, is incontrovertible.' He stopped. Again he waited, but this time there was no response. 'Rosalind – the manuscript – it's real. Can you hear me?'

Rosalind had to try and absorb Charles' news. She was paralysed to the spot, unable to move. The immensity of the moment overwhelmed her.

'Well, what is it, Rosalind?' Raveena asked, realising what was happening.

'It's genuine, Rav. It has been authenticated,' she said quietly. 'Charles, what do we do now?'

'Bernard said it's time for you to speak to your

professors at Oxford, or wherever they are. It's your turn to take the stage. You have to find out if Shakespeare wrote the bloody thing!'

'Right, I'll get on to it straightaway.' She ended the call. She turned to Raveena, and embraced her. Tears were streaming down her cheeks, the enormity of the discovery was now really beginning to sink in. She above everybody else knew that the poet had written it, but the rest of the world would not be satisfied with her endorsement. She needed the best experts in the land to validate what she already knew. She was also aware that the whole process was beginning to take on a life of its own. She would not be able to control it. Whatever Bernard had said, her and Charles' privacy would become a thing of the past. She let go of her best friend. 'I have to return to Oxford.'

'I know. Do you want me to come with you?' Raveena saw the strain in Rosalind's beautiful face.

'No, I must do this alone. I've got Charles ... and Bernard, who I think is the only one who understands the pressure and who's fully prepared for the public exposure.' She looked around the grass lawns of Roedean. She looked across the horizon towards the glinting sea, rolling in on to the stony beaches of East Sussex. 'This is where it all started, Rav.'

'I know.'

'Not just falling in love – also Shakespeare. The lessons with Mrs Robinson, and that very first reading of *The Winter's Tale*. Do you remember?'

'I remember "Robby", but I hated English. I

certainly don't remember us reading *The Winter's Tale.*'

'Oh, come on, you must remember. I played Perdita and you were Paulina. That's when my journey began. I was sitting gazing outside of that window.' She pointed to a small window on the ground floor ten yards away. 'And then I saw them, just as Perdita was glorifying them as spring's great symbol.'

'What?'

'*Daffodils ... that come before the swallow dares, and take the winds of March with beauty.*'

27

The Bodleian had passed on the manuscript, along with the Folio, to two leading professors of English, whose names had been given by Rosalind. Both of them knew Rosalind very well, and were delighted to help, especially when briefed on the extraordinary discovery. A date was set in the beginning of June. The dons wanted time to look at the manuscript, before making their opinions known. They were initially sceptical, despite being told of its origins, and of the positive report from the Bodleian. There was a lot at stake. People's reputations were about to be torn asunder if the document was authentic. Even with Rosalind Blackstone being involved, who was beginning to make a name for herself at the university with her brilliant thesis, the professors took the discovery with a pinch of salt.

But all this was to change when the document

arrived at All Souls College, where it was to be examined. Rumours started to spread around the halls and corridors of the great colleges. Noises reverberated around the cloistered quadrangles, as the news of the find swept across the academic institutions. Nor were the rumours confined to Oxford, as word spread to Cambridge, and then on to London. Keeping the discovery a secret was nigh impossible. By the time Charles, Rosalind and Bernard arrived at All Souls in June, a small piece in the *New York Times* appeared reporting that an original Shakespeare manuscript had been found in England, and was being verified.

'It hasn't even been authenticated, and it's in the *New York Times?*' Charles said in disbelief.

'I did warn you. And it hasn't even started yet,' Bernard replied.

'It's exciting. Everybody's so interested. It's just great that people recognise how important the whole thing is.' Rosalind felt a certain sense of justification that her hero, whom she had devoted more than just her academic life to, was receiving the proper attention he deserved.

'Bernard, I think your advice was right. You must take the pressure off us. Can you front everything with the public? You've been a fantastic support.'

'Don't worry just yet, but of course I will. I must tell you both something. Apart from getting to know you over the past few weeks, and becoming good friends, I have to be honest with you.'

'What about?'

'Well, I'd be lying if my offer was based on purely altruistic motives. If it all holds up, my

385

name, and my business, will become the most famous in the manuscript world.'

Charles and Rosalind laughed. 'It's all right Bernard, we'd worked that one out already. But we haven't got a problem with it.' He patted the bookdealer's back as they approached the college from the high street, to meet the waiting dons.

28

They were led through the front quadrangle, and then up the staircase to a study overlooking the back lawn and walled cloister. They sat down and waited for the professors. Rosalind knew the city so well, but she never tired of the views that each college afforded. She stared out of the window, across the grass lawn, and over the wall. She could clearly see the rounded cupola of the Radcliffe Camera, and then beyond, towards the roofs of Brasenose College.

'Good morning!' The two robed dons entered the study. The senior expert placed the Folio and the manuscript, in its protective plastic cover, on the table.

The three young visitors stood up, and greeted the academics. 'Rosalind!' He looked at his student. 'Well, you've certainly a habit of surprising me!' He smiled.

'What do you think, Professor Campbell?' she said impatiently. She knew Sir William Campbell extremely well. He had taught her at Christchurch for six years, and was one of the leading Shakespearian authorities alive. He was one of the very few people who could still teach Rosalind something new about her craft.

'Well, where do I begin? Given the fact that the age of the document has been authenticated, and having been briefed on where you found it,' he looked down. 'The writing – Hand D', he looked up at Rosalind, who was fully aware of the academic consequences of the find. 'Its style, the directions, the language.' He waited. 'I have no doubts! It's extraordinary, I know, but I'm convinced. We've studied at enormous length the writing and the notes and there is nothing there that turns me away from thinking that it's genuine and the poet himself wrote it. I'm also rather happy, I must admit, that certain matters can finally be put to bed.' He looked at Rosalind. It had been the subject of many discussions between them over the years. He smiled. She held the same view as him.

'The identity of the playwright has in the past been debated. Candidates have ranged from the Earl of Oxford to Sir Francis Bacon. Some most recently have raised the prospect of Sir Henry Neville. But with the initials 'WS' I think there is little doubt that the true identity is none other than William Shakespeare. The elitists and snobs will have to drop their claims, and accept that a working-class boy with a grammar-school education was the true author. Now, I know Roger has his own views on the manuscript.' He glanced across to his colleague from St Johns, another scholar and Fellow of All Souls. He didn't know Rosalind as well as Campbell did, but had advised her on parts of her doctorate.

'Well, it's certainly incredibly interesting, Rosalind, and exciting, tremendously so. It's been very hard to contain ourselves, but ... we have to be very careful, you do understand,' Roger Tennyson responded.

'You mean because of William Henry Ireland?' Rosalind asked.

'Precisely.'

'Who's Ireland?' Charles asked.

'He lived in the eighteenth century, and was responsible for one of the most famous forgeries in history. At one stage he actually produced, amongst others, an entire manuscript for *King Lear*. They were all believed to be authentic. Even the best scholars of the day thought them to be real. He was eventually found out, after he produced a "new play" by Shakespeare, called "Vortigen and Rowena". He eventually admitted that they were all forgeries. Since then, people are obviously, extremely wary.'

'Oh, I see. But you don't think that we–'

'No, no, not at all,' Tennyson replied. 'Absolutely not. But you can understand how careful we must be. We also have our reputations to protect. If we come out and say yes! This is a genuine manuscript of act II scene ii of *Romeo and Juliet*, written by Shakespeare himself, then we have to be completely certain.'

'I understand, Professor, but what's your view? Do you agree with Professor Campbell?'

Tennyson looked at the manuscript lying on the table, untouched, alone, its magnificence resonating throughout the room. He was sure, but not as sure as Campbell was. He was slightly worried that someone, somewhere, might have forged it, and then placed it in the Folio, without anybody knowing. It was doubtful, but possible. He wanted an insurance policy. 'I do ... but I would like a third opinion, just to be safe.'

Sir William Campbell raised his eyebrows at his younger colleague. 'How do you propose to get one? And who?'

'Let's get an opinion from across the pond!'

'You mean Drayson?'

'Yes. Not just because of his chair at Harvard, and because of his works on Shakespeare, but also because of his position at the Folger.' He was referring to the famous library in Washington.

'That's not such a bad idea, but you do realise, Roger, that by sending it there, the lid will come off? Everyone and his dog will have an opinion.'

'I do, William, but the importance of the find is so great, nobody wants to be made to look stupid.'

'Rosalind?' Sir William asked his star student. 'What do you think?'

'Well, Drayson is the most famous of the present-day Shakespeare critics. If you're happy about getting his view, and Oxford doesn't mind getting advice from Harvard, then who am I to demur!'

'Very good then. I'll speak to Bob, and ask him to come over. If we go there, or send over the manuscript, we haven't a chance of keeping out of the press.'

'I agree,' Tennyson said, clearly more reassured that Bob Drayson, the leading authority on the poet, was being brought in.

'Fine. As we still have a long way to go until everyone's satisfied–'

'Charles, patience! This is going to take time, they're right. You have to listen.' Rosalind held Charles' arm as he stood up to leave.

'I understand, but as Bernard will appreciate, things are going to get out. You guys don't understand commercially what this means. If, as we all deep down know, this is real, the value of the manuscript–'

'Mr Longhurst, we both fully understand. We also know of the pressure that you, Rosalind, and Mr Shapeman are under, but you have to wait. We are all on the same side. We know how important it is. We are desperately excited, and long for it to be genuine. But that, surely, in itself is a reason to get a third opinion.' Sir William got up, and smiled at Rosalind. 'We are on the threshold of perhaps the most important discovery in the history of English literature. We'll have to wait and see what our American friend has to say.'

'Do you think he'll believe you, and come over?' Bernard asked.

'Oh, I have no doubts about that!'

29

Bob Drayson, six foot six inches, broad shouldered, would not have looked out of place in an American Football team. His prodigious physical presence was only matched by his enormous personal charm and charisma. Holding the chair at Harvard in Literature, a trustee of Amherst

College, in charge of overseeing the Folger Library, and author of numerous works on literature, his towering work on Shakespeare remained the seminal text on interpreting the poet, overtaking the greats such as Coleridge, Hazlewitt and Bradley. For Rosalind, his work had been a seminal influence as an undergraduate, and although now in the final stages of her own doctorate, she was still extremely excited at the prospect of meeting him.

He was expecting the phone call. After all, everybody was talking about some fabled document written by Shakespeare that had been found in a First Folio shelved in a mythical library somewhere deep in the English countryside. There was not an institute of learning – from the Campanile at Berkeley to Harvard's Massachusetts Hall, and from the cloistered quadrangles of Oxford and Cambridge to the ornate lecture theatres of the Sorbonne – that was not infected by the talk of the manuscript. People were continually asking him about it, but he had nothing to say. For how long he didn't know, but it was only a matter of time.

'Drayson!' he shouted down the receiver in his throaty Brooklyn voice.

'Bob?'

'Sir William.' He instantly recognised the voice of his distinguished friend on the other end of the line. 'I've been waiting for your call.'

'I'm sure you have.'

'Is it true? Have you really got something?'

'Yes, I think we have, Bob. I think this is, as you would say, "the real thing".'

'My God! What's written ... we hear that it

consists of one page, it's in great condition, and the text's from *Romeo and Juliet,* but that's about it.'

'Well it's all that, old boy, but it's more than that–'

'What?'

'It's act two, scene two – it's the complete exchange, the heart of the play. And it's – how can I say it? Well it's utterly sublime.'

'You mean, you really have it in your hands, in its original form – with stage directions and alterations?'

'Yes.' There was a crack in his voice. The Oxford professor, normally so taciturn in communication, so measured in appraisal, was finding the moment exhaustingly emotional. The parchment he was now holding represented the apogee of his career. The enormity of the find was sinking in.

'When can I see it?'

'As soon as possible. We need you here. Roger feels we need a final opinion, although I have no doubts. Will you come?' He had recovered some of his composure.

'Of course.'

'Splendid. But Bob–'

'What?'

'Are you prepared to put your head on the line?'

'No question.'

'Thank you.' Sir William placed the manuscript back on the table. He knew that once Bob Drayson confirmed his and Roger's opinion, he would have to let the manuscript go back to its owners. He hoped beyond all hopes that it would find a resting place at the British Library for the world to see, but he somehow doubted it.

30

Bob Drayson arrived 48 hours later. By the time he arrived, speculation had further increased. The *Daily Telegraph*, picking up on the *New York Times* article, had made enquiries, and followed up leads eventually ending up at Christchurch College.

'You must understand, I cannot comment on this at the present time.'

'So you don't deny the existence of the manuscript, Sir William?' the reporter asked.

'No, but neither can I confirm it,' he replied. He knew it was only a matter of time before the story would break. The old don had to hold out, at least until the American had seen it, before releasing the news.

It was pouring with rain, when the 45 year old Harvard giant arrived in his car. He drove into the main quad, ignoring the signs directing him to leave the car around the back. He got out at the far right-hand corner, and walked up the wide stone staircase, and into the Dining Hall. He had spent his life in many of the great academic institutions throughout the world, but he never ceased to be impressed by the august surroundings of Christchurch College.

'Hello, William.' Bob Drayson strode into the Hall. 'You know, my heart almost misses a beat whenever I come here.'

'You're not alone, Bob.'

Drayson ignored the young woman standing next to his old friend Sir William, and walked around the perimeter of the room looking at the famous alumni, then up at one of the windows which showed characters from Alice in Wonderland. 'This place – it's so grand, so majestic. I suppose you're all used to it.'

'No, not really.' Sir William smiled. 'Let me introduce you to Rosalind Blackstone. She's the student I talked to you about last year. I had wanted you to take her on as a researcher, but she's about to get married. You remember, don't you?'

'Of course I do. Very pleased to meet you. I've heard a great deal about you. He thinks very highly of you – now that's real praise!' He looked at her, admiring her beauty, and immediately seeing something special. 'Your mother must have had great taste in choosing your name!' He shook her hand rather formally.

'I try very hard to emulate her, but it's just about impossible!' she replied jokingly, immediately creating a rapport with one of the finest critical minds alive.

'Don't worry, nobody can reach her level of brilliance and wit!' he said, trying hard to make her relax. He knew the effect he had on people. His imposing physical presence, coupled with his enormous brain frightened many students, particularly female ones. But he needn't have worried. Rosalind, although excited at meeting him, was fully composed, and in control.

'Now then, Bob. I fully briefed you on the

394

origins of the find, and have sent you the scientific reports, and all the analysis from the Bodleian. You also should have received both my and Roger's report.'

'I've had everything. And William, surprisingly I have read everything!'

'Good, well come over here.' Sir William took him over to the High Table where the manuscript lay.

The American stood still and bent over the document. Without moving from his fixed gaze, he asked gently, 'A huge coincidence, don't you think?' He then sat down.

'What?' Rosalind answered, for some reason knowing that the question was directed at her.

'You ... you finding it. I mean, of all the people. The brightest student in Oxford, certainly on Shakespeare, finding this.' He continued to study the writing in front of him. 'Don't you think it's a coincidence?' His words, although quietly spoken, had an air of menace to them.

'I like to think that it was meant to be. But if you want to call it coincidence, you can. For me it's fate, destiny.'

'Whatever ... but your love for the poet is unquenchable. Maybe the passion turned into obsession, and–'

'Professor Drayson, the manuscript's genuine. It's not a forgery. You have the evidence in front of you.'

'Ms Blackstone, why are you denying it's a forgery.' Rosalind had become Ms Blackstone, as the atmosphere suddenly darkened.

'It's a natural response for God's sake, Bob!' Sir

William interjected.

'It is ... and you're right, but I haven't yet accused her.' The American continued with his examination, never looking up. Tracing his finger through each line, inspecting every word, syllable and letter, he was lost in the manuscript. He looked closely at the writing, comparing it with everything he knew to be written by Shakespeare. There was, like with everybody else, precious little he could fall back on, apart from the unpublished Thomas More fragment, some signatures and various legal documents that were unsubstantiated. His examination lasted for two hours. Very little was said until he had finished.

'You say you found it in the First Folio itself.'

'Yes.'

'And that Folio had been in the library from the date of publication.'

'Yes... Well, as far as I know.'

'Oh come on. Either it was or it wasn't. William, you said—'

'Professor Drayson, the library at Hathaway House was a secret to the outside world, except to the privileged few. The collection started in Elizabethan times. It's certain that this came to the library at its inception. The book remained untouched since it was originally purchased, until it came into my hands. I can assure you of that, and that is the truth.' Rosalind interrupted, keeping complete control. However, she feared that Drayson's suspicions were growing.

'Where is it?'

'The Folio?'

'Yes.'

'Over there.' Professor Campbell fetched the book over to Drayson. He examined the Folio, looking at the place where the manuscript was found. He could see immediately that the Folio was in immaculate condition, the finest copy he had ever seen. This was made even more impressive since Drayson, through his trusteeship at Amhurst College was in charge of the unrivalled Shakespeare collection at the Folger Library in Washington, including over 80 copies of the First Folio that are housed there, and is regarded as the world's leading research centre on the poet. His position there, and not just his professorship at Harvard, gave him an unrivalled pre-eminence as an authority on Shakespeare. 'This the place?' he asked. Rosalind nodded to him. 'And William tells me it just fell out of the book while it lay open.'

'It didn't fall out. It came loose. I noticed the frayed edge.'

Drayson closed the book and got up. He had heard and seen enough. 'OK then, William, I've seen enough.'

'What? Is that it? For Christ's sake, how can you let your pride get in the way? Don't you see that it's genuine. Are you too scared to come out and confirm it, or are you too arrogant to let anybody else claim such a prize?'

'You better call a press conference,' he replied, staring at Rosalind.

'But what for? What's the point?'

'To announce the greatest discovery in the history of western culture.'

'What? But I thought–'

'Not at all, William. The manuscript is clearly original. I suggest you both get on to it right away.' He smiled at Rosalind. 'You do understand, I had to push you to see how you reacted.'

'I obviously passed the test.'

'Serenely.'

31

Sir Francis Sutherland had been kept up to date with the events leading up to the calling of a press conference. He was excited for his surrogate son, and inevitably anticipated what Charles was thinking. The enormous prize would be more than enough to buy Hathaway House back from the banks, and indeed replenish the library. However, any hope of reclaiming his family seat from the receiver suffered a devastating setback the day before the conference was called.

As the old lawyer walked into his office that morning, the newspapers were lined up by his secretary on his desk. He walked over and looked at the front pages of all the major broadsheets. All were dominated by the discovery of the manuscript. The hysteria was extraordinary, nowhere more so than in London. People could barely wait for the conference, which was to be held at the Empire in Leicester Square. The demand for tickets from the world's press was overwhelming, and the 1300-seat cinema's acoustic system and wide screen were perfect tools to describe the discovery.

As he scanned through the articles, he couldn't

help laughing at the irony of the whole situation. A few months previously the papers were concentrating on the flight of the twins, and the demise of the Longhurst family. Now, like a phoenix from the ashes, Charles, the heir to the family seat, was on the front pages with his fiancée, about to cash in on the most valuable family heirloom that nobody had known about. He continued to go through the articles, but was suddenly interrupted by one of his partners.

'Francis? Can I come in for a moment?'

'Of course you can, George. What do you think of all this? Quite extraordinary, don't you think?'

'Unbelievable! It's obviously true.'

'No question. In any case, we'll hear tomorrow! What can I do for you?'

'Well, it's a little awkward, Francis, and it's not entirely unconnected to this.'

'Really?'

'Yes. It concerns–' The young partner looked at his senior colleague preparing for his reaction to the information he was about to disclose. 'Hathaway House.'

'What about it?'

'I'm acting for the bank consortium.'

'Yes, I know, George, I assigned you the job. I felt I was conflicted.'

'Well, they've decided to sell it, quicker than we first thought.'

'But I thought that they were going to invest money into it, and refurbish the entire house, before putting it on the market.'

'That was the original plan. But they had an offer that was so good that they unanimously 'accepted it.'

'But it hasn't even been placed properly on the market.'

'I know, I know. It's strange, but as their lawyer, and having seen the price, I had no hesitation in advising them to accept it.'

'You did what? Didn't you think of coming to me, as your senior partner?'

'No, not really. It was a commercial decision, and I was clear in my mind that the advice I gave was correct.'

'You should have come to me, especially now that–'

'Forgive me, Francis, but that's precisely the reason why you gave me the brief in the first place. You were conflicted, and you still are.'

Francis Sutherland slumped in his chair. After all he had been through, he wasn't sure how Charles would react. He had been under intense pressure. 'I'm sorry, George, you're absolutely right. It's just that with all the excitement, my judgement–'

'Don't worry, Francis, I know. Look, it's very difficult, but the offer the banks got ... well, it's a very good one!'

'How much?'

'Seventy five million.'

'Is that such a good offer?'

'Have you seen its current condition? It's totally dilapidated. It will cost the new owner tens of millions to restore it to the glory that you once knew.'

Francis turned around and looked out of the office window. He didn't want his partner to see how distraught he was. 'Thank you, George.' He didn't move. 'George!' he shouted.

His partner stopped. 'Yes?'

'Who's buying it?'

'Abraham Bernstein. Personally.'

'You're joking.'

'I've never been more serious,' George Whittaker responded.

32

Francis decided not to tell Charles about the news until after the press conference. He had mixed thoughts on the old man Bernstein buying Hathaway House. He understood his anger at the twins. He knew how they behaved towards him, but at the time he could say and do nothing, due to the conflict of interest with him acting for the family. But he also knew that he was Sam's father, and as such knew Charles, and liked him. He hoped that he, or Sam could persuade him to transfer it back to the family, without suffering any financial loss. He was convinced that he could find another grandiose property for the old man. He had no idea how deep Abraham's revenge ran. The resentment against the establishment, that had propelled him forward in business, was now laced with a hatred directed against the Longhurst twins. As far as he was concerned, Hathaway House belonged to them, and the purchase had nothing to do with Charles.

The banks were delighted with the offer, not only because of the price, but also because it

401

came from such a reputable source. Abraham Bernstein's career was based on the twin bedrocks of honesty and integrity. Once he put an offer in for a property, his word was his bond. In fifty years of dealing he had never reneged, and he certainly wasn't going to start now. He hadn't told his wife, Leah, knowing that she was not keen on a country estate, preferring to stay in town near her family and friends. He hadn't even mentioned it to Sam, the one person in the family with whom he shared his most intimate business secrets. He knew that his son would be upset by the purchase, and would try and convince him to pull out.

With such opposition within the family, he wanted to produce a *fait accompli*, especially having read about Charles' incredible discovery. He realised that his son's friend would have more than enough to bid for his old family estate. Abraham wanted to exchange before the conference began. He didn't want to leave anything to chance.

'Their clients are in no rush. They're very happy with your offer, Abraham. Relax,' said Jonathan Shaffer, his lawyer, trying to hold back his client.

'I want to exchange by Wednesday morning at the latest.'

'But that's the day after tomorrow!'

'I know, but I want it done, and done quickly.'

The lawyer looked at his diary, and immediately realised that Wednesday morning would be a problem. 'We could possibly push for the afternoon, but the morning will be impossible. The press conference has been announced that

402

morning. The whole world's going to stop and watch.'

'It's Wednesday morning, or it won't happen.'

'But I haven't yet received the contract. I am at their mercy.'

'It's your problem.'

The lawyer replaced the receiver. He had been acting for Abraham Bernstein for five years, and knew that he meant everything he said. There was no pique or bravado. It was always measured. The lawyer understood the instruction and would have to deliver.

33

It was 11 o'clock on Wednesday morning, and the lights went down in the Empire cinema at Leicester Square. Television and radio stations from across the world focused on the stage set up for the conference. Every seat was taken by the countless newspapers that were represented. The aisles by the walls were filled with reporters standing, some with their pens and paper pads, but more with their pocket recorders. The anticipation was electrifying. Everybody was waiting for the entry on to the stage of the main players in this extraordinary tale of discovery.

Suddenly the spotlights were turned on, and five men followed by a solitary woman walked on to the stage. You could hear a pin drop as they all took their seats behind the long table. After a moment, and having gathered his papers, the eldest of the men – tall, slender, with his grey hair receded and combed tightly back – stood up and walked to the lectern.

'Good morning, ladies and gentlemen. Thank you for coming. My name is William Campbell, and I hold the Chair in English Literature at Christchurch, Oxford. On my left is Roger Tennyson, my colleague at St Johns. Seated next to him is Bernard Shapeman, a leading antiquarian book and manuscript dealer. The next person along needs very little introduction: Bob Drayson, the world's foremost critic on William Shakespeare. And finally Charles Longhurst and Rosalind Blackstone, whom you have all recently read about.'

He took his spectacles out from his jacket pocket, and placed them at the end of his nose. 'I have called this press conference sooner than I really wanted, but such has been the speculation and wild rumours that have swept across the globe, I and the rest of us here on the stage felt it was best to make an announcement. I won't take any questions until after I have finished.' He looked up. He only wished his students in the lecture halls of Oxford were as attentive as this audience. They were in the palm of his hand.

'Seven weeks ago, a manuscript was found, placed in a very rare Shakespeare First Folio. The Folio was the first publication of Shakespeare's plays in 1623. It was published by his friends and fellow actors as an act of homage to the playwright. This particular First Folio was part of the now dismantled Hathaway Library, and has therefore only had one owner. The manuscript, which was found by Charles Longhurst and

Rosalind Blackstone, contained the celebrated lovers' exchange between Romeo and Juliet from act two scene two of the play, in tacto. Ms Blackstone is presently doing a doctorate in Shakespeare's tragedies, and immediately recognised the potential importance of the parchment.

'Advised by Mr Shapeman, the manuscript was taken to the Bodleian and verified, scientifically, for its age. Having now established its authenticity with regard to its age,' he stopped and looked up, 'for example, to confirm that it dated back to the end of the sixteenth century, and also the materials that were used, such as the paper and the ink were consistent with the time, enough proof had been attained to take the next step, and to examine the contents of the manuscript itself. They approached myself and Roger Tennyson, both of us being professors on the subject and also being well known to Ms Blackstone, to see if the poet wrote it himself.

'We examined the document, paying attention to the style, the alterations, the stage directions ... and, of course, the handwriting. It was extremely difficult for us to authenticate this, given the lack of comparable material. We obviously employed experts in the handwriting field, using Shakespeare's signature, and other legal documents that he is said to have written. We also looked at the "Thomas More" manuscript from the British Library.' He took a deep breath. 'I don't want to go into the authentication process now, and I could talk for hours on this,' he looked up, 'but we have concluded, based on all of what has been said, that this manuscript...' He turned to the screen and pointed to the image that flashed on to the screen to the accompaniment of gasps from the audience '...is genuine, and that the poet himself wrote it.' He waited for everybody to calm down from their obvious excitement. 'You will of course note the initials – here', he pointed to the *"ws"* written at the bottom of the page. 'I think this will put to rest a lot of bogus argument about the identity of the playwright.' He waited for the audience to catch its breath. 'To complete the authentication, we asked Bob Drayson, trustee of Amhurst College, Governor of the Folger Library and Professor of Literature at Harvard, as well as being the pre-eminent Shake-spearian authority, to give his opinion. His view corroborated our opinions.

'I understand that a great many of you who are scholars or academics will want more time to study this, but for the sake of the wider audience I have to be brief. You will, I promise, be given more material as you leave, which will fully explain our conclusions, particularly with refer-ence to the textual debate.

'Ladies and gentlemen, this is probably the greatest find in the literary world, in modern times. Mr Longhurst and Ms Blackstone have agreed to lend it to the British Library for a period of four months so the public can see the manuscript. After that time, it will be placed in auction for sale, to the highest bidder.' He stopped, and took his glasses off. 'I'll now take five questions. Please be patient.'

The arms shot up in the air, each and every one of the audience having a desperate desire to learn more. Sir William Campbell took the questions at random.

'Whom does the manuscript actually belong to – Ms Blackstone or Mr Longhurst?'

Charles stood up. 'The First Folio belonged to the library at Hathaway, and therefore was part of my family's estate. Before my father, James Longhurst, died, he gave the book to my fiancée, Rosalind. Since we are to be married, we both agreed that we would share ownership.'

'Ms Blackstone, did you think it was genuine as soon as you read it?'

Rosalind adjusted the microphone, but remained seated. 'I couldn't actually believe it. My mind was rushing ahead as I read the script. I suppose at first I hoped more than believed, but after the Bodleian gave the results, I knew it was real.'

'Mr Shapeman, why are you involved?'

'I was asked for advice by Mr Longhurst and Ms Blackstone, as an expert in antiquarian books and manuscripts.'

'Two more questions – yes, sir.' The old don took the question from the back.

'How much do you think it's worth?'

'I think a manuscript in this condition, depicting the most familiar lovers' exchange in the English language, written by the most important playwright – indeed probably most important person of the millennium, is priceless. I know certain people from my country would pay more than $200 million.' Drayson had taken centre stage. His gigantic frame dominated the auditorium platform. His reputation as the greatest modern critic of literature coupled with his massive intellect hypnotised the audience. Everything that came out of his mouth had the air of not just legitimacy, but also authority.

As the gasps quietened down, Campbell asked for the final question.

'Why are you auctioning it? I mean, can't the manuscript stay here in England? Do you have to sell to the highest bidder? It's a bit mercenary, isn't it?'

Charles stood up again. 'No doubt most of you will have read or heard about the demise of my family. My elder brothers fled the country, having lost the family estate that had been with us for hundreds of years, and destroyed the finest library in the land. My ambition is to buy the house back from the banks, and slowly build up the library. I have plans, if I succeed, to open the house up to the public, with the library being the centrepiece of the attraction. Of course, if the government want to negotiate, I would be happy to listen to offers. But I've heard nothing to date.'

Sir William nodded to the technician at the side, who put the lights back on. 'Thank you, ladies and gentlemen. There are packs outside explaining in more detail the manuscript, the First Folio, and the written authentications from the Bodleian and various universities. My opinion, coupled with those of Professors Tennyson and Drayson, are also included.'

The conference came to an end. The excitement generated by the anticipation showed no signs of slowing down. The press left the cinema in a hubbub of activity. The television cameras turned to their presenters, who started making their own summaries of the drama that was now front-page news all around the world.

34

On that same Wednesday morning, at 11.15, Abraham Bernstein and Jonathan Shaffer were going through the contract to buy Hathaway House. The old man thumbed through the document. He had seen hundreds like it, but this one caused him more enthusiasm than any other. The taste of revenge was so sweet, he could hardly believe it.

'Is everything in order?'

'Everything. They want a five per cent deposit.'

'How generous,' he commented sarcastically.

'Well, it's better than the normal ten.'

'I'm Abraham Bernstein. They know I'm good for the money. They didn't need a deposit from me.'

'Well, they thought it was a concession. The title is fine, and everything seems OK.'

'Good.' He signed the contract. 'Exchange now. Go on, use the phone.'

Shaffer picked up the phone, not understanding why the old man was in such a rush. 'My client has signed. Are you in a position to exchange?'

'Christ! Why the rush? Normally it's the vendor who's pushing. It just so happens I can exchange now. My clients have given me the power of attorney.' George Whittaker picked the contract up. 'OK, let's do it.'

'Good ... thanks, George ... and we'll complete in four weeks?'

'Yes... Listen, can I go? I want to watch the conference.'

'Of course. I wish I could do the same, but my client, the only one in London, doesn't seem to be interested!'

'That's your problem, Jonathan.' George replaced the phone and returned to the television, only then to hear Charles' response to what he was going to do with the money he would receive from the sale of the manuscript. He immediately understood why Bernstein wanted to buy so quickly, and why Francis had been so upset when he had heard about the conveyance. He walked to Francis' office to break the news.

35

Charles and Rosalind left the cinema by the back door, and took a taxi back home. His mobile phone vibrated in his hand. He looked down at the screen and saw the name, 'Francis Sutherland'.

'Francis? Well how did it go? Was it OK?'

'Yes. I think you were fine. I must warn you, if you think your privacy was invaded when your elder brothers left, then you're going to be in for a nasty shock.'

'Well, the taxi driver didn't recognise us,' he laughed. 'But I do take your point. Listen. Why don't you come round for supper tonight?'

'No, I can't I'm afraid ... going to the opera. My favourite, *Fidelio*, is being performed at the Opera

House. It's a "no miss event". Charles–'

'Yes, Francis. What's the matter? I can tell by your tone that something's up.'

'I've just heard that the banks have sold Hathaway House.'

'What?'

'This morning ... they've sold the house ... for 75 million.'

'But I thought they were going to refurbish it, and then put it on the market in the autumn. At least that's what you told me.'

'I know ... I know but–'

'But what, Francis? Your firm were acting for the banks. I don't understand–'

'Charles, I had a conflict of interest. I couldn't control events. It was an enormous offer given the current condition of the estate. You must understand, I'm as upset as you are.'

Francis was greeted by silence at the other end of the line. 'Charles, the banks felt it was an offer that they couldn't refuse.'

'There's not much I can say or do, Francis.' He took a deep breath, and looked at Rosalind, who overheard the entire conversation. She took his hand and clasped it. 'Who bought it?'

It was the question that Francis was waiting for, but also dreaded. 'Abraham Bernstein.'

'You have to be joking!'

'That was my reaction, but no, I'm not.'

'But why, at his age, would he want Hathaway? It will take at least two years to get it back into some sort of order. He must be mad.'

'Well, he exchanged this morning and will complete in four weeks, just after your wedding.'

'Listen, I'll talk to Sam. Maybe he didn't realise at the time that I wanted to buy it back. He probably didn't see the conference if he has just exchanged, and when he hears what I want to do, I'm sure he'll understand.'

'I suppose you can talk to your friend, but I suspect that you are misreading the situation. Abraham Bernstein never does anything on impulse. He has a reputation for being methodical, and utterly ruthless.'

'I'll speak to Sam, and get back to you.' Perversely, the news that his friend's father was buying the family seat filled Charles with optimism. He sensed that he at least had a better chance of trying to convince someone he knew, rather than an unknown buyer, to listen to him and transfer the property back to its historical owner. He was convinced that when Abraham knew the full story, he would sell it back. He was sure that the old man had not realised that he himself would be in a position to buy the house. If he had seen the conference, everything would be clear to him. He smiled as his thoughts raced ahead, along this positive path.

Rosalind looked into Charles' eyes. She continued to hold his hand tightly. 'What is it, darling?' he asked.

'Nothing. It's just that, I know what you're thinking.'

'I can sort this whole thing out – I know I can.'

'Can you?' Rosalind asked, but not wanting an answer. She knew that Francis was right. She sensed, from her previous meetings with Abraham Bernstein, that this was not a sudden whim,

412

or an opportunistic purchase to gain more personal prestige. There was something more in this, and she feared the worst.

36

Sam received the call from Charles and was just as surprised as his friend was at the news.

'Dad? It's me, open the door.' The intercom released the front door, as he walked into his parents' home. He made his way into his father's study.

'Hello, Sam, how are you?'

'I'm fine, thanks.'

'Well, what is it? Why the sudden rush to see me?'

'You must know.'

'Really I don't,' the old man replied.

'Hathaway House.'

'What about it? I exchanged on it yesterday.'

'Exactly.'

'I'm sorry, Sam, but I just don't understand your interest – and your tone.'

'You know that it was Charles' family home. How could you be so insensitive?'

'Of course, I knew, but I had no idea that Charles was bidding on the property.'

'He wasn't, but with the proceeds from the sale of the manuscript, he would have been in the position to buy it back and restore it.'

'But Sam, it was an opportunity that I took. I was sure Charles didn't have the money. Besides he never said anything to me. I can't wait around

413

for announcements and press conferences, you know. The world doesn't work like that.'

'No – but your world does. It must have crossed your mind that, with everything you already knew from us about the manuscript, that the value was enormous and that Charles might want to bid on the property. From what I hear, the banks were going to put it on the market, after refurbishing it in the winter. Why did they suddenly sell it to you? And why the rush?' Sam was deeply suspicious of his father's motives.

'I have nothing to say, Sam. I can't wait around second guessing people's actions, waiting for them to make decisions. Hathaway House is a magnificent home. Charles doesn't have to worry, I will restore it myself to its former glory.'

'Second guess? Well let me second guess you... I think you leapt in and bought it, knowing that the press conference would reveal the value of the manuscript and confirm its authenticity to the world. I think you realised that Charles would make clear his intention about what he would do with the monies. I also think that the banks would have held off selling to you off the market, and given him a chance to bid. You needed to exchange before the conference, and that explains the rush in the legal work. Sir Francis Sutherland couldn't understand it ... but I did. It bore your hallmark.'

'Very good, Sam – most eloquent, but you are looking into things too deeply. I have always wanted a country estate. It's as simple as that. The fact that the house belonged to Gordon and Robert Longhurst, I must admit, does add to my pleasure.'

414

Sam looked at his father. He knew it was the final statement that had driven him to buying Hathaway. Abraham Bernstein was desperate for revenge, and this was the perfect avenue to achieve it. 'So what about Charles?'

'I'm sorry. He will always be welcome, of course.'

37

Sam realised immediately that his father was set on his path, and nothing could stop him. He understood his father's need for revenge, not only against the establishment that had cold-shouldered him for all his life, but also against the contemptible twins who had swindled him. He had a certain amount of sympathy for him, and if it wasn't for Charles he would have supported him. But it was because of Charles that his behaviour and actions were unsupportable.

'Believe me, nothing can be done,' Sam told the assembled group at Charles' house.

'What do you mean, "nothing"?' Raveena asked, implying that Sam should have done more.

'He wants revenge on Charles' brothers. To be fair I'd like to think he hasn't thought it through, and has forgotten about Charles' feelings, but–'

'No, I don't think so, Sam. He was terribly insistent on exchanging on Wednesday morning – and I stress, morning. Before the press conference, and thus before the banks could realise that another special bidder could join the fray. They would have definitely waited, given Charles' interest, and of course, newly-found wealth,' Sir Francis interrupted.

'Yes, I'm afraid I think you're right. The old man is extremely clever, with a very big chip on his shoulder.' Sam glanced at Charles. 'Look, I know this might sound mad, Charles, but although I suspect Francis is right, and he orchestrated the purchase so as not to give you a chance, he's got nothing against you personally. He's driven on by his hatred for the establishment, and by his loathing of your brothers. As far as he's concerned, you're an innocent victim. He even looked forward to you being a guest there!'

'Sensitivity is his strong point!' Charles said, as he got up, keeping control of his emotions. 'Look, there's nothing we can do now. I'll have to buy somewhere else, and try and create a new Hathaway House, and a new library. It's a shame, but I can't see what else there is to do.' He looked across the room at Rosalind. 'You've said nothing.'

'I know ... I'm thinking. I wonder if he'll come to the wedding?'

'Without a doubt,' Sam replied. 'He doesn't see it as an issue with you two. Obviously he understands that you will be upset, but he genuinely thinks that you will understand – even empathise with him. This is his battle, and as far as he's concerned, he's won.'

'Why do you ask, Rosalind?'

'No real reason.' She got up, and walked to the door. 'Anyone for some tea?'

Saturday 9 August was a day that Catherine and Alan Blackstone had looked forward to for a very long time: the marriage of their daughter to Charles Longhurst was to be a memorable event for the family. As hard as it was for Alan to give his daughter away, he was a happy man having met his soon-to-be son-in-law. The days leading up to the wedding were chaotic, but Rosalind remained in control.

'Mother, you must relax, everything will be wonderful. I saw Father Docherty this morning at communion. He was so funny, reminiscing about your wedding day ... he remembers everything, you know.'

'Yes, he's an amazing man. I still can't quite believe he has the energy still in him to marry you both. It seems such a long time ago when he married me!'

'He told me that Daddy was so serious, and very ambitious.'

'He was, but he was very sensitive, and look how well he did.'

'I know. It's so exciting, don't you think?'

'Of course I do. How's Charles?'

'Nervous, but looking forward to it. He's been so busy with the press, and now he's got the government pressurising him.'

'Why?'

'Well, the manuscript doesn't come under Treasure Trove Law, since it has always been in his family's possession, but the government is anxious to keep it here. Obviously it doesn't want to pay very much.'

'Does Charles need all this money, dear? I mean, it would be lovely if he gave it to the nation–'

'Well, he's a bit like you. But I've told him to go for the highest bid.'

'Why? You're not a materialistic type of girl.'

'No I'm not, but I have something to do, and if I succeed then he'll need every penny. If I fail – and I doubt I will,' she laughed, 'then he can always leave it to charity.'

39

As soon as the press conference had finished, Charles' life became public property. He and Rosalind were constantly being photographed or questioned by the press. Both of their pasts were suddenly under the microscope. There wasn't much that could be printed about Rosalind that the papers would find interesting, but with Charles it was a different matter. The legacy he inherited was the stuff that tabloids dreamt about. Everything was dredged up from the past, including his father's youth, his mother's death, the flight of the twins, the denouement of the family estate; nothing left out.

Against this backdrop, he had to deal with a force that he was not prepared for. The government had initially approached Bernard Shapeman to discuss a price for the manuscript. It felt that it was in the national interest for it to remain in the country, and it could not guarantee that if, as was planned, it would go to the highest bidder.

'I don't think my client should have any obligation to you over this.'

'Mr Shapeman, this is an historic find. Her Majesty's Government is very keen to keep it here. We are happy to pay, but I am not sure that we can compete. Can I persuade you, Mr Longhurst, into reconsidering the auction? It would be at the mercy of American hedge fund managers, Russian asset strippers, Japanese telephone magnates, or indeed, heaven forbid, the French government. It's a national treasure, for God's sake!'

'I appreciate your concern, but I want to try and reclaim my inheritance.'

'But I believe Hathaway House has been sold.' The civil servant was becoming increasingly aggressive.

'I know, but I have other plans. Besides, I would like to rebuild the library.'

'I am frankly surprised by your mercenary attitude. People will assume the worst, you know.'

'And what might that be?' Bernard asked, sensing there was an underlying threat.

'Oh, I don't know, but people might resent Mr Longhurst's greed.'

'Maybe, maybe not. Do you not think that the government itself might attract the wrong type of opinion if it failed to come up with the money? Can you imagine the outcry if the manuscript ended up in the Louvre?' Charles intervened, annoyed at the tactics adopted by the Home Office.

The civil servant looked straight back at him.

He realised that Charles was not going to be bullied, and was resigned to the fact that the manuscript would indeed go to the highest bidder. He himself would have to tell his bosses that if the government wanted to keep the manuscript in this country, then it would have to pay the market price – whatever that might be.

As Charles and Bernard left the building, it was clear to both of them that the press might well start questioning Charles' motives to sell for the highest price.

'Listen, you're not doing anything illegal or immoral. It's perfectly legitimate to sell it for what you can. Don't be bullied, Charles, and don't let them make you feel guilty. There are very few people out there who wouldn't do the same as you.'

'Yes, but I do feel a sense of loyalty to the place where I was born. I don't quite know what Rosalind has up her sleeve. She's being very secretive. But whatever it is ... if it fails, do I really need it all? I suppose I could set up a charitable trust of some sort.' Charles was beginning to doubt the whole purpose of it all. Without Hathaway House, there was little that he wanted to do with the money. A new house with a new library sounded wonderful, but he knew it was a hollow enterprise.

'Come on, let's get back. You've got a wedding to go to at the weekend. I've managed to talk to the press office, who have agreed to leave you both alone. It was a very rare show of restraint, I must say.' Bernard ushered Charles into the taxi.

40

The night before the wedding, Charles had dinner with Sam, Sir Francis and Bernard at the Grand Hotel. That anticipation and excitement that usually accompanies a stag night was tempered by the shadow of Abraham Bernstein's purchase of Hathaway House. There was nothing that they could do to prevent the old man from achieving his goal; he was utterly driven, and the four men dining that night knew it.

'It's not even that we're dealing with a rational man here – it's a nightmare,' Sir Francis said, shaking his head, looking into his empty wine glass.

'It's not so bad. We can create something special with a new library. We can make it into a modern wonder of the world. It doesn't matter where it is, but it will be open to the public. I have a real dream.' Bernard was far more upbeat. He didn't really understand the magnitude of the loss that Charles was feeling. He wasn't part of the Hathaway memory, unlike the other three. He had, of course, seen it, and had presided over its dismantlement, but he was never part of it. It was impossible for him to appreciate what the others felt.

'I know, Bernard, but my heart's not in it. Yes, you might be able to recover what...? including what you own, about seventy five percent of the old library, but even if you did ... even if you recover ninety percent ... housing them somewhere other than Hathaway just wouldn't be the same. I'm not sure what I want to do any more. I mean, what's the point in having all that money without any real purpose. If Hathaway, and the library there, cannot be recovered, then perhaps I should give it to the nation. After all, I've got enough.' Charles signalled to the waiter to bring one more bottle of the most expensive claret the hotel had on its menu. 'I think Rosalind wants to talk to your old man, but it's a fruitless exercise, don't you think, Sam?'

'I think you should just concentrate on tomorrow, and place everything else to one side.' The waiter brought the Chateau Talbot 1990 to the table, and poured a drop into Charles' glass. He sniffed it and looked at its colour. He nodded, and the waiter poured the contents equally into all four glasses. 'Gentlemen – to the bride and groom!' Sam raised his glass. Francis and Bernard raised theirs, and repeated the toast.

Charles sat back and looked at his three close friends. Sam was right; he owed it to Rosalind to make this day special. He had to ensure, no matter how he felt, that tomorrow would be her happiest.

41

The wedding was a small affair. Most of the invitees were friends rather than family. This was no accident. Alan Blackstone had no family, and Catherine only had one distant cousin surviving. Charles' family was a large but distant one. There were only a handful of cousins, from his mother's side of the family, whom he wanted to invite. Some of his relatives had naturally made contact following the discovery, hoping for an invite, but were doomed not to receive one. There was, however, one person he wanted there more than anybody else: Janet.

She had been like a mother to him, and although contact had been less frequent since she had moved away to Scotland, he still loved her. The feeling was mutual, and when she replied to the invitation that she was coming, Charles' personal relief was palpable.

The ceremony began at 11 o'clock. Although the wedding lacked numbers, there were 45 guests in total and formality was not sacrificed. The men were all dressed in morning suits with buff-coloured waistcoats, white shirts and ties of their own choice. The women were dressed in their best cocktail wear. The turnout perfectly befitted the occasion. Sam, the best man and true to his role, remained close to Charles throughout the morning, not letting him out of his sight.

'This is it,' he said quietly to the groom, standing in position near the altar.

'I am aware of that ... but I don't quite understand why you've stuck to me like a leech throughout this morning. I'm not going to run away or do anything stupid.'

'Well, I thought that's what a best man has to do. You know–'

'Do you have the rings?'

'Uh ... yes, I think so.'

'That, Sam, is the only thing you had to really do this morning.' Charles was remarkably calm, more so than the best man.

'It's all right, I've found them,' Sam replied, relieved at locating the gold bands in his waistcoat pocket.

The two young men stood silently, hearing the guests come in. Sam occasionally looked back, seeing who had arrived. 'My parents haven't come yet.'

'No? Maybe they won't.'

'Mother told me they were. It's unlike them to cut it so fine.' Sam looked around the room, recognising a few friends and acknowledging them. 'I see that Janet's arrived. Don't worry, she's in her reserved seat.' Sam smiled at Charles.

'What time do you make it?' Charles asked.

'Eleven ... exactly.' As he answered, he heard the familiar loud, heavy Eastern European accent of his father's voice. He looked around and saw his parents being guided to their seats.

'Is there anything closer to the front?' the old man asked.

'No, sir. Please, the bride will be arriving very soon.'

'But my hearing is terrible,' he protested.

'Please, sir, you have to sit.' Leah pulled at her husband's sleeve, whispering to him to sit.

'They've arrived, in case you hadn't heard.'

'Who?' Charles was so focused on his bride, or rather her absence, that he had failed to notice Abraham Bernstein's loud entry into the church.

'My parents!'

'Very good, Sam ... but I am slightly more concerned about Rosalind. She's never late.'

'Charles, it's only a couple of minutes ... and

it's her prerogative.'

At that moment, the doors opened. The sunlight that shot through the widening gap, combined with the shafts of light that had already pierced through the stained-glass windows, suddenly produced a golden glow that illuminated the entire church. Catherine Blackstone led the procession, followed by Raveena, the maid of honour. They made their way to the front row, and sat down. Sam looked back down from the altar. He looked at Raveena, and then looked behind towards the bright sunlight that was bursting through the back doorway, waiting for a first glimpse of the bride.

The statuesque figure, her white dress with a strapless, white bodice covered in glass beads, with a flowing train, walked out of the sunlight into the church, accompanied by her father. Her grace and elegance emanated throughout the church. Sam suddenly noticed the music, which up to now had been Pachelbel's Canon in D, had now changed to the Trumpet Voluntary on her entrance. It was the signal for Charles to know that she was coming down the aisle.

He only just managed not to look round. He fixed his stare on the octogenarian priest who was about to marry them. Rosalind left her father and took two steps to join her groom. Still he refused to look. He wanted to make sure she was there, before turning. Her smell drifted towards him and it was only at that point that he sensed her. He breathed in her fragrance, immediately feeling her presence. A sudden surge of strength, combined with confidence, filled his veins, as he now looked across at his bride. Her face was a picture of beauty. There was nobody in the world at that moment who was more radiant and elegant than Rosalind. Standing tall, her auburn hair was tied back, emphasising her face in all its majesty. Her pale complexion, with a hint of red in her angled cheeks; her wide pale-blue eyes, and her perfectly formed mouth, were all part of a perfect picture, a sublime impression of an English rose.

The Trumpet Voluntary stopped. The bride and groom were looking at each other as the old priest began to take the service. Whether it was because he could not stand for too long, or whether he had forgotten some parts of the ceremony, Father Docherty carried out his function in a very quick, almost perfunctory, manner. It took no longer than fifteen minutes before the bride and groom exchanged vows.

'Charles Longhurst. Do you take Rosalind Blackstone to be your lawful wedded wife?'

It was only then that he felt the full force of the nuptial rite and the splendour and sanctity of marriage. Charles at once realised, despite all the trials and tribulations he had suffered over the past few years, that he had at last won. Looking into her dazzlingly blue eyes, he saw that no house or manuscript came close to the prize he had now gained.

'I do.'

As he placed the ring on her finger, and was given permission to kiss the bride, Charles pulled her close to him. He closed his eyes as his lips kissed hers.

'Are you happy?' she whispered in his ear, as they embraced to loud applause from the audience.

'Never more so ... I understand now.'

'What?'

'That all I want from life, is you. Nothing more, nothing less. Everything else is irrelevant. And you? Are you happy?'

'I've waited over ten years for this. From the first glimpse of you three miles down the road. What do you think? Of course I'm happy!'

42

The reception took place in the Blackstone house in Kemp Town. It was a glorious sunny day and the garden was the perfect setting for the celebration. Rosalind was irrepressible, speaking and laughing with everyone. Charles mixed as best he could, avoiding Sam's father and mother. He concentrated his attention on Janet, catching up on old times, and promising to keep in better contact in the future. She was so proud of him that, quite out of character, she had found it difficult to keep her composure.

'Have you said anything to Abraham Bernstein?'

'No. Where is he? I must speak to him,' Rosalind replied.

'He's over there ... perhaps I'll come with you.' The newlyweds walked over to the elderly couple sitting at one of the tables.

'Hello. Thank you both for coming.'

'Oh, it was wonderful. We've never been to a Catholic wedding ceremony before! You look even more beautiful than ever, Rosalind,' Leah Bernstein said in her educated English accent.

'Thank you, Mrs Bernstein. And Mr Bernstein, did you enjoy it?'

'Very much. Congratulations to you both – well done,' the old man replied, shaking the bride's hand. 'So Charles, how are things going with the manuscript?'

'It looks like a December auction. I believe the government is going to try and fund a competitive bid through the British Library. They did try and persuade me to sell it to them for less, but–'

'Oh, you mustn't let the civil servants get the better of you. One must sell to the highest bidder ... it's the only, I should say the fairest, way. Everybody who can afford such a treasure should be given a chance. Nobody should be excluded.' He was forceful and lucid. Abraham Bernstein was one of those people who believed in everything he said.

'Well, without being able to buy Hathaway House, I don't see the point. I am a rich man, and perhaps the best thing would be to give it to the nation,' Charles replied, desperate to see the old man's reaction.

'Nonsense! The establishment in this country doesn't deserve it ... exclusive and privileged, they don't understand the meaning of fairness. You could buy the biggest, most wonderful estate for yourself.' He completely ignored the comment about Hathaway House, and had instead

428

concentrated on his favourite topic.

'No chance of you selling Hathaway on to me. I'd offer you a profit on the contract.' This was Charles' last throw of the dice.

'None at all, Charles. I want Hathaway House – it's my revenge. I want to own the house that your brothers once had. You understand, don't you? It has nothing to do with you. You are an unfortunate casualty in all this, but such is life.' He smiled, and sipped his tea.

Charles looked at him, and then glanced at Rosalind, who was in deep conversation with Leah. He understood now what Sam had meant. It had not entered the old man's thought process that he would alienate himself from Charles, by buying the latter's family seat from under his nose. Yes, he had manipulated events in order to succeed in his quest, and he knew that Charles would be upset, but he was convinced in his own mind that he was doing the right thing. Battle-worn from fighting a war against the establishment, he had lost sensitivity for others. In his own Machiavellian mind, he was justified in what he had done and was not prepared to think about the consequences of his actions on Charles.

'What are you going to do with Hathaway?' Charles asked, without any hidden agenda. For the first time, he now accepted the old man's stance.

'Oh, I'm going to refurbish it completely. Restore it totally, and then you and Rosalind must come down. It will be like old times for you!'

'Uh ... not quite!' He paused. 'What about your wife?'

'She's not so keen – she hates the country, but I'll convince her.'

Charles looked across at Rosalind, who was still talking to Leah Bernstein, and wondered what she was up to.

43

He slowly undid the buttons on the back of her beaded bodice. It had been a very long and emotional day, but she could feel her heart racing, and her fingertips tingled with excitement. As he finished unfastening her, she arched her back, letting the garment fall away from her. She stepped out of the collapsed dress, and turned around to face him. He looked at her. She undid her bra, and took one step towards him. He placed both hands on her shoulders, and gently stroked her. He lifted his hands and delicately removed the clip which had kept her hair tied back. Released from its constraint, the dark auburn hair fell down to her shoulders.

He moved closer to her and kissed her. His lips moved to her cheek, and then to the lobes of her ears. 'Charles?' she whispered, almost out of breath.

'Yes?' He continued to peck at the lobe of her ear.

'Please – just make love to me– I–'

'But don't you want me to–?'

'No! I'm 26, and still a virgin. I've waited long enough.'

He reached down, and slipped his hand inside

her white underwear, and felt her. His fingers touched her swollen moist vulva, and then pushed inside, probing her warmth. 'All right, darling. Are you sure?'

'Yes.'

They walked over to the bed. She took her panties off, and waited for him. He undressed, and approached her. Fully erect, he carefully pushed himself inside her. At first he struggled, but after several attempts, he finally eased his way inside. She groaned, from a mixture of pain and ecstasy, as she took the full force of his entry. The pleasure of him, pushing against her, and the delight of feeling his organ brush against her clitoris was almost too much. He continued to rhythmically thrust himself into her. She could hardly breathe, as he pushed and pushed, feeling that he was sinking ever more deeply inside her. After five minutes, her pleasure reached a crescendo, as she lost control of her senses, and she gave in to the utter bliss of an orgasm, the like of which she had never felt before.

He felt her orgasm, the contraction inside her, against him. He was determined that she should enjoy it, and was anxious for her to climax first. He now began to relax, and increased his stroke. She felt his increased physical exertion, and his breathing becoming heavier. He made one last thrust, and shook in a rhapsody of ecstasy. He groaned and slumped on top of her. Wet from sweat, they both lay still, neither able to move after the physical exertion they had just experienced.

'Was it painful?' he asked, as he finally rolled off her.

'Only at the start. Do you want to do it again?'

'You are joking, aren't you?'

She laughed, 'Well, if you're too tired, or perhaps too old – then–'

'No, come on then,' he said, as he began to climb on top of her. 'I love you, Mrs Longhurst.' He kissed her.

'I know you do.'

'No ... I mean, I really love you.'

'I know.'

44

A month after the wedding, when they had returned from their honeymoon in Europe, Rosalind received the call she was expecting.

'Hello.'

'Rosalind? It's Leah Bernstein.'

'Hello, Mrs Bernstein. How are you?'

'Please call me Leah. I'm very well, and how are you?'

'I'm fine, Leah. Well, do we have a date?'

'He's been very busy, the more so since he retired – isn't that strange? His charity work is unending. Anyway, I've got an ideal space – Friday, next week, 3rd October at 2.30.'

'And he's expecting me?'

'No, but his diary is open that afternoon and I've told him to keep it free to discuss the new curtains for Hathaway!'

'Rather apt, don't you think?'

'Yes, it is rather. So I'll see you then?'

'Yes ... and thank you.'

'It's my pleasure, Rosalind. I only hope that you convince him, for both of our sakes.'

'Oh, I will.' She was supremely confident in her own ability, especially now that she could count on the support of Leah Bernstein. It was the last chance to capture her husband's ancestral home, and she wasn't going to let it go without giving it everything she had.

45

Charles had no idea of what Rosalind had up her sleeve when she left their house that Friday afternoon and walked the short distance to Berkeley Square. She rehearsed what she was going to say to the old man, trying to prepare herself. She was very nervous, visibly so, as she rang the doorbell and was let in to the house.

'Who is it?' The booming question echoed around the marble hall, from upstairs.

'It's Rosalind Blackstone, Mr Bernstein.'

'Oh... What a surprise. I wasn't expecting you.' The old man came down the stairs. 'Let me take your coat.'

'No, I know you weren't. Here ... thank you.' She gave him her coat. 'Is it possible that we could talk?'

'Yes, yes, of course, come in. Would you like a drink ... a cup of tea?'

'No, nothing, thank you.'

'So, how can I help you?'

'Mr Bernstein – Abraham,' she wanted to make it more personal. 'It's about Hathaway House.'

'Ah, yes. I've completed you know – £75 million, plus stamp duty and fees. After refurbishment I don't anticipate being in for less than £100 million. It's a lot, but, thank God, I'm a very rich man.'

'But may I ask why you want it?' She, of course, knew the answer.

'I'm not going to discuss this with you, Rosalind. I've already spoken to your husband, not to mention my son. Leah and I are looking forward to the project, and staying there.'

'Leah? She hates the country – she told me so.'

He got up. He wouldn't look her in the eye. She was the most exquisite creature he had ever seen. She possessed the most perfect nature, coupled with a remarkable presence. She frightened him.

'Rosalind, I won't discuss it–'

'Why, Abraham? Why did you buy it? I know you have nothing against Charles–'

'It has nothing to do with him. I am very fond of him. His brothers on the other hand–'

'Revenge? Is that what it's all about? But why, it serves no purpose!'

'Rosalind,' he was now looking straight into her eyes. 'Do you know what it's like to be excluded, deprived from what you want and what you deserve? All my life I have worked against the odds, against prejudice ... against the establishment. I have been treated with contempt and have been sneered at.' He stopped and looked at her. 'You are a scholar of Shakespeare, aren't you?' She nodded. 'Then you'll understand these lines ... *laughed at my losses, mocked my gains ... thwarted my bargains ... what reason? I am a Jew. Hath not a*

Jew eyes? ... organs, dimensions, senses ... fed with the same food, hurt with the same weapons ... warmed and cooled by the same winter and summer as a Christian is? If you prick us do we not bleed? If you tickle us do we not laugh?... If you wrong us shall we not revenge?... I will have my revenge, Rosalind, because that's what I've learnt from them.'

She looked at him. At this moment Abraham Bernstein was Shylock. She had never seen anyone quite so bent on retribution. He must have hated Gordon and Robert, but it wasn't just about them. Yes, they had wronged him, but the fact that Hathaway House was theirs, was simply the icing on the cake. This was an attack on the entire establishment: his final payback.

'Are you satisfied?' she asked him quietly. She could see, almost feel, the anger that was seething from every pore of his body. There was a knock on the door.

'Yes? Ah! Leah, come in.'

'Abraham, I've been listening to you. But is it necessary? It's so pointless – you know we'll never move there.'

He sat silently, wishing that his wife hadn't entered the room. 'Leah, I will not be moved. I don't care if we never go there ... it's mine!'

Rosalind got up. She was desperately trying to think of a quotation from Shakespeare to throw back at the old man, but to no avail. Her hero provided her with nothing at that moment. She was about to leave when she noticed a book lying incongruously on top of the others. She walked over to the bookshelves and picked up the small volume which had obviously not been put back in its correct position. She stared at the title. Unlike the vast majority of the books in the room, this was a paperback. It had been well read.

'You're right, I do love Shakespeare, but it's not from him that I can find an answer.' She paused, collecting her thoughts. 'Almost ten years ago I first met you here, in this house. Do you remember?'

'Yes, I do. It was in the kitchen.'

'That's right. And do you remember what you were reading?' There was no response from the old man, but he remembered well enough. 'It was this book, *The Penguin edition of The Complete Greek Tragedies, Volume one, Aeschylus.*' She showed him the book.

'That may be so, Rosalind. I frequently read the Greeks, particularly Aeschylus. That particular volume I read a lot.'

She thumbed through the pages, trying to find the quotation as quickly as she could. Arriving at the page, she breathed in, and slowly read out loud.

And even in our sleep, pain that cannot forget,
falls drop by drop upon our heart,
and in our despite, against our will,
comes wisdom to us by the awful grace of God.

He sat motionless, going through her words in his mind. He knew in his heart that he was wrong, but before it didn't matter. Now, it seemed that it did. He knew the famous quotation from Aeschylus' first play in the

Oresteia Trilogy, *Agamemnon*. It made him think about his action in a different perspective. He understood the point she was trying to make. He had to find wisdom through his pain and suffering and not through revenge.

'Abraham, darling, you've won already. You don't need a country estate to prove it. You've beaten them. You have a family, your health and enormous wealth. You have to let the bitterness go or else it will bring you down.' Leah was tugging his arm.

He looked at his wife, a tear falling down his cheek. 'Do you really think so?'

'Yes, I do.'

He looked up at Rosalind, who was standing imperiously by the doorway. 'You are a remarkable young woman.' He looked down at the floor and said nothing. He knew he had lost the argument. Indeed, he was always aware that he was fighting a battle that was more destructive than constructive, but he had stuck to his task. It was only now that he questioned himself on the matter. Knowing that he was wrong, was he man enough to back down and concede? He had done it before with his son, over his relationship with Raveena; he'd reaped the benefits of his retreat in that argument. He pondered, and then suddenly sat up.

'You know that it's much easier to stand by a decision, even when you know you're wrong, than to back down gracefully.'

'Of course I do,' Rosalind responded, sensing victory was close at hand.

'Tell Charles I'll sell him the house – at exactly

the same price that I paid.'

'Can it wait until after the auction in December? We don't have eighty million lying around!'

'Oh, if you insist then!' He smiled.

46

As Rosalind was let out, the postman arrived with a letter.

'Mr Bernstein ... Abraham Bernstein?'

'Yes.'

'Special delivery, sir. Can you sign here, please.' Abraham signed the sheet of paper, and took the letter back with him into the study.

'Who was that?' Leah asked, sipping her tea.

'The postman – special delivery,' he replied, taking the letter-opener from the drawer of his desk.

'Who's it from?' she asked, but there was no reply. She watched her husband's face, as he read the contents of the letter. She saw his expression crack as he gave off the most enormous guffaw.

'Here, take it. What's your advice on this one, Leah? Do you think I should accept?'

Leah took the letter and smiled. She handed it back to him. 'How does it sound? Sir Abraham? Perfect!'

She got up and hugged him as they continued to laugh. 'Not nearly as good as Lady Bernstein!' he answered.

Part 11

SOTHEBY'S, THE PRESENT DAY

4.50 P.M.

1

Smith Luytens looked straight back at his old friend Hugo Samuels, not quite believing the bid from the British Library. It was far more than he had anticipated. 'I have £300 million ... and I will sell at this level.' He looked at the tall American standing, imposingly, almost imperiously, in the aisle. He seemed to dominate the proceedings, even though he was now losing the race. He didn't move. Everybody waited with baited breath, as the giant American weighed up his options. Of course, he knew he could afford it, but was he prepared to pay that much money for it? He knew that Samuels was representing the British Library, and he'd been advised about all of the potential bidders. Maybe it should stay in the mother country, he thought.

'It's still against you.' Smith Luytens was now anxious to bring the hammer down. He had achieved a higher than expected price, with the bonus that it would stay in the country. He waited, then finally the signal came. Bill Gaston shook his head, indicating that no higher bid was forthcoming.

'Thank you, sir – you are now out. Do I have anybody else?' He looked at the other bidders in the room, starting with the lady in the navy suit who had begun the bidding and who was representing a museum in the mid west of the

United States. She failed to respond. He then looked at the tall, black American who was acting for the Getty Museum in Los Angeles. He smiled and shook his head. Smith Luytens scanned the room, and came across the Russian billionaire who sat staring at the catalogue, not daring to look up in case of embarrassment. The auctioneer's eyes then settled on the Clouseau-type figure from France, seated in the front row. He gave a brusque wave of his hand that was definitely not a bid, but rather a signal of resignation. He finally looked up at Bill Gaston.

'I have £300 million for the manuscript written in William Shakespeare's very own hand, depicting Act two Scene two of the play, *Romeo and Juliet*. For the first time ... the second time ... and finally the third time.' The hammer came down. 'Sold for £300 million to my friend, the gentleman at the back.'

There were spontaneous cheers from all sides of the room. The press, and television cameramen moved in and surrounded Hugo Samuels. The latter remained calm, and took out a folded piece of paper.

'Please! I know you have questions but all will be explained in a press statement, which has now been released from its embargo. I would, however, like to say how delighted I am, on behalf of the British Library, which was so generously supported by the government, to have bought the manuscript for the nation. It is part of our heritage, and we felt that no price was too high to keep it on these shores. Thank you.' He made his move to the exit, only to be followed by the army of reporters.

<h1 style="text-align:center">2</h1>

The young couple, who had gone unnoticed up until now, turned to go, only to be spotted by another journalist.

'Mr and Mrs Longhurst, do you have a comment?'

'No, except to say how pleased we both are that the government found a way to buy it.'

'What are you going to do with all the money?'

'Do what I always said I would – complete the purchase of Hathaway House, restore it to its former glory, and then rebuild the library.'

'A lot has been written in the past weeks about the library and its mythical status. Nobody ever saw it. Will you open it to the public?'

'Yes, but we have to recover the books before we can open it. Now, please, can we go–' Charles made his way through the crowd, with Rosalind holding on to his arm. Finally reaching the hall-way, they went up the stairs and approached the back door. There, waiting for them, was Bernard Shapeman, his arms open, smiling. 'You did it! Well done!'

'No, Bernard, we all did it! Come with us and have a drink. Raveena and Sam are waiting for us at Claridges.'

'Thank you, but I can't ... I have to try and recover a library!'

Charles laughed, 'Yes, you do! We'll speak to-morrow.'

'Darling, come on, we have to go. Rav wants to discuss her wedding dress, and I promised I would come straight after the auction was over.'

'OK–' He looked at her. 'Have you put on weight?'

'Maybe...' She smiled.

The publishers hope that this book has given you enjoyable reading. Large Print Books are especially designed to be as easy to see and hold as possible. If you wish a complete list of our books please ask at your local library or write directly to:

Magna Large Print Books
Magna House, Long Preston,
Skipton, North Yorkshire.
BD23 4ND

This Large Print Book for the partially sighted, who cannot read normal print, is published under the auspices of

THE ULVERSCROFT FOUNDATION